Also by Ollie Ann Porche Voelker
Home at Last: An Acadian Journey

A Silver Lining

From Acadie to Louisiana

Ollie Ann Porche Voelker

Inspiring Voices®

Inspiring Voices books may be ordered through booksellers or by contacting:

Inspiring Voices
1663 Liberty Drive
Bloomington, IN 47403
www.inspiringvoices.com
1 (866) 697-5313

Because of the dynamic nature of the Internet, any web addresses or links contained in this book may have changed since publication and may no longer be valid. The views expressed in this work are solely those of the author and do not necessarily reflect the views of the publisher, and the publisher hereby disclaims any responsibility for them.

Any people depicted in stock imagery provided by Thinkstock are models, and such images are being used for illustrative purposes only. Certain stock imagery © Thinkstock.

ISBN: 978-1-4624-1057-6 (sc)
ISBN: 978-1-4624-1058-3 (e)

Library of Congress Control Number: 2014917291

Printed in the United States of America.

Inspiring Voices rev. date: 10/14/2014

In loving memory of my parents
Annie Erick Giroir Porche
who did the initial genealogical research
which provided the spark for me
to embark upon this journey
and
Roland Joseph Porche
who was a descendant of Pelagie Benoist

This is the story of my great-great-great-great-grandmother Pelagie Benoist (Benoit), an Acadian. It is also the story of thousands of Acadians who were deported from Nova Scotia between 1755 and 1759, and settled in Louisiana years later. They were people of strength, faith, courage, and love of family. This story is for their descendants, to help them take pride in their heritage.

Acknowledgements

In the early 1970s my mother, along with one of my paternal aunts, Ola Porche, and a paternal second cousin, Mona LeGrand, spent many hours in libraries pouring through books, researching one branch of my father's family as far back as Martin Benoist, who sailed from France to Nova Scotia in 1671. Although my parents mentioned a few of the events in the life of my great-great-great-great-grandmother Pelagie Benoist, I didn't take much notice until I went through my parents' papers after their deaths. I found family trees, copies of birth, marriage, and death records, and also several letters from Mona in which she mentioned additional genealogical information she had found. She made Pelagie so real that I knew this was a story that needed to be told. For all your time and effort before home computers, thanks Mom, Ola, and Mona.

Special thanks to three people who answered my many questions, and then read my manuscript for historical accuracy: Maurice Basque, scientific advisor at the Institute of Acadian Studies at the University of Moncton in Moncton, New Brunswick, Canada; Anne Marie Lane Jonah, historian at the Fortress of Louisbourg in Louisbourg, Nova Scotia, Canada; and Warren Perrin, chairman of the Acadian Museum in Erath, Louisiana and President of CODOFIL. I appreciate their time and input far more than I can say. If there are any mistakes, they are mine.

Thanks to A.J.B. Johnston, Canadian historian and author of five of the books about Louisbourg that I used in my research, who willingly answered my questions about religion in Louisbourg. To Alan Matherne at the LSU AgCenter for information about the flow of bayous, and Chris Bonura at the Port of New Orleans for information about sailing up the Mississippi River. Also, thanks to the staff of Wildlife and Fisheries in Lafourche Parish, and the county agent in St. Charles Parish for answering my questions about wildlife and crops in these two parishes.

Many thanks to my critique partners: Jodie Harris, Carole Ford, Renelle Folse, Judy Creekmore, Carol Ashley, Candy Olsen, and Regina Gautreaux for their friendship, time, support, and helpful suggestions, and also for the smiles and even occasional tears as we read what I wrote about Pelagie's experiences. They lived with this story for several years. Judy not only became familiar with Pelagie during our regular meetings, but also reread the manuscript after completion to see how it flowed. Again, thanks to all of you for making our meetings enjoyable and something to look forward to—even when we discussed the tragedies of Pelagie's life.

One of the important reasons for this venture was to give my family a glimpse of their heritage. Hugs to them for their encouragement and support: to my children Kathryn and Steve Walker, Heidi Voelker Davis, Eric Voelker, and Cindy and Stan Bonis; my grandchildren Kaitlin and Ethan Walker; Rhett, Tess, and Brynn Davis; and Annie and Blaine Bonis. To my husband, Bill, for reading my manuscript and putting up with my countless hours of research and writing. Many thanks.

Extra thanks to my daughter Heidi for drawing the picture for the front cover, and to my son-in-law Stan for removing the tourists from the pictures that my husband and I took at the Fortress of Louisbourg.

Thanks to Gerald and Helen Crochet who shared the information they had about Yves Crochet—Gerald's ancestor and mine. Also to Vic Estelle who sent information about Martin Benoist, and to Diana and Tommy LeBlanc for the use of his books for my research.

And to all of my family and friends who continue to encourage me—merci beaucoup.

Introduction

The majority of Acadians were unable to read and write at the time of the deportation. For this reason, accounts of the daily lives of these people are mainly stories passed down orally through generations until someone put them in writing. Much of the official paperwork during the lives of the Acadians was destroyed or lost, although some was found by historians in France, England, and Quebec.

I obtained my information about my great-great-great-great-grandmother Pelagie Benoist and her family from census records, church records of births, deaths, and marriages, and also ship records and land holdings. From these documents, I traced Pelagie's travels from Nova Scotia to Prince Edward Island (Île Saint-Jean), to Cape Breton Island (Île Royale), to France, and finally to Louisiana. I found enough information to know this is a story that has to be told. Through countless hours of research, I found general information about the Acadians in each area where Pelagie and her family lived, and used it to write a *probable* story of Pelagie's life. All of the dates are accurate except possibly the year of Pelagie's birth (listed by historians as either 1741 or 1742) and dates of births and deaths of her ancestors (sometimes listed "about . . .").

The information presented about Pelagie's parents, grandparents, siblings, aunts, uncles, cousins, husband, children, and grandchildren was found through similar research.

Some genealogists list Pelagie's parents as Abraham Benoist and Angélique Vincent, since they had a daughter named Pelagie, who was born in 1742. Initially, I thought *this* Pelagie was my ancestor, but further research provided different information.

- The marriage record of my ancestor Yves Crochet identifies his wife, Pelagie Benoist, as the daughter of Claude Benoist and Elisabeth Terriot.
- According to Stephen A. White, famed Acadian genealogist at the Center of Acadian Studies at the University of Moncton in Moncton, New Brunswick, Canada, and author of *Genealogy Dictionary of Acadian Families*, Abraham Benoit, Paul Benoit, their wives, and all their descendants (except for one of Paul's daughters) suffered the fate which I discuss in this book.
- Finally, I contacted Louis Benoit, author of *Histoire, Notes et Généalogie sur la Famille Acadienne Benoit*, who stated that the ancestor we have in common was Pelagie-Blanche, born in 1741, daughter of Claude Benoist and Elisabeth Terriot. He believes the reason for the confusion about her parents was because the eleven-year-old daughter of Claude and Elisabeth was listed as Lablanche in a 1752 Île Saint-Jean census.

Pelagie and her relatives were people who actually lived at the times and in the places discussed in this book. With the few exceptions listed below and those in the Author's Notes at the end of the book, their stories are factual, based on genealogical research and the history of the Acadians. Their friends and neighbors are representative of people who might have lived at that time. The priests and nuns were real people, and the events are all part of the history of the Acadians.

My book is historical fiction since I took the liberty to put thoughts into people's minds and words into their mouths. I also took Pelagie on a few adventures in Louisbourg and France that she *could* have had, since the things she did in the story happened, as reported, when she lived there.

When an Acadian woman married, her maiden name continued to be used on official records. However, her husband's surname was used when she was addressed as madame. The children's last name was the same as their father's.

For names of people in this book, I used the spelling found in the early records of Acadie, but in the Introduction and Author's Notes, I spelled the names as they were spelled by the authors of the books I discussed. Pelagie's family name is now spelled Benoit.

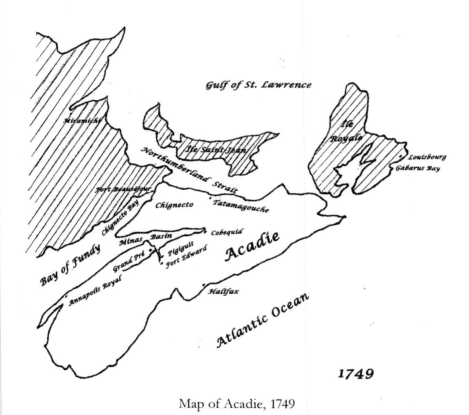

Map of Acadie, 1749

Map of Ile Saint-Jean, 1750

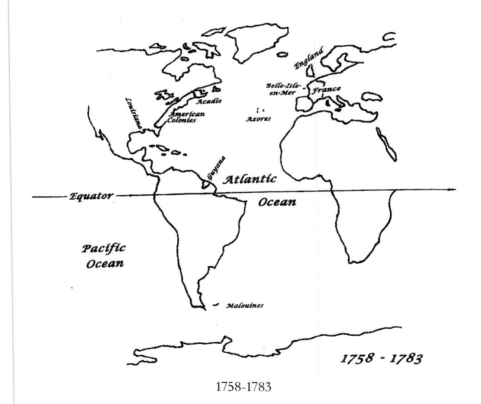

1758-1783

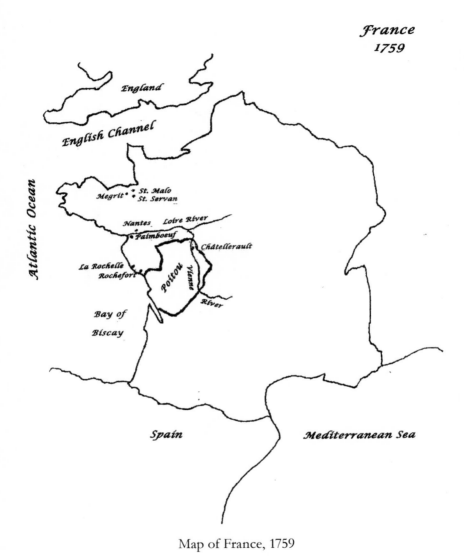

France
1759

England

English Channel

Atlantic Ocean

Megrit• •St. Malo
           •St. Servan

Nantes   Loire River

•Paimboeuf

Châtellerault

La Rochelle
Rochefort

Poitou   Vienne

River

Bay of
Biscay

Spain

Mediterranean Sea

Map of France, 1759

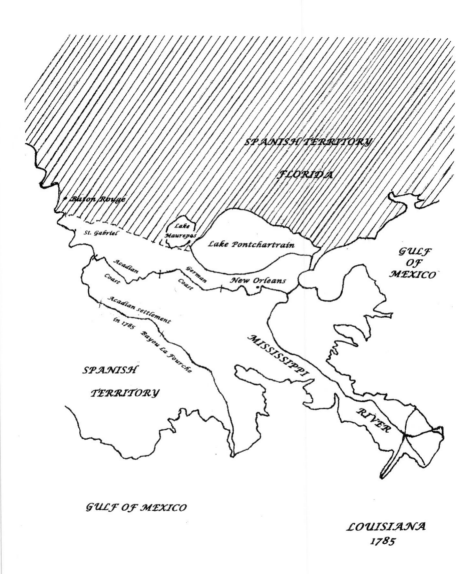

Map of Louisiana, 1785

1

English Soldiers

Pigiguit, Acadie, Winter 1750

Angry voices and the thunder of horses' hooves shattered the early-morning quiet. I dropped my basket of eggs, reached for my four-year-old sister's hand, and held her close. Trembling, Anne and I peeked out the henhouse door.

Twelve huge horses pawed the dusty road. The scowling soldiers astride them wore white trousers, long red coats, and black three-cornered hats.

"English soldiers," I whispered. My heart pounded. I couldn't breathe.

As Papa rushed out of the barn, the soldier in front shouted, "We have orders from Governor Cornwallis to build a road from here to Halifax, and your people will help us! We begin in one week. Be ready!"

As soon as the soldiers moved down the road, Papa stomped into the house. Leaving the basket on the henhouse floor next to the broken eggs, I pulled Anne to the partly-open door of our house.

Anne tugged on my sleeve. "Pelagie. . ."

"Shh. I want to hear what Papa says about the soldiers."

He threw his felt hat on the bed. "That's it. We're leaving."

Maman twisted her apron. "Why? What is happening?"

"With a road from here to Halifax, it will be easy for the English soldiers to get here in a few hours. They'll be watching us all the time, and we'll always be waiting to see what they're going to do next."

"Where will we go?"

"Île Saint-Jean. It's the closest French-controlled land. My brother Augustin moved there almost a year ago and is happy. The only way we'll ever live in peace is by getting away from the English."

"How will we survive?"

"The French leaders have promised to provide food until we can take care of ourselves. I'm going to talk to my brothers. I'll be back as soon as I can."

I couldn't believe what I just heard. Leave Pigiguit! How could we leave our home—the house where I was born and had lived all of my nine years! At first I couldn't move, then I hurried to pull Anne away from the door, so Papa wouldn't know I had been listening.

Grand'maman and Oncle Paul arrived the next day from their homes nearby. Oncle Abraham and Oncle Charles had come with their families from Grand Pré, along with Tante Claire and her husband, Pierre LeBlanc. The men were dressed in linen shirts, knee-length pants, and long socks. The women wore blouses and long skirts in shades of tan and brown. Caps covered their dark hair. The children were dressed like their parents; everyone wore moccasins or wooden shoes.

My favorite cousin, Françoise, and I brought the younger children outside to play, but she and I stayed near the door. I had to hear what the grown-ups were saying.

Papa paced up and down. "I was worried when the governor brought several boatloads of people from England to live in Halifax last summer, but I knew it would take several days for them to get here through the forest. Last week we were told we must sign a new oath of loyalty to the king of England, and now we have to build a road to Halifax. I will *not* build a road and I will *not* sign the oath, no matter what the governor says."

"If we don't take the oath, we'll have to leave our homes and our land," said Oncle Abraham.

"Non," said Oncle Pierre. "I think Governor Cornwallis wants to scare us, so we'll promise to fight with the English against the French. He'll never make us leave Acadie."

Papa shook his head. "The oath will be a promise to fight our own people if there is another war. I've had enough! I refuse to fight, and I'm not going to wait for the governor to send us away. We're leaving before the soldiers return to start building the road."

"Oh, no!" I whispered. "I hoped he would change his mind. We're really leaving!" Françoise just sighed.

"Claude, we have a good life here," said Oncle Pierre. "Your farm is doing well. Why would you want to start all over again? Don't worry; the governor won't make us leave."

"I don't trust him. My mind is made up," said Papa. "I hope you'll all come with us."

"I'll have to think about it," said Oncle Paul.

"So will I," said Oncle Charles.

With tears streaming down their faces, my aunts hugged Maman. "I'll probably never see you again," said Tante Claire. "Pierre refuses to leave."

"I don't know what Abraham will decide to do," said Tante Angélique. "I hope we'll all live near each other again someday."

Maman sighed, wiped her tears with her apron, and then turned away, as if she couldn't bear to say goodbye.

I didn't say a word as I held Françoise tightly, wondering if I would ever see her again.

* * *

Usually after supper, Maman and I mended clothes while Gregoire helped Papa clean and repair his tools. However, that night we all sat quietly, staring at the flames dancing above the logs in the fireplace.

After a while I had to have an answer. "Papa, why do we have to leave Acadie? The English soldiers aren't bothering us."

"Not yet, but England and France have been fighting over Acadie for years. The English leaders want our land because of the fish, furs, and good trading routes. We have worked hard to make our farms prosper, so they want their settlers to live here."

"But it's our land," I said.

"I know, but they envy us because we have plenty of food for ourselves and enough grain and cows to send to our people at the fortress in Louisbourg. Maybe the English leaders don't realize that our soil isn't fertile because of luck, but because our ancestors spent years of backbreaking work building our dikes."

"Do we hate the English?"

"Non, ma chère enfant. We don't hate anyone, and it doesn't matter to us which country is in control as long as the governors don't try to change the way we live. We've been ruled by the English for almost forty years. They've left our people alone, except for demanding every few years that we sign an oath promising to fight with the English, if the two countries ever go to war again."

"But Papa, you can't read or write. How could you sign the oath?"

"It's true that many Acadians can't read or write. Then, an English soldier writes the man's name, and the Acadian makes a cross next to it.

"Until this year," Papa continued, "whenever we were asked to sign the oath, we refused. But we were always told that the English king only wanted us to be loyal to him, and we wouldn't be forced to fight against our people if the two countries went to war. We were also told we could continue to worship God as Roman Catholics. So we signed the promise to be loyal to the king."

"If you signed the oath, why do we have to leave?" I asked.

Papa sighed. "Edward Cornwallis is our new governor. He insists that we sign a *new* oath, and we *will* have to fight against the French if there is another war. We'll be permitted to worship God as Catholics, *as far as the laws of England will allow us.* I'm not sure what that means, but I don't like the sound of it. I'm afraid the English leaders will start telling us how to live and worship God, and will *make us fight.*"

"We don't want to fight," said six-year-old Gregoire.

"Non," said Papa. "We are peaceful people. We don't want to fight anyone, but especially not the French. Our ancestors came from France and many of our relatives still live there. And we don't want to be told how we should worship God.

"Some of the English governors have treated us fairly, but we don't know if we can trust Governor Cornwallis. We can't wait to see what he is going to do next. We must leave. Soon."

The next day Maman and I cooked, cleaned, and washed clothes as usual, but instead of spinning thread or making cloth, we helped Papa take Maman's spinning wheel and loom apart. Then we packed them on one of our Indian dragging trains, which would carry everything we were taking with us.

In the evening Papa came in from the barn with a big smile on his face.

Maman stopped stirring the soup and wiped her hands. "It's been days since I've seen you smiling."

"My brother Paul brought a message; my maman and all three of my brothers in Acadie will accompany us to Île Saint-Jean."

"That's the best news I've heard in a long time," said Maman.

I took a deep breath and twirled around the room. "Bon. Grand'maman, Françoise, and lots of other cousins will go with us."

Papa smiled. "I knew that would make everyone happy. Maybe it will be a little easier for us to leave."

"But what about your sisters?" asked Maman.

"Anne will come with us, but Judith's and Claire's husbands refuse to leave."

Maman sighed. "I was afraid that would happen."

I stopped twirling and sat down. "I wish Tante Judith and Tante Claire would come, too."

After supper I went for a walk; I had to think about what was happening. In front of the house lay the fields that had been golden with wheat before our fall harvest. Past the fields were dikes, which the first Acadians in Pigiguit had built to hold the water back from the bay so they could plant crops in the fertile soil. Beyond the dikes, the river flowing into Minus Basin lay in shadowy darkness.

Papa and Gregoire were always busy outside, except on extremely cold days. They planted wheat in the spring, raised farm animals, and took care of the dikes. Maman and I helped them cut and bundle the wheat in the fall.

Behind our house was Maman's big vegetable garden where we grew many different vegetables and herbs for seasoning and medicine. Her maman and the Mi'kmaq Indians had taught her which herbs to use if one of us got sick, but that rarely happened. We were healthy because, as Papa often said, we worked hard, enjoyed life, and had lots of good food to eat.

I always spent my days helping Maman in the garden and with our household chores. We also made candles and soap, and preserved food for the winter. Anne helped as much as she could. We were constantly busy, but we talked, sang, and laughed as we worked. But during the week that we prepared to leave Pigiguit, there was no laughing or singing, and little talking.

I gazed around as far as my eyes could see, hoping I would remember my home and land forever.

* * *

The following evening as Maman and I wrapped dishes in towels and packed them in a cooking pot, we heard a knock at the door. My first thought was *English soldiers*. I didn't realize I was holding my breath until my cousin Paul walked into the kitchen. "Good evening, Tante Elisabeth, Oncle Claude, Pelagie. Antoine is waiting in the woods with our animals; we'll take yours and follow the path to Cobequid until the rest of you catch up with us."

Papa had just finished cleaning his gun; he hung it on the wall over the fireplace and grabbed his jacket. "Bon. I hope you get away without being seen by the English soldiers. I'll help you lead my animals into the woods. May God watch over you and keep you safe."

After they walked toward the barn, I turned to Maman. "Why are they leaving now? We're not ready to go yet."

"It will be difficult to keep the animals quiet so as not to alert the English soldiers. If the soldiers hear them, the boys can say we don't have food in our barns for the animals, and they're hunting for food in the woods. It will be safer for all of us that way."

When he came back inside, Papa told us we would leave Acadie the next evening. "We'll walk all night so we will be far away before the sun comes up. If the English soldiers catch us leaving without permission, we'll be thrown in jail."

That night, lying in the darkness trying to go to sleep, I thought again about what we were leaving. Tears wet my pillow. I loved our house that Papa had built with the help of our neighbors when he and Maman married. My family gathered, ate, and slept in the one big room downstairs. Gregoire slept in the loft upstairs where the other boys were supposed to join him when they were older.

I thought about the fun we had when our work was done. On Saturday nights we got together with our neighbors, taking turns at different houses. Everyone brought food. The men pushed the furniture against the walls and played music. We sang and danced—even the babies who were just learning to walk.

I longed for my happy life in Pigiguit to continue.

* * *

The following morning Maman looked around at our almost-empty kitchen and sighed. "Papa put our cooking pots and barrels on the dragging trains; Pelagie, please fill them with food for our journey."

"Come help me, Anne," I said, as I walked to the garden.

Cabbage was the only vegetable there. Gregoire and I had cut the heads in October and turned them upside-down so the snow would protect the cabbage all winter. Carrots, turnips, peas, and beans that had grown in the nearby rows were stored in our cellar, along with herbs that Maman had dried.

After loading the dragging trains with as much cabbage as we could, I took Anne's hand and we wandered through the fruit orchard. In the summer we picked cherries, and in the fall we harvested pears and shiny red and yellow apples.

I smiled at my little sister. "Do you remember the fun we had in the orchard, running between the trees, and helping Maman gather the fruit when it was ripe? I think you and Gregoire ate as much as you picked."

Anne's shoulders drooped. "I wish we could do that right now."

I pulled her close for a hug. "So do I. But now we have to pack our food, or we'll get very hungry just eating nuts and plants on our way to Île Saint-Jean." In the cellar were shelves of enough dried food for the winter—pork, fish, beans, and peas. There were also rows of jam and jelly from our fruit trees. In another section of the cellar were barrels of turnips and carrots packed in dry leaves, and barrels of apples packed in straw.

We made many trips up and down the cellar stairs, until the barrels and cooking pots on the dragging trains were filled with food.

I ached inside as I looked around the empty cellar. Would we ever return to our home that I loved so much? Would we ever see Tante Judith, Tante Claire, and their families again? Would we survive? Why was God letting this happen to us? It would be years before all of my questions were answered.

2

Leaving

I had to find the doll—a little rag doll that I had made for my two-year-old sister, Marie Josephe. How would she sleep without it? I was still searching when the door suddenly opened.

Cold air swirled around the room as Papa rushed in. *"Allons! Vite!* (Come on! Hurry!) We must leave. Now! The moon is hidden by clouds so it's dark enough for us to get away without being seen. Follow me quietly, one at a time into the woods."

Everyone was ready to leave, but I still hadn't found the doll. Marie Josephe sat on the bed crying, "Ma poupée."

I patted her hand. "Don't worry. I'll find it." I hoped that was true.

Gregoire and Anne picked up their bundles of clothes, as I glanced around one last time. The house that I loved looked as sad and lonely as I felt. There was no warm, crackling fire in the fireplace and only a lingering smell of fresh, hot bread and Maman's vegetable soup. The beds were bare. Maman's loom, always next to the fireplace, was gone. There was nothing on the table on the other side of the fireplace: no pots, dishes, food, or candles to show that a family lived here.

"Will we come home again, Papa?" I asked.

"Je ne sais pas, ma petite Pelagie. (I don't know, my little Pelagie). We can only hope and pray that France and England settle their problems so we can live in peace once again."

There was another blast of cold air as Papa opened the door, picked up Marie Josephe, and followed Gregoire and Anne into the woods.

Maman whispered, "Allons, Pelagie, allons," then walked through the door carrying two-year-old Daniel, who was sound asleep. I knew I should follow Maman but I couldn't move. I opened my mouth to call her, but nothing came out.

I had to find Marie Josephe's doll. Leaving home was hard enough; she needed her doll. I couldn't stop looking. I said a prayer, and finally, I saw it under a mattress. *Thank God.* I looked around one last time, took a deep breath, and left the only home I had ever known.

I stood for several minutes in the shadow of the house. Looking. Listening. Everything was quiet. Nothing moved.

I wished I could stand there forever, breathing in the sweet scent of the land and the clean night air. Pulling my cloak closer, I ran behind the house past the vegetable garden, past the empty barns, and through the fruit orchard with its bare trees, until I reached the woods. I held my breath.

No one was there. Had they left without me?

For a moment the moon peeked out from behind the clouds. Several men stood near the edge of the woods, watching me. Were they soldiers waiting to grab me and throw me in jail? Should I run back to the house? I couldn't scream. I couldn't move.

Then I heard Papa whisper, "Pelagie, *viens ici* (come here)."

I hurried over to hug him. "Oh, Papa, I was so scared!"

His arms tightened around me.

Maman rushed over. "I thought you were right behind me. I was so worried when I reached the woods without you."

Then I recognized the other men: Oncle Paul, Oncle Charles, and Oncle Abraham. More people stood deeper in the woods, motionless, not making a sound. Some of them stood beside dragging trains loaded with furniture and household goods. Almost everyone was there: Grand'maman Elizabeth, Tante Angélique, Tante Madeleine, Tante Anne, and lots of cousins. Altogether my three uncles had twenty-one children, and Oncle Paul had a newborn grandson. The only ones missing were my oldest male cousins, who had gone ahead of us with the farm animals.

Even the youngest children were as still as the night animals that lived in the woods—animals that were probably watching us.

Oncle Paul looked around. "It's time to go."

Papa said, "Walk through the woods without making a sound, the way our friends the Mi'kmaq Indians do. We can't let anyone hear us, so we won't talk. Don't even whisper. Our lives could depend on this."

There was nothing I could do except walk silently through the woods and pray. So I made every step a prayer that someday we would come home again.

* * *

With my heart thumping in my chest, I stayed close to Papa as we walked through the woods on a trail that had been made by the Mi'kmaq Indians. Last summer after finishing my daily chores, I had often followed this well-worn path for a few miles with my cousin Elizabeth. She and I pretended that we were going to Cobequid to visit Tante Marguerite. We ran, picked berries, and hid behind the trees, without a care in the world.

But tonight every tree, every stump, every sound in the dark woods was an English soldier waiting to shoot us or take us to jail. Even the night sounds of insects and the hoot of an owl—sounds so familiar to me—caused me to stop and look around.

Suddenly, there was a rustling in the underbrush. It had to be an English soldier hiding behind the tree right next to me. I stood still. I couldn't breathe. Then a tiny white-footed mouse scurried through the leaves. I wondered how something so small had frightened me so much, but every shadow continued to make my throat tighten until I could hardly swallow.

We trudged slowly and carefully through the forest. Roots and rocks tried to trip us in the darkness, but we couldn't allow the slightest sound to alert the English soldiers of our escape. Even the babies were quiet, sleeping peacefully in their mothers' arms.

The boys took turns pulling the dragging trains piled high with furniture, dishes, pots, clothes, and food. Older girls carried the younger children or held their hands. Men carrying guns and knives guarded our group, front, rear, and sides.

I knew I should help Maman with my younger brothers and sisters. I took a few slow steps away from Papa toward the group of ladies and small children. Immediately my heart began to thump. My breath came loud and fast. My first thought was that if there were any English soldiers nearby, they would hear my breathing and my heartbeat. I couldn't move another step away from Papa. My aunts and cousins would have to help Maman.

* * *

My aching feet and legs reminded me that we had been walking for several hours. We had stopped only for brief rests and a refreshing drink whenever we were lucky enough to find a running stream. When I thought I couldn't take one more step without falling, we reached a clearing.

Papa stopped to wait for the other men. "I think we have walked far enough for one night. I don't think the English soldiers will be looking for us here."

Oncle Abraham nodded. "It should be safe for us to stop and get some sleep, but we're still too close to Pigiguit to light a fire."

We snuggled together, lying on quilts and covered with furs. I fell asleep immediately, too tired to think about home, the cold, or the English soldiers.

Bright sun, filtering through the trees, woke me. I was too tired to open my eyes and I wondered why my legs ached; then I remembered that we had walked for hours late into the night. The adults and older children were already busy folding quilts and piling everything back on the dragging trains. After a quick breakfast of dry bread and cold water, Papa said, "Allons. It's time to get started."

"But Papa," I asked, "Don't we have to wait until dark?"

"Non, we had to get away last night without being seen, but we're probably far enough from Pigiguit that the English soldiers won't be looking for us. It will be easier to travel during the day."

"*Oui* (Yes)," said Oncle Paul. "Soldiers stay close to the villages to catch people who are trying to leave. I don't think they'll waste their time coming this far into the woods looking for us."

Oncle Charles nodded. "From now on, we can talk softly and make a fire at night to keep warm, but we don't want to make any loud noises, just in case there are English soldiers nearby."

As my cousin Françoise and I walked together, I whispered, "I still can't bear to think that I'll never return home. I wonder if we'll ever be happy again."

Françoise shook her head. "I don't know. We'll have to keep praying."

We still looked around, watching for strangers, but we felt safer and safer as each step took us farther away from the dreaded English soldiers, and sadly, from our beloved home.

* * *

We walked until mid-afternoon, sometimes surprising a few animals that were near the trail. After the men found a place to camp for the night, my aunts looked for a safe spot for a campfire.

"Girls, it's time to prepare supper," said Maman. "We need firewood for cooking and to keep us warm through the night. Also, search for anything we can eat, but stay close enough so you can see us and we can see you."

"Come on, Françoise," I said, "let's see who can find the most." We filled our aprons with berries, nuts, roots, and plants that our mothers and the friendly Mi'kmaq Indians had taught us were safe to eat.

I sighed when Maman called us back. "She must need help preparing the carrots and turnips we brought with us."

Back at the camp, I looked around for the men and boys. "Where is everyone, Maman?"

"Some of the men found a stream and brought back water; now they're trying to catch some fish. Others went farther into the woods to hunt for meat."

I put carrots into the pot. "I hope we'll have turkey for supper."

Maman wiped her hands. "We'll cook whatever they're lucky enough to find, and it will be delicious."

As we sat around the fire after supper I asked, "Papa, why did the first French people come here to live? If they had stayed in France, we'd live there, and we wouldn't have to worry about fighting with the English."

After filling his pipe with tobacco, Papa lit it with a glowing stick from the fire. "And you would have missed all the joy of living in Pigiguit! Your uncles and I will tell you about our people. You must all listen carefully so that someday you can tell your children and grandchildren. That's the only way our story will be remembered. It *must* be remembered!

"For hundreds of years, only Indians lived in this area. Then French fishermen began to come here every spring to fish in the waters around Acadie. When they returned to France in the fall, their ships were loaded with fish."

I interrupted him. "Grand-père once told me the fishermen dried some in the sun, and put others in big barrels of salt. French people couldn't wait to buy that fish." Then I held my breath, waiting to see if Papa would scold me for being rude.

Papa only nodded. "That's right, Pelagie. Explorers from Europe also crossed the ocean, each one searching for land to claim for his own country. Jacques Cartier claimed this beautiful area for France, and the first French settlers arrived almost one hundred fifty years ago. Two years later, the first English settlement was begun farther south, in the American colonies. But the English wanted our land too."

"Why did they want our land? They had their own," said Gregoire.

"They wanted to sell the fish and furs," I said.

"Oui," said Oncle Charles. "Our waters are teeming with fish, especially cod, which the French people love. People in Europe also like the coats and hats made from beavers and other animals that are trapped here, and the shipping routes are perfect for trading with other countries. All of this adds to the riches of the country that owns this land."

"When did our family come to Acadie?" I asked.

Maman spoke for the first time. "That's a story for another night. We should all get some rest."

"Oui," said Papa. "We still have a long way to walk. We'll have more stories tomorrow night. Sleep well. And don't forget to say your prayers."

3

Traveling through Snow

After a quick breakfast the next morning, we were on our way again, trudging farther and farther north. Oncle Paul, who was at the head of our group, stopped suddenly and said softly, "Listen."

Everyone stood still, not making a sound. My heart was in my throat. I trembled and moved closer to Papa, but I breathed a sigh of relief when I saw the smile on his face and heard the soft lowing and shuffling noises of cattle. He said, "It must be the boys with our animals. Stay here." He and my uncles strode ahead for a few hundred paces and then motioned for us to join them. I was surprised and delighted to see the two cousins who had been missing from our family group. For the rest of our journey, the boys and girls who were old enough helped to keep the cows from wandering away.

Since Françoise had lived in Grand Pré, which was at least a half day's travel from Pigiguit, we had been unable to see each other often before we left our homes. Now she and I walked together whenever our mothers didn't need our help. Since we were the same age, we shared many secrets, hopes, and dreams as we trudged through the woods.

"What are you smiling about?" she asked late in the afternoon. "I haven't seen you this happy since the week before we left Acadie."

"I'm thinking about our cows," I said. "I'm tired of drinking water all the time. Now we'll have milk for breakfast and supper."

"And butter and cheese when we finally get settled."

While walking through the woods, we occasionally met small groups of Mi'kmaqs. We shared our food with them and they shared what they had. They often walked with us for a few hours, and sometimes for a whole day. We spoke to them as we always did, with a mixture of their native language, gestures, and some French and English words. The Mi'kmaqs always had good news for us; there were no English soldiers nearby.

As we traveled farther north the first few flakes began to fall. I flung out my arms and shouted, "Snow!" Later it fell harder and piled up on the ground. "Françoise," I whispered, "let's throw some at the boys." Soon all of my cousins were laughing and throwing snowballs or making snow angels. The adults watched us, smiling.

I bent over to make another snowball, then looked around and gasped. Pulling my cloak closer, I hurried to find Papa. "Look at all the tracks in the snow! Will the English soldiers follow us?"

"Non, Pelagie. We've been walking for days. I don't think they're looking for us now. Every step brings us farther from the English forts and soldiers. But we'll have to be careful when we get closer to Tatamagouche. Soldiers will probably be there, watching for Acadians who are trying to cross the strait to Île Saint-Jean."

We walked slower and slower as the snow got deeper. My fur cloak helped to keep out the cold and my snowshoes made walking easier. But the bottom of my skirt, sometimes dragging in the snow, was cold, wet, and extremely uncomfortable when it touched my legs. My hands felt frozen because my gloves were wet from playing in the snow.

That night while we prepared supper, the older boys dug caves in the snow so each family would be sheltered from the wind. As soon as the dishes and food were put away, I joined the others around the campfire. "Papa, you promised to tell us why our family came to Acadie."

He smiled at me. "About eighty years ago, your great-grand-père Martin Benoist sailed from France with your great-grand'maman Marie when he was twenty-eight and she was only fifteen years old. More than fifty men were in their group, but just five women."

"Did their mamans and papas and their brothers and sisters come, too?" I asked.

"Non. Their families stayed in France."

I sighed loudly. "Then why did they come to Acadie? How could Great-grand'maman leave her maman and papa to cross the ocean when she was only fifteen?"

"Louis XIV, king of France, wanted colonists to settle here," said Oncle Paul. "He paid for the trip and also gave people land to encourage them to move. The people in France had small farms, and had heard from earlier settlers about large land grants and the abundance of food that grows in Acadie for those who are willing to work. In France, frequent wars, famines, and terrible diseases made life extremely difficult. The colonists were told that their lives would be much better here."

"But, Oncle Paul, were they?" I asked.

"Yes. I was ten years old when my grand-père Martin died. He and my grand'maman Marie often told me they were happy they had moved to Acadie, even though they never saw any of their relatives again."

"I wish I could cross the ocean," said Gregoire.

"I hope you never have to," said Oncle Paul. "It may sound like fun, but my grandparents often talked about the trip. They said it was terrible. It took about six weeks to sail across the ocean, which was stormy at times—six weeks, crowded in a wooden boat with only hard bread, dried fish, and dried meat to eat and stale water to drink."

Papa nodded. "You children are unhappy about leaving your homes, but it must have been much harder for them. You're lucky enough to be with your families."

"What did Great-grand-père and Great-grand'maman do when they finally got off the boat?" I asked.

"The group joined the settlers who were already in Port Royal. Even though they were probably exhausted from their long journey, each family had to build a house. The new settlers had to hunt for food, plant vegetables and fruit trees, and build dikes. The Acadians already living there helped as much as they could, but they had their own farms to care for. It was a hard life."

"Did they ever leave Port Royal?" I asked.

Oncle Paul nodded. "They lived in Port Royal for thirty years and raised their ten children there. Then they moved to Pigiguit along with nine of their children; most of them were ready to start farming their own land. At that time Pigiguit was a new settlement with plenty of land where they could have large farms near one another. All of your Grand'père Pierre and Grand'maman Elizabeth's children were born in Pigiguit."

Grand'maman Elizabeth smiled as we all looked at her. "Oui, but that's a story for another night."

* * *

The next day several Mi'kmaqs who were also going north caught up with us. Papa and my uncles greeted them, *"Mes amis."* (My friends). The Mi'kmaqs repeated the greeting, told us they were going to Cobequid, and asked if we'd like to accompany them.

"Gladly," said Papa. "I was afraid we'd lose our way since we can no longer see the path because of the deep snow.

While we were eating supper around the fire that night, I asked the question that had been on my mind all day, "Why do we have to go to Île Saint-Jean? It's so far from Acadie."

Papa said, "Île Saint-Jean is still controlled by the French. We'll be happier with our own people who speak French and are Roman Catholics. Most of the English people are Protestants. In Île Saint-Jean we'll be allowed to speak French, keep the faith we grew up with, and not have to worry about fighting against our own people."

"But why didn't we wait until spring to leave?" I asked. "It would have been easier without all this snow."

Papa looked around at everyone sitting around the fire. "We were afraid to wait any longer to leave. We didn't know what the English might be planning to do to the Acadians."

"But, Papa," I said, "a lot of Acadians are still in Acadie. Why aren't they leaving too?"

He sighed. "They don't think the English leaders will make our people fight or make them leave Acadie. I hope they are right, but we didn't want to take a chance."

"Like Tante Judith and Tante Claire," I said.

"Yes, like Tante Judith and Tante Claire," said Papa. "We can only hope and pray their husbands made the right decision for themselves and their families."

4

The Mountains

Fifteen days after we left our beloved home, we dragged into the village of Cobequid. I didn't have the energy to talk to anyone; I only wanted to sleep.

While the women washed our dirty travel clothes in a stream the next day, the men tried to find relatives or friends in Cobequid. I knew I should help Maman but I shivered whenever I put my hands into the freezing water. Instead I told her I'd watch our two-year-olds, Daniel and Marie Josephe, as they chased each other around the trees, rosy-cheeked and laughing.

Papa and my uncles returned to our camp with big smiles on their faces. "A large number of Acadians are preparing to leave for Île Saint-Jean," said Papa. "They plan to travel in small groups so they won't attract attention, but everyone will be close enough to be safe. They asked us to join them, but I'd better let Paul tell you the rest of our news before he bursts from excitement."

Oncle Paul said quickly, "The best news is that we found our sister Marguerite who lives here in Cobequid. We will travel with Marguerite, her husband Paul Doiron, and his father and brothers."

"Oh, Papa," I said, "it's been so long since we've seen them. I want to see them *now*."

"Tomorrow, Pelagie. You'll have lots of time to spend with them."

We were greeted with many hugs and smiles the next morning when we visited Tante Marguerite and many of the other people we would travel with. They had good news for Papa and my uncles. "If you make a small cart for each family in your group," said one of the men, "we will to give you an ox to pull each one."

Papa smiled. "Thank you. That will be easier than traveling with our wooden dragging trains."

"And we'll have room for the old and the very young to ride when they get too tired to walk," said Oncle Paul.

"We are planning to leave in about two weeks," said Tante Marguerite. "That will give you time to build your carts."

As soon as we returned to our campsite, some of the older boys left to hunt while others went fishing. The men began cutting down trees to make the carts. Soon they were sawing, hammering, and cutting wheels.

After watching for a while, I asked, "Why didn't we bring carts from home instead of the dragging trains?"

"Two reasons," said Papa. "We were trying to get away quietly; sometimes wheels squeak and animals make noise. Also, we knew there was only a rough path from Pigiguit, making it difficult to travel with carts and oxen. The Cobequid Acadians built a road all the way from here to Tatamagouche to send supplies to our people in Île Saint-Jean and Île Royale. Except for the mountains, the rest of our trip should be easier."

"We have to go through mountains?"

"Yes. I hope that won't be too hard."

I wished I could go fishing with the boys, but I knew Maman needed help, so I churned butter, then helped prepare and salt the meat and fish the boys brought back for the rest of our trip.

When we were finally ready to start our journey to Tatamagouche, we followed the Cobequid River for a short time, then the North River.

"Fresh, cold water to drink, whenever we want it," I said one morning. "This makes me happy."

"And water to wash dishes, hands, and faces," said Maman. "That makes me happy."

But our smiles disappeared a short time later when we saw what was ahead of us.

Oncle Charles suddenly stopped walking. "Look at those mountains! I didn't know they'd be that high."

I sighed. "What are we going to do? Can we go around them?"

"Non, not if we want to get to Île Saint-Jean in a few weeks," said M. (Mr.) Richard, an Acadian from Cobequid who was walking with us. "That would take much too long. It will be difficult, but many of our people have made it through the mountains before."

"Papa, you said this would be easier than walking from Pigiguit," I complained.

"Since there's a road through the mountains, I thought it would be easier. I never saw mountains before and never dreamed they would look like this!"

I don't think we could have made it without the Mi'kmaqs and the Acadians from Cobequid who knew the route well. We went up narrow paths on the sides of the mountains, then down through valleys. There was often little room to pass between boulders. Since spring was finally here, the snow had started to melt in spots, and no more fell during our trip.

The road was frequently bumpy with rocks. Sometimes, as we got higher and higher in the mountains, we were right on the edge of a steep drop, and one slip would have meant falling down farther than we could see. The adults and older boys and girls carried the small children or held their hands. I was relieved that no one asked me to take care of one of the little ones, because I had enough to do taking care of myself.

Once, only once, I looked down. My head began to spin. I shook all over. I knew if I moved, I would go over the edge. Maman, carrying Marie Josephe, walked behind me. She took my hand. "Come on, Pelagie. You can do it. We'll walk together." It was only because she was beside me that I was able to continue through the mountains.

Somehow the oxen and carts made it without any problems. Just when I thought I couldn't go one step farther, a soft sound caught my attention. After a few more turns in the path, a rushing stream poured down the mountain right in front of us.

"Bon," said M. Richard. "Our journey will be easier now. This is the beginning of the Tatamagouche River. If we follow it down to the valley, we'll reach the Northumberland Strait, which we have to cross to get to Île Saint-Jean."

Maman squeezed my hand and smiled at me. "I knew you were my brave girl."

Even though I wanted to lie down and never get up, I kept walking, knowing that we would soon be able to rest. When we were finally on flat land again, I joined the younger children as we hopped, skipped, and ran around.

Putting a finger to his lips, M. Richard said, "We're near the strait, so we'll hide in the woods and be very quiet. The Mi'kmaqs told me that English soldiers sail up and down the strait, trying to catch our people who are leaving Acadie. They are probably watching for us."

That quieted us in a hurry.

5

Crossing the Strait

My feet and legs ached. I was tired and dirty. I wanted to jump into the water, no matter how cold it was. I wanted to dance for joy because we had walked so far and were finally close to the island that would be our home. "What are we waiting for, Papa?" I asked, as we sat under the trees deep in the woods.

M. Richard spoke softly. "Acadian fishermen watch for our people; they will bring us across the strait. But we have to be patient. We don't want to get caught now, after the exhausting weeks we spent getting here."

"*Regardez!* (Look!) There's a boat now," said my four-year-old cousin, a little too loudly.

"Quiet," whispered M. Richard. "Don't anyone move or make a sound. That's an English boat."

We held our breaths, afraid that the English had heard Jean-Charles's shout. On the boat, sailors in uniform looked up and down the coast—searching for us! To my horror, the boat pulled to shore and a few sailors got out and walked close to our hiding place in the woods. My hands shook; I trembled all over. We were going to be caught!

I held my breath. It seemed like forever, but the sailors finally went back to the boat and sailed away. We all breathed a sigh of relief, but it was a long time before any of us moved.

That night, as we still waited in the woods watching the water, a light flashed—one, two, three times. "Look!" I whispered, pointing.

Everything was quiet, and then it flashed again—one, two, three times.

Oncle Paul stood up. "That's our signal. Everyone wait here and stay quiet."

He lit his lantern, held it high, covered the light, and quickly uncovered it, one, two, three times. Silently he crept to the shore and signaled again. Just when I thought I would burst if I had to sit still another minute, he crept back into the woods.

"It's the Acadian fishermen. They brought four rowboats," said Oncle Paul. "Each one can carry twenty people. They'll bring the ladies, children, and older men to Île Saint-Jean now, and come back with larger boats to get the animals. The rest of us will wait here. Come. We must hurry before the English patrols return."

We scrambled into the boats as quickly as we could. It seemed to take forever to cross the strait. I knew I should be thankful that we were close to Île Saint-Jean, but I could only think of how miserable I was—cold, hungry, and tired. The wind blew steadily. The spray of icy water chilled us as the men dipped and raised their oars, pushing us closer and closer to our new home. I wanted to complain, but I couldn't say a word because I didn't want to attract the English soldiers, if there were any patrolling nearby.

Then I thought of Papa waiting in the woods with our animals. I knew what he would say if he were with me. "Be thankful our family is together and we're safe."

So I closed my eyes and prayed for God to make me strong and help me appreciate what I had: my loving and healthy family, our new Acadian friends, our animals, and the safe end of our journey through the mountains.

6

Île Saint-Jean

I nearly fell asleep listening to the soothing sound of waves lapping against the fishing boat, but my thoughts kept whipping around, keeping me awake. Would our house be like the one in Pigiguit? Would the land be ready for planting wheat? What about a vegetable garden and a barn? Life *had* to be as good as it was in Pigiguit. No, it would be better. The French officials *want* us here. I whispered softly, "I hope I never hear the word *English* again."

A large icy wave splashed me. I looked around the small boat, shivered, and snuggled closer to Maman who was holding Marie Josephe and Daniel. One of the fishermen rested his oars and pointed. "Look to the front of the boat."

I sat up straight. "Is that Île Saint-Jean?"

"Yes, your new home. You came at the right time. The English burned the buildings and fields when they seized the island in 1745. The French regained control two years ago, in 1748. Our new governor brought soldiers who are rebuilding their living quarters, and then they'll build a fort to protect all of us."

As soon as our boat pulled close to shore, I stood up, but my legs wouldn't hold me. They were numb from sitting still so long in the cold. As I rubbed them, a soldier carrying a lantern hurried to the boat. "*Bienvenue,*" (Welcome), he said. "Follow me. I'll show you where you will live." He walked toward a cluster of wooden buildings, which didn't look at all the way I had pictured our new home. I stopped and stared. My heart sank. Where was our house? Where was our yard? This couldn't be it!

"Are we going to live *here*?" I whispered to Maman.

The soldier heard me and smiled. "Non. These are soldier's barracks and warehouses for supplies. We have several empty buildings where women and children arriving from Acadie stay while the men build a small house for each family. You'll be given land nearby."

I wanted to cry. There was no house waiting for us. That had only been a dream.

By the time we were settled and had fixed something to eat, Papa and the other men arrived with our animals. "Bring your carts tomorrow," said one of the soldiers. "We'll give you your supplies, and tell you where your land is."

I couldn't stop smiling the next day when Oncle Augustin came for a visit. He had left Pigiguit a year before we did. "I missed you so much," I said.

After hugging everyone, he said, "You're finally here to share my happiness. Come meet my sweet wife, Marguerite Le Jeune; we were married in February."

I danced around the room, but stopped long enough to hug my new aunt.

Oncle Augustin continued. "Her parents think life will be better in Île Royale in the Fortress of Louisbourg; they plan to leave as soon as a ship arrives. Marguerite and I have decided to go with them."

"You're leaving?" I stopped dancing, sighed, and sat near the fireplace.

"I hate to see you go," said Papa. "I wish we had gotten here sooner to have more time together. Please let us know how you like Louisbourg."

Later Papa put on his coat and walked to the door. "Come help me get our supplies, Pelagie."

One of the officers put several containers of flour, a barrel of dried fish, and a few vegetables in our cart. "I'm sorry, but this is all we can spare. The Acadians living here have been unable to grow enough to feed their families this year—even those who have been farming here for twenty or thirty years."

"Where did this food come from?" asked Papa.

"We're surviving on supplies from Louisbourg and Quebec. The officers at the Fortress in Louisbourg aren't happy about having to share their food with us. They expect *us* to send food to *them,* because their land isn't fertile. The reason the French officers want people to settle here is to provide food for the people in Louisbourg. I wish you good luck. We'll help you as much as we can."

When we returned with our supplies, Papa told Maman, "Our land is in *Anse au* (cove of) Matelost, along with Charles and Abraham. Unfortunately, Paul and his son were given land almost a day's walk from us."

"Oh, Claude," said Maman, "I wish they would live closer to us; we could help Paul with the children."

"I know. Paul has been a widower far too long with four children under age nine. The two oldest girls should be married with their own families instead of taking care of their brothers and sisters."

"I'll pray for all of them," said Maman.

Two days later Papa left with Oncle Charles, Oncle Abraham and his oldest son, some other men who had traveled with us from Cobequid, and a guide. They were going to build homes across the bay in Anse au Matelost. They carried tools, food, straw mattresses, and other supplies in small ox-drawn wagons. Oncle Paul also left with his three oldest sons, a guide, and other men from Acadie, who would live in Grande Ascension.

The rest of us spent the next two weeks resting from our long journey, cooking for the soldiers, and getting to know the other women and children who had arrived from other parts of Acadie. Maman had brought cloth that she wove before we left Pigiguit; we sewed whenever we had any spare time. We visited Oncle Augustin and his wife as often as possible, since we didn't know if we would ever see them again after they left for Louisbourg.

*   *   *

Every day I watched the road for Papa and the other men and boys. Finally one evening Oncle Paul's sons, Paul and Antoine, appeared alone. They walked slowly, dragging their feet.

"Maman, they're coming. Hurry!"

We ran to meet them, all of us talking at once.

"Where are the men?"

"Are the fields ready for planting?"

"What about a vegetable garden?"

"Is the land near water?"

"Do we have a house?"

Cousin Paul took a deep breath. "We've been working hard, and we're ready to bring our family to our new home. On our way here, we stopped in Anse au Matelost. The men wanted to continue working, so they asked us to bring their families when we return.

"Do *we* have a house?" I asked again.

"Your Papa has worked hard; you have a place to live. We're tired and need to rest; we'll leave in the morning."

Maman took my hand as we went back to prepare supper. "Why are you frowning, Pelagie?"

"Cousin Paul didn't really answer any of our questions. When I asked if we have a house, he said we have a place to live. What does that mean?"

"We'll find out tomorrow. Now we must tell the soldiers we're leaving. It won't matter what we live in. We'll manage as long as we're together."

7

Our New Home

After we crossed the bay in a boat, Papa and my uncles met us to walk the rest of the way to our new home.

"You look exhausted," said Maman.

Papa wiped his face with his handkerchief. "Yes, we've worked hard. We cleared a piece of land, cut down small trees, and built a house— really just a hut—for each family. Luckily we have good Acadian neighbors, who spent all of their time helping us. They promised to help us clear land for farming, too."

"Do you mean there's no cleared land?" asked Maman.

Papa shook his head sadly. "All the good fertile land on this island is being farmed by Acadians who moved here twenty to thirty years ago. Our land is heavily wooded, not like the rich marshland that we're used to. It will be difficult to farm."

Maman rubbed her hands together. "What are we going to do?"

Papa took a deep breath. "Whatever it takes to survive, just as Acadians always do. We'll work hard, but with the help of *Le Bon Dieu* (the good God), and that of our friends and neighbors, we'll make it. We have no other choice."

Walking next to them, I said, "Oh, Papa, what's going to happen to us? How will we live without wheat and vegetables, and our house?"

"We have a place to live, and it will be adequate until we can build a bigger house. We'll work together to clear our land and plant enough wheat to feed our family. We'll also prepare a place for a vegetable

31

garden. That's all we'll need for a few years, until we have time to clear more land to grow additional crops.

"I don't know why we left Pigiguit," I mumbled.

"Pelagie, haven't I always told you that we have to expect difficult times in life? Sometimes dark clouds hide the sun, but when we see the bright glow around the edges—the silver lining—we know the sun is still there. Better days are ahead if we keep working hard and have faith in God.

"Let's thank Le Bon Dieu for all the good things we have. Even if we don't have everything we *want*, we have everything we *need*. And Oncle Charles and Oncle Abraham will live near us."

I clapped my hands and skipped around. "Oh, Françoise and ten other cousins nearby!"

Papa smiled. "Yes, there's your silver lining. And Oncle Paul is not far away. We'll see his family often. Look, our land is just ahead. Charles's land is next to ours, and then Abraham's.

I hurried to catch Françoise, who was walking ahead of us with her family. "We'll live close enough to visit every day after we finish our chores," I said.

She smiled and reached for my hand as we skipped down the road. I no longer dreamed of a house as nice as the one we had in Acadie, but I wasn't prepared for what I saw. I stopped skipping and stared. I couldn't say a word.

Our new home was smaller and rougher than the barn for our animals in Pigiguit. I thought about the house we had left—with its big loft upstairs for the boys, and the large room downstairs, with a fireplace big enough for Maman to cook a meal for our aunts, uncles, and cousins. Papa had spent many long winter evenings making furniture—a long table with enough benches and chairs for everyone, Maman's rocking chair close to the fireplace, and her loom and spinning wheel. He had also made their large bed, which was at the other end of the downstairs room, and the smaller bed where Anne and I had slept.

The hut wasn't just tiny; it was built with small poles standing on end next to one another and tied together with small twigs. Branches of trees served as a roof. I stood there, unable to move. I couldn't believe we were going to live in this *shack*.

Papa put his arm around me. "What's wrong? Did you expect a house like the one we had in Pigiguit?"

"Yes, Papa, I mean, no, Papa." I stared at the ground. I couldn't look him in the eye. He had worked hard to build this hut for us, and I knew I should be grateful to have a place to sleep.

"Pelagie," he said, "think about your Great-grand'maman Marie. When she came to Acadie with her new husband, she was just six years older than you are now. She left her parents, brothers, sisters, and all her other relatives and friends in France, never to see them again. She had to help your Great-grand-père Martin build their house, plant crops and vegetables, make furniture, build fences, and raise animals. Do you think her house was any better than this one?"

"No, Papa," I said, barely able to get the words past the lump in my throat.

"We have much more than they did when they started out," said Papa. "We have our family and many relatives. We have our animals and enough food to keep us from starving. The hut will protect us while we get started in this new land. It's cold inside but our furs and quilts will keep us warm. As soon as your brother and I clear enough land to plant wheat and vegetables, I will build a bigger, warmer house. That is my promise to you."

After breakfast the next morning Papa looked outside. "Let's go, Gregoire. It's time to prepare the ground for Maman's vegetable garden."

Gregoire finished his last bite of bread. "But, Papa, we can't plant seeds with all those tree stumps in the ground."

"Farming forestland will be different from the way we farmed the marshland in Pigiguit," said Papa. "Your uncles and I chopped down some of the trees, but we couldn't remove the big stumps. We'll dig the ground around them so we can plant the seeds. When the stumps rot, we'll have more room for planting."

They prepared a small plot of ground where we would plant turnips, peas, beans, cabbage, and onions as soon as the weather was warm enough. I was so hungry for fresh vegetables that I didn't think I could wait for them to grow.

A few mornings later, I pulled up vines while Gregoire and Papa cut down small trees on the land that would be their wheat field. "Someone's coming," said Gregoire, "with a saw."

Papa looked up. "That's our neighbor, M. Haché."

"Bonjour," said the man, nodding to Gregoire and me. "Do you need any help?"

Papa wiped his face on his sleeve. "Bonjour. We'd welcome your help."

We had a large pile of trees and vines when Maman brought cool water for us to drink, and we rested for a few minutes. "I'm wondering about the crops here," said Papa. "Before we left Pigiguit, we were told we'd be able to feed our families if we moved here, and the French government would provide food until we were able to grow our own. But the officer in Port-la-Joie said the Acadians have been unable to grow enough for their families this year. What has happened?"

M. Haché sighed. "I've been here nearly thirty years. Our soil is good, much better than that in Louisbourg. When everything goes well, we have an abundant harvest and everyone has plenty to eat. There's even enough to send flour, vegetables, and cattle to Louisbourg."

"That's good," said Papa.

"But much too often, something happens and we have nothing to eat. Between 1724 and 1738, the entire wheat crop on the island was destroyed three times by swarms of black field mice."

I gasped. "Field mice?"

He nodded. "Yes, the worst year was 1738. The greedy little creatures moved rapidly, eating everything in their path, and kept running and eating until they reached a stream or a river, where they quickly drowned."

"Ugh," I said. "I'm glad I wasn't here. I don't like mice."

M. Haché smiled at me. "Neither did my children. They hid in the house under their quilts. The mice didn't go into houses; they just kept running in the fields eating our wheat. They didn't even leave any seeds for planting the following year, so we had to get them from Louisbourg. That could happen again, anytime."

Papa put his arm around me, and then turned back to our neighbor. "It's been difficult for you. If our people had known what was happening, we would have sent food and seeds from Acadie. Our crops were usually abundant. We were always told we should send everything we didn't need to Louisbourg. So we sent wheat, vegetables, and large numbers of cattle."

M. Haché sighed. "I wish mice had been our only problem. Twice forest fires destroyed all the crops on part of the island. Last year we had a plague of locusts. Then in the summer, all of our wheat died because of a severe drought. And to make things worse, our streams dried up. We were lucky to have wells which supplied water for drinking and cooking, but not nearly enough for our crops."

"What did you eat?" I asked.

"The officials in Louisbourg sent flour so we could make bread, but not enough to keep everyone from starving. Every day when the tide in the harbor went out, the townspeople gathered on the shore and collected lobsters, oysters, and clams."

"But only poor people eat lobsters," I blurted, and then blushed because I had spoken without thinking.

M. Haché shook his head. "We were thankful to have lobsters, because when we ran out of flour we had nothing else to eat. By the grace of Le Bon Dieu, we salvaged enough seeds to plant this spring, but not enough to make our bread. We can only hope the officials in Louisbourg and Quebec continue sending supplies to us, and pray that nothing happens to our crops, especially with so many people arriving from Acadie. I must go now. I will come back tomorrow to help you. May God be with you."

* * *

We quickly fell into a routine. Papa and Gregoire planted wheat for our fall harvest; then they built fences and a barn. Maman, Anne, and I had plenty to do—planting vegetables, cleaning, and cooking. Several of our new neighbors gave us wool which we spun into thread, then used a neighbor's loom to make cloth.

"When will we use our own loom, Maman?" I asked.

"We hardly have room to move in our little hut. Where would we put a loom? It will have to stay in pieces in the barn until we have a house to live in."

Whenever Maman could spare me for a short time, I visited my cousins. We enjoyed the pleasant spring weather as we tried to forget our problems. When Françoise and I were alone, we shared our thoughts and dreams.

"Françoise," I said one day, "sometimes I miss Pigiguit and our life there so much I can hardly stop my tears. But I try not to cry, because that makes Papa and Maman sad. I want my old life back! I want to live in Pigiguit again."

"So do I, Pelagie," she said. "But when I complain, Papa tells me this is better than worrying about being forced to fight against our people, or having to give up our religion as well as our land. He says we must do our best with what we have."

I sighed. "All of the Acadians who recently arrived here live in huts just like ours. We'll work hard and pray that God will watch over us. Someday, everything will be better again. It has to be."

I had finally realized that my dream of a life better than we had in Pigiguit was just that—a dream. I wondered what would happen in the next weeks, months, and years. Then I wondered if it was better that I didn't know.

8

Good Times and Bad

Oncle Paul came to visit after dinner one afternoon. "You must have good news," said Papa. "You look happier than I've seen you in a long time."

With an even bigger smile, Oncle Paul said, "I'm going to marry Marie Josephe Viger. You might remember her—she's a widow who came here from Cobequid with our group."

Papa hugged his brother. "Congratulations; it's about time. I had just about given up on you. You've been a widower far too long—and with a houseful of children."

I clapped my hands. "When's the wedding?"

"I'm on my way to make arrangements with the priest in Port-la-Joie. I'll let you know."

Maman made new caps for Anne, Marie Josephe, and me. We decorated them with brightly colored flowers made out of tiny scraps of material. Françoise and I collected flowers, berries, nuts, leaves and anything else we could find to decorate St. Jean the Evangelist Church and the room where we planned to gather following the ceremony.

The wedding was a happy occasion, which helped us forget for a while the many problems we were facing. All of the Acadians in the area attended. Following the church service, we had cake and apple cider in the building where we had lived when we first reached the island. Usually, after an Acadian wedding, everyone walked with the newlyweds to their new house, which all of the men and boys had helped the groom build. They also helped him plant his first crops. But

Oncle Paul already had a hut and some crops planted. His property was too far away for everyone to accompany the couple home, so Oncle Paul and Tante Marie made the trip with his children.

Two months later Tante Angélique, Oncle Abraham's wife, died. Since we lived close to their family, I had visited them often. I grieved for her, Oncle Abraham, and their six children.

* * *

The following year, hundreds of cows died in Île Saint-Jean. One morning I followed Papa into the barn. Our cows looked too weak to lift their heads. "Oh, Papa," I said, as tears ran down my cheeks, "they're so thin. Are they going to die too? Several of Oncle Charles's and Oncle Abraham's cows are already dead. What's wrong with them?"

"I don't know, Pelagie. The sickness seems to move from one farm to the next. And because of the weather, we don't have enough hay to make them fat and healthy as they were in Pigiguit. I wish we could save them; we need their milk."

This was a terrible loss. We depended on our cows for milk, butter, and cheese, and we traded extra milk for whatever we needed. We were supposed to send cows to Louisbourg since they didn't have enough land to raise large animals. Everyone was going to suffer because of this sickness.

* * *

Since we had arrived in Île Saint-Jean, Grand'maman Elizabeth and her daughter, Tante Anne, had lived with Oncle Paul. They moved to Oncle Abraham's to care for his children after Tante Angélique died. I had visited Grand'maman almost every day when we lived in Pigiguit, then several times a week when she lived with Oncle Abraham.

At the end of 1751, over a year after Oncle Paul's wedding, we finally had another occasion to celebrate. Papa smiled when he told us that Grand'maman was going to marry François Michel. "Your grand'maman has been alone too long, since Grand-père died before we left Acadie. It's good to see her happy again."

Anne and my brothers and I were delighted. A wedding meant cake and apple cider—if someone in the family was lucky enough to have everything that was needed to make the cake. In Acadie, we hadn't needed a reason to celebrate, and ate cake often, but here we were grateful if we had enough flour to make bread.

Even this day was tinged by sadness. François Michel and his six children lived in Anse à Pinet, which was a day's walk from our house. Since everyone spent most of their waking hours struggling to put food on the table, we would seldom see Grand'maman and Tante Anne. This left an ache in my heart when we said goodbye.

* * *

Our whole family was working in the wheat field one pleasant spring day in 1752. Seeing a sailor walking down the road, Gregoire shouted, "Someone's coming!"

Papa leaned on his sickle. "Bonjour."

"Bonjour," said the sailor. "I just arrived on a ship from Louisbourg. We brought supplies for the people of Île Saint-Jean, so you don't starve while your crops are growing."

"Praise God," said Papa.

The sailor smiled. "I also have a message for the Benoist brothers from Augustin Benoist in Louisbourg. He has a small house and works in a bakery, making bread for the king's soldiers and people who can't make their own. Augustin misses his relatives and friends, but he wants you to know his life is better than it was here in Île Saint-Jean because his family always has enough to eat. He wants you to join him in Louisbourg."

"Merci," said Papa.

The sailor continued, "Whenever we sail here, our ship is filled with food and supplies for your people, but we carry little on the return trip, and usually there is extra room. If you ever want passage to Louisbourg, tell the commandant at the fort in Port-la-Joie. He'll give us the message."

"Merci," Papa repeated. "Maybe someday."

That night Papa told Maman he'd been thinking about leaving Île Saint-Jean. "I'm not going to give up yet, because I'm not ready to start over again, but we might have to. Maybe we shouldn't continue to depend on farming here. We cleared enough land to plant a sufficient amount of wheat for our family, but we don't have enough seeds to plant. Our cows are dead and we have only one pig. Everyone else has lost many cows. I don't know how long we can go on like this."

Even though the French officers in Quebec and Louisbourg continued to send food and clothing to our people, often all we had to eat was bread and peas. Maman made soup with the peas; it was usually enough to fill us up. Acadians are proud people and we wanted to take care of ourselves as we always had in Acadie, but that was impossible because we couldn't produce enough in good times to put food aside for the times when we had nothing to eat.

* * *

That summer Papa found time to build a house for us with the help of neighbors and relatives. It was not as nice or as big as our Pigiguit house, but was larger and more comfortable than the hut.

In September 1752, my sister Marguerite was born. Acadians usually had large families and welcomed babies. Maman often said that new life brings hope, and the smile of a baby makes everything worthwhile.

I loved my baby sister; I especially liked to rock and cuddle her to keep her warm. But a new baby didn't change the fact that we were all hungry and our clothes were thin and ragged. I hoped, with one more child to feed and clothe, that we'd have enough to eat, and enough wool for cloth to keep us from shivering during the winter.

"Papa," I said one bitterly cold day that December, "we're freezing and starving. I pray, but nothing changes. Maybe Le Bon Dieu has forgotten us."

"Pelagie, never give up. Don't forget that dark clouds have a silver lining. Keep praying. Le Bon Dieu loves us and cares for us. It may take a long time, but things *will* get better."

9

Hunger

By the end of 1754, our fourth winter in Île Saint-Jean, everyone on the island was cold, hungry, and discouraged. Our clothes were in rags. Long ago Maman had used all of the cloth we brought with us from Pigiguit. We couldn't grow flax to spin thread for cloth, and since we didn't have any sheep, we didn't have wool. Our neighbors didn't have enough wool for themselves, and certainly none to give away.

"Papa, what are we going to do?" I asked one freezing day as we huddled near the fireplace, eating a little bread and the last of our dried fish. "All of the Acadians are starving. Many can't even go outside during the winter to care for their animals because their clothes are too ragged and thin. They just sit by the fire and try to keep warm, as we do."

"I know, Pelagie," said Papa. "The people in Louisbourg and Quebec can't help us, because they're getting very little food from France and Acadie. And we're still not able to grow enough to survive."

"Why can't we go fishing?" asked Gregoire. "I know I could catch enough to keep us from starving."

Papa shook his head and sighed. He seemed to have aged twenty years in the four years since we left Acadie. "The French officials in Louisbourg allow only a few Acadian families in Île Saint-Jean to fish. The rest of us are required to farm."

"Why, Papa?" I asked. "Do they know how hungry we are?"

"The officials probably think if they allow us to fish, we won't try to farm anymore. They're afraid *they'll* starve if we don't send food to them, since they can't farm the rocky ground around the fort. They're not considering the fact that we've hardly been able to grow anything in the time we've been here."

"What about the cows that Oncle Charles and Oncle Abraham still have?" asked Gregoire. "They could butcher them and share the meat with us."

"The officials told them they must keep their animals for the people in Louisbourg. I don't think anyone realizes how hungry *we* are."

My baby brother, Pierre, born three months earlier in September 1754, began to cry. I picked him up and sat in Maman's rocking chair, holding him close. "Why did we have to leave Acadie?" I asked, for probably the hundredth time. "And why didn't everyone leave when we did? A lot of our relatives and friends are still there. They weren't sent away by the English."

"I know," sighed Papa. "Some of our relatives left after we did. Others, like Tante Judith's and Tante Claire's husbands, said the English would never send our people away from their homes and land. Maybe they were right and I was wrong. If we still lived in Pigiguit, we wouldn't be cold and hungry. I'm sorry this has been so difficult for everyone. We probably should have stayed in Acadie for a while longer to see what the English officials would do."

I put the baby in his cradle and hurried to stand in front of Papa. "Then we can go back. Oh, Papa, let's go back now," I pleaded. "We were happy there—living close to our relatives. We always had plenty to eat, and enough flax and wool to make all the clothes we needed."

Papa took a deep breath and shook his head. "I wish we could. We had an abundance of food for ourselves, and enough to send to the Acadians in Louisbourg. One reason we are hungry now is because so many of our people left Acadie. There aren't enough farmers left to feed those of us who moved to Île Saint-Jean and Louisbourg."

"Then let's go back and grow food for them," said Gregoire. "I don't like being hungry all the time."

"We can't," said Papa. "It's too late. From the news I've received, things seemed to get better for a while after we left. Governor Cornwallis went back to England and was replaced by Governor Hopson, who treated the Acadians with more understanding and kindness than most English governors did."

I clapped my hands and twirled around. "That's good. We'll have a good life again."

"I'm afraid not," said Papa. "Unfortunately, Governor Hopson got sick and returned to England. Lieutenant-Governor Charles Lawrence replaced him. Acadians who arrived here recently told me things are worse than ever now. They left Acadie because they didn't feel safe with him in command."

Papa sighed. "In addition to the forts in Port Royal and Halifax, the English have built others in Pigiguit and Chignecto. Can you imagine living in Pigiguit with a fort right there in our village, and English soldiers watching every move we'd make? From the way he's acting, Lieutenant-Governor Lawrence won't be happy until he chases every one of the Acadians away and controls all of Acadie."

* * *

Oncle Charles came to visit after finishing his work the next day. "Our brother Guillaume sent a message," he said.

"A message from Île Royale?" I asked.

"Yes, he heard that we are starving and wants us to move there. He lives outside the fortress and can't grow crops because his land floods every spring, but the land is crowded with good trees. He built a sawmill and is doing well, selling the wood for building houses. He has never had a problem providing for his family."

"We might have to leave Île Saint-Jean someday," said Papa. "We were promised that the French government would take care of us, but many unexpected things happened in the years we've been here. It seems that the king of France has spent so much money on wars that he can't afford to help us any longer."

"Maybe we should all go to Île Royale," said Oncle Charles. "Guillaume is happy there, and Augustin has a good life inside the fortress of Louisbourg."

"What makes you think that will be any better than this?" asked Maman. "We were told our lives would be better here, and look at us—we're all starving."

"That's true, Elizabeth," said Papa. "But King Louis XV wants to protect his land. The officials in France know if they don't send supplies to Louisbourg, the English will take over the fortress and also Île Saint-Jean, Quebec, and the French-controlled land along the St. Lawrence River. I think they take better care of the people in Louisbourg than of us. Also, fishing is a big industry there. We wouldn't have to get permission to catch fish to feed our families."

Oncle Charles nodded. "The people inside the fortress walls have small gardens for vegetables and herbs, so they always have food to eat. Augustin has been in Louisbourg for four years, and he says no one is starving. His family gets tired of dried and salted meat and fish during the winter because ships can't cross the ocean to bring flour and vegetables, but they have more to eat than we have."

I knew I shouldn't join an adult conversation unless someone spoke to me, but I couldn't keep quiet any longer. "Are we going to move?" I asked. "What about Oncle Paul and Grand'maman? Will they come with us?"

"Don't worry," said Papa. "They're coming here tomorrow to discuss moving to Louisbourg. We'll talk about it, but I'm not ready to leave yet. Maybe someday, but not now."

Our relatives gathered at our house the next day. The younger children played outside while the cousins near my age gathered to talk. But since I always wanted to know what was going on, I sat near the door so I could hear what the adults were saying.

"I'm staying here," said Oncle Paul. "I don't want to make my family move again."

"We're staying, too," said Oncle Abraham.

"I can't decide," said Oncle Charles. "We've been here four years, and we have nothing to show for all our work except the land we've cleared, but I don't want to start over again."

"If we can't feed our families we'll have to go to Louisbourg," said Papa, "but I'd like to wait until next fall. That will give us a year to see if any crops will grow."

Grand'maman sighed. "I wish we could agree. Either all go, or all stay here."

After much discussion, it was decided that everyone would stay in Île Saint-Jean until fall. By that time we'd know if our wheat would provide enough flour for bread for the next winter. We'd continue to work hard and pray that we were making the right decision. But nothing could have prepared us for the news that was to come before another year passed.

10

Terrible News

One morning in November 1755, Oncle Abraham hurried into the kitchen without knocking. He was trembling and his face was as pale as his clean white shirt.

Papa looked up from his breakfast. "What's wrong, Abraham? What has happened?"

"Come. Sit down," said Maman. "Pelagie, hurry. Bring a chair and a glass of water."

"Tell us what's wrong," said Papa.

Oncle Abraham sat down and took a deep breath. "I went to the fort to ask the soldiers if they had received any flour from Louisbourg. A large group of women and children, accompanied by several men and a few old people—about one hundred Acadians in all—had just arrived; they escaped from Acadie. They told me that English soldiers captured Fort Beauséjour in Chignecto in June of this year. All Acadian males age sixteen and over, who lived in the area around Chignecto, were commanded to go to Fort Beauséjour on August 10 to hear the governor's orders.

"Since they don't trust English officers, the men refused to go. Later that day, they were told the governor planned to return their land to them, so about four hundred Acadians went to the fort the following day. You probably remember that the English officers think the land belongs to their king since they took control of Acadie, but they allow Acadian farmers to live there and grow crops."

"Yes, I remember," said Papa. "Was their land given back to them?"

"Non. They were imprisoned in the fort."

"Dear God!" Papa jumped up from his chair. "What's going to happen to them?"

"They were told they would be sent away from Acadie as soon as enough ships arrived to transport them. Their families were also told to prepare to leave. The wives were ordered to bring food to the fort every day for the men and the soldiers."

Papa paced from the fireplace to the kitchen door. "I was always afraid our people would be sent away, but I find it hard to believe it actually happened."

"Believe it," said Oncle Abraham. "The men were imprisoned for two months before they were forced onto the ships. Soldiers searched for the rest of the men who lived in the area, but many were hiding in the woods. From a distance, they watched the English soldiers push their relatives and neighbors onto sailing ships where they were packed tighter than the cattle we shipped to Louisbourg."

"How can anyone treat people that way?" asked Papa. "And where is Lieutenant-Governor Lawrence sending the men who were imprisoned?"

"They weren't told where they are going, only that they could take small household articles and money. But how many Acadians have money? They were also promised that families wouldn't be separated."

"Thank God," said Maman. "That's a relief."

"But the worst thing possible happened. Many families *were* separated. The men were already on the ships when the soldiers started boarding the women and children, so it was probably difficult to keep families together. Hundreds of people were waiting to be sent away. It must have been a terrible scene as husbands begged for their families to be put on the ship with them. Many parents were separated from their children; they searched with tears streaming down their cheeks until they were forced onto a ship without them. Screaming children were pushed onto other ships without their parents."

Tears ran down Maman's face. "I can't bear to think about so much sorrow. Our people are suffering, and we can't help them."

"And that's not all," said Oncle Abraham. "As the ships sailed away, the soldiers ransacked the houses and barns; they took everything of value, including the animals. Then they set fire to the town; thick black smoke covered the sun as the ships sailed away. Everything burned: the houses, the church, trees, even the crops in the fields. Everything is gone." He put his head in his hands and his shoulders shook. "It was dreadful hearing these poor people talk and seeing the looks on their faces."

By this time, we were all crying. Maman, Anne, and I sobbed. Papa and Gregoire had tears streaming down their cheeks. The younger children were also crying, even though they couldn't understand everything that had happened. For a few minutes, no one moved except to wipe away tears. Then Papa asked, "How did the Acadians who escaped get here?"

"A missionary priest told the wives to save themselves and their children by coming to Île Saint-Jean. Most of them didn't listen. Wanting to be with their husbands, they went to the ships.

"Those who just arrived hid in the woods and traveled at night. During the month it took to get here, they often met Mi'kmaq Indians and Acadians who had escaped from other parts of Acadie. These people told them that at the same time their husbands were imprisoned at Fort Beauséjour, the men in Pigiguit were imprisoned at Fort Edward and the men in Grand Pré were locked inside their own church."

We all gasped and stared at Oncle Abraham.

"Oh, no!" said Papa, "Not Pigiguit and Grand Pré, too. What about our sisters Judith and Claire? Have they been sent away as well?"

Oncle Abraham's voice shook, so I could hardly understand what he was saying. "If they didn't get away before the meeting they were ordered to attend, they're gone now, and the towns were burned. We don't know where the ships are taking them. We might never see them or hear from them again."

Maman covered her face with her apron and her shoulders shook. "Nooo! Not Judith and Claire, too. Forced onto ships and sent away from their homes. Our relatives, friends, and neighbors are all gone," she moaned.

"You weren't able to get any information about Judith and Claire?" asked Papa.

Oncle Abraham sighed and shook his head. "Non. The people who arrived from Acadie only knew that the Acadians were sent away from their homes. No one knows where. But I will never stop trying to find them."

"So we were right, after all. It happened as we thought it would," said Papa. "I'll never forgive myself for not trying harder to convince Judith's and Claire's husbands to come with us."

Maman knelt on the floor in front of her chair. "We must pray for the people of Acadie, especially for Judith, Claire, their husbands, and children. We'll ask Le Bon Dieu to give them strength. We'll pray for their survival. We'll pray that we'll find them someday." We joined hands, bowed our heads, and prayed as we never had before.

Sadness surrounded us like a dark cloud, choking us. Could our lives get any worse? Had we done something wrong to make God punish us? Had I complained too much? I promised God that I would always remember this day and the sufferings of our people, especially when my life seemed too difficult to bear.

11

A Difficult Decision

A few days later our family held a meeting: Grand'maman Elizabeth, Oncle Abraham, Oncle Paul, Oncle Charles, their wives, and grown sons and daughters. The younger children, happy to be relieved of chores for a short while, played outside. Françoise and I sat nearby and listened along with our cousins who were close to our ages, old enough to understand the importance of this meeting. We were too anxious to find out what was going to happen to wait to hear about it later.

"We're going to Louisbourg as soon as there is room on a sailing ship," said Papa. "I want to get as far away from Lieutenant-Governor Charles Lawrence as I can. I'm afraid we'll be next—he'll send us away, too. Guillaume seems to be happy in Île Royale, and Augustin has asked us to move to Louisbourg. He sent a message about a carpenter named Philippe Gautreau, who always needs good workers to help him make and repair furniture, as more and more families continue to move to that fortress town."

"I don't want to make my family move again," said Oncle Paul. "I'm staying."

"I think we're safe here, far enough from the lieutenant-governor," said Oncle Charles. "The French soldiers will protect us."

"But Charles," said Papa. "Several thousand soldiers and sailors protect Louisbourg, compared to a hundred here. And we'll live inside the fortress walls."

"*We're all farmers,*" said Oncle Abraham. "And now, Augustin is a baker, Guillaume has a sawmill, and Claude, you're talking about repairing furniture! That's not for me. I'll stay here and someday, maybe next year or the year after, I know we'll have a good harvest. Until then, we'll survive."

"I don't know what we should do," said Grand'maman.

My heart dropped. None of my uncles wanted to leave. My aunts, uncles, and cousins would stay in Île Saint-Jean, and I would never see them again. I would never see Françoise, never talk to her again. No more working together, laughing, and whispering secrets. How could I bear it?

We had been in Île Saint-Jean for five years, and every night I had prayed for our lives to get better, but everything continued to get worse. How could I live in a new town without my relatives, especially Grand'maman and my favorite cousin?

After everyone left, I asked Papa, "How can we leave if everyone else stays here?"

"I'm sorry, Pelagie. I hoped they would agree to go to Louisbourg with us. But each of my brothers has to make his own decision, just as I do. We must do whatever we can to make our lives better. We have to move because doing nothing will accomplish nothing."

"Why are you going to repair furniture instead of farming? What will we eat?" I was thinking about Pigiguit and our acres of wheat fields, spacious fruit orchards, Maman's large vegetable garden, and pastureland for cows, sheep, and goats. Even in Île Saint-Jean, Papa had grown wheat when the weather cooperated; Maman had a small garden, and we had raised a few animals.

"If we're lucky we'll have room for a few vegetables and our animals, but it won't be the kind of life you're used to."

"You won't grow wheat in Louisbourg?" I asked.

"No. The weather is too cold, the growing season is too short, and the soil isn't thick and rich like that in Pigiguit."

I stared at him. "I can't imagine not growing wheat and lots of vegetables. And what about Grand'maman and Grand-père François? Will they come with us?"

Papa sighed. "I hope they do." But the next day he seemed to carry a heavier weight on his shoulders.

"What's wrong, Claude?" asked Maman.

Papa shook his head and sat down. "M. François decided to stay here. Maman said they're too old to move and start over again, and my sister Anne will stay with them. I'm disappointed, but I still think we must leave."

It was hard to swallow with the big lump in my throat. I wanted to cry. I couldn't leave all of my relatives. How would I live without them? But what could I do? Papa had made his decision.

The next day he walked to the fort in Port-la-Joie. He asked the administrator to notify him when a sailing ship arrived, and tell the sailors that our family wanted to make the trip to Louisbourg. Then he said, "If a messenger passes through before a ship with room for us gets here, please ask him to contact my brother Augustin for me. Tell him we're going to move to Louisbourg; I will need a job and a house."

It didn't take us long to get ready. Each of us had only one set of work clothes and one set of church clothes—all ragged and worn. We had quilts, sheets, towels, pots, and pans. We'd take our chickens and goats, but we would give everything else to Grand'maman and our uncles. Furniture would take too much room on a sailing ship, since other families might also be moving.

That afternoon, Françoise knocked softly and rushed in to hug me, as tears streamed down our cheeks. "Oh, Pelagie, I can't bear it. Your family is leaving, and everyone else is staying here. I don't want you to go."

I sat down and sighed. "I don't want to go. I don't want to leave my relatives, especially you—my best friend. I wish I could stay here with you. I might never see you again."

Françoise frowned. "You have to go, Pelagie."

"I know," I said. "Maman needs me. But since we have to leave, I wish we could go back to Pigiguit. I can't stop thinking about how happy we were there. We were never cold and always had plenty to eat, and enough to share with anyone who needed it."

"Yes," said Françoise, "I don't think we really knew what sadness was when we lived there."

"So many families thought life would be better here, and look at us—thin, hungry, and dressed in rags. How does Papa know Louisbourg will be any better?"

"But we don't know if our lives will get better if we stay here either."

I picked up my sewing. "I just hope Papa is right *this* time."

I knelt next to my bed that night to pray that we were doing the right thing. I prayed that my life would get better, but I should have prayed for courage to face the problems that were to come.

12

Louisbourg

Thick fog swirled around our sailing ship as we drifted slowly toward the Fortress of Louisbourg, our new home. "Please let this be the last time we have to move," I prayed. The wide stone walls of the fort loomed above us and a lone soldier watched our approach. Dozens of cannons were aimed in our direction. It was a forbidding sight.

I shuddered, pulling seven-year-old Marie Josephe and three-year-old Marguerite closer. "Papa," I whispered, "is this where we're going to live? If these people are French, they're not very friendly."

"Yes, Pelagie, we're going to live inside the fort. The soldiers are watching for our enemy, the English, not for us. Come, everyone help with the little ones; don't forget any of our belongings."

One of the sailors jumped onto the dock and said, "I have the password. Follow me."

"What's a password, Papa?" I asked.

"It's a secret word known only by the people who are allowed to enter the fort."

"A password!" I mumbled. "This is getting unfriendlier all the time."

Dauphin Gate, Fortress of Louisbourg

We walked over a drawbridge and entered the town through a large gate guarded by two French soldiers wearing blue breeches and waistcoats. Papa asked where we could find M. Gautreau, the carpenter. Pointing down a narrow street, one of the soldiers gave Papa directions.

The entire town appeared to be surrounded by high, thick walls, wide enough for several people to walk side-by-side. Our wooden shoes echoed on the cobblestone streets, interrupting the quiet of the early morning. Soldiers in uniform were everywhere, some of them wearing a longer coat of light gray over their blue breeches and vests to protect them from the early-morning chill.

The houses resembled Acadian houses in Pigiguit and Île Saint-Jean, made of wood with shutters covering their windows.

I whispered to Marie Josephe, "Look at this; how can we live here?"

She just shook her head.

"Papa," I asked, "why are all of the buildings so close to the street? The houses don't have any front yard at all."

"Because, my dear Pelagie, this is a fortified town—a big town inside a fortress. There isn't any land to waste. Oh, this must be the place we're looking for." He stopped in front of a wooden building, took a deep breath, and walked through the front door.

A tall man with gray hair and glasses hurried to greet Papa. "Welcome! You must be M. Benoist," said the man.

"Yes," said Papa, "Claude Benoist. This is my wife and these are my children."

The man smiled broadly. "I'm happy you're finally here. I'm Philippe Gautreau. Your brother told me you're the excellent helper I'm looking for. Over five thousand people live inside the fort, and several hundred others live just outside the walls. Not all of the people can make or repair their own furniture."

"Are there really that many people inside these walls?" asked Maman.

"Yes, it's a large fortress town. About half of the people are living here for protection from the English. The rest are soldiers. Come, I'll show you around." We followed him through the small room that contained several rough tables; a few chairs without seats or with broken legs stood near the wall. Saws of several sizes hung on the wall; chisels and a pile of wooden pegs covered one of the tables.

"This is where we repair furniture, and you will live there," he said, pointing out the window to a small building next door. "My wife and I lived in that house until we built a larger one a few years ago. There's room for a small garden and some chickens and goats, if you want them."

"Will we be able to grow vegetables?" asked Maman.

"Yes, almost everyone has a small kitchen garden for vegetables and herbs. The weather is cold and damp, and the growing season is short, so a garden won't provide all the food you need, but it helps."

"I'm so glad. It was difficult trying to grow anything for much of the time we were in Île Saint-Jean," said Maman, looking happier than I had seen her in a long time.

"I'll tell my wife you're here. She's been waiting for you." M. Gautreau looked at Gregoire. "I could use a strong young man like you to keep the shop clean. Come with your papa tomorrow if you want the job."

Gregoire stood up straighter and beamed. "Yes, sir!"

Fortress of Louisbourg

The house was a typical Acadian house—smaller than ours in Pigiguit, but bigger than the one Papa built in Île Saint-Jean. It had one room downstairs and a loft upstairs for the boys. Near the fireplace was a table with two benches and a few chairs. There was a bed for Maman and Papa and several rolled-up mattresses, which would be beds for my sisters and me. A small chest completed the furniture.

I looked out the window. "Such a small yard," I murmured.

"It's different from what we're used to," said Papa. "I just hope Maman can grow the vegetables we loved at home."

She smiled at him. "We'll make the best of it as we always do. Come on, children. Let's get the house straightened up. There isn't much to do because it looks very clean."

Anne and I quickly hung our cloaks on the pegs near the door and opened the flat top of the chest to put away the few pieces of clothing we owned. Maman had already tidied up the kitchen when we heard a knock at the door. A dark-haired lady walked in carrying a large pitcher; she was followed by a young girl with a big basket. They wore long skirts, long-sleeved blouses, vests, aprons, and caps similar to the ones we wore. The blouses and caps were made of white cotton and their aprons were striped. The vests and skirts were the most beautiful light blue I had ever seen. I couldn't stop looking at them.

The little girl put the basket on the table and smiled shyly. I finally realized I was being rude, so I stopped staring and smiled back.

"Bonjour," said the lady. "I'm Marie Gautreau and this is my daughter Louise. My husband told me you arrived, so we brought some food. My children and I got the house ready when we heard you were coming." She put the pitcher on the table, opened the basket, and pulled out two loaves of bread, several fresh fish, a cabbage, and apples.

"I told the girls some kind person cleaned the house for us," said Maman. "Thank you for that, and for the food. This looks wonderful. We haven't eaten fresh fish since we left Acadie five years ago. We weren't allowed to fish when we lived in Île Saint-Jean."

"Why not?" asked Madame Gautreau.

"The authorities wanted us to grow crops for ourselves and to send here. They thought we wouldn't try to farm if they allowed us to catch fish. They didn't know that farming is in our blood."

"The cod is very good here—my sons caught these early this morning. My girls and I made the bread because we knew you and your family would be hungry. We'll go now so you can eat. I'll come back later with my older daughter Hélène to show you around town." She looked at me. "She's probably your age. But before we go, I must warn you about the town wells. We don't drink that water because it has a bad taste. I don't think it's clean; many of us are afraid it will make us sick."

"Then what do you drink?" asked Maman.

"We have our own well, but since you don't, you can boil the water from the town well to make herb tea. Angelica tea is very good; that's what we brought in the pitcher. Many people raise goats so their children can drink milk. And, of course, men drink wine and spruce beer."

"What can we grow here?" asked Maman.

"Lots of vegetables: cabbage, turnips, carrots, onions, beans, and peas. You'll want to grow herbs: mint, parsley, sage, thyme, chives, angelica, and others. I'll bring some seeds and plants to you. Your little kitchen garden will be quite full. After you've eaten and rested from your journey, Hélène and I will bring some clothes that I put aside for you—we heard how bad things are in Île Saint-Jean."

I watched Madame Gautreau leave, hoping that Hélène and I would be friends. Everything I saw and heard made me realize how much I needed a friend, someone to help me learn how to live in this strange, new place.

13

Our New Town

As we finished cleaning the kitchen after dinner, there was a knock at the door. A girl walked in carrying a basket. She looked like every Acadian girl I had ever known with her dark hair and eyes, her long skirt, vest, and cap. But her smile and her sparkling eyes seemed to light up the room. I liked her immediately.

"Bonjour. I am Hélène. Maman is at the workshop with Papa. She wants us to meet her there." Turning to me she asked, "How old are you?"

"Fourteen."

"Bon, so am I," she said, swishing her skirt and clapping her hands. She opened the basket and took out several packages of seeds and some small plants.

"Merci," said Maman. "This will help us get started. Anne, please watch the little ones while Pelagie and I take a short walk around town with Madame Gautreau and Hélène."

They showed us the closest town well to get water for cooking and cleaning, and where we could buy household goods. We walked past the warehouse where food from France and Quebec was stored. Suddenly, the clatter of marching feet and a sound I had never heard before made us all turn around. A large group of soldiers marched past us down the street. I looked at Hélène. "A few of the uniforms are different from the others. Who are they and what are they doing?"

Drummers & Fifers, Fortress of Louisbourg

"Drummers and fifers. They're practicing. Listen to the drum calls and watch what the soldiers do. Drummers communicate using different calls to tell the soldiers whether to turn right or left, to advance, or to retreat."

"Why don't they just tell them what to do?"

"Soldiers might not hear an officer giving orders during a battle, but they can hear the drum. Since it's very important for the drummers to beat the correct call given by the officers, and for the soldiers to immediately know the meaning and follow the directions, they practice every day.

"Why are the drummers' uniforms different from those of the soldiers?" I asked, looking at their bright red pant-socks and vests, blue coats trimmed with red, and three-cornered hats.

"So the commanders can easily see the drummers to give them orders to pass on to the troops," she said.

"They do stand out from the rest," I said. "I like their uniforms."

Hélène nodded. "I can see that you do. You'll often hear the drummers' calls during the day, and you'll soon recognize what many of them mean. Drummers wake the soldiers in the morning, call the troops to duty, and let them know when they can take their breaks. Some of their calls are important to *us*; they signal the opening and closing of the fortress gates and when public announcements will be made."

"They have a lot to learn. What does a fifer do?"

Hélène smiled. "Makes pretty music."

"Very interesting." I watched until the soldiers turned a corner and I couldn't hear the drumbeat or the marching feet any longer.

"You can stop looking now," said Hélène with a big smile. "We'll walk around town often, so you'll see them again."

"I'm enjoying our walk, but Hélène and I must go home," said Madame Gautreau. "We have to prepare supper."

"Thank you for showing us around," said Maman. "We'll buy some flour and go home, too."

"Tomorrow we'll see more of the town," said Hélène. "I'll show you everything."

A warm feeling in the pit of my stomach told me that I had a new friend who was fun to be with, and I hoped we would be friends forever.

"Maman," I said after Hélène and Madame Gautreau left. "How can we buy flour? We don't have anything to trade and we've never had money."

"You're right," she said. "We always traded crops or animals for anything we needed in Pigiguit. But most people have money here, since they either have their own business or they work for others. Papa will be paid with coins, but until then, M. Gautreau told him the merchants will allow us to charge whatever we need, since they know he has a job and will pay them back."

As we left the shop where household goods were sold, I said, "I'm glad we're almost home; this flour is heavy."

Just then we heard gunfire and I almost dropped the flour. We ran close to a building and stood there trembling until a fisherman carrying a string of fish walked over to us. "Don't be afraid, Madame, Mademoiselle," he said. "The soldiers shoot their muskets and cannons often, practicing so they'll be ready when the English come. You'll know when it's really a battle and not just practice. Soldiers watch the harbor day and night to warn the citizens if they see an English ship."

"Merci," said Maman. "We just arrived and the noise frightened us."

"You'll get used to it soon enough," said the fisherman as he tipped his cap to us. "You'll hear it every day."

Maman and I hurried back to tell the rest of the family everything we had learned about our new town.

After supper we walked to Oncle Augustin and Tante Marguerite's house. We hadn't seen them since they left Île Saint-Jean shortly after we arrived there five years earlier. They now had three adorable children, Marguerite, Simon, and Elisabeth.

The grownups had lots of catching-up to do. Oncle Augustin and Tante Marguerite wanted to hear all the news about our relatives who were still in Île Saint-Jean. My brothers and sisters and I spent the time getting to know our new cousins.

As we left, Oncle Augustin said, "Be sure to come to the garrison bakery to see how we make bread for nearly three thousand soldiers."

"Bread for three thousand soldiers! That's a lot of baking," I said.

I had many things to be thankful for when I said my prayers that night. I thanked God for my new friend Hélène, our relatives who lived in Louisbourg, my new cousins, Papa's and Gregoire's jobs, our house, and a yard to grow vegetables. I prayed that we would finally get settled and not have to move again. I prayed that we would all be happy again.

14

A New Friend

Bells woke me early the following morning. I had never before awakened to that heavenly music. It was a beautiful sound, one I hadn't heard since we left Pigiguit when I was nine years old. There we heard the church bells when we were in the village at noon or at six o'clock in the evening, but our house was too far away to hear them at six o'clock in the morning, and we never went to the village that early.

I lay on my straw mattress and wished the bells would ring forever, but their sweet sound was soon replaced by a loud, grating noise. Marching feet on the cobblestone street had me jumping out of bed and running to the window. A group of soldiers marched past our house; I watched until they turned a corner and I couldn't see them any longer.

I had just finished dressing when Hélène knocked at the door and handed me a basket filled with fresh fish, dried meat, vegetables, flour, and herbs. "Maman sent this so you'll have something besides bread to eat until you go to the warehouse for supplies. I'm on my way to school now, but I'll be back as soon as I get home."

"School? You go to *school*?" I said. "What is it like? Does everyone in Louisbourg go to school?"

"Wait, one question at a time," she said, laughing. "Yes, I go to school. No, not everyone does. I'll tell you all about it when I see you this afternoon."

Maman and I spent the day making vegetable soup, baking bread, and mending our clothes. Papa and Gregoire went to the workshop for their first day of work.

That afternoon, Hélène breezed into our kitchen as if we had known each other forever. "Come on, let's go for a walk. I've been thinking all day about the places I want to take you."

I hadn't stopped working since early that morning, so Maman said I could leave for a little while. Hélène and I watched the waves crashing on the shore below us as we walked along the wide ramparts. Guards patrolled the walls while searching for enemy ships. Back on the street, soldiers were everywhere: moving through the streets, keeping order, and guarding the entry gates and military buildings.

"Why are there so many soldiers?" I asked.

"They're here to protect us in case the English try to capture the fortress again—as they did in 1745. At that time they wanted fishing rights and control of the shipping routes."

"What happened?" I asked.

"England won. There weren't enough French soldiers, sailors, or ships to defend the fort. All the Acadians who lived here were sent to France."

"How horrible," I said, shuddering. "Did you live here then?"

"No, we lived in Grand Pré, Acadie. We moved here in 1750 when I was nine years old. Since England and France signed a peace treaty in 1748, many Acadians who had been deported returned from France. Papa knew they would need furniture."

"We left Pigiguit the same year you moved here," I said.

When we passed the king's storehouse, Hélène said, "The food in that building is brought by sailing ships from France, Quebec, and the American colonies. We used to get lots of food from Acadie, too. The warehouse is supposed to hold enough to feed everyone in Louisbourg for a year, but often the food is spoiled, either because of the long trip from France or because it was already bad when it was put on the ships. Come back with your papa to get your supplies and hope everything is edible. Oh, look, there's the bakery."

"My Oncle Augustin works there; he makes bread for the soldiers," I said.

"Most of the bread is for the soldiers; they eat the kind of crusty brown bread that we eat. But some people with lots of money also buy bread; the bakers make soft white bread for them." We went into the bakery and waved at Oncle Augustin who was hard at work.

After watching for a few minutes, we walked down the street and stopped in front of an immense building. "What's this," I asked. "I've never seen such a huge building in all my life."

King's Bastion, Fortress of Louisbourg

"It's called the King's Bastion. It's where the governor and military officers live; the hospital for wounded and sick soldiers is on the ground floor. We go to Mass in the chapel on the second floor because we don't have a church. You'll see the chapel on Sunday. You'll also see a priest in a brown robe walking around town, going to visit Catholic families.

"Oh, let's walk down this street; I want you to see my school. I'll ask if you can visit one day."

"You were supposed to tell me about school. What do you do there?"

"We learn about our religion, and how to read and write . . ."

"You can read and write!" I said, interrupting her. "I didn't know girls went to school. And I didn't know they learned to read and write.

I thought only important men who need it for their jobs had to learn anything in school."

"No, three nuns . . ."

"Nuns? What are nuns?"

"I'll never finish telling you about school if you keep interrupting," said Hélène.

"I'm sorry. I won't do it again."

"Nuns are ladies who belong to a religious order. They live together, pray together, and teach Louisbourg girls whose families can afford to pay for their daughters' education."

"What about boys? Do they go to school?" I asked. "Oh, I'm sorry. I promised not to interrupt."

"Boys don't go to school because there isn't anyone here to teach them. The nuns only teach girls. Some families with lots of money send their sons to school in France. My older brothers had a tutor, a man who came to my house to teach them. When they were my age they went to work for Papa to learn how to make and repair furniture."

I stopped walking and stared at Hélène. "You're not going to work in the shop, are you?"

"No, I'll go to school another year or two, then I'll stay home to help Maman until I get married."

"What else do you do at school?" I asked.

"Fancy sewing. I'm learning to make lace. I'll teach you, and one of the shop owners might sell it for you. Ladies like fancy lace collars."

The ringing of the chapel bells reminded me that I had to go home. "I have to help Maman get supper ready," I said. "I'd better hurry."

Hélène smiled as we parted. "See you tomorrow."

When I said my prayers that night, I thanked God for my new friend and for what seemed to be a pleasant and safe place to live. It was probably best that I didn't know what was to come.

15

Learning to Enjoy Life in Louisbourg

I wanted to smile, to laugh, to dance because we no longer had the constant worry about what might happen that day or the next. With soldiers everywhere, I felt secure and protected. Nothing could happen to us behind the thick fortress walls.

Our family soon settled into a pleasant routine. Chapel bells woke me every morning at six o'clock. After I said my prayers, I helped Maman fix breakfast. We spent the rest of the day cooking, cleaning, baking, spinning thread, making cloth on Maman's new loom, sewing, and caring for the younger children. "Maman," I said a few weeks after my long walk with Hélène, "I'm glad I don't have to go to school. It's fun to cook when we have enough food, and I like working on the loom; it's been so long since we had new clothes."

Maman smiled at me. "Yes, we're fortunate your papa has a job so we can buy what we need."

Papa and Gregoire spent long hours at work every day except Sunday. When Gregoire finished sweeping up sawdust and making deliveries, he helped Papa repair furniture. They were tired, but happy. Neither one was used to being inside all day, but they liked the work and were paid well.

Sunday was my favorite day of the week. The priest was always at the chapel to say Mass. In Pigiguit our priest had alternated Sundays on each side of the river. It had been difficult for us to cross the river, so we joined our neighbors for prayers and hymns when the priest was at the other church. St. Jean the Evangelist Church in Île Saint-Jean had a resident priest, but it was a long trip to Port-la-Joie and it had often been impossible for us to get there.

In Louisbourg we cooked dinner and cleaned the kitchen after Mass, and then the afternoon was mine to do as I pleased. Since Catholics weren't allowed to do any unnecessary work on Sunday, we didn't sew or work on the loom or in the garden. Sometimes our whole family went for a walk in the woods outside the fortress walls to explore and collect spruce boughs that Papa used to make spruce beer.

While walking with Hélène one day I said, "It's so noisy here. Sometimes I miss Pigiguit where it was so peaceful that only children's laughter and the sounds of animals broke the silence."

Hélène laughed. "I thought you liked our chapel bells."

"I do. I love listening to them three times a day when they remind us to pray, but why do they have to ring so many other times?"

She laughed again. "They peal a few notes every half hour during the day so that people know what time it is. You'll get used to it."

"Maybe," I said, "but the clatter of marching feet, the shouts of soldiers, and the blast of cannons and guns sometimes make me want to jump out of my skin."

"Soon you won't notice those sounds at all," she said. But I found that hard to believe.

* * *

I rushed through my chores every day so I would be finished if Hélène came by on her way home after school. She arrived at my house several times a week, always planning to take me somewhere in our fortress town. These trips were exciting because everything was so new to me, and because Hélène never stopped laughing and made everything an adventure.

One morning Maman and I were making dresses for the girls and shirts for the boys. She was humming and smiling as she worked.

"Why are you so happy this morning, Maman?" I asked.

She stopped working to smile at me. "I was worried when we arrived here. You and the younger children were as pale as your apron. Your clothes had to be pinned to keep them from falling off. Now all of you have rosy cheeks and have filled out so your clothes fit again. It makes me happy to have a healthy family."

"We're not hungry anymore," I said.

Marie Josephe looked up from the butter she was churning. "I always thought we were supposed to be hungry."

With a sad look on her face Maman said, "No, ma chère. We didn't have enough to eat in Île Saint-Jean. You don't remember Pigiguit because you and Daniel were just two years old when we left. We always had plenty of food there."

"When Gregoire has time, he promised to hunt for rabbits and birds," I said. "We . . ."

The door banged against the wall. I gasped and looked up. Eight-year-old Daniel stood in the doorway with a smile that reached his eyes. "Look what I caught!" He held a bucket full of fat codfish.

"If you keep catching beautiful fish like that," said Maman, "we'll never be hungry again."

"Please, Maman, let's make fish soup or stew for dinner," I said. "With the herbs and vegetables Madame Gautreau gave us, we'll have the best meal we've had in years."

"Delicious," I said later when we finished eating. "That's my favorite food."

"I like chicken stew best, with big pieces of brown bread," said Gregoire. "But the only time we can have it is when a chicken stops laying eggs."

"I'm thankful we have goats and chickens to give us milk and eggs," said Anne.

"We have a lot to thank Le Bon Dieu for," said Papa. "We have everything we need and we even have money to buy food that doesn't grow here. In the spring the ships will bring fruit from the American colonies and Quebec. And with molasses and sugar coming from the West Indies, what more could we want?"

One Saturday afternoon Hélène asked me to go with her to buy flour. Turning a corner on our way home, we almost bumped into a fisherman. He was tall with dark hair, dressed as all fishermen in this fortress town, with a heavy linen shirt, dark knee-length pants, thick black socks, and wooden shoes.

He tipped his cap and said, "Bonjour, Mesdemoiselles." We smiled at him and kept walking. Hélène looked back and whispered, "That fisherman is watching you, and he's nice-looking."

"Why would he be looking at me?" I asked.

"Because you're pretty, especially now that you smile a lot. Maybe he wants a wife."

"What are you talking about, Hélène?" I asked, laughing. "I'm not ready to get married."

"You're fourteen. Lots of Acadian girls marry at fifteen or sixteen."

"Maybe he recognized me. I think he's the same man Maman and I met when we bought flour the day we arrived."

For the rest of the day, all I could think about was the fisherman and what Hélène had said. I knew I would get married and have a family someday, because that's what Acadian girls did. Maman was teaching me to take care of a house and family, but I was just fourteen, and finally beginning to enjoy life again. I hoped Papa wasn't thinking about finding a husband for me so soon. When I said my prayers that night, I asked God to send me a good husband—but not yet.

16

Bad News

I was surprised to see M. Gautreau at the door as we finished washing the dishes after supper one evening in February, a few months after we arrived in Louisbourg. Hélène and Madame Gautreau visited frequently, but not M. Gautreau. "Please pardon my intrusion, Madame Benoist," he said, "but I just spoke to a friend who is an army officer, and I felt I should warn you about something that he told me."

"Warn us?" said Maman. "What's wrong?"

"The officers received orders from France to prepare for war. England and France are fighting many battles not far away from us, and it probably won't be long before war is declared in Europe. The officers are afraid the English will attack Louisbourg again, as they did in 1745. I hate to tell you this when you're still getting settled, but you must be prepared."

"Surely, the fortress is better protected than it was eleven years ago," said Papa.

"Yes, we might be able to withstand an attack, but getting food can always be a problem during a war."

"We have plenty to eat," said Maman. "We haven't eaten so well in several years."

"I know," said M. Gautreau. "But even though we have plenty now, we always have a shortage of food in the spring. Oh, we won't starve, because fish are waiting to be caught, and almost all citizens grow vegetables in their kitchen gardens. But since we depend on bread for our main food, we need flour. That's a bigger problem now than it ever was. Before the Acadians were deported to the American colonies, they shipped flour to us. The farmers in Île Saint-Jean also sent flour when their crops grew as they should—when no droughts, fires, locusts, or mice destroyed the wheat."

"Yes, we know about the problems in Île Saint-Jean," said Papa.

M. Gautreau nodded. "Unfortunately, the only place left for us to get flour now is France. But ships usually don't cross the ocean between November and late April because of strong winds and high waves. This year, because of the threat of war, a ship arrived during the first week in January with supplies from France. Our officers were so concerned about running out of food that they asked the captain to go back to France and return with another shipload of food for us. If he gets here safely in March, or even in April, we should have enough for everyone in Louisbourg for at least a year. However, some of the food usually spoils. I felt I had to warn you."

Papa sighed after M. Gautreau left. "Have I made another mistake by bringing my family here? Maybe we should have stayed in Île Saint-Jean."

Maman put her hand on Papa's shoulder. "Claude, you know we couldn't stay there. The children were starving. And if we hadn't left Pigiguit when we did, we would have been forced to leave with everyone else last year. Our poor friends and relatives who were sent to the American colonies are being mistreated and are very unhappy."

Papa nodded. "You're right, Elisabeth. But it's so hard to make decisions for the family."

"Let's pray that we won't have to make another decision about moving," said Maman.

At Mass that Sunday the priest read a letter from the bishop of Quebec. He wrote that the people of Louisbourg must pray and follow God's laws so Louisbourg would not be lost to the enemy again.

* * *

Hélène lacked her usual smile the next time she visited. "I can't believe it! Papa told me last night that we're not having Carnival in Louisbourg this year!"

"Why not?" I asked. "And what is Carnival, anyway?"

Hélène stared at me. "Don't tell me you don't know what Carnival is! It's a time of celebration before the beginning of Lent. We don't have school for two days, and no one works. Wealthy people go to dances and parties or listen to music. Sometimes one of the girls at school invites me to a party. Then I get a new dress; it's lots of fun."

"We didn't celebrate Carnival in Pigiguit or Île Saint-Jean," I said, "but I know all about Lent. That means no meat except on Sunday for six-and-a-half weeks. In Pigiguit, I complained about eating fish every day, but in Île Saint-Jean, I would have been delighted to have fish to eat—dried or salted, I wouldn't have cared.

"What do you do for Carnival if you don't go to a party?"

Hélène's frown turned to a smile. "I watch the dressed-up people go to dances given by the governor at the King's Bastion. I'm sure you've never seen dresses like the ones those ladies wear. They buy beautiful silk and wool material from France and have their dresses made by dressmakers, using the styles worn by royalty in France. Silk shimmers in the light, and the colors—you wouldn't believe your eyes!"

She pranced around the room with her hands pressing her waist. "They wear corsets with strips of whalebone that squeeze their waists tight. This makes the dresses so narrow, I don't know how the ladies can breathe. And their skirts poof way out, so they can hardly get through a door."

I laughed at her antics. "What makes their skirts so big?"

"Maman said the dressmakers make narrow pockets inside the skirt, which hold long strips of whalebone. The ladies have trouble sitting down with their big skirts, but they look beautiful, and I love to watch them."

"What about the men?" I asked.

"They're so handsome; I love watching them, too. Their knee breeches have buckles fastening the pant legs just below the knees. The cuffs on their coats fold back, and their shirts are trimmed with linen or lace ruffles in front and at the end of the sleeves. Their shoes also have buckles, and most of the wealthy men wear a wig and a three-cornered hat."

"You still haven't told me why Carnival is going to be cancelled this year," I said.

"Because of the threat of war. Everyone is too worried to celebrate." She shook her head and frowned again. "Men are too serious. If they spent more time having fun, they wouldn't have time to fight with other countries."

After a little prance around the room, Hélène smiled again. "I'm glad you're here so we can find something fun to do. My friends at school are learning to act like *proper ladies*. They hold their little finger in the air when they drink tea, walk with tiny steps, and curtsy without falling down. I don't want to be proper, and I'm not ready to be a lady. I want to sing, dance, run, shout, and have fun, fun, fun!" With these last words she twirled around until she fell into a chair, too dizzy to stand.

* * *

In 1756 Carnival fell on Tuesday, March 2. Since the people in Louisbourg didn't celebrate the holiday that year, Hélène invited me to her house in the afternoon after we both finished our chores. Her mother had made tiny, delicate teacakes for us, and a drink I had never tasted before.

"What *is* this?" I asked.

"Hot chocolate," said Hélène. "Papa buys cocoa for special occasions; he got this the last time a ship came from the West Indies, before we knew that Carnival was cancelled."

"I've never tasted anything so delicious in all my life," I said, as I drained my cup.

"Next time you come, we'll drink coffee; it also comes from the West Indies, but I don't like it nearly as much as hot chocolate."

* * *

At the end of March while we were eating dinner, Papa said, "It's good we arrived here when we did, because now the harbor is blocked by ice drifting from the north. Nothing can get through, not even small boats. The sailors probably would have dropped us farther down the coast, wherever it was safe to pull to shore. We would have had a long, cold walk to reach the fortress."

"What do fishermen do if they can't go out in their boats?" I asked.

"They fish along the coast. M. Gautreau told me that even though the harbor doesn't freeze over, the drifting ice prevents big ships from docking for a week or two every winter."

After work that day, Papa said, "I have more news. Sails appeared outside the harbor this morning; it was the *Rhinocéros*, the same ship that arrived early in January with supplies. The captain tried to get through the ice, but it damaged his ship."

"What will happen to the *Rhinocéros*?" asked Daniel.

"I don't know. I hope the sailors are rescued and the food can be saved. The officers in France must be extremely worried about war. They wouldn't send a ship across the ocean twice during the winter unless they think no supply ships will be able to get here in the spring."

Every day after he completed his chores, Daniel hurried to the ramparts overlooking the harbor to watch for the ship. The following week he rushed in, shouting, "Great news! The wind changed direction, and it's blowing the ice out of the harbor. Now ships from France can dock safely."

"Unfortunately, so can ships from England," murmured Papa.

That evening we watched another ship tow the damaged *Rhinocéros* into the harbor. The sailors quickly unloaded the supplies, repaired the ship, and departed within a few weeks.

"Why were they in such a hurry to leave?" I asked. "Hélène told me the sailors like to stay in town, playing cards, eating, and drinking."

Papa frowned. "M. Gautreau said the captain was anxious to begin his voyage back to France, knowing he would face ice and high waves, because he was afraid of a bigger springtime danger—English warships!"

We continued to hear rumors about the British plans to attack Louisbourg, but we felt secure within the fortress walls, protected by nearly three thousand soldiers. And the king's storehouse was packed with flour. Everyone in Louisbourg would have bread until the next ship arrived from France.

17

Waiting for News

Early in May 1756, Gregoire dashed in after work. "English warships are patrolling the water close to Île Royale," he said. "But they're not coming into the harbor."

"Why are the ships here, Claude?" asked Maman, as Papa followed Gregoire into the house.

"M. Gautreau thinks England isn't ready for a big battle; instead, the sailors will attack every ship arriving in Louisbourg or leaving our harbor. He said if the English can prevent ships from delivering supplies, they'll take control of us without firing a shot. That would be the easiest way to win a war. They know we can't survive without food and other goods from France, Quebec, and the West Indies, and the only way for supplies to get here is by ship."

A few days later, a small group of soldiers rushed down the street in front of our house. Hélène was right; I didn't notice the sound of marching feet any longer. However, the rhythm of this drumbeat was so unusual that we all stopped what we were doing and ran to the window.

Maman picked Pierre up, holding him tight. "Pelagie, run next door. Find Papa and ask him what's happening."

I almost bumped into Papa as he left M. Gautreau's shop. "Go home," he said. "Tell Maman that everyone must stay inside. That drumbeat is the signal that the officers will make a public announcement. I'll hurry back with the news."

It seemed like forever before Papa came home followed by M. Gautreau. Papa's hands shook as he filled his pipe. "A French ship got past the English warships. They brought supplies and bad news. England and France have officially declared war in Europe."

"That means we *will* be attacked," said M. Gautreau. "If the British capture our fortress, they can easily take control of Quebec and the settlements along the St. Lawrence River. All the French-controlled land will be theirs—and *that's what they want.*"

"Doesn't France have a strong army and navy?" asked Papa.

"Yes," said M. Gautreau, "but the English Royal Navy far outnumbers the French Navy in men, warships, and guns. And the English warships are much bigger. It will be difficult for us to defeat them."

Our soldiers were everywhere. Those not on guard duty or patrolling the streets were hard at work strengthening the fortress and its defenses. They had to make sure that the English couldn't get inside the fortress easily. They lowered some of the hills on the landside of the fort to keep the enemy from having a good target from higher up. They also removed the high rocks on the seaside by lighting gunpowder, which they had placed in holes drilled in the rock.

The usual blast of cannons and guns, when the soldiers practiced their routine drills, no longer startled me. But the new noise of rocks being blown to bits made me tremble. I couldn't concentrate on my sewing or cooking. I darted from one window to another, trying to figure out what the soldiers were doing, but seeing only plumes of smoke. "What's going to happen to us, Papa? How long will this go on?"

"I don't know, but I hope we're safe inside the fortress. The only thing we can do is pray."

"Will our lives ever be normal again?" I asked. "I was so happy here for a few months, and now, look at what's happening!"

Papa ran his hand through his hair. "I'm sorry, Pelagie. But we had to leave Île Saint-Jean, and there was nowhere else for us to go. I didn't expect the English to follow us here."

We went on with our lives the best we could while anxiously waiting for news about the war, hoping the English were too busy fighting in Europe to attack Louisbourg. We planted vegetables and herbs; Gregoire and Daniel caught fish whenever we needed food.

Papa came home with a smile on his face one evening. "Today I heard that France recently won several victories over England in the war in Europe."

"Are we safe?" I asked.

"Not yet, but it gives us hope." He turned to Maman. "A young fisherman named Yves Crochet came to the shop this afternoon to ask if he can call on us."

"A fisherman!" I said.

"Yes, he'll come tonight."

After supper, Maman told me to comb my hair and wash my face and hands. Just as I was putting on a fresh apron, there was a knock at the door. Standing with his cap in his hands was the fisherman who told Maman and me not to worry about the gunfire on our first day in Louisbourg. He was also the same fisherman who spoke to Hélène and me when we were out walking.

Papa introduced us and we sat and talked—Papa, Maman, Yves, and I. Gregoire was busy making a chair as Daniel watched, hoping to help. Anne sewed, and the little ones played on the floor with scraps of material. I said little because I didn't know what to say. Mostly Papa and Yves talked, and Maman joined in at times. Papa told Yves about our life in Pigiguit, our escape to Île Saint-Jean, and our life there.

"Yves, have you heard anything about the war in Europe?"

"A fisherman told me that the English Royal Navy captured one of our ships a few days ago. They chased a second one, but it docked safely south of Louisbourg instead of trying to get here. Fortunately for us, small boats that can sail near the coast are bringing the ship's supplies to the fortress."

"Thank God," said Papa. "We need all the supplies we can get. Yves, are you still fishing even though the English are patrolling right outside the harbor?"

"I caught trout in the lakes and streams all winter. I should be fishing out in the ocean now. This is the best time to catch cod, but I don't want to get captured by the English, so I stay close to shore. I'm afraid I'll have a bad year if this blockade continues."

"Where do you sell your fish?" asked Maman.

"The townspeople buy some of the fresh fish. When I go out into the ocean, I always have enough left over to dry. I store it, and sell it whenever a supply ship departs for France. The French people love our good codfish. But I probably won't have enough to dry this year."

"I wish I could go fishing in a boat," said Gregoire.

"I do need one more strong young man," said Yves. "My boat is a three-man shallop and I have only one helper. Every spring, French trading ships bring hundreds of fishermen who want to work until fall—but not this year. There are no trading ships and no fishermen. If your Papa and Maman will let you, I'd like for you to work with me."

"You want Gregoire to fish with the English close by?" asked Maman.

"M. Benoist, Madame Benoist, I promise if you allow Gregoire to help me, he'll be safe. We'll fish close to the coast; we won't go anywhere near the English warships."

"Tell us exactly what Gregoire would have to do," said Papa.

"The three of us will row out as far as we can go safely. Each of us will care for a number of fishing lines lowered over the side of the boat. We'll stay out for several hours until our boat is full or the fish are no longer biting. When we reach shore, we'll bring the fish into town to sell."

Yves stood up. "I'll come back tomorrow evening for your answer. I must go before the guards close the gates. If I wait, I won't get home tonight, and then I'll be late getting out to fish in the morning."

"You live outside the gates?" asked Gregoire.

"Yes, I have a little fisherman's hut on the water. It's better for me than living inside the fortress because I go out at first light to see if I have enough herring in my bait nets. My boat is in the water near my house, ready to go."

Papa walked to the door with Yves. "How would Gregoire get there on time if the gates are closed?"

"If he's waiting at the gates when they're opened, that will be soon enough. My fisherman, Henri, and I will have everything ready."

"We'll discuss it," said Papa. "Maybe M. Gautreau will allow Daniel to take Gregoire's place in the furniture shop."

Yves thanked Papa and Maman for a nice evening, smiled at me, and left.

I knew from the look on Gregoire's face that he would do anything for a chance to fish with Yves, but he would have to wait until Papa made a decision.

That night I prayed for Yves's safety and Gregoire's, if Papa allowed him to work with Yves.

18

Yves

Hearing a noise at the kitchen door the next evening, my breath caught in my throat and I jumped. Could it be an English soldier? Was my secure little world inside the fortress walls falling apart already after such a short time?

I relaxed when I saw Yves holding a wooden bucket. "I hope you can use these codfish," he said. "I just caught them this afternoon."

Maman gave him a big smile. "Merci, Yves. We'll enjoy them."

Papa looked up from his chair near the fireplace. "Come in, Yves. Sit near the fireplace with me. I was afraid Gregoire would burst if you didn't get here soon. He's ready to start working for you—just tell him when."

"Bon, he can start tomorrow. With his help Henri and I will catch more fish. If we're lucky enough to catch more than we can sell, I'll teach Gregoire how to preserve them for the winter."

Maman wiped her hands on her apron. "How do you do that? I know you don't just clean them and put them in barrels of salt, the way we do."

"Non, we split the fish, clean them, remove the bones, and then salt them lightly. We put the liver aside for cod liver oil. After several days in the salt, we lay the fish on racks to dry in the sun. I've always hired a skilled man for this job, because we send only the finest white cod to France, where it gets the best price. It must be turned on time, get enough air, and not too much heat. At night, it is laid skin-side-up, so the cool air doesn't ruin it. But this year, since we can't go out into

82

the ocean, I don't expect to catch enough fish to send to France, even if there were any French fishermen here to be hired, or any boats carrying fish to France."

"Why did you come to Louisbourg, Yves?" asked Papa. "Your accent tells me that you're not from Acadie."

"Non, I was born in Megrit, France, and my parents still live there."

I sat down next to Maman and picked up my sewing. "Why did you want to be a fisherman?"

"Mon père had a friend, M. Latour, who was a fisherman in St. Malo, France. Whenever he visited us, he told wonderful stories about crossing the ocean to catch fish in Acadie. He said they were so plentiful that he could almost sit and wait for them to jump into his boat. I listened to him as long as he would talk.

"My parents never left France, and they had no reason to think I would ever leave. But we visited St. Malo in the spring when I was ten years old. I watched fishing boats sail away and asked where they were going. Mon père told me they were crossing the ocean to catch fish, and would return to France in a few months."

Daniel stopped sanding a piece of wood to listen to the story. "Did you believe him?"

Yves shook his head. "Non. I watched for those boats every day. I looked out as far as I could, and since all I ever saw was water, I didn't believe they would ever come back. But we went to St. Malo again in the fall and I finally saw sails in the distance. The sailors returned with ships loaded with dried and salted codfish. I wanted to spend every minute of every day listening to them tell about their adventures."

"Why did they come to Acadie to fish?" I asked. "Couldn't they catch them in France? Why would anyone want to go so far from his home and family?"

"Life is hard in France," said Yves. "There are epidemics, plagues, and wars—always wars. We were often hungry because we couldn't grow enough food for our family. Fishermen came to Acadie because of the abundance of fish. They knew they would sell them because French people love codfish.

"I was filled with curiosity. I had to learn more about this magical place and why the sailors were gone at least six months of the year. I wanted to know about the enchanted water filled with codfish. The sailors caught so many, I thought they must scoop them right out of the water with their hands."

"What did you do until you sailed here?" asked Gregoire.

Yves gazed into space, as if he could see that curious boy in France dreaming about fishing. "My parents struggled to put food on the table while M. Latour made a good living selling his dried and salted fish to the rich people in France. I convinced mon père to let me spend a few months in the fall and winter with his fisherman friend. That kind man taught me everything he could about fishing and sailing. He was patient, and answered my endless questions. With each of his answers, I knew what I wanted to do with my life. I spent every spare minute learning everything I could about fishing and sailing. I went out on small boats and soon realized that was what I had to do."

"When did you come to Acadie?" I asked.

"I wanted to come here when I was thirteen. I planned to convince mon père to let me sail to Acadie with M. Latour. Unfortunately, that was the year the English attacked the Louisbourg fortress. French fishermen were afraid they would be captured by the English, so they stopped coming until after the peace treaty in October 1748. In the spring of the following year, fishermen again made the voyage across the ocean, and Acadians who had been deported to France began to return to Acadie.

"By that time, I was seventeen and still dreamed about crossing the ocean and catching the fine Acadian codfish that my family couldn't afford to buy. Almost before I knew what was happening, I was on a ship, watching St. Malo get smaller and smaller as we sailed away."

"Did you like it as much as you thought you would?" asked Gregoire.

"It was a long, rough voyage. I often wondered if I would ever get back to France, or if I would ever see my parents again. However, when we sailed toward Louisbourg harbor, my doubts were gone. I was captivated. Sails fluttered in the breeze as far as I could see—French ships filled with supplies, trading vessels, fishing boats.

"I asked one of the sailors why there were so many ships in the harbor. I had never seen so many at a time in St. Malo. He told me the trading ships bring food and goods from the Caribbean, France, Quebec, and the American colonies; the ships return to their ports laden with dried fish and furs. I was surprised when he said that up to one hundred fifty ships sail into the Louisbourg harbor every year, and that's usually in the six months it's safe to sail across the ocean."

Daniel moved his stool nearer Yves. "What else did you see?"

"When we got closer, I saw wharves piled with fish waiting to be loaded on the departing ships, while sailors on incoming ships unloaded sugar, spices, coffee, wine, flour, and other goods for the people in Louisbourg.

"We spent six months in Acadie. Every morning we woke before the sun rose, and went out in a large boat that held eleven men. Sometimes we stayed out on the banks for several days before going back to shore. It wasn't easy, but I learned a lot. I missed my family, but I knew I was helping them put food on the table. My pay at the end of six months took care of my family for the rest of the year."

"How did your parents feel when you crossed the ocean and were gone for six months?" asked Maman.

"It was hard for them. My maman and grand'maman worried the whole time I was gone, and said many prayers for my safe return. They had no way of knowing if I was alive or dead until our ship arrived in France in the fall. Unfortunately, every year several fishermen didn't return, having drowned while fishing during one of the sudden storms here.

"In the fall, families spent hours every day watching the horizon for their first glimpse of sails, hoping and praying to see the ship they were waiting for. It was especially difficult for the wives and children of sailors."

"I don't know how you could leave your family for such a long time," I said.

"I love to fish, so I looked forward to my life here. The work is difficult, outside in all kinds of weather, up to eighteen hours a day, seven days a week."

"Seven days a week? You don't work on Sunday, do you?" I asked. "Nobody works on Sunday except priests and those who care for the sick."

Yves smiled at me. "Fishermen often do. We can't catch enough to sell in fall and winter, so we have to work when the fish are biting. My days aren't nearly as long now because there aren't as many fish near shore."

"Why did you decide to live here, instead of returning to France?" asked Papa.

"Even though I love to sail, after several years of spending four to six weeks crossing the ocean twice a year, often on rough, violent seas, I had enough. And I had fallen in love with Acadie. Before I left France in the spring four years ago, I told my parents that I wanted to stay here. I told them I would sell my fish to traders, who would take it to France for me. They weren't happy about my decision, but they had gotten used to not seeing me for more than half of every year. I think my maman was slightly relieved that she wouldn't have to worry about me during the long voyages twice a year."

Maman looked up from her mending. "Have you ever regretted your decision, Yves?"

"Non. I miss my family, but I'm happy here. I'm doing well with my small boat, and someday I'll have enough money to buy a large boat." He looked across the room at me and smiled. "Then I'll get married and have a family of my own. I have a good life."

I blushed and quickly picked up my sewing. Why had he looked at me that way?

19

Excitement

"Four French naval ships bypassed the English and entered the harbor today," said Gregoire as he hurried into the house one evening near the end of July. "I saw them as I walked on the ramparts on my way home. A soldier told me they're here to help protect the fortress."

I breathed a sigh of relief. "We're safe."

However, a few days later, Gregoire raced into the house again, stopping to catch his breath before he could talk. "The fighting is getting close to the fortress. French warships were escorting a supply ship into the harbor when a battle broke out. Seventy-five Frenchmen were either wounded or killed."

Maman made the sign of the cross. "May God protect us."

One day blended into the next. We worried about the possibility of more battles, and whether our soldiers and sailors would be able to protect the fortress. However, besides praying, there was nothing we could do other than go about our routine tasks, always waiting for the drumbeat alerting us that something was happening.

Hélène continued to visit whenever she could after school. She taught me to make lace, which I enjoyed, but I didn't think I would ever make collars beautiful enough for anyone to want to wear them.

Yves was a frequent visitor, coming after supper at the end of a long day of fishing. I didn't know whether he came to see Papa, Maman, Gregoire, or me. Hélène teased me, saying I would soon be a bride, but Yves and I spent no time alone; that wouldn't have been proper.

On the first day of August 1756, Hélène knocked, then rushed into the house without waiting to be invited. Her eyes shone, and her smile was bigger than it had been in weeks, maybe months.

Maman looked up from her sewing. "What has happened, Hélène?"

"Today is the first of August," she said, waiting for our reaction.

"So?" I asked. "What's so special about August?"

"Don't you know? The Catholic Church celebrates four holy days in August—*four*. As we did for the two in June, we'll go to Mass, and return to the chapel for prayers in the evening. The rest of the day is ours to do whatever we want, except work, of course—no unnecessary work is allowed. The best holy day is the Feast of St. Louis, King of France, on August 25th."

"Why is it so special?" I asked.

Hélène sighed. "Don't you know anything? Didn't you celebrate the Feast of St. Louis in Pigiguit or Île Saint-Jean?"

"No, we didn't, Hélène," said Maman. "The ancestors of the people in Acadie were cut off from France for over one hundred years, so we developed our own celebrations and dropped many of the French traditions. The people in Louisbourg cling to French customs because they've been here such a short time, since France regained control of the fortress in 1748."

"Tell us about the Feast of St. Louis," I said.

"Louis IX was king of France five hundred years ago. That's his picture hanging above the altar in the chapel. Since it's a state holiday and a religious feast day, it's the biggest and best celebration of the year. Just like Sundays—no work or school. Papa and my brothers will spend the day at home and we'll eat a fancy dinner.

"In the afternoon there's a religious procession, gunfire on the ships, cannons shooting on the ramparts, and music and prayers in the chapel. In the evening there are fireworks and an enormous bonfire. Some of the wealthy people go to dances and fancy dinners, and we can watch them walk around in their expensive clothes. I'll just die if they cancel everything because of the war, the way they did for Carnival."

In the next few weeks we were told that the Feast of St. Louis would be celebrated, although it wouldn't be as elaborate as usual because of the war. "A soldier told me," said Papa, "there won't be any fireworks, gunfire, or shooting of cannons because ammunition can't be wasted."

When the feast day finally arrived, our whole family went to morning Mass, except for Gregoire who was excused because he was a fisherman. We prayed that God would protect our people. After a delicious dinner, we watched the religious procession, and then went to the chapel for the *Te Deum*—music and prayers praising God. Gregoire came home from work in time to go to the bonfire with us; Yves, Hélène, and her family met us there. I had never seen such a large fire. The flames reached toward the sky as the wood crackled and popped.

Walking home in the darkness, I felt like dancing down the street. "I understand why Hélène said this is the best day of the year. It was wonderful. I hope the war will be over next year so we can enjoy everything, including the cannons, gunfire, and fireworks."

On September 29 we were getting ready for bed when the beat of drums alerted us that something was happening. My heart immediately began to thump, and my breathing was loud and fast. Papa grabbed his jacket and hat and opened the door. The street was crowded with men and boys running past the house shouting, "Fire! Fire!"

"Where?" asked Papa.

"The army bakery," yelled several people who ran by without stopping.

Papa looked at Maman. "I'm going to help. Gregoire, you'd better come, too."

I hurried to the door. "May we watch?"

"If Maman wants to take you. But stay far away so you don't get in the way or get hurt. And help Maman with your brothers and sisters." He and Gregoire raced down the street.

Maman picked up two-year-old Pierre, and I took four-year-old Marguerite's hand. Anne held Daniel and Marie Josephe's hands. "Stay together," said Maman. "I don't want anyone getting lost."

Red flames lit the night sky. The acrid smell of burning wood filled the air as choking smoke wrapped around us. When we were about a block from the bakery, we could see hundreds of men and boys forming lines from the harbor to the burning building. More lines formed from the town wells as people continued to come from every direction to help. Soldiers, sailors, merchants, bakers, and men of every occupation and class, rich and poor, passed buckets of water from one person to the next, to be poured or splashed onto the fire, causing the hot wood to sizzle.

As we watched, thick, gray smoke climbed high into the sky, permeated our clothes and the air around us, and filled our nostrils until we could smell nothing else. Fortunately, by the grace of God, there was space between the bakery and nearby buildings. There was no wind to spread the fire. It was early enough that people had not yet gone to sleep, so they were able to reach the bakery quickly to help. The soldiers were close by, and every able man and boy in town joined the bucket brigade. The fire was put out; soldiers stayed on guard all night to be sure it didn't start burning again.

"The building was destroyed; it will have to be rebuilt," said Papa, when he finally came home. His clothes, face, and hands were covered with soot. He looked too tired to even hold up his head.

"What will the soldiers eat, with no bread?" I asked.

"The governor already made an announcement. Private bakeries and the one in the King's Hospital will increase the amount of loaves they make every day so the soldiers will have enough to eat."

"Was anyone hurt?" asked Maman. "What about your brother Augustin? Is he all right? Will he still have a job?"

"No one was hurt. The bakers, including Augustin, had all gone home for the evening, since they start baking very early every morning. No one seems to know what started the fire. All of the men will have jobs in the smaller bakeries because the soldiers will still need bread."

* * *

A French supply ship or warship occasionally managed to bypass the English blockade and land in the harbor, providing the only excitement for the next month. News spread quickly around town, and people gathered with many questions:

"What supplies did you bring?"

"What's the latest news about the war?"

"Did you see any enemy ships?"

"Did you see any French naval ships?"

Our constant thoughts and our prayers were for protection from the English, and for France to send enough food to keep us all from starving.

20

French and English Ships

One afternoon at the end of October 1756, I walked on the ramparts and was pleasantly surprised by what I saw. High waves pounded the shore at the entrance of the harbor, and not a sail was in sight. "Where are the English ships?" I asked a soldier.

"Mademoiselle, they all returned to England. The sailors didn't want to be caught here all winter without supplies. They weren't concerned about ships arriving from France to deliver food to us, because the frequent storms make it foolish to cross the ocean in the winter."

"Will the enemy return?" I asked.

"They'll be back in the spring. They won't give up their plan to capture the fortress, not without a fight."

By the beginning of November, Maman frowned every time she reached into the flour jar to make bread. "What's wrong, Maman?" I asked.

"We don't have enough flour to last until the ships bring supplies in the spring."

The next time Madame Gautreau visited, Maman asked, "Do you know if we'll be given any flour from the king's storehouse?"

"My husband told me there isn't much food left on this island. Everyone in town is worried. This is the worst winter since we've been here. Always before, when French ships couldn't cross the ocean, we continued to receive supplies from Acadie, Quebec, Île Saint-Jean, or the American colonies. With the war, we won't get food from the

American colonies. And none from Acadie, since it's now controlled by the English."

Maman sighed. "The harvest in Île Saint-Jean was poor again this year. The settlers don't have any wheat for us; they don't even have enough for themselves."

"We'll continue to share what we have with them, and hope they have cattle to send to us," said Madame Gautreau. "And we'll pray that God will take care of all of us."

Maman smiled. "I know we won't starve. We have dried fish, but the children miss eating soup and stew. In Pigiguit, we always had vegetables and fruit in our cellar—enough for the winter. But I must stop thinking about the past. If we had stayed in Pigiguit, we would have been deported, and would be suffering in the American colonies now. The English don't want the Acadians there. Our people are starving and can't find work. Some of their children have been taken away from them. That has to be worse than this."

"Thank God we're here," said Papa. "We have to worry about the war, but my family is together, and we aren't starving."

* * *

As we reached the end of 1756, the news continued to get worse. At least twenty-three French ships had been lost in battles while crossing the ocean, or had been driven ashore as they neared Louisbourg harbor, their supplies captured by the English Royal Navy.

It seemed as if winter would never end. The constant cold winds, the fog, our worries about the war, and the shortage of food made my thoughts often go back to our lives in Pigiguit. I tried not to complain, because that made everyone else unhappy. The ringing of the chapel bells three times a day—at six o'clock in the morning, noon, and six o'clock in the evening—reminded me to pray. I discovered that was the best way to keep myself from dissolving into tears whenever thoughts of the war and our unhappy lives came to mind.

By the spring of 1757, we had nothing to eat except the rations we were given from the king's storehouse. The fish we had dried and the vegetables we had grown and stored were gone. I often had to remind myself that the years of starvation in Île Saint-Jean had been worse.

The first of May brought an unusual surprise to brighten our lives. I looked out of the window in the morning and shouted—*very unladylike, I know*, "Look! Snow! Just when we thought the weather was finally going to be a little warmer."

Everyone gathered at the window. The flakes were big and fluffy, filling the air and covering the ground.

"It's beautiful," whispered Maman. "Like a gift from heaven."

The children dressed quickly, spending hours outside making snow forts and throwing snowballs. More than eighteen inches finally covered the ground, and lasted almost two weeks. It was so unexpected that our whole family ignored our chores for once, and stayed outside enjoying its beauty until we couldn't stand the cold and had to go inside.

* * *

Between May 23 and June 19, three groups of French ships reached Louisbourg. After the arrival of the last fleet, Gregoire rushed in after work, breathless. "I counted twenty-three French ships! A sailor told Yves they carry over fourteen hundred cannons. They left France months earlier than usual to get here before the English blockaded the harbor. The sailor said this is the biggest French fleet that has ever been here. The English had better stay far away from Louisbourg this year!"

Three weeks later, M. Gautreau appeared at our door one evening. Shaking his head and sighing, he said, "Six of the French ships in the harbor sailed to Quebec to protect the people there. I think they should have stayed here. Louisbourg is England's primary target, so we need all the protection we can get."

"We still have seventeen ships," I said softly, hoping that would be enough.

"There's more bad news," continued M. Gautreau. "Before the second fleet of ships left France, two sailors were very ill—with typhus. It spread so rapidly that four hundred sailors who were supposed to make the voyage were left in France. The captain thought everyone on board was well, but more got sick while crossing the ocean, so many that there isn't enough room for them in the King's Hospital. Some are being cared for in private homes outside the fortress walls. The governor hopes this news won't spread; he's afraid we'll all panic. But I think we need to know what's going on."

I worried that Yves would be asked to house sick sailors. Maybe it was because of his long days at work or because his cottage was so tiny, but he was spared. I begged him to stay away from the houses where the sick were staying.

"My neighbor," said Yves one evening, "told me his son got sick a few days ago. It started with high fever and a bad headache. Today he woke up with a red rash all over his body. I'm going to ask the brothers who care for the sick in the King's Hospital if it could be typhus."

"Oh, Yves," I said, "please stay away from everyone who is sick."

"I'll be careful," he promised, "but I must do whatever I can to help."

The following week, Yves's young neighbor died from typhus. I prayed that Yves would remain healthy. I didn't want anything to happen to him.

Our prayers for food were finally answered. Several large privately-owned vessels captured a few English supply ships. They carried grain, which we fed to our chickens and geese, and flour—enough for the people in Louisbourg and Île Saint-Jean. The news that the sailors brought back after delivering the flour to Île Saint-Jean was not good; they had less food than we had, and many people had recently died.

In early August 1757, Louisbourg harbor was filled with French warships—so many that the entrance was blocked. It was a beautiful sight, but frightening as well, seeing the tall masts and knowing there was no hope for us without them.

"No English warships will get into the harbor," said Gregoire. I prayed that he was right.

By the middle of August, Yves rushed in breathless one Friday after work. "A sailor told me twenty-two English ships are outside Louisbourg harbor. Don't worry. They won't attack us; they're not carrying enough men to fight the large number of sailors on our warships and the soldiers in the fortress."

The English ships remained just outside the harbor all day, their white sails fluttering in the breeze. Strangely, they were gone the next day.

To celebrate—the following week was the Feast of Saint Louis, King of France—the governor ordered the sailors to fire every gun on the French ships, one after another. What a racket!

By the middle of September, the English ships were back. They were too far away to be hit by the fortress cannons, but unfortunately, they were close enough to capture any French ship that sailed in or out of the harbor. It was again time to start worrying about food for the coming winter. We prayed that God would keep us safe and provide enough food for all of our people.

21

September Storm

I missed Hélène. M. Gautreau wouldn't let her come to visit unless one of her brothers had time to walk with her and return for her later, so I hadn't seen her since the English ships began patrolling outside Louisbourg harbor.

When they finished fishing earlier than usual, Yves often accompanied Gregoire to our house where they made or repaired nets while Maman, Anne, and I sewed. One Friday afternoon in September, Yves said, "Pelagie, I haven't seen your friend Hélène in quite a while. Does she still visit you?"

"No, I wish I could see her. It's the English soldiers' fault. They're ruining my life. Hélène used to come here often. Sometimes her twelve-year-old brother or Madame Gautreau would accompany her, but not anymore, because the English soldiers might attack the fortress. Papa said we must stay in the house unless it is absolutely necessary that we leave, and then we must always have an adult with us.

"I know you miss her, Pelagie," said Maman. "I'd like to go with you, but I can't take the little ones, and I can't leave them alone."

Yves looked at me, then at Maman. "Madame Benoist, I'd be happy to escort Pelagie to Hélène's house, and return for her in an hour. These nets can wait until tomorrow."

Maman stared at Yves, but said nothing. Even with his sun-darkened skin, his cheeks reddened. "Oh, no, I didn't mean that she and I would walk alone in the streets. I thought Gregoire could accompany us."

I didn't move. I didn't breathe, waiting for Maman's answer.

"Yes, I think that would be acceptable," said Maman. "Get your shawl, Pelagie; it's windy today."

I jumped up, twirled around, and kissed Maman's cheek. "Merci, Maman."

Hélène and I had a wonderful time catching up on everything that had happened since we last saw each other. She teased me about Yves, and I teased her about a young merchant who visited M. Gautreau often. It seemed that she and I had just started talking when Yves and Gregoire returned for me. When we reached our house, I said to Yves, "Come in. Eat supper with us."

"Non, I must get home. Gregoire and I walked on the ramparts while waiting for you. The wind is blowing hard and the waves are high. I must secure my boat. Gregoire, if the weather is like this tomorrow, we won't go out. I'll come here and we'll work on the nets."

The next day the wind was much stronger. Coming into the house, Yves said, "I've never seen the waves so high. I'm afraid a storm is on its way. Sometimes we have violent weather at this time of year."

By Saturday night the wind howled and whistled. Our poor little house seemed to shiver and shake. The shutters rattled with every gust of wind. "Will the roof blow away, Papa?" I asked, as I trembled and wrapped my shawl tighter around my shoulders.

"I hope not, but M. Gautreau told me that September storms are sometimes fierce, and houses can be damaged."

In the middle of the night, the wind roared so loudly that none of us could sleep. We gathered around the table and prayed for God to protect us; that was all we could do. Even though it was Sunday, we couldn't leave the house to go to Mass. Finally, around noon, the intensity of the wind began to decrease.

As soon as it was safe, we went outside to see if our neighbors needed help. The shed where our goats and chickens lived had lost two walls and part of the roof. Our yard and the streets were a mess from branches, leaves, and small objects that had been blown around and broken. No one seemed to be hurt, so we spent the rest of the afternoon cleaning up even though it was Sunday; this was necessary work.

That night when I said my prayers, I thanked God for sparing us from the storm. Then I said another prayer of thanks for Yves, Hélène, and my family.

22

A Busy Winter

We continued to worry about food and the war. However, there was one bright spot in our lives. My little brother Sébastien-François was born on October 20, 1757. He was baptized five days later in the Chapelle de Saint-Louis in the King's Bastion. Anne and I spent all of our waking hours working in the house and garden, trying to make life a little easier for Maman. She always seemed to glow when she had a new baby to care for and rock to sleep.

Yves continued to visit two or three evenings a week. At first, it was always the same; he and Papa talked while Maman and I spun thread, made cloth on the loom, or mended clothes. But as the weeks passed, Yves looked at me more and more while he talked to Papa. I know, because I watched him as I worked. He always smiled at me when he got up to leave, and sometimes Maman asked me to walk to the door with him.

"I can't wait to see you again," he whispered one evening as he was leaving. "But I wish we could be alone."

My heart fluttered. I couldn't answer him; I could hardly breathe. Wouldn't tongues wag if we ever met alone!

"That young man has a smile that lights up the room," said Maman as I returned to my sewing.

The next evening I jumped up and ran to the door when I heard a knock. "What's your hurry, Pelagie?" asked Gregoire, with a big grin on his face.

Yves stood at the door, nervously twirling his cap in his hands. He cleared his throat. "Please ask your Papa if I may speak to him outside."

"Is something wrong, Yves?" I asked.

"Non, I just need to speak to him."

Papa went outside and closed the door. After what seemed like forever, he returned alone.

"Where is Yves?" I asked.

"He left so I can talk to you and Maman. He will visit tomorrow. Pelagie, do you like Yves?"

"Yes, Papa. I'm very fond of him."

"He asked for permission to court you."

My heart started to beat so hard that I was afraid it would jump out of my chest. I finally managed to ask, "What did you tell him?"

"I said your Maman and I would be happy to have him court you. I'll rest easier knowing I have someone to help care for my family if anything should happen to me, especially in time of war. I wouldn't worry so much if we still lived near all of my brothers and sisters; there would always be plenty of family to help. But only Augustin is here. His three children are so young, I would hate to ask him to care for my family, too."

"Papa, nothing will happen to you and Maman."

"I hope you're right, but you never know."

After that, when Yves visited, we were allowed to sit on one side of the room, our chairs next to each other, with the rest of the family on the other side of the room. We could talk softly to each other, but never touch, not even our hands. I always walked to the door with Yves when he left. He smiled at me when he said goodnight.

A few days after we began to court, Maman said, "Pelagie, we'll have to spend all of our spare time sewing so that we'll be ready when Yves wants to get married."

"Maman," I said, "I'm not seventeen yet."

"You will be soon, and we have a lot to do. I've put aside several sheets and quilts, but you'll also need pillows, towels, a mattress, a few new dresses, nightgowns, and caps. I hope I'm not forgetting anything."

* * *

Days grew shorter, and everyone talked and worried about whether our food would last until supply ships could cross the ocean in the spring. Whenever Yves visited us, that was his and Papa's main topic of conversation.

"Papa," I said one evening as they discussed their concerns, "before we moved here, you said we would never have to worry about being hungry in Louisbourg."

Papa sighed. "That was before England and France went to war."

Yves said, "He *was* right, Pelagie. We always had enough to eat, although it could be tiresome without fresh fruit, butter, and molasses during the winter. We had dried meat and fish, and enough flour in the storehouse for everyone. However, since the war started, it's been difficult for supply ships to bring food from France and Quebec at any time of year."

"Isn't the storehouse full of flour?" I asked.

"Non, we're afraid we won't have enough for everyone this winter. Unfortunately, we can't grow grain or enough vegetables or animals to survive, so we have to depend on imports. Lately, between storms and blockades, no ships have been able to get through. Winter will soon be here and it won't be possible to get any supplies until spring. It's a terrible problem."

* * *

As Maman and I sewed and Anne worked on the loom one dreary evening, we heard a drumbeat. Gregoire jumped up from the net he was making and grabbed his coat and hat. "That's the signal for a public announcement," he said. "I'll go, Papa, to find out what it is."

"Hurry back," said Papa.

It wasn't long before he returned with a big smile lighting up his face. "A ship flying the Portuguese flag arrived with salted meat, flour, vegetables, and butter. We'll have food for a little while longer. The captain said the English warships didn't bother him because Portugal and England are still at peace."

"I'm surprised he was able to cross the ocean this late in the year," said Maman.

The following week, Papa returned home from the storehouse with our rations. "Several supply ships were captured by the English soon after they left French ports. The administrator doesn't think any more ships will arrive until spring. He is very concerned about the shortage of flour. He wants everyone, even those who bake for the soldiers, to substitute rice for one-third of the flour in our bread. The bakers aren't happy about that."

"We'll do whatever we have to," said Maman. "We've certainly gone without before. At least we'll have something to eat." It seemed strange at first, but we soon got used to our "new" bread.

"Rumors are flying," said Papa, "among the soldiers, the people who come into the workshop, and on the street, that the English will attack us in the spring. When their ships sailed away from our harbor in October, they went to Halifax instead of returning to England. It will be easy for them to reach our harbor before ships arrive from France to protect us."

"We must pray for our safety," said Maman.

Not knowing what would happen if, or when, the English attacked us, the people of Louisbourg decided to celebrate the beginning of the New Year in 1758. The merchants and their families ate fancy meals and went to dances. Hélène convinced her brothers to take her to watch the dressed-up people who were going to a dance given by the governor. Papa allowed Anne and me to go with them since Gregoire agreed to accompany us. It was a wonderful evening, especially being with Hélène again.

"Look at those dresses," said Anne.

"Look at the handsome men," said Hélène, laughing.

The ladies were stunning in their fine wool dresses made in the styles the French ladies wore. "I've never seen anything as beautiful as those dresses," I said as we walked home.

"We'll do this again soon," said Hélène. "On January 12 the pre-Lenten parties begin, and this year Louisbourg is going to celebrate

Carnival. The administrators won't cancel it as they did two years ago. Everyone realizes that being miserable didn't keep the English away. I can't wait. My brothers will take me, and you'll come with us."

Gregoire and Daniel grudgingly came with us to watch the people going to parties. "Why would anyone want to look at people who are so dressed up they can hardly walk?" asked Gregoire. "Then they go to the governor's party where they eat and drink so much, they really can't walk. What's the fun in that?"

"Hélène and I want to see what the ladies are wearing. Their dresses are beautiful, nothing like the plain clothes we wear."

I went with Hélène several more times because the wealthy people of Louisbourg celebrated with many parties. "I wish I had a soft wool dress from France, or a shimmery silk one," I said on our way home one evening, "but I know that won't happen."

"Maybe you'll have one someday," said Hélène.

"Maybe. And I'll wear it to cook dinner and work in the garden. That's the way I spend my time." We laughed all the way home.

On the last Sunday in January 1758, Yves again stood at the door after supper, twirling his cap and looking very nervous. After chatting with Papa for a while he cleared his throat and said, "M. Benoist, will you give me your daughter's hand in marriage? We can live in my rented fisherman's cottage now, but by the end of this fishing season, I'll have enough money to build a small house of our own. In another year or two I'll buy a larger boat. I'll be able to support a family and I want Pelagie to share my life."

I couldn't breathe. I thought I was going to die right there if Papa didn't hurry with his answer.

"Yes. I think you'll make a good husband. You must promise to take good care of our Pelagie."

"I will."

"When do you want to get married?" asked Papa. "Of course, it can't be during Lent or Advent. The church doesn't allow that."

"No, and it can't be during late spring, summer, or early fall when I fish from dawn to dusk. We'd never see each other. The best time is before Lent."

"That's not possible!" said Maman. "Ash Wednesday is less than two weeks away."

"I'll talk to Père LaGrée tomorrow," said Papa. "With all of the administrators in Louisbourg thinking that the English will attack in early spring, I'd feel better knowing that Pelagie is settled and will be taken care of, along with the rest of my family if something happens to me."

"I don't want anything to happen to you," said Yves. "But of course, I'll take care of everyone if I have to."

The priest agreed that the wedding could take place before the beginning of Lent. He promised to read the first bann announcing our marriage at Mass the following Sunday, the fifth of February; he would dispense with the other two banns because there wasn't time for them before Lent.

"It's a good thing we made your sheets and towels and all the other things you'll need for your house," said Maman. We had been so busy sewing that we hadn't thought about what I would wear. I opened the chest where I kept my clothes and looked at my two everyday dresses and my one Sunday dress. "Mama, what am I going to wear for the wedding?"

"I have a few yards of beautiful material that the dressmaker, Madame Babin, gave me after I helped her make wedding dresses for some of the merchants' daughters. I've been saving it for a special occasion, and it will be perfect for you."

Maman had wrapped the material in a sheet to protect it. It was the palest pink I'd ever seen, so soft and fine that I was almost afraid to touch it. "Oh, it's beautiful," was the only thing I could say. "Like the fancy ladies wear."

As soon as she heard the news about our wedding, Madame Babin hurried to our house. "Elisabeth," she said, "you have helped me make many wedding dresses and ball gowns. Now I want to help you with Pelagie's dress."

"We would be happy to have your help," said Maman. "We have only a week and want to take our time so we don't make a mistake and waste even an inch of the precious material you gave me."

I had never before sewn anything except the homespun we made with our spinning wheel and loom. When it was finished, my wedding dress was simply made, as all of our clothes were, but the material made it lovely. When I tried it on, I danced around the room, twirling to watch the skirt as it swirled from side to side.

"I could wear this to a party given by the governor's wife," I said.

"You'll have to get invited first," said Gregoire with a laugh.

My prayers that week were for a happy marriage with many children, and the health and safety of Yves's family and mine. If I had known what we were going to face in the future, I would have doubled, no, tripled, my prayers.

23

Our Wedding

On Friday, three days before our wedding, Yves asked Maman and Papa if they would accompany me to his cottage the following day. "I'd like Pelagie to see it," he said. "I want her to be happy."

"That's a good idea," said Maman. "We'll bring the things we have for the two of you. Anne will help us and Gregoire will stay home with the younger children."

After Papa got home from work the next day, we walked through town carrying our bundles as Papa pushed a cart he borrowed from M. Gautreau. Just before I walked through the fortress gates, I stopped, looked around, and said, "Except for a few walks in the woods with my family, I haven't been outside of the walls surrounding our town since we arrived in Louisbourg a little over two years ago. So much has happened in that time."

Maman put the things she was carrying on top of the cart and hugged me. "You have many years ahead of you. I pray the rest of your life will be wonderful and will bring you much happiness."

Fisherman's Cottage, Fortress of Louisbourg

Papa smiled at me as he pushed the cart through the gates. In the distance were many small fishermen's cottages near the bay. Next to the water were racks that would soon be covered with fish drying in the sun. As we got closer, I was amazed to see an animal on one of the roofs! "What is that goat doing up there?" I asked.

Yves stood in the open door of that cottage, waiting for us. Seeing my puzzled look, he smiled. "Do you like my goat, Pelagie?"

"What's it doing on the roof?"

"Eating."

"Why is it on the roof? And how did it get up there?"

"Lots of fishermen raise goats for their milk," he said. "My roof is made of a thick layer of sod, which helps to keep the cottage warm in winter. The grass stops the sod from washing away, and the goat prevents the grass from getting too long. If you look at the roof, you'll see that one side angles down close to the ground, making it easy for the goat to jump on and off. Come in; put your bundles down."

"I hope you have room for all of this," said Maman. "I made a new mattress and two pillows stuffed with small feathers from our chickens for your wedding present. Claude made a rocking chair for Pelagie. I see that you have a chair for yourself. Pelagie, Anne, and I made new sheets, towels, quilts, and pillowcases. We will also give you a hen and a rooster if you build a pen for them."

"Thank you. I'll do that today so Pelagie will have fresh eggs for cooking. How do you like our little cottage, Pelagie?"

"It's tiny, but big enough for two," I said. "It's so clean and neat; I love it."

"You didn't think I could keep a cottage clean, did you?" asked Yves with a sparkle in his eyes. "I made a chest for you to keep your clothes in. Look around to see if you need anything else."

"It looks perfect," I said. I could hardly wait to call it mine.

On Sunday morning I sat in the chapel with my family at High Mass. I shivered when the priest announced our wedding bann, stating that we wanted to be married. Père LaGrée asked the congregation to notify him if anyone knew of any reason why we shouldn't marry. I looked across the aisle and saw Yves smiling at me; that calmed me. After Mass everyone congratulated us on our upcoming marriage, which would take place the following day.

Chapelle Saint-Louis, Fortress of Louisbourg

Monday, February 6, 1758 was a beautiful day for a wedding. My whole family walked to the King's Bastion and upstairs to the small white chapel where the large painting of King Louis IX hung over the altar. I had gone to Mass there every Sunday for the last two years, but it felt different. I trembled and wondered if I was going to faint. Papa put his arm around me. "Don't worry. You'll be happy, my sweet Pelagie. Yves is a good man."

The candle flames danced in front of the picture of St. Louis, who was king of France from 1226 to 1270. The first person I saw was Yves, looking handsome in his dark Sunday coat, white shirt, dark knee-length pants, and long socks. Next to him stood Père LaGrée in his brown habit, rope belt, and sandals. Already seated were Oncle Augustin, Tante Marguerite and their three children, M. and Madame Gautreau, Hélène, her sister and brothers, four of Yves's friends, and a few neighbors.

The priest asked Yves and me to stand in front of the communion rail. I was so nervous, I remember little about the ceremony except that Père LaGrée asked us several questions about our Catholic faith, and we repeated our vows to love and be faithful to each other. The priest signed the parish record, wrote Yves's name and mine, and asked us to put a cross next to our names. Yves's friends also put a cross next to their names. When we sat in the front pew for Mass, my new husband took my hand in his and smiled at me—the smile that I loved. "You are beautiful," he whispered. I was no longer nervous; I knew I was doing the right thing.

"Come to our house to celebrate," said Maman to everyone as we walked out of the chapel. We served spruce beer for the adults and angelica tea for the children. Maman had made a cake; where she found the ingredients with the shortages, I don't know. The gifts we received took my breath away: a beautiful handmade quilt from M. and Madame Gautreau, a delicate lace collar from Hélène, two hens from Oncle Augustin and Tante Marguerite, and a goat from Yves's friends.

In the afternoon everyone walked with us to our little cottage, then left us to begin our lives together.

That night I knelt next to our bed and prayed that I would be a good wife to Yves, that someday I would have his children, and that I would always be as happy as I was that day. It was a blessing that I didn't know what we would face in the future. That would have ruined the wonderful day.

24

Married Life

The day after our wedding, Yves and I walked to town to watch the Carnival celebrations. After eating a delicious meal that Madame Gautreau had prepared, my family spent the afternoon and evening strolling around Louisbourg with their family.

"I love watching the governor and his friends going to parties and dances dressed in their expensive clothes," said Hélène. "I always pretend I'm invited, too."

"Everyone is having fun today," I said.

"They seem to be determined to enjoy themselves before Lent starts," said Yves. "Since almost all of the people in Louisbourg are Catholics, they probably don't want to think about fasting and abstinence."

"Don't remind me," said one of Hélène's brothers. "Sundays are the only days we're allowed to eat meat and three full meals a day for six whole weeks."

Papa sighed. "I think most people are trying to forget that we'll probably soon be at war."

* * *

Yves and I were happy living in our tiny one-room cottage near the water. We took long walks along the shore in the evenings, enjoying our quiet life. It was a peaceful time with no warships in sight.

Yves was busy even though fishing season hadn't started. He cared for the goats and chickens, prepared a plot of ground for my kitchen garden, cleaned and readied his boat and nets, constructed a new fish drying rack, and made a small loom for me. I always had something to do—cleaning, cooking, sewing, and visiting my family.

The week after our wedding, Yves and I walked hand-in-hand along the shore of the harbor. Suddenly I stopped. "Look at all the ice."

"Yes," said Yves. "That's drift ice. It flows in from the north and fills the harbor at this time every year. Ships can't get in or out. But that's an unusually large amount; it will probably take longer to float away."

"Good," I said. "That will keep English ships out of the harbor for a while."

February was quiet except for two fires in town that damaged buildings. It was still too cold for fishing. The soldiers usually spent much of their time making repairs on the outside of the fortress, but they had to stop because of the cold. The guards walked the ramparts, but no English warships or supply ships were expected.

As we ate supper one evening with my parents, Papa said, "Pelagie, M. Gautreau asked me to tell you that Hélène wants you to visit her. She's anxious to see you."

The next afternoon Yves and I walked to Hélène's house, because I couldn't wait any longer. "Pelagie, at last I can tell you," said Hélène. "Joseph and I are getting married on the first Monday in May. He's the merchant who has been calling on me. He finally asked Papa's permission to marry me."

"I'm so happy for you," I said as I hugged her. "What can I do to help you get ready?"

"We have lots of sewing to do. Come help us as often as you can."

Maman and I immediately began to make a quilt for a wedding present. Whenever Yves had time to walk with me to Hélène's house, she and I spent the afternoon sewing and enjoying each other's company as we always had.

It was good to have sewing, quilting, and talking about Hélène's wedding to distract us from worries about war. Beginning in mid-April, many English ships were seen sailing outside of Louisbourg harbor.

Several French warships arrived, bringing news that others had been delayed or captured by the enemy.

May was a long month of worry and wondering about what was going to happen to us. The one bright spot was Hélène and Joseph's wedding on Monday, May 2, held in the chapel in the King's Bastion. On our way there, Yves said, "Since Joseph is a merchant and so is his father, he and Hélène will probably have a fancy wedding and a fancier house. I wish I could provide for you in the same way."

"Yves, I couldn't be happier if I had a big house full of servants. I have everything I want in life except children, and someday we'll have a houseful, God willing." As we climbed the stairs to the chapel, he squeezed my hand and looked at me with the smile that I loved.

Hélène wore a shimmery pale yellow silk dress similar to those worn by the ladies we liked to watch going to parties at the governor's house. It was trimmed with lace in the front; in the back, pleats fell gracefully to the floor over a wide hooped skirt. She looked elegant. Joseph's pants had buckles below the knees; his shirt had lace ruffles in front and on his wrists. His leather shoes also had buckles on them.

After the wedding, my whole family attended the reception at M. and Madame Gautreau's house. The table was covered with fancy cakes and cookies made by Madame Gautreau and her friends. There were drinks for everyone: spruce beer, wine, tea, coffee, and hot chocolate. Such luxury! Later, as was customary, we all walked with Hélène and Joseph to their new house.

"That can't be their house," I said to Yves as we walked down their street. "It's two stories high and looks big enough to have two separate rooms on each floor. Why would Hélène and Joseph need so much space?"

"Maybe they're hoping to have a big family."

"Well, I hope she invites me to visit soon; I'm dying to see the inside," I said as the newly-married couple walked in and closed the door.

A few days later, after Yves came in from fishing, he and I went to Maman and Papa's house. The streets were crowded with soldiers; many of them wearing uniforms trimmed in green instead of the familiar red.

"Yves," I said, "those soldiers aren't French. Their uniforms are different, and I can't understand a word they're saying to each other."

"I know. Maybe your papa can tell us what's going on."

We hardly had time to greet my family before Papa started talking about the war. "Several French warships arrived yesterday with hundreds of soldiers."

Yves nodded. "We saw them in town, but many of them speak different languages."

"I was told," said Papa, "that they are from several countries in Europe—mostly from Switzerland and Germany. Groups of Indians have also come to help; I even met a few Mi'kmaqs from Île Saint-Jean."

I smiled. "That's good. We'll defeat the English with the extra help."

Papa walked to the fireplace and lit his pipe. "I'm afraid that's not good. If the French government is willing to pay hundreds of soldiers from different countries, and even Indians, that can only mean the king knows we can't win the war without their help. England must have a tremendous army and navy ready to attack us."

Maman put a pitcher of spruce beer and glasses on the table, and then turned to look at us. "Pelagie, you and Yves should stay with us. "We're safer inside the fortress than you are outside the walls."

"I don't think we're in danger yet," said Yves, "and if I don't fish, we won't have enough food to last through next winter. I promise we'll come if the news gets worse, or at least, I'll bring Pelagie here. I won't let her stay in our cottage if there's any danger."

"Pelagie, don't go out of your cottage alone," said Papa. *"Not ever."*

"I won't, Papa. I promise."

For the rest of the month, news was sometimes good—occasionally a ship reached Louisbourg safely—but it was usually bad. "First the English blockaded the harbor, then they captured several French ships," Yves said, as he paced the floor. "Now, soldiers are sick—so many that the Brothers of Charity can't care for all of them. A large number of the soldiers who were stationed at the landing beaches south of the fortress had to be hospitalized. It isn't good for them to live outside in this cold, wet, foggy weather."

On May 25 priests, brothers, and important lay people walked in procession through Louisbourg to celebrate Corpus Christi, the feast of the Blessed Sacrament. Since it was a holy day of obligation, parishioners watched the procession, attended Mass, and spent the rest of the day with family. We also planned to celebrate the octave of the Feast of Corpus Christi on June 1 in the same way.

However, on May 29 loud noises broke the usual quiet of the evening and brought us running to the door. "That's gunfire," said Yves. A loud blast was followed by several more. "That's cannon fire. Get your shawl and cap, Pelagie. We're going to your papa's house." Before we reached the town gate, the drummers were beating the emergency signal. "Hurry!" said Yves. "We must get through the gates before they're closed."

We ran over the drawbridge, breathlessly. My heart was beating so hard, I was sure the soldiers manning the gates would hear it. Yves gave the password, and asked, "What's happening?"

"Guns and cannons north of the fort. Both French and English ships are there—lots of them. That's all we know." The soldiers closed the gates and pulled up the drawbridge.

With Yves's arm around me, we rushed through the streets, which were jammed with soldiers hurrying to their posts. Civilians were rushing in all directions. I shivered. "Don't let go of me."

"Of course, I won't, Pelagie. I'll always take care of you."

When we reached Papa's house, he and Gregoire were leaving. "Do you know what's happening, Yves?" Papa asked.

"No, I wanted to get Pelagie here safely. I'm going back to get news and see if I can help."

I rushed to hug my husband. "Don't leave," I begged.

"Pelagie, I'm going with your papa and Gregoire. We'll do whatever we can to help. We can't let the English capture the fort without trying to stop them."

Papa started to close the door. "Stay here, Pelagie. Help Maman with the children."

For the next two hours we paced the floor, praying and wondering what was happening and what Yves, Papa, and Gregoire were doing. I thought I would lose my mind with worry, but they finally returned.

Walking through the door, Yves said, "We're safe, for now." I ran across the room and threw my arms around him, not wanting to ever let go.

"What happened, Claude?" asked Maman, taking his coat and hat.

"The authorities sounded the emergency signal because they were afraid the English were coming ashore just north of the fort. We'll be in great danger if their soldiers decide to attack us on land instead of by sea. By the grace of God, that didn't happen. Instead, three French ships sailed safely into the harbor."

Yves nodded as we walked to the door to return to our cottage. "Hundreds of townspeople were out in the streets, ready to help protect our town. Gregoire, I'll see you early tomorrow morning."

Maman twisted her apron in her hands. "English ships are everywhere. You can't go fishing."

"We have to fish every day so we don't run out of food," said Yves. "We'll stay in the harbor, near the shore. The English aren't there yet. I promise I won't risk my life or that of my helpers."

Looking at Papa, Yves said, "M. Benoist, Thursday is the octave of the Feast of Corpus Christi, but Gregoire and I are excused from the obligation of attending Mass. Pelagie can't go alone."

"Corpus Christi and its octave are my favorite feast days," I said. "I love the procession and the festivities. I'll meet Maman and Papa in front of the chapel."

"No, Pelagie," said Papa. "That's not safe. Since it's a holy day, I don't have to work. I'll walk to your house early in the morning so you can come to the celebration with us. You mustn't miss it."

On Thursday morning Papa and Daniel greeted me with excitement. "There are so many English ships outside the harbor that you can't see anything except sails fluttering in the breeze," said Daniel.

"Are they going to attack us?" I asked.

"Possibly," said Papa. "But *probably* they're going to blockade the harbor again to keep French ships out."

As we walked over the ramparts to the chapel, I clutched my cap and cloak to keep the strong wind from snatching them away. A soldier stood watching someone near the water. "What's happening?" asked Papa.

"With so many English ships patrolling outside the harbor, Governor Drucour was notified. He stood on the ramparts and counted sails—there were seventy!"

"Oh, we're in danger," I said.

"No, no, Madame. The good Lord sent powerful winds to keep the ships from getting close to shore. Our troops are protecting the three places where the enemy might land outside the fortress. We're safe *for now.*"

Even with the threat of war, the streets were crowded with people observing the feast day. We met Maman and the children near the chapel. Soon after we arrived, the priests, along with a few lay people, led a procession through town. Everyone sang hymns until the priest carrying the Blessed Sacrament grew near; then people knelt in the streets, worshiping God. The procession was accompanied by an artillery salute, gunshots on the ramparts and ships, signaling respect. When the priests returned to the chapel, Père LaGrée said Mass, reminding us in his sermon that we must continue to ask God to protect us.

After Mass, civilian volunteers helped the soldiers at the landing beaches and the fortress wall facing the ocean. Watching them hurry to their posts, I wondered what the future would bring for the people of Louisbourg, but some things are better left unknown.

25

Threat of War

A week of strong wind and high waves prevented the English from bringing their ships close to shore. Listening to the wind howling around the cottage, Yves reached for a piece of hot, crusty bread to eat with his steaming bowl of vegetable soup. "I hope the wind keeps blowing; that makes it difficult for the enemy to attack. It also gives extra time for Quebec and France to send supplies and soldiers to us."

That afternoon I clutched my cape and cap as Yves and I walked to visit Hélène and Joseph for the first time since their wedding. She served hot chocolate and cookies as we sat at the table near the fireplace.

Yves tasted his drink and smiled. "Delicious! Pelagie told me to try the hot chocolate at your wedding reception, but I drank wine instead. "What's the news around town, Joseph?"

"The rumor is that almost two hundred English ships are prepared to attack. Some are sailing just outside the entrance to the harbor, and others are anchored southwest of Louisbourg in Gabarus Bay."

"What does that mean? What's going to happen to us?" I asked.

Joseph sighed. "I don't know. We don't have anywhere near that many ships. However, Governor Drucour asked his officers for numbers of soldiers, troops on the ships, Indians, Acadians, and others who are trained to fight. Counting all of them, we have over four thousand men who will do whatever they can to save Louisbourg."

I reached for another cookie. "That's a lot."

"Yes, but not enough," said Yves. "Unfortunately, those men must protect the fortress, the islands, and the whole rocky coast. The English claim to have at least three times that many fighters."

As Joseph and Yves continued to talk about the war, I whispered to Hélène. "I'd like to see your house." In the large room upstairs, I twirled around, pretending I had a partner. "We could have a dance and invite Governor and Madame Drucour."

She smiled, "Maybe we will someday, if this war ever ends."

Walking home later, I enjoyed the peaceful night and hoped it would last forever.

Yves left the cottage about five o'clock the next morning, just as the sky began to lighten before sunrise. I stood in the doorway watching him walk along the shore and saw Gregoire hurrying to meet him. Just then, the sound of gunfire made us all look toward the southwest; the booming of the cannons went on and on.

Yves ran back to the cottage. "We'll fish near the shore and return if the gunfire sounds closer. Don't leave the cottage alone. Gather our clothes and some food in case we have to leave in a hurry."

My hands shook and my voice trembled. "I'll be ready."

A short time after the chapel bells chimed the Angelus at noon, the sound of running feet and shouting brought me to the window. Daniel banged on the door and almost fell into the room, breathing hard.

I dropped the shirt I was mending. "What's wrong? What's happening?"

Daniel stopped to catch his breath. "English ships are everywhere, and they all have guns—too many to count! A short time ago, our drummers beat the signal for troops to go to the closest landing beach south of Louisbourg. The governor thinks the English will attack there. The soldiers inside the fortress are manning their cannons and waiting to see what the English are going to do."

"What are *we* going to do?"

"Papa said you're to come home with me, *right now*. He went to look for Gregoire and Yves. He said we must all stay together inside the fort in case the English attack."

"Daniel, do you think Yves and Gregoire are safe?"

"They must have stopped fishing an hour or two ago; they're probably cleaning their catch."

"I wish they'd forget the fish and come home."

Daniel shook his head. "You know Yves isn't going to let a boatload of fish spoil."

"Just this once, I wish he would."

Daniel helped me close the shutters and he picked up the basket of food. I took a bundle of clothes and as many quilts as I could carry. After one last look around, I shut the door of the pretty little cottage that Yves and I shared. I thought about leaving our house in Pigiguit eight years before, and I never saw that house again.

The knot in my stomach loosened slightly as we hurried through the gates of the fortress. I gave the password and the guards allowed us to pass without question.

Maman breathed a sigh of relief when we walked into the house where she and Papa lived with my seven sisters and brothers. "I'm so glad you're here—I was sick with worry. As soon as Papa, Gregoire, and Yves get home, we'll eat dinner." The house smelled wonderful. Maman had baked bread and made vegetable soup; no one could make soup or bake bread like she could.

Time dragged as we waited and wondered where the rest of our family was. I couldn't sit still. I walked to the window every few minutes, praying to see my handsome, twenty-six year old husband. Maman put her arm around my shoulders and pulled me away from the window. "Don't worry, Pelagie. He'll be here soon."

I thought my heart would stop beating when at last I heard the door open. Gregoire walked in, followed by Yves and Papa. They were bent under the weight of the barrels they were carrying. I ran to Yves and tried to hug him before he put his barrel down. "Oh, Yves, I was so worried."

A smile lit up his face. "Pelagie, don't you think I can take care of myself?"

Maman hugged Papa, then turned to Yves. "What's in the barrels?"

"Dried codfish. We weren't going to leave it in the fishing shed for the English to eat."

"Bless you. Now we won't have to worry about food. But we need water."

Yves picked up the empty buckets in the kitchen. "Pelagie and I will go."

We didn't stand around the well talking to friends and neighbors as we usually did. Everyone was in a hurry, peering around to be sure there were no enemy soldiers lurking close by. We whispered as if the sound of our voices would attract the English and cause an attack. In the distance two of our soldiers guarded the thick wooden gates at the entrance of the fort. The gates were closed and the heavy drawbridge was up; no one could enter the fortress. Soldiers stood watch near the cannons on top of the high walls surrounding our town. I breathed a sigh of relief. Louisbourg was secure. We were safe.

After dinner, Papa and Yves left to get the latest news. "It's not good," said Papa when they returned. "When we heard the guns early this morning, English ships were shooting at the soldiers who were protecting our landing beaches. Earlier, a large number of their sailors lowered themselves into small boats so quietly that our lookouts didn't know they were coming until they were very close to land. Some English soldiers were hit by French gunfire and several of their boats overturned in the heavy waves, drowning the men in the cold ocean water. Since many English soldiers were dying, a retreat was called."

"A retreat—that's good news," said Maman.

Yves shook his head. "As the English soldiers rowed back to their ships, three boats reached an area where they were able to land out of sight of the French lookouts. The soldiers on several other boats joined them. When they came on shore, they climbed a cliff, surprised the French, and attacked."

"But the French fought back and won, didn't they?" asked Gregoire.

"Non," said Papa. "Thinking they were outnumbered, the French retreated to the fortress. The commanders don't know how many French soldiers were lost—killed, captured, or deserted. The soldiers from the other landing sites are back in Louisbourg. The governor and the commanders are shocked that our men couldn't keep the enemy from landing. What they will do next, no one knows."

I shivered as I thought of the English army and navy so close to us, with their guns and cannons pointed at our fortress town. I was only seventeen and already had faced more sadness than I wanted to think about, but I had not lived through war, at least not close to my home.

I was tormented by my thoughts. What was going to happen to us? My family had always been nearby to guide me and keep me strong. Would they always be there to protect me? Were we going to be forced to leave Louisbourg? Why couldn't we stay in one place and enjoy a peaceful life? I had many questions, but no one had any answers.

26

Closer and Closer

A few days after the English sailors reached the first of our landing beaches, Yves left early in the morning to get news, and soon rushed back, stopping to catch his breath before he could talk. "Thousands of English soldiers have landed south of the fortress and are putting up tents, building dirt and stone walls for protection, and even making roads to move their cannons. They must be planning to attack us."

Yves took a drink of water and continued. "Governor Drucour is afraid the enemy will set up their cannons in the hills overlooking the fortress."

"Didn't the French soldiers lower those hills?" asked Papa.

Yves nodded. "They lowered some, but there were too many to get rid of all of them. I'm going to help our soldiers. I'll do whatever I can to keep the fortress and our people safe."

Gregoire rushed to the door. "I'll go with you."

Papa reached for his hat. "So will I."

"How can you help, Yves?" asked Maman.

"We'll go outside the walls to fill bags of dirt to protect the cannons in the King's Bastion. We'll also make a shelter for women and children."

I grabbed Yves's arm. "You can't leave the fortress walls. It isn't safe."

"The enemy won't see us; the fog is too thick, and a group of soldiers will protect us."

Giving me a quick hug, Yves left the house followed by Papa and Gregoire. Maman, Anne, and I kept busy as we waited and worried about our men until they finally returned just before supper—dirty, tired, and hungry. Papa sank into his chair with a sigh. "We did as much as we could; let's hope it helps."

Hearing shouts in the street the next morning, we ran outside. Large plumes of smoke filled the sky south of Louisbourg. Our neighbor, M. Robichaud, told us what was, for me, the worst news of all. "The governor sent soldiers to set fire to the cottages and buildings outside Dauphin Gate."

I shuddered. "That's the gate we use. Does that mean our cottage?"

Yves put his arms around me. "Probably."

I shook with sobs. "Why would the governor want to burn down our beautiful little cottage?"

"It's for our safety," said M. Robichaud. "The governor didn't want to give the enemy a place to hide so close to the fortress."

"But, Yves, the chest and loom you made for me, the rocking chair Papa made, the sheets and towels that Maman, Anne, and I made were all in the cottage."

"Pelagie, those are just things," said Papa. "Don't ever grieve for anything that can be replaced. Your family is what's important. We're together; that's the only thing that matters."

I wiped my eyes. "What do you think happened to our goats and chickens?"

Yves hugged me. "Maybe the soldiers let them go. We might find them after the war is over."

* * *

M. Gautreau knocked at the kitchen door a few days later. "Three French ships sailed out of the harbor late yesterday. A soldier told me one is sailing to France, the other two to Quebec."

"Why did they leave?" asked Yves.

"I don't know. I hope they're going to ask for more ships and men to fight."

Papa shook his head. "I'm afraid it's too late for that. It would take months for a ship to sail to France and back. I doubt there are enough soldiers in Quebec to make a difference. Maybe the captains left to keep their ships from being damaged or destroyed in the war."

Hard rain and thick fog kept everyone inside for several days in mid-June. One morning, Papa put on his jacket and picked up the empty buckets. "I'm going to the well for water." He was barely outside when he ran back into the house, frightening us all as he dropped the buckets. I rushed to get a chair for him. "Papa, what's wrong?"

Yves brought a cup of water. "Sit down and catch your breath."

Papa sipped the water. "The British have captured Lighthouse Point."

"But those guns and cannons are supposed to protect Louisbourg harbor," said Yves.

With shaking hands, Papa wiped his face. "I know. The fog was so thick for the last few days that our sailors couldn't see the English ships moving north toward Lighthouse Point. When the fog lifted, the English had already landed."

Yves paced to the window and back. "So now they're on land north and south of us. Soon we'll be surrounded."

Papa nodded. "I always thought we were safe, but the enemy continues to move closer and closer to us. They have many more ships, soldiers, and sailors than we have. I'm no longer confident that we can win this war."

"But we'll keep the English out of the harbor; we have to," said Yves. "We still have soldiers guarding us with cannons and guns on two islands and on our ships.

* * *

Later, M. Gautreau came to our house, looking tired and discouraged. "I wanted to be sure you and your family are well. Claude, if you need anything, send a message to me."

"We have everything we need. How is your family?"

"Afraid of what might happen to us. Did you hear that the governor sent Madame Drucour and some ladies on a ship to deliver letters to the governor of Quebec? It was a foggy morning, so they should have been able to get away without being seen, but the fog lifted soon after they left the harbor. An English ship chased and captured them."

"What happened?"

"They were sent back here; Madame Drucour said they were treated well. Our governor was so happy that his wife was safe, he sent a letter to one of the English generals saying he would send his own surgeon if any injured English officers ever need him. The general replied by sending a letter to Madame Drucour praising her courage, and asking her to accept several pineapples."

"Pineapple!" I said. "Hélène told me about them; I'd love to taste one. Did Madame Drucour accept them?"

"Yes. Then the white flag of truce was raised, all shooting stopped on both sides, and a French messenger brought a basket of wine to the English general from Madame Drucour. As soon as the messenger returned, the fortress gate was closed, and the cannons began firing again."

I shook my head. "Maybe Madame Drucour and the English general should work together to find a way to end the war."

* * *

The rest of June passed in a blur. Our ships in the harbor kept up a constant attack on the English on Lighthouse Point, trying to keep them from setting up their guns and cannons. For more than a week, the English didn't return the fire; but then their signals were seen in a new area close to the fortress. That was the beginning of continuous shooting at our ships.

Some nights the emergency signal was sounded so often that we hardly slept at all. Whenever we heard it, the men dashed out to see what they could do to help. At times it was a real emergency; at other times it was a false alarm.

By the end of June, another island had been taken over by the English. Not long after, guns and cannons began firing from a hill a little over a half-mile from Dauphin Gate. "That's the end," said Papa. "The enemy is close enough to open fire on the town."

"What will we do?" asked Daniel.

Papa sighed. "We'll pray harder. There's nothing else we can do. We're too far from France to get help from them."

That same evening, M. Robichaud stood outside shouting, "An English cannon hit one of our ships in the harbor. Soon they'll all be captured or destroyed." The following morning, the neighbor's news was even worse. "During the night *our* soldiers sank five or six of *our own ships* at the entrance to the harbor."

"Why would they do that?" asked Papa.

"The governor and council decided that blocking the entrance was the only way to keep English ships from entering the harbor."

Papa wiped his face with his handkerchief. "Our soldiers turned some of the cannons on the ramparts to face the hills where the English are setting up their cannons. If our sunken ships keep the enemy out of the harbor, the only way they can attack us is by land. That puts us all in danger, not just our soldiers and sailors.

* * *

Since our family arrived in Louisbourg, we had always enjoyed spending time outside after supper in the spring and summer. We took long walks on the ramparts, looking at the blue water, smelling the salty air, and enjoying the warmer weather. Sometimes we visited with our neighbors while children played games in the street. But by the last week of June 1758, no one left the house except Papa and Yves, and they went out only for water and news. We closed the shutters tightly before dark and sat near the fireplace with a single candle burning. The enemy was too close; we didn't want to attract them with light or the slightest sound.

I shivered whenever I thought about the guns and cannons pointed at our fortress town.

Papa had often talked about how, less than three years before, the English had forced thousands of our people in other parts of Acadie to leave their homes. Was that going to happen to us, too? Would our family survive? Would our people survive?

27

War

At the beginning of July, the constant blast of guns and cannons on the ramparts and from our ships in the harbor was deafening. Since we couldn't get away from it, we kept the shutters and doors closed tightly even during the day to muffle the sound as much as possible. The noise went on for such a long time that we almost got used to it. However, by the end of the week the explosions seemed to be closer and louder than before. Papa put on his coat and went to the door. "I must find out what's happening."

Maman squeezed her apron into a knot. "Don't go, Claude. It's too dangerous."

"I'll be careful." He walked away into the foggy night.

We paced the floor, listening for Papa's returning footsteps. At last the door opened and we ran to hug him before he slowly lowered himself into his chair. "Most of the gunfire we've been hearing was ours, even though some of the officers think it's a waste of French ammunition. There's such a shortage that our soldiers are shooting any scrap of metal they can find and are even reusing enemy bullets."

"Do we have a chance of winning the war?" asked Yves.

"No, it seems that our officers are only trying to delay having to surrender. French soldiers acting as spies learned that the English are increasing and enlarging their fortifications, and are getting closer to us. They haven't been shooting as much because they're busy setting up another camp just a few hundred yards from the fortress walls. Last night, several English bombs hit the King's Hospital, killing a soldier and injuring two Brothers of Charity. If the English keep firing at the fortress, many houses will be destroyed and more people will be killed."

Five-year-old Marguerite stood next to Papa's chair. "Papa, why are the English soldiers angry at us?"

He hugged Marguerite. "They don't want us here. They're hoping that we'll all go somewhere else to live so they can have the fortress for their people."

My whole body shook. "How will we survive?"

Yves put his arms around me. "We'll do what our people have always done. We'll pray, and help those who are in need."

Before he could say another word, a whistling sound was followed by a tremendous explosion that shook our house. We all screamed and I covered my face with my apron. When I looked up, the air was cloudy with dust. Papa jumped up and ran to the wall near his bed. "The bombs are hitting too close; our walls are separating. I don't know how much more this poor little house can take."

The following week, our soldiers continuously fired their cannons and guns all night and throughout the next few days; this time the English returned the gunfire. Since they were so close to the fortress walls, a number of people on both sides were injured, and some were killed.

Late one day, a loud explosion in the direction of the harbor was followed by several more blasts. The noise continued as heavy smoke and flames rose high over the water. Early the next morning, Papa left to find out what had happened. When he returned, he said, "An English cannonball hit another French ship in the harbor. It caught fire; sparks quickly spread to two other vessels that burned all night. All three were destroyed. We have very few ships left to protect us."

"Why were there so many explosions?" asked Maman.

"That was the ammunition on the ships; it exploded when it got hot.

"One of our officers told me that we had more than four thousand soldiers and sailors when the war started. Now we only have about two thousand who are able to fight because many are sick or injured; others deserted or were killed. The few who can fight won't be able to protect us much longer.

"The governor's wife, Madame Drucour, seems to still have hope because she walks on the ramparts every day and has three cannons fired to inspire the men. However, I am afraid. Elisabeth, I want you, Pelagie, and Anne to take the younger children to the shelter in the King's Bastion. It was made to protect women and children; you'll be safer there."

With tears rolling down my cheeks, I kissed Yves, Papa, Gregoire, and Daniel good-bye, not knowing if I would ever see them again. Maman led the way to the shelter carrying eight-month-old Sébastien-François. Anne and Marie Josephe followed closely behind, holding hands. I took Marguerite's and Pierre's hands, not noticing where I was going, just keeping up with the others until we reached the King's Bastion.

For hours the thud of cannonballs hitting the fortress walls filled the air. I shuddered whenever a cannon was fired, especially when one of the gates in the fortress wall was hit. I thought nothing could be louder until we heard a deafening sound and the whole building seemed to shake. Children screamed and cried. A soldier who was nearby shouted, "That one hit the roof! There's no other damage. Ladies and children, stay where you are. You're safe in the shelter."

After we finally quieted the children, Maman said, "I smell something burning."

Someone shouted, "The roof is on fire! The King's Bastion is burning! Get out! Hurry!"

"Not the King's Bastion!" Maman and I grabbed the younger children and scrambled out of the building as fast as we could as cannonballs continued to hit houses around us. We ran until we found a covered place to stand and catch our breath, and then turned around to look at the largest building in Louisbourg. Flames raced from the roof and down the sides of the building as thick grey smoke covered the sky. It burned for hours. That night, a bomb also struck the Queen's Bastion. Like the King's Bastion, it was badly damaged, along with two nearby houses. Only a change in the direction of the wind saved many more buildings.

"I'm sorry I sent you to the shelter," said Papa when we reached our house. "You're safer at home, where Yves and I can take care of you." The cannon fire continued all night and the following day.

When I couldn't stand the noise any longer, I shouted, "Is the enemy trying to destroy the whole town and everyone in it?" Yves held me tightly in his arms, but he didn't have an answer for me.

Sometime after midnight on July 26, the emergency signal was sounded, followed by shouts of "*aux armes!*" (to arms). Papa and Yves hurried to the village square before the sun rose. When they returned, Yves's jaw was clenched and Papa was pale and trembling. "The last two French ships in the harbor were captured during the night. Because of the thick fog, our sailors couldn't see the English in their small boats; the enemy boarded our ships and took over before our sailors knew they were there. Now one of our ships flies the English flag; the other was destroyed by fire."

Papa paced to the door and back several times. "We have only four cannons that work, little ammunition, and no ships to protect us. English scaling ladders are in the trenches near a large hole in the fortress wall. In other places, parts of the walls have fallen into the water. Many houses have been destroyed; the rest are damaged. We are doomed."

Shivering, I clutched my shawl around my shoulders, "What will our soldiers do?"

Yves took my hand. "Pelagie, we can't fight any longer; our soldiers will have to surrender."

Papa nodded. "The English will take us as their prisoners. I don't know what they'll do with us—send us to France, or maybe to the American colonies as they did with our people in Acadie a few years ago. I pray to God that we'll be allowed to stay together."

Daniel chewed on his fingernails. "But, Papa, won't they let us stay here if we promise not to fight?"

Papa shook his head. "The English rulers don't want us here; they want all of the land for themselves. The commanders of the English army and navy will be praised and rewarded if they can get rid of us. And all we ever wanted was to farm, care for our families, enjoy life, worship God, and live in peace with everyone. I pray we'll be allowed to do that if we're sent to France."

Anne twirled several strands of her long, dark hair around her finger. "Will we have a good life in France?"

"The men and women will welcome us; they're our people," said Papa.

"Papa, do we have any relatives in France?" I asked.

"Only distant ones. Martin Benoist arrived here fifty years before I was born, and I'm thirty-seven. Four generations of Benoists were born here."

"We'll probably find some of my relatives in France," said Yves. "I hope they'll help us get settled."

The roar of a cannonball followed by a tremendous explosion interrupted Papa. The house shook. We all cringed and gasped because it was different from the continuous firing of the enemy guns that we had almost become used to. Papa made the sign of the cross. "That was too close. We must pray now. There's nothing else we can do."

28

Surrender

Around mid-morning that day, July 26, the drummers beat a different signal—one we had heard only once or twice before. This was followed by complete silence since all gunfire had ceased. It seemed eerie for the day to be so still; we had gotten used to the almost constant sounds of war. Papa opened one of the shutters and looked out. "It hasn't been this quiet in a long time. Yves, let's find out what's happening."

My pleading look didn't stop Yves from walking out the door. Gregoire followed them saying, "Please let me go with you, Papa."

"Come."

Maman moaned. "No, Claude, he's just a boy."

"He's old enough. Bolt the door behind us."

Maman and I spent the rest of the morning preparing dinner and worrying about our men. My hands trembled and I nearly dropped a stack of dishes I carried to the table. "Where can they be, Maman? The chapel bell rang the half hour five times since they left."

"Be patient, Pelagie. They'll be here soon." Maman moved the soup away from the fire as she tried to sound calm, but she frequently twisted her apron.

It seemed like forever before I heard Gregoire call, "Let me in, Pelagie."

I ran to open the door, then had to sit down before I fainted. Gregoire was alone. "Where are Yves and Papa? Are they safe?"

"They're walking around the fortress. Papa sent me back to tell you not to worry—they're not in danger. You won't believe what's happening! It's so exciting. This morning our soldiers raised a white flag near the Dauphin Demi-Bastion where there's a huge hole big enough for the enemy to get through the fortress wall. The drummers' signal that we heard earlier was a request for a ceasefire."

I interrupted. "What's a ceasefire?"

"It's an agreement to stop fighting. We watched a French officer leave the fortress to deliver a message to the enemy. The rumor is that Governor Drucour wants to surrender, but would like to discuss the terms: what will happen to the soldiers, and to us. Word got around quickly after the officer returned. The English commander replied that the Royal Navy will sail into the harbor tomorrow morning and attack with every gun and cannon they own, unless the governor surrenders without conditions."

Maman rubbed her hands together and twisted her apron. "What does that mean?"

"The governor can't make any requests. We'll all be prisoners of the English, and our lives will be totally under their control."

Maman and I gasped. The little ones looked at us with fear on their faces. I picked Pierre up and hugged him tightly at the same time that Maman put Sébastien-François on her lap. She asked, "What's the governor going to do?"

"No one knows. The enemy demanded his answer in one hour."

The chapel bells rang several more times before Yves and Papa finally returned. The whole family surrounded them, and I took Yves's coat. "Where have you been? We were so worried."

"Sit down. We have a lot to tell you." Maman and I sat on the edges of our chairs while the rest of the family gathered around. Yves looked at me and continued, "We walked around the fortress to find out everything we could. The members of the council are said to be in shock because they aren't receiving the respect and consideration that is due the French after this long battle. The enemy refuses to recognize the importance of our officers."

Maman tried to hide her trembling hands. "What does the governor want?"

Papa sat next to Maman and put an arm around her shoulders. "Governor Drucour sent another message asking the English to treat our soldiers and sailors with honor, and transport them to Brest, a port in France. He requested that the rest of us be brought to Rochefort, France, with our belongings. He asked for the usual method of transferring power after a war . . ."

Gregoire jumped up from his chair. "Can't you picture it? Our soldiers marching out of the fortress carrying their guns to the beat of drums, with our flags flying high while eight cannons fire twenty shots each. That's the way to finish a war!" He looked at Papa and hung his head. "I'm sorry I interrupted, Papa."

Papa smiled at him. "The governor also wants several small enclosed boats that won't be inspected by the English soldiers."

"Whatever for?" I asked.

"No one knows."

Yves exhaled loudly. "I heard two soldiers talking; they think the English leaders won't give our troops the honors of war because they're still angry about a battle last year. French soldiers, joined by a large number of Indians, attacked the English at Fort William Henry—far from here, in Canada."

"The battle wasn't in Acadie, was it?" asked Papa.

"No, it had nothing to do with our people. The French far outnumbered the English, who surrendered after a few days of fighting. The French gave them the respect that was due; the English turned their guns over to the French, and then marched out of the fort with their colors flying, with honor. But the Indians wanted more, and attacked the English as they marched away unarmed. Many soldiers were killed and several hundred were captured. The French commander soon regained order, but according to the men I overheard, the English want revenge."

I rubbed my aching neck and shoulders. "What do you think will happen?"

Yves stood up and paced around the room. "As soon as the messenger left with the governor's letter, the officers were ordered to find a suitable place for the next battle—the last one if the English commanders refuse to honor their requests. Our fortifications were so badly damaged by the English cannons that only two places are left which can provide protection for our soldiers. When the officers tried to inspect these two bastions, they were greeted by a mass of shouting people."

I watched every step Yves took in his nervous pacing. "What did they want?"

"The people are afraid of an attack. Our ships are gone, half of our soldiers are injured or sick, and we're running out of ammunition. We can't win—everyone in the fortress will probably be killed if we have another battle."

Papa ran his hand through his hair. "But our war council thinks that would be better than surrendering without terms, the way the enemy wants us to. Fighting until everyone is killed would be an honorable end to the war!"

I had been trembling, but I couldn't hold back my tears any longer. "Did the English officials reply to the governor's request for leaving the fortress with honor?"

"They replied. There will be no discussions and no honors. Governor Drucour has a half hour to agree to the English terms. But our governor and war council won't change their minds, so the English will attack, and we'll all suffer the consequences."

By that time, tears were streaming down everyone's faces. I couldn't stop shaking. "Are we just going to sit and wait to be killed?"

Yves put his arms around me. "Our troops are at their posts. They won't give up without a fight. We'll have to protect ourselves however we can."

Papa stood up. "We must get ready. Gregoire, check the shutters and doors—be sure they're securely bolted. Yves, help me push the table close to the wall. If we're in danger, Elisabeth and the children can crawl under the table and we'll surround them with mattresses. That's the best we can do."

When our meager preparations were made, Papa called us to sit near him. "We've done all we can. Our lives have been difficult since we left Pigiguit, but we can't give up now. We'll never give up. Continue to pray that things will be better someday—Le Bon Dieu will provide. Pelagie, you're not a little girl any longer. If something happens to Maman and me, you must be strong—you can't expect Yves to do everything. Can I depend on you to care for your brothers and sisters? Will you promise?"

I sobbed for a few minutes, then wiped my face and nodded. "Yes, Papa, I'll do whatever is necessary. I promise."

"Good. That makes this a little easier. And remember what I've often told you. If you survive this, someday your lives will be better. We've had lots of dark clouds; it's time to start looking for the silver lining.

"Now, we'll pray—and wait." We knelt in front of the crucifix on the wall over Maman and Papa's bed. Holding hands, we prayed as we never had before for deliverance from our enemy. "Dear God," said Papa, "we know you have a plan for us. Give us the grace to accept your will."

Later, shouts in the street disturbed our thoughts and prayers. I jumped up and grabbed Yves's hand. "Is that the enemy?"

Papa walked to the door but didn't open it. "I don't think so, but I want to be sure."

The shouts grew louder, followed by banging on the door. "Claude, it's Alexis Robichaud, your neighbor. The governor surrendered. The English won't attack tomorrow."

Papa opened the door. "Why did he change his mind?"

"No one seems to know, but the French flags were taken down, and white flags of surrender are flying."

"Thanks to Le Bon Dieu. We don't know what will happen to us, but at least we won't all be killed in a battle in which none of our people have a chance of coming out alive."

I'll never forget the date—July 26, 1758—the day the French surrendered the Fortress of Louisbourg to the English for the second time.

29

Prisoners of War

I should have been thankful that the thousands of us living in the fortress wouldn't be killed in one last tremendous battle so the French commanders' lives could end with honor, but I couldn't stop worrying about our future. I stood at the front window for a long time, feeling the pounding of my heart, and trying to keep my wobbly legs from giving out under me. People walked up and down our street; it seemed that every Acadian in Louisbourg was outside.

Yves put on his hat as he opened the door. "Let's go for a walk, Pelagie. You haven't left the house in weeks, except to go to the shelter in the King's Bastion."

I shuddered. "Don't remind me. Do you think it's safe to go out?"

"Yes. The fighting has stopped, and the English soldiers haven't entered the fortress yet. But don't ever go out without your papa or me."

The town was crowded with civilians, but no soldiers walked on the ramparts or patrolled the streets. I breathed deeply of the night air. "Oh, it feels so good to be outside."

Yves took my hand. "You'd better enjoy it now, because we don't know what will happen tomorrow."

The sound of footsteps behind us made me jump. It was our neighbors M. and Madame Robichaud, their daughter Marie, and a young man. Marie greeted us with a big smile. "Jacques and I are on our way to get married. The priests promised to keep the tiny chapel next to their house open all night for weddings, even without banns."

"Why tonight?"

"No one knows what kind of laws the English will pass tomorrow when they take over. We're afraid the enemy might not allow me to stay in Louisbourg if I'm not married, or they might force me to marry one of their soldiers."

I shook my head. "What a strange place we live in. Good luck."

It was late when we returned home, but Papa was waiting for us. "Good, you're back. Please sit down; we have several important matters to discuss. Pelagie, I already asked you to take care of your Maman and your brothers and sisters if we're separated by the English."

"Oh, Papa."

"I know. You don't want to talk about this, but I can't put it off any longer. No matter what happens, you must continue to tell our story to your brothers and sisters. The little ones are too young to remember everything that has happened to us, so they'll have to hear about our people again and again over the years. And another thing—please try to find the relatives that we left in Île Saint-Jean and Acadie."

"Of course I'll search for them. Yves and the little ones should meet your brothers, sisters, and their children. And I'm anxious to see them again."

Papa walked to the fireplace, lit his pipe, and sat down again. "If only we could have stayed in Acadie, they would all still be our neighbors. My parents lived in peace even though they were ruled by the English for much of their lives. But the days of freedom and tranquility didn't last; our people were deported soon after we left Pigiguit. My sisters Judith and Claire stayed there when the rest of our family left, and they were forced to leave almost three years ago. They're probably living in one of the American colonies."

Papa sighed. "Paul, Abraham, Charles, and your Grand'maman Elizabeth stayed in Île Saint-Jean when we came to Louisbourg. I hope the English leaders allow them to live there in peace."

Maman looked at Papa. "Don't forget your youngest brother, Augustin," she said. "He and Marguerite have three sweet children who at ages seven, five, and three are too young to remember what it's like to live without war. I'd like to live close to them so Marguerite, Pierre, and Sébastien-François could play with them."

Papa nodded and sighed again. "Pelagie, I have one more brother I want you to look for—Guillaume. We came to Louisbourg because of his many messages that this was a good place to live, and we've never found him. He lives somewhere north of us, outside the fortress walls, but I'm not sure where. I hope to see him again someday or hear from him and know he's well. He might be allowed to stay where he is; the English soldiers might want just the fortress, not the whole island."

I walked over to Papa and kissed him on the cheek. "We mustn't be separated, but if anything happens to you, I promise to look for all of them until I find them, or at least know where they are."

"Thank you. That makes me feel much better."

As we prepared dinner the next day, marching footsteps and the beat of drums disturbed the midday quiet. I peeped through a crack in the shutters. "It's our soldiers—the ones who announce the orders for the troops."

Maman twisted her apron as the color drained from her face. "Not another emergency! How much more bad news can we take?"

Yves set down the two buckets of water he'd brought in, and put his arm around her shoulders. "That's the signal for our soldiers to gather at the parade grounds. They're going to surrender their guns to the English officers, and each company will hand over its flag. English soldiers marched into town a few hours ago and are guarding the streets and the ramparts."

I stopped setting the table and looked at him. "Why?"

"To keep order—although I don't think they'll have any problems. The Acadians, and even some of our soldiers and sailors, seem to be relieved that the war is over without thousands of people getting killed."

I opened the shutters all the way and looked out the window. "Will we be allowed to watch the soldiers surrender their guns and flags? I enjoyed the walk last night, but I want to feel the sunshine on my face; we've been in the dark too long."

"It's not safe outside," said Maman.

Papa took his hat from a peg near the door. "The war is over. I don't think the English soldiers will bother us today. Look at the Acadians crowding the street already; everyone wants to watch the surrender ceremony. If there are any problems, we'll come home, but we can't continue cowering in the house."

Maman pulled the pot of stew away from the fire; it would stay warm so we could eat it later. The bright sunshine and the gentle breeze made me want to dance down the street, but I had to act like a lady. I hoped we would see Hélène and Oncle Augustin and his family, but several thousand people were at the parade grounds, probably everyone who lived inside the fortress, so it was too crowded to search for anyone.

At noon, Governor Drucour saluted English Brigadier General Whitmore. The French soldiers were ordered to hand over their firearms, but instead of putting their guns on the ground, many soldiers threw them down in anger. An officer of each company handed its flag to the English. The exception was one military group whose members were so upset at having to surrender without honors that they broke their guns into pieces; they had burned their flag the day before, rather than give it to the English soldiers.

As English soldiers filled wagons with the French guns and ammunition, a murmur rose through the crowd. We watched as General Whitmore walked beside Governor Drucour toward the restaurant where the wealthy people of Louisbourg often ate.

"What are they doing?" Papa asked a French soldier who had watched the ceremony with drooping shoulders after he turned in his gun.

"The English General Whitmore is going to dinner as Governor Drucour's guest. Can you believe it? And we weren't allowed the honors of war!"

We walked home quietly; none of the people around us had much to say. On the way to the parade grounds, I had been so happy to be outside in the fresh air that I didn't look around. On the way home, however, I no longer felt like dancing. "Yves, look at our town. The fortress walls are falling into the water. Every house in Louisbourg that wasn't destroyed must have been damaged. What are the poor people going to do? And the barracks are totally destroyed. Where will our soldiers live?"

"I don't know. They'll probably find shelter wherever they can."

Through the mist that settled above the water in the harbor, waves gently lapped at the skeletons of masts and sails. "Look at the harbor; there's trash floating everywhere," I said. "The French ships that were supposed to protect us were all wrecked or burned."

"Yes, many of them are completely underwater."

Two days later, Gregoire rushed in after a trip to the town well. "Several English warships are near the entrance of the harbor, decorated with many flags. Come on, Yves. Let's go watch them."

Yves grabbed his hat. "Come with us, Pelagie."

I stared at him. "How will the ships get into the harbor? It's full of trash and sunken ships."

"The English soldiers have been cleaning the harbor and fixing the buildings they destroyed. It's their town now and they need a place to live."

"Is it safe to go out?"

"Yes, they won't bother us," said Yves.

Walking through town, we saw English soldiers in their military uniforms at work on every block, but they paid no attention to us as we passed. We reached the harbor as the warships pulled close to the wharf. "Look at the dressed-up soldiers," I said.

"Those are officers in their dress uniforms. Something important must be planned."

A horse-drawn carriage stopped close to the wharf. Governor Drucour alighted and helped Madame Drucour out. They were quickly ushered aboard the first ship. "Where can they be going?" I asked.

A French soldier standing nearby exhaled loudly and shook his head. "They're going to eat with the English officers, acting like they're all friends again. And we're sleeping outside because they destroyed our barracks and took over every building that still has a roof."

* * *

Approximately three thousand French soldiers remained in Louisbourg at the time of the surrender. The sick officers were sent to France; the sick and wounded soldiers and sailors stayed in the hospital in Louisbourg, while the rest of the military, the prisoners of war, were transported to England. This took several weeks; then ships had to be found to deport three to four thousand civilians.

The first ship left for England on August 9 carrying French commanders, soldiers, and sailors. Armed English soldiers stood guard. As Governor and Madame Drucour boarded a warship, she waved her long white scarf. I shuddered. "Yves, why do the guards have guns? Our men don't have any way to protect themselves."

"The English don't want to take any chances."

Several days later Yves rushed into the house. "Many Acadians living in nearby villages are being brought into the fortress by the English. They'll be deported, too."

Papa immediately went to the door. "I'm going to try to find Guillaume. Come help me, Gregoire."

They returned several hours later. As soon as I saw Papa, I knew they hadn't found Oncle Guillaume. "We looked everywhere and asked everyone; no one knows where he is, but I won't stop trying to find him."

For the first time that I could remember, we didn't have chores to keep us busy from dawn to dusk. After meals were prepared, dishes were washed, and the floor was swept, we had nothing else to do. "I'm not going to make furniture to leave here for the English to use," said Papa. "We have enough food to last a few months—enough to take with us if we're sent away, thanks to Yves and Gregoire's dried fish and Maman's vegetables."

Maman and I didn't plant a garden or make candles, soap, cheese, or wine. We each had two sets of work clothes and one set of church clothes, and quilts, sheets, and towels that we could carry aboard the ships. There was nothing for us to do except wait and worry. Papa spent his days smoking his pipe and pacing the floor. Maman often sat staring into space, wringing her hands or twisting her apron while her lips moved in silent prayer.

I heard my parents' whispered conversation one night as they shared their worries, thinking that we were asleep. Papa's deep voice murmured, "I can hardly bear the thought of leaving, knowing that we'll never return. Except for our troubles with the English, Acadie was a wonderful place to live and raise our children. If only our whole married life could have been as it was in Pigiguit when Pelagie and Gregoire were small. We could have raised our children and watched our grandchildren grow up there. I'm afraid our lives will never be as good as they were then."

"We can never give up hope," answered Maman's soft voice. "I know God will take care of us, but I'm so afraid of a long sea voyage. Our people who were sent to the American colonies were miserable, and even though theirs was a shorter trip than crossing the ocean, many got sick and died."

"My fear is that we won't be allowed to stay together," said Papa. "I can't bear to think about never seeing my children again."

Every day Yves and I walked to town to see what was happening. We wanted to be prepared for whatever was to come. About two weeks after the surrender of Louisbourg, we returned home with news that I hated to share with my parents. "The English commander has sent five ships and five hundred military to deport the Acadians in Île Saint-Jean."

Papa collapsed into his chair. "I hoped they would be left alone and allowed to live there in peace. Why do the English want that tiny island?"

Yves paced around the kitchen. "They're determined to get rid of all of the Acadians. They don't want any of us here; they'll probably send all of us to France."

Maman sighed. "That means Paul, Abraham, Charles, and their families will have to leave their homes."

"And my maman," said Papa. "She and her husband, François, thought they would be safe if they stayed in Île Saint-Jean with my brothers. I hope she is strong enough for the voyage."

A sudden thought made me smile. "Papa, maybe we'll see them again if we're all sent to France."

"Maybe."

When the first two ships arrived to transport civilians from Louisbourg, sailors loaded the vessels with boxes and barrels of food and water. A few days later, I couldn't stop tears from pouring down my cheeks as about six hundred of our people were forced on board, not sure about where they were going. The English soldiers seemed to try to keep families together, but sometimes wives were separated from their husbands, or children from their parents. I had to cover my ears to keep out the sounds of their misery.

The next day I put on my shawl and walked to the door. "I'm going to visit Hélène. I haven't seen her in almost three months, way before the fighting started. Think about it—I might never see her again."

Yves immediately put down the pair of wooden shoes he was making and followed me. "Wait, Pelagie, you can't go out alone; the English soldiers haven't bothered us, but we can't trust them. I'll go with you."

As soon as Hélène saw us at her door, she stopped packing clothes and food into boxes. We hugged as tears ran down our cheeks. "Oh, Pelagie," she said, "I've missed you so much; I don't want to leave you."

"Wherever they send us, we'll find each other; we have to."

"Joseph is in town trying to get information about where we'll be sent."

Yves went to the door. "I'll look for him and come back for you in a few hours, Pelagie."

Hélène and I couldn't stop talking about all the fun we had together before the war started. I promised to visit her again in a few days.

However, the next ship that sailed from Louisbourg took my best friend and her family away from me. I had lost some of my cousins when we left Pigiguit, Grand'maman and more cousins including my special friend, Françoise, when we left Île Saint-Jean, and now Hélène. Would my life ever settle down so that I could hold on to those who were dear to me? I might have lost all hope if I had known how many more loved ones I would never see again.

30

A Letter

During the next weeks we said tearful goodbyes to our friends and neighbors. One morning I was sitting at the window when a sailor stopped in front of the house and tipped his hat. "Good morning, Madame. I am Edmund, a friend of Joseph Savoie."

"Hélène's husband," I said.

"Yes. Before the war between England and France, I sailed on a trading ship that often came to Louisbourg. We brought wood and other building materials from the American colonies and exchanged them for rum and molasses from the West Indies. Joseph was a new merchant in Louisbourg and we became friends."

"Do you have news? Do you know where Hélène and Joseph are?"

"Yes, Madame. When the war ended I was hired to help transport Acadians from Louisbourg and Île Saint-Jean to France. They sailed on my ship to St. Malo, France. Madame Hélène asked me to bring this to you." He handed a letter to me and tipped his hat again. "I must get back to the ship. Get ready—you don't know when it will be time for you to leave."

As he hurried off, I ran to find Yves. "Please come with me to the chapel. I'll ask one of the priests to read Hélène's letter to me." I was lucky. Yves wasn't busy and Père LaGrée, the priest who performed our wedding ceremony, invited us in and read aloud:

Dear Pelagie,

I am writing to you in sorrow because of the many sufferings that my family and friends have had to endure. You probably know by now that my family was forced to leave Louisbourg a few days after you visited me. It was a foggy morning, and I brought a basket of food to the convent for the three nuns from the Congregation of the Sisters of Notre Dame, where I attended school. While I was in the parlor talking to two of the nuns, we heard a loud knock and a shout. "Open the door or we'll break it into pieces."

We all stood and dear Sister Saint-Arsène went to the door. Six English soldiers dressed in bright red coats, white pants, and three-cornered hats held rifles. My legs shook and my hands trembled so much that I had to sit down. "What do you want?" asked Sister.

"Get your extra linens and march quickly to the ship," growled the tallest soldier.

"Please, sir, please let us wait a few more days. We'll gladly leave on the next ship. Sister Saint-Thècle is too sick to sail. She has been very ill with high fever for four days."

"Get her and leave now. We don't have time for your whining."

The two other sisters supported poor sick Sister Saint-Thècle and walked slowly out of the house, as the soldiers prodded them with their bayonets. "Hurry up, old women. We don't have time to waste on you."

I tried to hide behind the drapes, so the enemy wouldn't see me. But as soon as the nuns left, a soldier turned to me and motioned toward the door. "You're next. Get your family and go to the ship." I ran to Papa's house, thinking I would be safe there with Joseph, Papa, Maman, my sister, and my brothers. But the soldiers soon banged on Papa's door. We had to gather our things quickly and accompany them.

It's hard to describe how terrible the voyage was. As soon as we boarded, we were ordered to go below deck. It was dark, cramped, smelly, and damp. There were a few wooden benches nailed to the walls where the older people sat, very uncomfortably, I'm sure, although they didn't complain. We were so crowded that only about half of the people were able to lie down at a time, and that was on the cold, damp floor. Some people slept sitting up all night.

We soon finished the food we brought with us, so for the rest of the voyage, we ate the rations that the guards gave us—hard, dry bread twice a day and salt pork in the evening. The water was soon green and slimy, and the bread was full of insects. Many of us refused to eat during the day, because we didn't want to take the chance that one of the guards would open the trapdoor and there would be enough light for us to see what we were eating and drinking.

The voyage was extremely rough. We went through a violent storm about a week after we left Louisbourg. The waves were so high that one side of the ship was always above the other. Since we had nothing to hold on to, everyone would slide to one side, piling on top of one another, and then we would slide to the other side. Sometimes the front of the boat was at the top of a wave, and other times the back was.

Freezing water poured through the trapdoor and dripped through the cracks in the deck, which was our ceiling. Our teeth chattered from the cold, and we couldn't change our clothes, because everything we owned was soaked.

In the darkness, the cries of frightened people shattered the quiet. We tried to be brave, but sometimes we couldn't stop our screams. Babies wailed and children clung to their parents. Many people were sick; others stopped eating during the worst part of the voyage because we were afraid we wouldn't keep food on our stomachs.

My dear friend, Sister Saint-Thècle suffered terribly for ten long days. One of the sisters made a drink for her from some leaves which the Mi'kmaqs use for fever. We put cool cloths on her head and tried to make her comfortable, but she soon alternated between high fever and such terrible chills that we had to pile all of our quilts on her. To our sorrow, nothing did any good.

One day, she prayed for everyone on the ship, and everyone who was still in Louisbourg. She cried, "Dear God, be merciful to us." Then she died. We wrapped her in a clean sheet and the men carried her onto the deck. The Acadians who were well enough to walk followed, crying. Sister Saint-Arsène led us in prayer. We sang a hymn or two, and the men slowly lowered Sister Saint-Thècle's body into the sea.

This has been such a terrible ordeal. It seemed that the voyage would never end; we were on the water for over a month. My only blessing has been that Joseph, Maman, Papa, my little sister, and my brothers are still with me. Over a third of the people on the ship died, and many more were so sick when we docked in France that I fear for their lives.

I hope and pray that you won't have to go through this suffering. I try to remember that this is God's will and there is a reason for everything that happens. I pray every day for courage to accept the life that has been given to me. Please remember me in your prayers, as I will continue to pray for you.

Your devoted friend,

Hélène

I cried while Père LaGrée read the letter and even harder after we left the chapel. I could hardly see where I was going, and I don't know what would have happened to me if Yves hadn't been holding me close. How could anyone endure so much misery? I prayed for strength for all of us to face whatever the future would bring.

31

Leaving Again

"I can't bear to leave my home again," I said after telling my family about Hélène's letter. "When I was only nine years old, we had to leave my beloved Pigiguit. Although we were hungry and cold in Île Saint-Jean, I loved living near Grand'maman and my other relatives. I even saw my cousin Françoise almost every day until we moved here. Now the little cottage where Yves and I lived after we married has been destroyed and we're going to be sent away from Louisbourg. Will I ever live somewhere and not have to worry about being sent away or leaving everyone who is dear to me?"

Papa sighed, and I noticed how old, tired, and sad he looked. "Maman and I had good lives in Pigiguit," he said, "but my children have known nothing but sadness. If I could have prevented any of this, I would have."

I couldn't hold back my tears as I ran to hug him. "I'm sorry, Papa. None of this was your fault. You did what you had to do. We had good lives and lots of happiness because of you and Maman. I know I shouldn't complain. I'm just making everything worse, instead of trying to help you."

I wiped my eyes. "If we had stayed in Pigiguit, we would have been deported to the American colonies. If we still lived in Île Saint-Jean, we would be deported, probably to France. And I wouldn't have met my dear Yves. I promise, I'll stop complaining and crying, and look forward to a better life."

Papa gave me a weak smile. "Pelagie, please promise me one more time that you'll help Maman if anything happens to me, and you'll take care of your brothers and sisters if Maman and I can't. I'm not concerned about myself, but I worry about the little ones who can't survive on their own."

"Of course, Papa. I'll do whatever I have to, but nothing worse can possibly happen."

Much too soon, English soldiers banged on the door, and then pushed it open. "Come with us *now*. Your ship will sail tomorrow morning at dawn. We can't wait to get rid of you and let the people in France deal with you."

We grabbed our bundles—bread, dried fish, and dried meat wrapped inside a change or two of clothing. Maman walked out of the house clutching one-year-old Sébastien-François. Ten-year-old Marie Josephe's arms were filled with small wooden animals that Papa had carved for the children. Papa and Yves held as many quilts and towels as they could carry. Gregoire, Anne, Daniel, and Marguerite followed, carrying extra food and quilts. I took four-year-old Pierre's hand, stood in the doorway for a moment, and looked around saying a silent good-bye—once again. A soldier nudged me roughly with his gun. "Move," he shouted. "We don't have time for your tears."

I hurried to catch up with my family. We tried to stay together, but there were eleven of us, and the streets were crowded with Acadians who didn't want to leave their homes, but had no choice. Some protested; others quietly complied. When we reached the harbor, several hundred people were being forced onto the sailing ships; soldiers were everywhere, hurrying us along, shouting and threatening. I had thought nothing worse could possibly happen to us. I wanted to cry, to scream, but I knew if I started, I would never stop. What would the soldiers do to me then?

Walking ahead of me in the crowd, Marie Josephe stumbled, dropping her carved animals. She screamed as a soldier pushed her and stomped on her treasured possessions. Papa whispered, "I'll make more for you." No one could do anything else.

Only small bundles of clothing, food, and quilts were allowed on board. Everything else was ripped from people's arms as many sobbed about losing special treasures. Broken furniture, dishes, and other household goods littered the ground.

It was impossible to keep track of everyone in my family, but I held tightly to Yves and Pierre. After we were shoved onto one of the waiting ships, I looked around to be sure the rest of my family was with us. I soon found Gregoire, Daniel, Anne, and Marguerite clinging to one another. Fourteen-year-old Gregoire had a scowl on his face, ready to fight with anyone who tried to separate them. When Anne saw us in the crowd, she ran over and hugged me as if she would never let me go. Marguerite sobbed as Daniel tried to comfort her, even though tears ran down his own cheeks.

"Where are Maman and Papa?" asked Pierre.

"And Marie Josephe and Sébastien-François?" asked Marguerite.

"They were right ahead of us," said Yves, "but the soldiers pushed people between us and I lost sight of them. They might be on this ship, but it will be hard to find them; there must be several hundred Acadians sailing with us."

"If they're on this ship, we'll find them," I said, trying to be brave for my brothers and sisters. "If they're on another ship, we'll find them when we get to France."

A frowning soldier shoved Yves. "Stop talking and move. We have to cram more people onto this ship, so go down into the hold."

I shuddered as I looked into the dark opening of the damp, smelly hold. Was that where we were going to live for several weeks? I wanted to curl up and hide. I wanted to cry until I had no tears left. How could I live through this and also care for my five brothers and sisters?

I'm too young, only seventeen. I don't even know if I can take care of myself. I can't do this. But I promised Papa I would.

I took a deep breath, closed my eyes, and prayed. "Dear God, give me strength. Help me get through this ordeal. Let us find Maman and Papa, and have a better life in France."

I looked at the damaged fortress and thought: *God sent Yves to me. With his help, I'll do whatever it takes to care for my brothers and sisters and give them the kind of life we had in Pigiguit. The people in France are our people. Unlike the English, who want to get rid of us, the French will welcome us. Maybe we'll find Maman and Papa, or Yves's family, or some of my distant relatives who live in France. Whatever happens, we'll be with family and life will be better. It has to be.*

"Move!" shouted the soldier. I looked at the sky and thought of the silver lining behind every dark cloud that Papa had often talked about. "I'll work hard, pray, and do whatever I can to provide a better life for my brothers and sisters until we find you and Maman again," I whispered. "I'll find that silver lining, Papa."

* * *

I shuddered as I went down the ladder into the hold below the deck of the ship. I knew from Hélène's letter that it would be bad, but this was worse than I expected. The hold was dark, cold, and damp. It looked big at first, but as many more Acadians were squeezed in, there was hardly room to move. The ceiling was so low that only young children could stand upright. Since there were no benches, we sat on our quilts on the floor. That was bad, but it got worse.

Six-year-old Marguerite clung to my hand. "I can't see anything down here, and there aren't any windows."

I pulled her close. "If you look up at the top of the ladder, you can see a little light." The words were hardly out of my mouth when the trapdoor slammed shut. There were sounds of dismay from many Acadians as we sat in what seemed to be total darkness.

Daniel whispered, "Look at the ceiling. You can see little bits of brightness."

"The ship's hold was already small, but then it was divided into three levels for transporting us away from Acadie," said Yves. "We're lucky to be at the top because light can get through the cracks in the deck, which is our ceiling. I pity the poor people below us. They're in complete darkness."

* * *

The next morning the ship rocked gently at first as it moved away from shore, but soon the motion increased as we left the safety of the harbor and sailed into the Atlantic Ocean.

I missed Maman and Papa. Talking to them about problems had always made me feel better; I could hardly hold back my tears thinking about them now, knowing that I might never see them again. Only seventeen years old, I was responsible for my three brothers and two sisters. I wanted nothing more than to sit in the darkness and scream until my throat was raw, but I knew I had to be brave for all of them.

Even though there were several hundred Acadians on our ship, we saw only the ones squeezed into our section of the hold. The soldiers allowed only a small group to take a short walk on deck at one time. Yves said they were afraid we might try to take control of the ship. But we were soon so weak in body and spirit from the lack of good food, exercise, fresh air, and sunshine, that the whole shipload of Acadians would not have been able to defeat a few soldiers and sailors if we had wanted to.

Sometimes I cried quietly, but I soon realized that Yves had enough to do caring for my brothers and sisters without worrying about me. With a lump in my throat and my heart pounding, I tried to keep the children busy by talking to them, telling stories, and making up games we could play in the darkness of the hold. This helped until we were hit by a terrible storm, probably as bad as the one Hélène told me about in her letter.

Icy water poured through the trapdoor and dripped through the cracks in the deck. We couldn't get warm, and we couldn't put on dry clothes because everything we owned was soaked.

We were so crowded that some of us had to sit up all night. Even when it was my turn to lie down, the roar of the angry ocean kept me awake. Pierre spent days sitting on my lap and nights curled up next to me. The warmth of his little body was comforting and I prayed that I would soon return him safely to Maman and Papa.

* * *

We ate very little during the storm, afraid that we would be sick as many others were, but it wasn't long before we finished the food we brought with us. For the rest of the voyage we had to eat the hard bread and dried pork the soldiers gave us.

One day Gregoire said, "I would do anything for a bowl of Maman's vegetable soup." Then he chuckled. "I'd even eat the soup Pelagie makes."

The other children giggled and each added to Gregoire's wish:

"A piece of fresh, hot bread."

"I wish I could walk on dry land."

"And sleep in a bed."

"I want all of that," said Pierre.

We all laughed and I hugged Pierre. "Wait until we get to France."

"What will it be like?" asked Daniel.

Yves had been quiet for a long time. "We don't know where we'll land in France, but if we work hard, we should have enough to eat and a place to live. Remember, I lived there for seventeen years."

"Do you still have family there?" asked Anne.

"I don't know. I haven't heard from any of my relatives for several years. If we live near Megrit, I'll look for them."

Besides too little food and not enough room for everyone to lie down at night, we had no sanitation and no way to keep clean. Even though the water the soldiers gave us tasted terrible, we couldn't waste it washing faces, hands, or clothes. Since from a very early age Acadians are taught to keep themselves, their houses, and yards neat and clean, this was extremely difficult for all of us.

When the door to the hold was occasionally propped open, I was shocked at how pale and thin everyone was. Many people were sick. An old man who had lived near us in Louisbourg died one night. In the morning his wife hugged him for the last time and wrapped him in a sheet. We prayed together and sang a hymn. Two men carried the body onto the deck. When someone died, the soldiers allowed more people on deck than usual, so everyone well enough to walk followed. We were permitted to pray together and sing a few hymns before the men lowered the body into the sea.

A sailor who was standing near me said to another sailor, "That's the trouble with these people. As soon as they're all together on a ship, they get sick."

After we were forced back into the hold, we were quieter than usual. Probably everyone was praying for the sick and the dead, and wondering what was going to become of the rest of us.

32

Sickness

As days passed, many more people got sick, especially the very young and the elderly. Some had smallpox; others had typhus or other fevers. The voyage was even worse than Hélène wrote in her letter because it seemed that it would never end. I prayed night and day for strength to get through it, although sometimes I thought it would be easier to die.

But then I always said a prayer thanking God I was alive. I was having a terrible time coping with our losses and misery, but I had Yves to lean on. What would my brothers and sisters do if something happened to me? Yves couldn't care for them alone. Gregoire was fourteen, Anne twelve, Daniel ten, Marguerite six, and little Pierre only four years old. How could they survive without me? I needed to be strong for the children until we found Maman and Papa again.

Early one morning Pierre woke me, crying. "I don't feel good," he said. "My head hurts; I hurt all over."

Cradling him on my lap, I kissed his forehead. "Yves," I whispered, "Pierre is burning with fever."

"Oh, no, not one of ours."

Yves knocked on the door of the hold. "Please give us a bucket of water so we can bathe a sick little boy."

"We don't have water to waste," said the soldier who opened the door.

"Then give me a bucket of salt water. There's plenty of that in the ocean—it won't run out."

The soldier stared at Yves a minute and moved away. "Get your own water," he snarled.

We bathed Pierre's skin with the cool water until he fell asleep. His fever didn't drop even though we used every bit of water the soldiers allowed us to have. The next day when it was time for us to take our walk on deck, Yves carried Pierre, thinking the fresh air might make him feel better. I gasped when I saw him in the light. "Look at the flat rash on his face and arms. What can it be?" I raised his shirt; his stomach and back were covered as well. Yves and I looked at each other and he slowly nodded his head. I had never seen my husband with such a sad look on his face, not when we knew our little cottage had been destroyed, not even when we were forced to leave Acadie. That's when I knew—Pierre had smallpox!

A few days later, the bumps were raised and filled with fluid. I held Pierre day and night; I was afraid to let him go. He was uncomfortable and seemed to feel better in my arms. His body grew hotter and hotter, no matter how often Yves and I sponged him with cool water. One night after Pierre and the other children fell asleep, I asked Yves, "Why do so many people on the ship have smallpox? I never even *heard* the word smallpox until some soldiers and sailors in Louisbourg got sick after their long voyage from France. And, Yves, a lot of them *died.*"

"Several hundred of our soldiers were sick right before the English attacked the fortress and some could have had smallpox. With so many soldiers and sailors, French and English, coming to Louisbourg, someone may have brought it from Europe, where there are lots of different kinds of epidemics. Someone on our ship might have been sick before we left Louisbourg, then got sicker after we sailed and gave it to others."

"Papa always told us that we were healthy because we worked hard and had plenty of fresh air, good food, and lots of fruit and vegetables," I said.

"And we don't have any of that now," said Yves.

"What can we do to make Pierre better?"

"Try to keep him comfortable and pray. That's all we can do."

I prayed harder than ever before. When Marguerite and Anne woke during the night with fever the week after Pierre got sick, I thought I would lose my mind, but I continued to pray. My brother and sisters couldn't die. I was exhausted from caring for the three children, even though Yves, Gregoire, and Daniel worked as hard as I did. Other people in the hold wanted to help, but they had their own family members to care for, or they were sick themselves.

A few mornings after the girls got sick, I woke to Marguerite's cries. She and Anne were still very hot, but when I felt Pierre's forehead, it was cool.

"The fever broke. Thank God, he's well," I said. But then I felt his body, arms, and legs and knew something was wrong. "*Nooo!*" I cried. Yves touched Pierre and took me in his arms.

"I'm sorry, Pelagie. He's gone."

I cried harder than I ever cried before. I wanted to die, too. After a little while, Yves said, "We still have to take care of Marguerite and Anne. We have to be strong for them, and for Gregoire and Daniel. We can't give up."

I hugged my little brother and wrapped his body in a quilt Maman and I had made in Louisbourg. I held him tightly until everyone in our hold was awake. Two other people had died during the night. We held hands and prayed for our dear ones and sang a few hymns. When our guard opened the trapdoor to the deck to bring water, Yves told him we had three more deaths.

The families and close friends of the dead made our sorrowful way to the deck. That was the first morning that I wasn't thankful to be outside. After another group prayer and song, I kissed Pierre for the last time. I didn't want to let him go and I screamed when Yves gently lowered my little brother's body over the railing into the rolling ocean. Yves had to guide me back into the hold because I could hardly stand, and I couldn't see through my tears.

I sat in the darkness of the hold—just sat. I couldn't think, I couldn't sleep, I couldn't eat, I couldn't even pray. I had no more tears. I just stared at nothing. When I did speak, I wailed, "What will I tell

Maman and Papa when we see them again? I promised to take care of the younger children."

Yves put his arms around me. "I'll tell them how hard you tried to make Pierre comfortable and how good you were to him. Many people on their ship are probably sick, too. They'll understand."

"Then Maman and Papa could die, and so could Sébastien-François and Marie Josephe. I couldn't bear that."

"As your papa often told us, we'll pray for strength to face whatever we must."

Yves cared for Anne and Marguerite, sponging their burning faces, arms, and hands. After a few days I had to put aside my sadness for their sakes; if they died, too, then I would surely go mad. My days were a blur of sponging Anne and Marguerite, urging them to drink a little water, holding their hands, singing to them, and hoping they wouldn't break out in a rash. Their fever remained high. At times they shivered violently and we piled every quilt we had on them. I left the hold for a few minutes every day because Yves insisted, but I went back after a quick walk around the deck.

"If we had some of Maman's soup for them, they'd soon be well," I said one day.

I nibbled at the food the soldiers gave us, but only enough to keep up my strength. I gave the rest to Gregoire, Daniel, and Yves, hoping and praying they wouldn't get sick. After a week of little sleep and many prayers, I touched Anne and Marguerite's faces one morning. I couldn't breathe. Their skin was cool. Had they died, too? I almost collapsed onto the floor of the hold, but Yves was at my side.

"What's wrong, Pelagie?" he whispered.

"Anne and Marguerite. Their fever is gone. Have we lost them, too?"

"No," he said. "Thank God, their fever has broken. It wasn't smallpox. They're getting better."

Once again I cried, but this time with tears of joy. The girls grew stronger every day and began to eat the terrible bread again. By the end of another week they were sitting up. "When can I go on deck?" asked Marguerite one morning.

"It's a warm day and the sun is shining. It'll be good for her," said Yves. The girls were weak, but with our help, they got up the ladder to the deck. Feeling the sun's warm rays, I lifted my eyes to the beautiful blue sky, thanked God for the girls' recovery, and prayed for the health of the rest of my family.

There were no more new cases of smallpox or typhus in our hold. Almost half of our group had been sick, and about a third of the sick had died. I continued to mourn for Pierre, but I thanked God every day that the rest of the family had been spared. I prayed that we had endured the worst that life had in store for us. It's a good thing I didn't know about the other tragedies that awaited us.

33

France

After five miserable weeks we woke one morning to a strange sensation. The ship was swaying gently from side to side, but it wasn't moving forward. "What's wrong?" I asked.

"We're probably . . ." began Yves, but he was interrupted by the shout of a soldier who banged the trapdoor open.

"Get your things together. It's time for you to get off the ship. We've put up with you people long enough."

I gathered our belongings and took Marguerite's hand. "Take your clothes, quilts, and pillows, and *stay together.* I don't want to lose anyone else." As I followed Yves, Gregoire, Anne, and Daniel, my thoughts went back to the day when we boarded the ship in Louisbourg. I was holding Pierre's hand and I thought Maman, Papa, Sébastien-François, and Marie Josephe were right ahead of us. Tears filled my eyes and my throat ached, but I blinked back my tears. I refused to cry; I had to be strong.

"Yves," I said, "I don't know if I want to get off this ship."

He gasped. "Why not?"

"For the first time in my life, I don't have a house to live in. I don't know where my parents are, and my little brother is dead. I'm exhausted and we're supposed to start over again with the four children. I don't think I can."

Yves put his arms around me. "Oh, Pelagie, we have to be strong for your brothers and sisters, and each other. God still loves us and watches over us. Somehow we'll get through this. Together we'll replace

163

the bad memories with good ones." He took my hand as we slowly followed my brothers and sisters off the ship.

It felt strange to walk on land because I was used to the movement of the ship as it was tossed around by the waves. Yves turned to me. "I wonder where we are. We were on the ship long enough to be in France, but I know this isn't St. Malo. I hoped if we were brought to France, it would be St. Malo because my parents live not far from there, in Megrit. If they're still alive, we must find them someday."

A man standing on the dock watching the people get off the ship said, "You're in Rochefort, France."

"Rochefort!" said Yves. "That's a long way from St. Malo. Are there any Acadians here?"

"Yes, a few families. We were told that most of the Acadians from Louisbourg and Île Saint-Jean were brought to St. Malo."

"That's where we hoped to go," said Yves.

"I am Henri Comeau from Île Saint-Jean. We arrived two weeks ago; all of us live in the same area. Come, I'll show you."

I had trouble getting the words out. "Have you seen my parents, Claude Benoist and Elisabeth Thériault? Are they here?"

"Non, I'm sorry. I knew your parents when your family lived in Île Saint-Jean, but they aren't here. I know all of the Acadians who live here; there are so few of us. Several families who were on my ship sailed for St. Malo already, but I haven't seen or heard anything about your parents since you left Île Saint-Jean."

"What about my papa's brothers? They lived in Île Saint-Jean."

"Non, I don't know where they were sent."

Marguerite looked around. "Where are Maman and Papa? I thought they would be here, waiting for us to get off the ship."

"And Marie Josephe and Sébastien-François," said Daniel.

I pulled Marguerite and Daniel close and hugged them. "We'll look for them. We'll ask everyone we meet if they know anyone in our family."

Yves looked around and then turned to M. Comeau. "Will I be able to make a living here fishing or farming?"

"Non, I'm afraid this isn't a good place to live. The French government gave each family a small piece of land to farm, but I don't think we'll be able to grow anything. The soil is poor and rocky. I catch some fish, but without a boat, I can't catch enough to sell. You'll have a difficult time feeding all those children. Come on, I'll show you where we live," he added. "We must all stay together to help one another."

With other families from the ship, we followed our new friend down narrow streets until he stopped in front of a group of tiny, shabby sheds. "This is all there is," he said.

"At least we'll have a roof over our heads," said Yves.

"You'll be lucky if it doesn't have holes in it," said M. Comeau.

Our little shed contained a rough table, two benches, and a small fireplace. Anne, Marguerite, and I gathered twigs that we used to sweep the floor and remove spider webs from the walls. After we folded the quilts and sheets we had brought with us, Marguerite looked around. "Pelagie, where will we sleep?"

"On the floor until Yves and Gregoire have time to make beds for us. But right now, they have more important things to do."

Along with other Acadians, Yves, Gregoire, and Daniel spent all of their time looking for work on fishing boats. They managed to catch a few fish nearly every day, so we didn't starve. Sometimes they caught enough for us to trade for a cooking pot or a little flour. Anne, Marguerite, and I planted seeds the neighbors gave us, but we had little luck growing anything. M. Comeau was right—the ground *was* hard and full of rocks.

The French government gave each Acadian a few sols a day, but it was never enough to pay rent for our shabby shed, and buy a few vegetables and flour for bread. Almost every day I walked to the ocean, watching to see if any ships had arrived from Acadie, but I was always disappointed. I spent the rest of my time trying to find a way to feed my little family, begging for food if I had to.

I didn't mind the shabbiness or the lack of space in our little shed. Since I was separated from part of my family, I wanted the rest of us to be close together. One day blended into the next as I mourned for my little brother Pierre, wishing he could have had a proper burial. I thought constantly about Maman, Papa, Sébastien-François, and Marie Josephe. I longed to see them and was torn apart inside, wondering what had happened to them. Where were they? Would we ever find them? But I saved my tears for the middle of the night when everyone else was asleep.

One afternoon Yves raced into the shed with a big grin on his face. As I tried to remember when I had last seen him so happy, he said, "No one can give me any information about your family. I've talked to everyone around here, and I ask every sailor on every boat that docks in Rochefort."

I sighed. "You look so happy that I thought you had good news."

"I do, Pelagie. Several people told me that the place to go is St. Malo where most of the ships from Louisbourg disembark. Hundreds of Acadians live there. If we can't find your parents, at least someone might know where we can look for them. And we'll be closer to Megrit; maybe we'll find my family. We have to go."

"But, Yves, how will we get there? We have the four children."

"Pelagie Benoist! Of all people to ask how we'll get there! Aren't you the same Pelagie Benoist who walked with her family from Pigiguit to Tatamagouche, Acadie? Didn't you have to climb mountains and cross water? And weren't you just nine years old?"

"Yes, but . . ."

"If you could do it then, we can do it now."

"But, Yves, we're just getting settled."

"What kind of life do we have here? The soil is no good. We can't farm; you can't even grow vegetables. Gregoire, Daniel, and I catch only enough fish to keep us from starving. There aren't any jobs on boats. I don't even have time to make a loom or beds so we can be more comfortable. Why would we want to stay here?"

"Will we have to walk?"

"No, a ship just arrived with sick and wounded soldiers from Louisbourg. They'll be cared for here, but the ship will leave for St. Malo in two days; a few other Acadian families are planning to go. The sailors are tired after their long voyage, so they'll allow us to sail with them if we work aboard ship. Gregoire and I will help with the sails and

166

anchors, and anything else there is to do, and Daniel will run errands. This may be our chance to find your family and mine."

Yves smiled, hugged me, and left to tell our new neighbors we were going to St. Malo. I knew this was the right thing to do, but I didn't know how I could leave another home, shabby as it was. Leaving is especially difficult when you don't know what life has in store for you.

34

St. Malo

Our voyage to St. Malo was long because we sailed north, then east, following the coast of France. Sailors worked four hours, slept four hours, and then were back at work for four more hours, continuing day and night. Yves, Gregoire, and Daniel followed the same schedule, working as hard as the sailors. Anne, Marguerite, and I rarely saw Yves or the boys; as soon as they finished working, they fell into their sailors' hammocks, exhausted.

The girls and I spent most of our time on deck because this time we weren't prisoners confined to the cramped darkness below. I loved to stand near the rail, feeling the wind in my face, smelling the fresh air, and tasting the salt on my lips. The air was sweet and clean; I couldn't get enough of it, even though months had passed since we crossed the ocean from Louisbourg in our smelly prison.

Marguerite, just seven years old, chattered constantly, hardly able to stand still. "We're going to see Maman, Papa, Sébastien-François, and Marie Josephe," she said over and over. "They'll be waiting for us when we get off the ship."

Each time I reminded her, "Marguerite, we don't know where they are. They might not be in St. Malo. They might not even be in France."

"But they got on their ship the day we left Louisbourg. They *have* to be waiting for us."

I hoped and prayed she was right. If they sailed the same day we did and went directly to St. Malo, which is what the sailors told Yves almost all the ships did, they should be there. I might also find Hélène and Joseph.

One morning one of the sailors on deck called us, pointing, "There's land ahead. Keep watching; you'll soon see St. Malo."

"Look!" shouted Marguerite. "St. Malo is floating on the water! It looks just like Louisbourg."

"Marguerite, don't shout. Yes, you're right. It does look like it's built on water and it is a walled fortress with rocky ramparts, like Louisbourg."

Yves passed us on his way to help the sailors drop the anchor. "The old walled city is on a small island and is connected to the mainland by a bridge. Many of the buildings are hundreds of years old."

I was as excited as Marguerite was. When we finally got off the ship, a well-dressed man stood on shore smiling and saying, "Bienvenue," as each group reached him. Then, "*Viens avec moi.*" (Come with me.)

We waited anxiously for Yves and the boys, and then went into the building the Acadians had entered. It was an old military barracks, empty except for a large number of cots. The man who had met us on shore introduced himself as a government official whose job was to help Acadians get settled. He told us we could stay in the building until we found another place to live. He also said the French government would continue giving us our subsidy to help pay rent and buy food. Since we were all over seven years old, we would each receive six sols a day.

As the man was leaving, I stopped him. "Monsieur, do you know Claude Benoist and Elisabeth Thériault? They're my parents; we hope to find them here."

He shook his head. "The ships bring many Acadians to St. Malo, but few live here."

"Oh, no, we were told this would be the best place to find my family. Are you saying we came here for nothing?"

"Non, Madame, don't be upset. You came to the right place. The Acadians arrive here, but they make their homes in many of the villages and towns around St. Malo, especially in St. Servan. If your family is in France, you'll probably find them in this area."

Yves said, "My family lives in Megrit—at least they were there when I left twelve years ago. I'd like to find them."

"Megrit isn't far from here," said the official.

After a long walk, we found an empty shed in St. Malo, but unfortunately, we had to pay most of our monthly subsidy for rent. "The boys and I will try to find work," said Yves. "We'll manage somehow."

I spent my days doing chores and looking for Maman, Papa, and Hélène. I walked many miles because the Acadians were spread around the countryside. I knocked on every door in every Acadian settlement. I received hugs and listened to many sad stories as we shared our tears. I asked everyone I met, "Have you seen my maman and papa, Claude Benoist and Elisabeth Thériault?"

The answer was always, "Non, chère, not in St. Malo."

Some people added, "There are only a few Acadians here, but many live in nearby towns. Several hundred people were on our ship, but we were imprisoned below deck for most of the day. We didn't see anyone in other parts of the ship, so I don't know if your parents traveled with us."

Several people said, "Many died—so many—crossing the ocean and after we arrived in St. Malo."

Yves, Gregoire, and Daniel spent weeks trying to find work, any kind of work. One afternoon, Yves returned, frowning and walking slowly with his shoulders slumped. "Pelagie, I don't know if we'll ever find work. Even though this is a port town, there aren't any jobs, not fishing or sailing on ships or small boats. We're not trained for anything else. Too many people are here for the work that needs to be done, and there's no land available for farming. I don't know what to do."

I sighed. "Maybe we should go to one of the towns where more Acadians live. I've searched everywhere, and I've asked everyone I met, but no one knows anyone in my family, not Maman, Papa, my uncles, aunts, cousins, or Hélène."

"I've been thinking that we should go to Megrit," said Yves. "If my family is still there, they'll help us get settled. They might even be able to help us find your family."

So the decision was made; we would go to Megrit. We were told it was a day's walk, or we could go by horse and buggy, which would also take a day because the roads between towns were so bad.

The day before we left, Yves said, "Pelagie, there's something I want you to see before we leave St. Malo, because we might never come back." He led us to St. Vincent Cathedral.

"This beautiful church is special for several reasons," said Yves. "Construction began in the twelfth century. Then in 1534, before Jacques Cartier's first voyage to Canada when he claimed land for the King of France, he knelt here in front of King François."

The beauty of the building amazed me. We had attended a small, plain church in Pigiguit and a tiny chapel in Louisbourg. The size and ornateness of this cathedral overwhelmed me, especially the beautiful stained-glass window that made the interior of the cathedral shimmer with a glow of violet. I'd never seen anything like it before. I hated to go back to our cramped shed, but I knew we had a long walk to Megrit the next day.

When we reached the town late the next evening, Yves stopped the first man he saw. "I left Megrit twelve years ago. I'm looking for my parents, Guillaume Crochet and Julienne Durand. Do you know them?" After the man shook his head, Yves continued. "We'd like to live here; do you know where we can find a house?"

The man shook his head again; so did everyone else until one man pointed down a nearby street. "There are some empty sheds; you might find one that is big enough."

We found a shed that looked livable. The next day, the girls and I cleaned our new home and gathered firewood while Yves and Gregoire looked for work, and Daniel tried to catch fish in one of the streams.

Days passed with little change. Every morning Anne, Marguerite, and I swept, gathered firewood, baked bread if we had flour, and cooked vegetables if I could afford to buy them. We planted seeds the neighbors gave us and tried to coax a few vegetables to grow, but we had little hope that anything would survive in the rocky, hard ground that was our yard. We had nothing else to do. We had no animals, no loom, and no spinning wheel to keep us busy.

I talked to my sisters about Acadie as we worked because I wanted them to know that things could get better. "Anne, you were just four years old when we left Pigiguit, so you probably don't remember much about our life there. And Marguerite, you were born after we moved to Île Saint-Jean.

"In Pigiguit we spun wool and flax into thread, made cloth on our loom, and sewed clothes. Papa had a large wheat farm and raised cows, sheep, pigs, and chickens. Maman had a big vegetable garden. We had lots of fruit trees in our orchard. We dried meat and fish, and preserved food that we grew. We churned butter and made candles, soap, wine, and cheese. We collected eggs, planted vegetables, picked fruit, weeded the garden, and shelled beans and peas. We baked pies and made jam and jelly. We were always busy, but we were very happy."

"Did I help?" asked Anne.

"You helped in the garden. You also collected eggs, picked fruit, and tried to do everything Maman and I did."

I smiled at the girls. "Life was harder in Île Saint-Jean because we didn't have enough seeds to plant, and we were often hungry. Louisbourg was different since it's a fortress town, but we were happy there. You must remember living there. We bought yarn to make cloth since we couldn't grow flax or raise sheep; our yards were too tiny. We didn't have fruit trees and had just a small garden so we didn't preserve lots of food, but we did everything else that we did in Pigiguit. We were lucky to have the two of you and also Marie Josephe to help us."

Marguerite frowned. "Why don't we have a spinning wheel and a loom here?"

"Yves doesn't have time to make furniture, a spinning wheel, or a loom. He's too busy trying to find work, and he looks for his parents when he isn't working. I don't need a loom and spinning wheel, anyway. We don't have room in our tiny yard to raise sheep for wool or grow flax to make cloth. Even if we had room, we don't have money to buy sheep. I just pray that the clothes we have will last until we are able to provide for ourselves."

After our chores were done, I left Anne in charge of Marguerite while I spent my days exploring Megrit. I continued to ask about my parents and Yves's relatives, but I didn't find anyone who knew them.

One day Yves came home smiling. "I found three of my cousins, Jeanne, Jean, and Julien Crochet. I had a nice visit with them, and we'll all get together on Sunday after Mass. They told me everyone else in my family has moved away or died. I had hoped my relatives would be able to help us get settled and find work, but my cousins are as poor as we are, trying to make something grow in this unproductive soil."

Days, weeks, and months passed as we worked to feed our family. Yves, Gregoire, and Daniel found enough odd jobs to keep us from starving, but that was the best they could do. We grieved for Pierre, and I promised my brothers and sisters I would never stop looking for Maman, Papa, Sébastien-François, and Marie Josephe.

We celebrated two joyous events in Megrit; Yves and I became parents. Jean-Guillaume was born in September 1760 and François-Louis in December 1761. I loved holding those two little miracles, but I often sobbed when I looked at them and thought of how Maman and Papa would have loved their two grandchildren.

With two babies, I had less time to try to grow vegetables or to search the markets for cabbage or beans that the farmers were ready to throw away. Our small subsidy from the government, when we received it, wasn't enough to pay our rent and buy food.

After months of no steady work and no vegetables in our garden, the children were hungry and cold, and our clothes were in tatters. Yves said it was time to move again. "We'll go to St. Servan; we might find some fertile land so we can grow enough food to eat. We probably should have gone there from St. Malo, but I was sure my brothers would be in Megrit and would help us get settled. Since that hasn't happened, we'll go to St. Servan."

"Why St. Servan?" I asked.

"That's where most of the Acadians from Louisbourg and Île Saint-Jean are living. We're sure to find your maman and papa there."

"Do you really think we'll find them, Yves?"

"I don't know, but I promise we'll never stop trying."

"Where is St. Servan?" asked Gregoire.

"Close to St. Malo," said Yves. "We might be able to rent a plot of land to farm, but if we can't, we'll be close enough to the Gulf of St. Malo and the Rance River to fish or get work on boats. We'll wait until spring when the trip will be easier, especially with the babies."

It was simple to pack our belongings. Even though we had lived in Megrit for two years, we owned nothing but the clothes on our backs, a few chipped dishes, and a cooking pot. Once more, we left the shabby shed that was our home. Again I hoped and prayed that we would find some members of our family, and work for Yves and the boys.

35

Françoise

When we reached St. Servan we found temporary shelter in the military barracks until Yves came across an empty wooden hut with a roof of straw—just what we had become used to. When he brought us there, I walked in, looked around, and sighed. I was only twenty-one years old but I was exhausted and felt much older. I had lived in Pigiguit, Île Saint-Jean, and Louisbourg; and in France, we lived in Rochefort, St. Malo, Megrit, and now St. Servan. Would we ever have a permanent home? I knew I'd be happy if we could settle down, knowing we'd never have to move again. That would be peace and contentment for me.

My thoughts wandered to my great-grand'maman Marie Chaussegros, and my life suddenly seemed a little easier. I told the girls about her as we removed cobwebs and swept up dust. "Great-grand'maman sailed across the ocean from France to Acadie in 1671 and married Great-grand'père Martin Benoist when she was only fifteen years old," I said.

Anne stopped sweeping to stare at me. "She was younger than I am."

I reached high for several cobwebs near the ceiling. "Yes. What a hard life they must have had! The two of them left their families to settle in a strange new country, knowing they would never return to France. Sixty new colonists were sent to Port Royal, and only five of them were women. Great-grand'maman and Great-grand-père and their eleven children lived in Port Royal for thirty-one years. When

Acadians began to settle in Pigiguit in 1702, and their sons wanted more land, our great-grandparents decided to move there, too."

"Our Grand-père Pierre was one of their children," sang Marguerite as she danced around the room.

"Yes, he and Grand'maman Elizabeth were married the following year and lived in Pigiguit all their married life; in 1750 Grand'maman left for Île Saint-Jean with us to escape from the English."

"I was just four years old," said Anne.

"And I wasn't born yet." Marguerite suddenly stopped dancing. "Where is Grand'maman now?"

I sighed. "I wish I knew. Grand-père died before we left Pigiguit, and Grand'maman married François Michel in 1751, a short time after we reached Île Saint-Jean. She was sixty-two but she was healthy and strong, and acted much younger. They stayed in Île Saint-Jean when we left for Louisbourg. Just before we were forced to leave the fortress, a French soldier told Yves that the English were sending ships to Île Saint-Jean to bring those Acadians to France, too. If they're here, I'll find them. If I see Grand'maman's smiling face one more time, I'll be happy."

* * *

As soon as we were settled, I started searching for family and friends, anyone I knew. The first morning I asked a neighbor, "Do you know where my parents, Claude Benoist and Elisabeth Thériault are?"

"Oh, my dear, you're a Benoist. I know some of your relatives are here. Françoise Benoist has been looking everywhere and asking everyone about you."

"My cousin Françoise? She's here? Oh, thank God." I stopped for a moment. "But I have two cousins named Françoise Benoist. The daughter of Oncle Paul is about seven years older than I am. Or can it be the daughter of Oncle Charles? She's my age and my best friend. Our families moved to Île Saint-Jean when we were nine years old, but they stayed on the island when my immediate family left for Louisbourg. Do you know which cousin is here?"

"Chère, are you all right? You look very pale. Come inside, sit down, and drink a glass of water." She gave me a few minutes to catch my breath, and then said, "I'm sorry, chère, I only know she is Françoise Benoist."

"Oh, I must see her, whoever she is. My cousin, at last. Where does she live? Do you know where my parents are?"

"I haven't heard anything about your parents, but Françoise lives in a small Acadian settlement about a half mile from here. She might have found your parents because she's been searching for relatives since she arrived in France."

I set out immediately and, in my excitement, I ran almost all the way. I soon reached her street and was directed to Françoise's hut, which looked much like ours. My heart pounded as I knocked on her door. Suppose she wasn't home? I decided I'd sit in front of her hut all day until someone arrived. What if this was neither of my first cousins, but a different Françoise Benoist? Oh, I wouldn't care—she was a Benoist and an Acadian. Whoever she was, I had to see her and talk to her.

I heard a voice inside the house, and suddenly I felt faint. By the time she opened the door, tears had flooded my eyes so I couldn't see. But I fell into her arms and we held each other for a long time, unable to speak. Oncle Charles and Tante Madeleine's daughter! My first cousin and my best friend! Memories overwhelmed me. I couldn't remember such happiness except for the day I married Yves and the days when I first held my two sons in my arms.

"Pelagie, is it really you? I've searched all over St. Servan for you and your family. Come in and let me look at you."

"Françoise, I can't tell you how happy I am to have found you. I thought I'd never get over my loneliness for Grand'maman, my aunts, uncles, and cousins when we left Île Saint-Jean seven years ago. We visited Oncle Augustin as often as we could, but his children are so much younger than I; it wasn't like having you to talk to. Except for Yves and my brothers and sisters, you're the only family I've seen in the four years since we were deported from Louisbourg."

I clung to her hand; I didn't think I'd ever let her go. "Oh, Françoise, I've longed to find my relatives. I always ask everyone I meet, but until now, no one knew anything about our family. It's wonderful to finally be with someone from Pigiguit."

"What happened to you?" she asked. "Where have you been since the English captured the fortress in Louisbourg?"

I told her about our family and everything we'd lived through in Louisbourg and in France.

"You haven't heard anything about our relatives since you left Île Saint-Jean?"

I shook my head. "No, nothing. What happened after we left?"

Françoise gripped my hand tighter. "Life in Île Saint-Jean got worse, if that's possible, after you moved to Louisbourg. My parents and uncles often said we should have gone with you. We were always hungry and cold; that became the way we lived. After a while I didn't remember anything different. I refused to think about our wonderful life in Pigiguit; I was afraid I would lose my mind if I thought about being warm with a full stomach. Then the English came for us with their ships. We sailed on the *Tamerlane* and arrived in St. Malo in January 1759."

"Tell me about your life in France," I begged. "Who's here with you?"

"My mother, my brothers and sisters, Tante Anne, and her husband, Pierre Hébert, live here. Oncle Augustin was here for a while." Her eyes suddenly filled with tears and her shoulders shook as she sobbed. "But, Pelagie, my eight-year-old brother, poor little Pierre-Paul, died on the ship. It was horrible."

I held Françoise and cried with her. "I'm so sorry. My four-year-old brother, Pierre, died on the way to France, too. So many people died, especially the young and very old. Where are your parents? I want to see them. And where is Grand'maman Elizabeth? Did she come to France, or did the English soldiers let her stay in Île Saint-Jean?"

"Oh, Pelagie. There's so much you don't know; terrible things have happened. Grand'maman was forced to come with us; only a few people escaped to Quebec or New Brunswick before the soldiers came to our village and brought the Acadians to France. The voyage was long and difficult; you know how bad it was, and she was seventy years old."

"Grand'maman seemed so energetic when we left Pigiguit and walked for weeks through forests and mountains," I said. "Her health was as good as anyone's in Île Saint-Jean."

Françoise nodded. "Yes, but in the last few years without good food and warm clothes, she became frail and weak, hardly able to walk. It was almost too much for her when her husband, François Michel, died. But she hung on, still enjoying her children and grandchildren. When the soldiers came, she said she wouldn't stay in Île Saint-Jean even if they allowed her to, because everyone in her family was leaving for France."

Tears ran down my cheeks. I thought of the years with Grand'maman that I had missed. "What happened to her? Where is she?"

"The voyage was too much for her. She didn't complain but we knew she couldn't last much longer. One morning an old man died on the ship; I'll never forget what Grand'maman said, 'I hope I live long enough to die in France.' When I asked her why, she said, 'I can't bear the thought of being thrown into the ocean.' She was determined; she lived until July 11, 1759, almost six months after we arrived here."

I couldn't stop my tears and sobs. Françoise held me until I could talk again. Then she said, "Let's talk about something else. This is too much sadness for you in one day. I'll get a drink of water for you."

"No, no," I said, "I want to hear everything. Oh, why didn't our ship bring us to St. Malo instead of to Rochefort? Or if we had come here from Rochefort instead of going to Megrit, I might have found you before Grand'maman died. I wish I could have been here to talk to her and hug her one last time."

"She spoke of you often, Pelagie. She missed you, too. I think she was holding on to life, hoping to see all of her children and grandchildren again."

"Françoise, please tell me some good news."

She smiled. "One good thing probably wouldn't have happened if we hadn't been forced to come to France. I met Honoré Caret on our ship, and we were married three years ago, a month-and-a-half after we arrived. Papa and my sister Anne came to our wedding, but Papa died the following year, and my sister Judith died a few weeks later. All the years of hardship were too much for them, too."

"Oh, no, Oncle Charles and Judith died, too? Where is your maman?"

"She lives close by, with my sister Marie. You'll see them soon."

I smiled. "Are your sisters Marie and Anne married?"

"Yes, Anne married Charles LeBlanc in Île Saint-Jean in 1758." Françoise's smile changed to a frown. "Marie married René Rasicot two years before we left Île Saint-Jean. Unfortunately, that's another sad story. Do you want to wait for another day to hear this?"

"No, please go on," I said.

"Marie's husband, René, is a navigator. He and Oncle Augustin . . ."

"Oh, Oncle Augustin is here, too? I can't wait to see him and his family."

"I'm afraid you're going to have a long wait. Oncle Augustin and René found jobs as sailors on the corsair, *L'Hercule.*"

"A corsair? They're pirates?"

"No, privateers. King Louis XV granted them permission, along with others, to raid and seize vessels belonging to any nation at war with France. They're given part of the profit from the ships they capture."

"But Françoise, isn't it dangerous?"

"Very. A friend sent word to Marie that René and Oncle Augustin were captured by the English two years ago. No one has heard anything about them since then."

"Things just keep getting worse and worse. Marie and Tante Marguerite must be sick with worry," I said. "We visited Oncle Augustin, Tante Marguerite, and their children often when we lived in Louisbourg. Oncle Augustin baked bread for the soldiers there."

"Wait, I haven't told you the very worst yet. Oncle Augustin and Tante Marguerite were deported from Louisbourg on the ship *Supply.* All three of their children died on the way to France. If that wasn't bad enough, two months after they arrived in France, Tante Marguerite gave birth to another daughter, Perrine-Jeannine; Tante Marguerite and the baby died within days of each other."

I stared at her in horror. "Oh, no! Not Tante Marguerite and all four children! Poor Oncle Augustin. How much sorrow can a person have and still survive?"

"I don't know, but we have to pray and keep putting one foot in front of the other every day."

"I'm not surprised that Oncle Augustin became a privateer. He must have needed to get away from his sorrow—if that's possible. I'll pray for all of them, for strength to bear their losses. God knows I need strength, too. I'll also pray that all the news from now on is good, like finding you. I don't think I can handle any more tragic news. I can't bear to lose anyone else in my family."

36

More Bad News

When the sun peeked over the horizon each morning and brightened the sky, I dragged myself out of bed, exhausted. I rarely slept more than three or four hours. Maman, Papa, Marie Josephe, and Sébastien-François were constantly in my thoughts. I had been sure I'd find them in St. Servan. Where were they? Would I ever see them again? How could I continue to live without them, not knowing if they were alive or dead?

I was also haunted by a deep sense of loss: for my little brother, Pierre, for the many other relatives who had died on the way to France, for those who reached France but were too weak and frail to go on, for the aunts, uncles, and cousins we left in Île Saint-Jean and were unable to find, and for our relatives who had been deported to the American colonies. And where was my friend, Hélène?

My morning and evening prayers were for strength to face the future, knowing that my babies needed me. Slowly I began to feel better until, while praying one morning, it seemed that a weight had been lifted from my shoulders. I knew I would never forget Pierre, Grand'maman, or my uncles, aunts, and cousins who had died. I would never stop looking for Maman, Papa, Marie Josephe, and Sébastien-François. But, instead of crying for the ones who were no longer with me, I promised to thank God every day for the family I still had: my babies, Yves, my brothers and sisters, Françoise and her family, and Oncle Augustin, who was still alive—as far as we knew.

My daily routine never changed. I cooked breakfast for my family and hurried through my chores. I washed the dishes, swept the floor, made bread if I had flour, played with the babies, and went to market. Sometimes a friendly farmer gave me a few vegetables that were too small or misshapen for him to sell. Then my steps were lighter as I walked home with enough vegetables for a thin soup.

One afternoon, I hurried to visit Françoise. It had been almost a week since I'd seen her. We sat in rocking chairs near her fireplace, watching our little ones as they played together on the floor.

"Do you have any news for me today?" I asked. "Have you heard anything about any other members of our family?"

"Well," said Françoise slowly, "I didn't tell you everything I knew on our last visit. It seemed too much to burden you with all at once, when I told you about all the deaths in the family."

I gasped. "Oh, no! Are you about to tell me more bad news?"

"I'm afraid so," said Françoise. "Our cousin Marie-Marthe Benoist is living in a town in the south of France. A friend of our family heard from someone who lives near her."

"She's one of the daughters of Papa's brother, Oncle Paul." I said. "His family went to Île Saint-Jean with us, but stayed there when my family left for Louisbourg. Thank God she survived. Is she well?"

"*She* is. Eleven ships left Île Saint-Jean at the same time. My family sailed on the *Tamerlane*. The ships were separated during a terrible storm. We reached St. Malo first, on January 16, 1759, but three of the ships never arrived. On one of those, the *Duke William*, was Marie-Marthe's whole family—her parents, husband, nine brothers and sisters, a niece, and a nephew."

"Oh, no. What happened to them?"

"As the *Duke William* neared France, it approached the *Violet*, which was leaking and taking on water. Before the *Duke William* could get close enough to help, the *Violet* sank with its four hundred passengers and crew. Marie-Marthe said the captain of the *Duke William* stayed close, watching for survivors, but there were none."

"That's terrible," I said. "Thank God, Oncle Paul's family was on the other ship. But it must have been horrible watching the *Violet* sink."

"Yes, I'm sure it was, but you haven't heard the whole story yet, Pelagie," said Françoise. "Soon after the *Violet* sank, the *Duke William* started leaking. For two days, the passengers and crew worked frantically, trying to remove the water, but the ship began to sink. Two small lifeboats were launched and twenty-seven people, including some of the crew, reached France a few days later. Marie-Marthe was the only one in her family who was saved. Except for her, all of Oncle Paul's family was gone. Oncle Abraham and his whole family were also on one of the ships; none of them survived."

I sat without moving. Tears poured down my cheeks as I pictured each person in those two families. I knew them so well, and they had all drowned. "What a terrible way to die, knowing what is happening and unable to do anything about it. Please tell me that no one else in our family was on either ship."

"No one that I know of," said Françoise. "But news travels very slowly here."

* * *

A few months later, in March 1763, our third child, Jean-Joseph, was born. My sister Anne, who helped with the delivery, looked serious when she handed the baby to me. "What's wrong?" I asked.

"He's so tiny and weak," said Anne.

I held, cared for, and loved my little baby boy. I counted each day, hoping and praying that he was a little stronger as each day passed.

When I woke and checked on Jean-Joseph the morning he was ten days old, he was so still and cold, I knew he was dead. He had been too frail to survive. Yves and I mourned together; alone, I cried many tears, wishing that Maman and Papa were with me. Talking to them had always helped me feel better, but I didn't think there was anything anyone could say this time that would help. I felt as if a part of me had died.

A few days later I remembered my promise. I thought of the many Acadians whose children died on the ships or after reaching France. A large number, like Oncle Augustin, had lost several children. I prayed for our people who were suffering and I thanked God for my good husband and my two healthy children. I kept my tears for the times I was alone.

A couple of months later Françoise brought news that she thought would cheer me up. "England and France have finally signed a peace treaty. Almost four hundred Acadians who were held in England are now in France. Some of them had been sent to the American colonies in 1755, but they weren't wanted there so they were brought to England. Others were deported to England from Louisbourg and Île Saint-Jean in 1759."

"Where are they now?" I asked.

"Some are living in the military barracks in St. Malo, and others were brought to Morlaix, another port town. The guards won't allow them to leave or have visitors because the Acadians are exhausted from the heat and unhealthy conditions on the ships. Some have smallpox, and the officers are afraid many others will get sick. Just think, Oncle Augustin and Marie's husband, René, could be back in France."

"Oh, I pray that's so," I said. Suddenly I gasped, jumped up, and twirled around the room.

Françoise stared at me. "Pelagie, what's wrong?"

"Do you think Maman and Papa could have been in England, too?"

"It's possible," said Françoise. "My husband, Honoré, promised to go to St. Malo next week to ask about René and Oncle Augustin. He'll ask about your parents, too."

The following week I visited Françoise. When she opened the door, she smiled, and pulled me inside. "Come in and see who's here—it's Oncle Augustin."

I was delighted to see him, but shocked because I wouldn't have recognized him if Françoise hadn't told me who he was. He looked much older than he did the last time I saw him in Louisbourg. At that time Oncle Augustin had a wife, three delightful children and another on the way, a nice home, and a good job baking bread for the soldiers. Just four years later he had nothing and no one, and his health had suffered from being imprisoned in England. Losing one baby was terrible, but losing his wife and four children had to be impossible to endure.

185

I fell into his arms. "I'm so happy to see you again, but I can't bear to think about all you've gone through." I didn't want him to let me go. Finally I couldn't wait any longer and asked, "Have you seen my parents? Were they in England?"

"No, Pelagie. I'm sorry. They weren't on my ship or in the barracks in St. Malo."

"What about René?"

Oncle Augustin sighed. "We were imprisoned in England. He was very weak the last time I saw him, and he wasn't with the prisoners who were brought here."

"Marie must be worried sick," I said. "Thank God you're back. I couldn't lose you, too."

He shook his head. "I wish René had come back instead of me. I have no one in this world except a few nieces and nephews. I've lost everyone else who was important to me."

I hugged him. There was nothing I could say that would make him feel better.

* * *

That afternoon, Yves brought news of two settlements that were being considered to provide land for Acadians. "One is in Guyana, South America, in the tropics very near the equator. People are needed to work on sugar plantations."

"Will we go?" I asked.

"No, I'm a fisherman; I don't want to work on a plantation. I don't think many Acadians want to live in the tropics. However, some are interested in going to the Malouines to start a new colony. King Louis XV promised that France would continue the subsidy for Acadians who settle there. That colony will be for farmers, and the soil is supposed to be excellent."

"Should we go there? Would our lives be better?"

"No," said Yves. "We'll do whatever is necessary to give our children a better life. But I don't think we should go to the Malouines. That's off the *southern* coast of South America, much too far away.

Think about how long it would take to get there in a sailing ship! Someday we'll find a better place to live, a place that's right for us. We'll just have to be patient."

Two months later we had a happy occasion—at last! Oncle Augustin married Marie-Madeleine Gotreau in July 1763 in our village church. I was delighted that he had found someone to share his life, after all the sadness he had endured in the last four years. Our relatives in St. Servan attended the wedding and the celebration that followed. We needed a pleasant occasion to get together. It was a small gathering, with nothing to eat or drink; no one could afford any extras when we had to struggle every day to put food on the table.

I still missed everyone and everything I had lost; I knew I always would. It was sometimes difficult getting through the day, but I had to remember to thank God for His blessings, including the newest one; Oncle Augustin was happy again.

37

Hoping

Time passed slowly, as little in our lives changed. Our hut was much like the ones that poor French people lived in—one room with a wooden table and benches, straw mattresses, and a chest for clothes. And like poor French natives, we lived on bread, soup, and, when we could get them, cabbage, peas, beans, or turnips.

Yves and Gregoire continued to work at any odd jobs they could find, usually fishing or sailing. Daniel worked for a farmer who needed help plowing, planting, and harvesting his crops.

Anne, Marguerite, and I were constantly busy with cleaning, cooking, trying to grow vegetables in our rocky yard, and caring for the little ones. We also did small jobs for people who could afford to pay us with money or food. We knitted, wove cloth, spun thread, and sewed clothes, anything that would help to put food on the table.

Sunday was the only day we could spend with family and friends. We went to Mass in the village church, and then socialized with our own people, the Acadians.

One evening twelve-year-old Marguerite put her sewing in her lap and looked at me. "Pelagie, Papa often said if we were sent away from home, he hoped it would be to France. Why did he say that? Many people treat us as if they don't want us here."

I smiled at her and nodded my head. "I know, Marguerite. I, too, hoped and expected to be accepted by the French people, but I didn't realize what life was like here. Most of the people in the villages are poor peasants who have to work as hard as we do to feed their families. Many of them have to work two jobs."

Yves looked up from the net he was mending. "France is deep in debt because of the many foreign wars they've fought in, so taxes are extremely high. Few peasants can afford to own land, and they pay more taxes than we do, not only on the land they rent, but also on wine, salt, and bread. They're taxed by the church and the king, too."

I sighed. "I guess they're so busy working, they don't have time to think about making us feel at home."

"And," said Yves, "some of them resent us because the government gives us a subsidy, even though we couldn't survive without it. I've heard some people say their taxes wouldn't be as high if it weren't for *those Acadians.*"

* * *

The only changes in our lives were births, deaths, and moving from place to place. In May 1764 Oncle Augustin and Tante Marie had their first baby—a boy, Mathurin. I prayed that he would be healthy because Oncle Augustin had suffered enough, after losing his first wife and four children.

The following week I had another infant to pray for. Our first daughter was born, a beautiful baby we named Françoise-Pelagie. Yves was so proud of his baby girl; she had to live! With Jean-Guillaume almost four and François-Louis two-and-a-half, my days were full.

According to custom, since many babies died within their first few days of life, Françoise-Pelagie was baptized the day after she was born. My cousin Françoise stayed with me while the rest of the family took the baby to church. "I brought a bowl of soup for you," Françoise said. "I made it this morning. I wanted to bring enough for everyone, but I know you'll understand that isn't possible."

"I don't want you to deprive your family, but I'll enjoy your soup. Thank you. Now please tell me all the news. I've been housebound for months while waiting for the baby's arrival."

Françoise nodded. "My sister Marie was contacted by the French government. They now list her as a widow. Poor Marie. René never returned to France after he was captured by the English, so he probably died in prison."

"How will she survive without her husband?" I wondered.

"I don't know," said Françoise. "But there are many young Acadian widows here."

She walked to the window before sitting down again. "Yves probably told you about the small number of our people who decided to move to the tropics in South America. Some of them have already died, and the rest are back in France."

"I wonder if our lives will ever get better here."

"Many Acadians must ask the same question. That's probably why another group of our people from St. Malo is planning to join the Acadians who are already in the Malouines."

"Oh, that's too far away, and too cold. But Yves said some are willing to go anywhere if they're told there's land for farming. I can understand that. If someone told me today that moving would provide more food, better jobs for Yves and my brothers, or fertile land where we could grow crops as we did in Acadie, I would leave in an hour—as long as I wouldn't have to cross the ocean. Look at the number of times Yves and I have moved since we arrived in France. I pray that someday we'll find a place to live where we'll have lots of family nearby, enough food, a warm, comfortable house, and clothes that aren't so raggedy they're falling off our backs. That would be heaven for me. That's all I want and need."

"I'll continue to pray for that for all of us," said Françoise.

38

Joy and Sorrow

February 1765 brought a happy day tinged with sadness; my sister Anne married Louis Haché. Anne and I had always been close, but especially during our six years in France without Maman and Papa. She was such a help to Yves and me that I didn't think I could survive without her. Anne was just nineteen years old when she got married, but so much had happened in her young life that she seemed much older. And at twenty-four, I certainly felt old and tired. It was good to see Anne happy; she and Louis lived close to us, but I missed her constant company.

At the end of 1765, Yves told me about another settlement that was planned for our people. "Acadians are anxious to leave France. They continue to work hard, but live in misery and poverty. Seventy-five families from Morlaix and St. Malo—almost all had been prisoners in England—recently sailed to Belle-Isle-en-Mer where they will be given land for farming."

"Where is *that*?" I asked.

"It's a small island off the western coast of France," answered Gregoire who had followed Yves into our hut. "The settlers will be given land, tools, a house, a few animals, and food until they grow their first crops. When I hear about the attempts to begin colonies for the Acadians, I always wonder if we should join them. I don't think anything could be worse than our lives here."

"But we're not farmers," said Yves. "I want to stay where we can at least catch a few fish to feed the family. We don't know if we would be able to make anything grow. Anyway, Father Le Loutre, who led this group, didn't come here when he was looking for settlers. Maybe someday we'll be given a better opportunity."

Gregoire sighed. "I just hope we have the sense to take advantage of that opportunity if it comes along."

Oncle Augustin's second child, François, was born in October. I loved seeing my uncle with his babies, but soon felt the familiar sting of tears, a reminder that Papa should be with us, enjoying *my* children.

Another pleasant family occasion was the wedding of Françoise's sister Marie who married Joseph Hébert in January. We were happy she had someone to share her life with, since her first husband René had been captured four years before and probably died in prison.

I was overjoyed when my sister Anne and her husband, Louis, had a beautiful baby boy in March 1766. I don't remember ever seeing Anne so happy.

Yves dragged home one day, plodding along like an old man. "What's wrong, Yves?" I asked. "Are you sick?"

"No, I'm just discouraged. Daniel, Gregoire, and I never stop working, but we can't put enough food on the table to keep everyone fed. We catch a few fish if we're lucky, but barely earn enough to buy flour for a loaf of bread. You can't grow anything in our rocky yard. How can we continue to feed five grownups and three children this way? Look at you. You hardly eat so the babies will have enough. I heard things are better in Megrit now. We should go back."

"Must we go, Yves? We're finally with family here, and everyone lives the way we do. Why do you think things will be better in Megrit?"

"We have to try. The children are much too thin. I'm afraid we'll lose them if we can't give them more to eat."

"Come with us," I begged when we told my brothers and sisters we were leaving.

Gregoire shook his head. "I'm tired of moving. Life is bad everywhere. I'm staying here."

"I'm staying, too," said Daniel.

I couldn't believe we would leave Gregoire and Daniel. They had been more like my children than my brothers in the seven years since

Maman and Papa were gone. I was thankful my sisters and Anne's husband, Louis, decided to come with us. I needed their company and their help with my three little ones.

I missed everyone terribly. Daniel, Gregoire, my cousin Françoise, and Oncle Augustin were still in St. Servan. There would be no more weddings, baptisms, and family get-togethers for me to attend. Once again I wondered how I would survive without lots of family close to me.

* * *

The years dragged by—the monotony of trying to hold our lives together was broken only by births and deaths. In May 1766 we were blessed with another beautiful baby girl, Marguerite-Perrine, and my sister Anne had her second child, Marguerite-Yvonne, on September 3, 1767.

Three weeks later our smiles turned into tears. On September 25, my precious sister Anne died. She was five years younger than I, only twenty-one, and hadn't had a chance to enjoy life. She was four years old when we left Pigiguit, and just twelve the last time we saw Maman and Papa. The only life she knew was hardship in Île Saint-Jean, a few good years in Louisbourg, and much suffering in France, struggling and working from morning to night for our family. She was more than an aunt to my children; she was their second mother. She had been married for only two and a half years; her marriage and her babies had finally brought her joy. Poor Louis. I grieved for him, for his children, for my children, and for myself. It was a terrible loss for all of us. I wondered, probably for the hundredth time, how would we go on?

Yves and I had four children, the oldest just seven years old, and we expected another baby soon. But I had to help Louis care for his children; he had no one else in Megrit. It was hard for Marguerite and me, grieving and taking care of so many little ones. When Louis decided to return to St. Servan where his mother, five brothers, and their wives could help him, Yves agreed that it was time for us to move back, too.

We stayed in St. Servan for a little over a year, and then returned to Megrit. Those years were a blur of endlessly searching for family, food, jobs, fertile land for growing vegetables, and better houses. When we arrived in France I had vowed that I would never stop looking for my family. I kept that promise, searching every village we lived in. Yves did the same, always looking for his relatives.

No matter where we were, nothing changed. Our huts were drafty and cramped; we were always hungry, exhausted, and discouraged. We sometimes received our subsidies, but other times the government had no money, so our debts mounted. Luckily, we were usually able to find a sympathetic merchant or renter who was willing to give us what we desperately needed with a promise to pay when we could.

One day M. Aucoin, an Acadian who spent much of his time petitioning the king's council on our behalf, visited our neighborhood. "I've brought exciting news," he said with a big smile. "A friend of mine recently received a letter from his son Jean-Baptiste who lives in Louisiana. He wrote to his father about his travels from Halifax to Saint Domingue with Joseph Broussard, who was called Beausoleil. They arrived in Louisiana in February 1765 with a group of almost six hundred Acadians.

"Jean-Baptiste was sent with several other men to find a site where the Acadians could settle. They were told they would find the 'best soil in the world' in the grassland at Attakapas, in southwestern Louisiana. It was May by the time the rest of the Acadians joined them and were given land grants. They cleared land and planted crops, but in the terrible summer heat, many got sick and thirty-three or thirty-four died."

"We don't want to go where the heat causes people to die," said Yves.

"No, no," said M. Aucoin. "That was unfortunate, but you must wait to hear the good part. Jean-Baptiste said their fall harvest was good, and now they're growing grain, vegetables, and fruit of all kinds. They also hunt for deer, turkeys, bears, ducks, and much more. Each man has been given land, and those who work hard are doing well. He urged his father to find a way to sail to Louisiana, and to tell everyone that we should do whatever we can to join our people there. It sounds like the promised land."

"Where is Louisiana?" I asked.

"Across the ocean, south of the American colonies," he said.

I shivered. "I'm not crossing the ocean again."

Yves smiled at me. "I thought you couldn't wait to leave France." He turned to M. Aucoin. "How would we get there? We're in debt, so we can't pay for passage."

"I know," said M. Aucoin. "A group of us met with the king's council. They said it would be too expensive to send us to Louisiana. But don't give up; we'll keep trying to find a way."

Fortunately, Yves and I celebrated a few happy occasions, such as the births of three more babies—Yves-Jean in December 1767, Julien in March 1770, and little Pelagie in February 1772. Other joys were soon tinged with sadness. Both of my brothers knew joy and sorrow in St. Servan while Yves and I spent our last four years in Megrit where we received the news months later. My brother Daniel, now a maker of wooden boxes and packing cases, married Henriette Legendre in March 1768. Gregoire married Marie Rose Caret in February 1770. Daniel and his wife had a son and a daughter; the son survived but the daughter lived only seven months. Gregoire's first child, a son, lived only two months. I mourned for them, their wives, and babies. I also cried for myself because I couldn't be with them to share their tears.

During that time the French government continued to try to improve the lives of Acadians by starting different colonies for them, but nothing worked. Some of our people who had moved to the Malouines with high hopes returned in July 1769, after six years there. They had tried unsuccessfully to grow corn. Because of the strong winds off the ocean, they couldn't grow other vegetables unless they built high walls around their gardens.

Many of those who tried to settle in Belle-Île-en-Mer also returned to France. Their crops failed and their animals died after a drought, so they couldn't pay their taxes or feed their families.

When our Acadian friends talked about these failed settlements, someone always said that maybe we would be successful in Louisiana, if we could find a way to get there.

Yves was always exhausted, working many more hours than he should have, eating and sleeping little, trying to improve the lives of our seven children. When he wasn't doing odd jobs for anyone who needed help, he sat near the fireplace in winter, or outside if the weather was pleasant, making shoes, ropes, and wooden furniture. He traded everything he made for flour, fish, and vegetables. I worried about him day and night, but there was nothing I could do to help him. I was exhausted, too, from little food and sleep, never-ending cleaning, cooking, and caring for our children, and spinning, sewing, and weaving cloth whenever I had a spare moment.

My sister Marguerite still lived with us, working as hard as Yves and I did. She was the only sister I had left; she and I had lived together since she was born, except for the few months Yves and I lived in our fisherman's hut in Louisbourg. I wanted her to have a life of her own, but I didn't have the energy to think about how we would manage without her. The children helped as much as they could, working with Yves or with me, learning very early that there wasn't time for pleasure in our lives.

I dragged through days with little hope for our future. However, I never forgot what Papa had often told me, "Pelagie, you might have dark days with many sorrows, but you must remain close to God. Have faith, trust in Him, and do whatever you can to make your life better. Pray, work, help others, and believe that things will change, and someday you'll find a silver lining behind all of the dark clouds."

My daily prayer and my promise to our children was that, together, and with God's help, we would find a way to change our lives for the better. Even though most of the time, it didn't seem that God was listening, we couldn't give up hope. We had to keep praying and putting one foot in front of the other. We might not be able to change anything, but if we stopped trying there was no hope for anyone's future.

39

Hope and Sorrow

After living in Megrit for six years, Yves and I were as discouraged as almost all of the Acadians in France. One evening Yves brought news when he came in for supper. "I keep hearing rumors that a commissioner to King Louis XV is considering another plan to help us. The Marquis de Pérusse des Cars owns a large plot of land in Poitou in central France, and he hopes to find someone to farm it for him."

"Oh, Yves, maybe this is what we've been waiting for. The upper class here owns the good land. Nobody wants the poor, rocky soil they give us."

"We'll get more information before making a decision."

On a Sunday in the middle of 1773 our priest stopped us after Mass. "I received a letter from the priest in St. Servan," he said. "Gregoire and Daniel sent a message to you. They think the settlement in Poitou is the opportunity you've all been waiting for. They want you to join them there."

In my excitement I almost forgot to thank the priest. I squeezed Yves's hand. "Can we go? We could live near Gregoire and Daniel and their families again."

He smiled at me. "I'll have to find out more about this settlement. I'll ask around."

"Please ask until you get some good news."

By the following month we had enough information to give me something to look forward to. "The plan," said Yves, "is for 150 families made up of farmers and laborers to move to Poitou."

"Not fishermen?" I asked as my heart dropped.

"Don't worry, Pelagie. Gregoire, Daniel, and I are considered laborers as well as sailors because we can build houses. We're included in the 150 families. My father was a farmer; I can learn to grow crops if I have to."

I didn't realize I had been holding my breath. "Thank God. Tell me more about it."

"Each family will have a house and thirty arpents of land for farming. Animals and tools will be provided, and the marquis will supply food until January 1776. The families will share a large pasture. The farmers will pay rent to the marquis, but won't pay taxes to the government for thirty years. After six years, the farmers will own the land and houses."

I could hardly breathe. "Oh, Yves, it sounds wonderful. We have to go."

He smiled at me. "I'm afraid; it sounds too good to be true. All the plans for our people have failed so far, and the French government refuses to give the marquis any loans. This could fail, too."

Our next message from Gregoire again begged us to move to Poitou with them. "Oncle Augustin and his family are going, and so is Papa's sister Tante Anne. You must come with us. The Acadians who met with the king's council warned us that subsidies will end in January 1774 for Acadians who choose to remain in the ports instead of moving to Poitou. That's just a few months away. What will happen to us without the subsidy?"

"I don't want to go, Pelagie," said Yves, "because the marquis's section of Poitou is inland. We'll have no chance to work as fishermen or sailors. I heard that several Acadians were sent to look over the area. They said the soil is poor and there's little water. If we can't grow vegetables and can't catch fish, we'll starve."

I sighed. "Then we can't go."

"I don't know what to do. The Acadians who met with the marquis are so anxious to own land and to live close to their people instead of spread out in many different towns that they decided to accept the plan for settlement. If what Gregoire said is true, that our subsidy will soon end, we'll have to go. We can't properly feed seven children, Marguerite, and ourselves on the little money Jean-Guillaume, François-Louis, and I struggle to make, and the few fish we catch with Yves-Jean's help. I can't work any harder, and neither can you, Marguerite, or the girls. But you have to realize that either here or in Poitou, there's a chance we could starve."

"I hope we can go. Nothing would make me happier than to live near family again," I said.

* * *

In September 1773 Gregoire sent word that Oncle Augustin and his family and Tante Anne and her family had sailed from St. Malo to La Rochelle. From there, they would travel to Poitou. Gregoire and Daniel hoped to leave with the next group of Acadians. Plans were being made for those of us in Megrit to leave in the spring.

Yves had finally agreed to move to Poitou. "Pelagie," he said, "I have many misgivings about this move, but we have no other choice. Without our subsidies, this appears to be our only chance to survive."

One morning in the middle of November as my sister, Marguerite, and I cleaned our hut with the help of Françoise-Pelagie and Marguerite-Perinne, I danced around the room. "I can't wait to move to Poitou. It's been four years since we've seen Gregoire and Daniel. And we'll live near Oncle Augustin and Tante Anne again. Marguerite-Perinne, you're too young to remember any of these relatives, but you'll love getting to know them and their children. You'll find out how wonderful it is to live close to family and spend time with them, working, praying, and having fun. It will be like living in Pigiguit again."

"I can't wait," said Marguerite, as she twirled around.

Our happy chattering stopped when we heard a noise outside. It was too early for Yves and the boys to get home from work. My daughters looked up, and Françoise-Pelagie hurried to open the door. I gasped when I saw Yves looking pale and weak; only the support of our sons Jean-Guillaume and François-Louis kept him from falling. I ran to him. "Yves, what is wrong? Are you hurt?"

He looked at me with a weak smile. "Don't worry, my dear Pelagie; I'm just exhausted. It was cold and windy on the water today. I'll be fine after a good night's rest."

We took off his shoes, helped him to bed, and covered him. He closed his eyes and was soon asleep.

I turned to the boys. "What happened?"

Jean-Guillaume shrugged. "I don't know. We were working when I heard a noise. He had fallen forward and couldn't get up. He was too weak to walk without our help."

"We'd better pray for him," I said as I knelt next to his bed.

I woke Yves later and convinced him to drink a little broth, but he was soon asleep again. The next morning he tried to get up but couldn't. "I'm too tired to work right now. Tell the boys to go without me. I'll meet them later."

In the sixteen years I had known Yves, he was always dressed and ready to leave the house before the sun rose. He had worked outside in all kinds of weather for his whole life and never missed a day except for Sunday, and that was to go to Mass, and because of the church law to do only necessary work on Sundays. In Louisbourg he even worked on Sundays from early spring to late fall. The Catholic Church there allowed fishermen to work after attending Mass because the fishing season was short; the fishermen needed the work and the people needed the food.

Yves grew weaker and weaker. The following day, November 23, 1773, as I sat next to the bed holding his hand, Yves opened his eyes, looked at me, and whispered, "I'm sorry, but I can't go on. Take care of the children for me. I love you." Then he took his last breath. He was only forty-one years old. I screamed, "Noooo!" Then I screamed at God. "What are you trying to do to me? Haven't I lost enough of my loved ones? Haven't we suffered enough? How will I go on?"

I *couldn't* face it. I *wouldn't* face it. *I'm only thirty-two years old, a widow with seven children and another on the way. What am I going to do? It has been difficult enough with Yves working from morning until night, but without him, how can I possibly care for my children? What is going to happen to us?*

40

Coping

My dear husband was buried the following day. Marguerite took care of the house and children while I sat near the fireplace for hours in the rocking chair Yves had made for me. My pain was like nothing I had ever felt before. Three-year-old Julien and one-and-a-half-year-old Pelagie spent their days lying on the floor near my chair, sucking their thumbs and looking at me with pleading eyes.

A few days after the funeral, I realized with a jolt that the children needed me; I was depending on Marguerite too much. She couldn't, and shouldn't have to take care of everything. The only thing I could think of as I held my babies was that the love of my life was gone, and somehow, I would have to take care of our children. I thought of Maman and Papa as bitter tears ran down my cheeks and I shook with sobs. They had loved Yves, too; I wished they could comfort me in my grief.

I whispered to Julien and Pelagie, "You poor children. You won't remember your papa, who loved you so much. His life, since we arrived in France, was nothing but worry, stress, hopelessness, and hard work, until his poor, tired body gave out. He worked himself to death for us. And you'll probably never know your grand'maman and grand-père."

Then, hugging my two youngest children tightly, I took a deep breath, wiped my tears, and thanked God that Yves and I had decided to move to Poitou. Maman, Papa, and Yves wouldn't be there, but at least I would have family to help me, lots of family.

Days and weeks crept by slowly as the boys did odd jobs every day in exchange for flour for our bread; our good neighbors shared the little they had with us. I was still lost, going through the motions of living, but I managed to get through each long day, comforting the children as much as I could and doing what was necessary for survival. I spent my nights tossing and turning, unable to sleep, often sobbing all night. I couldn't pray, I couldn't eat, I couldn't sleep, I couldn't think. Looking around the church at Sunday Mass a few weeks later, I thought of the many Acadian families who had lost loved ones, and how they somehow managed to go on. Many of the ladies in church were widows, and they were coping; I prayed for help and strength.

Later that week, I received a message from Gregoire. "Come to Poitou with us. We'll all help you as much as we can. Don't forget, Acadians take care of their people."

"We must go," I told Marguerite. "We'll be with family again." So in the spring Marguerite, the children, and I sailed with a large group of Acadians. I hated to leave Yves buried in Megrit, but I had to do this for our children.

A large group of Acadians arrived in Châtellerault, looking forward to this new venture with hope. Everyone was talkative and happy, knowing this could be the chance we had been waiting for. Gregoire and Daniel met us and brought us to a building where their wives and children were waiting.

It was wonderful to be with my brothers again, to meet their wives and children, to hug, shed tears, and yes, even laugh. I felt warm inside for the first time in months. I don't remember ever seeing my children so happy. For the first time in years, they were surrounded by loving aunts, uncles, and cousins.

I thought I couldn't be happier, until my favorite cousin Françoise rushed in to hug me. We had many things to talk about; so many years had passed since we last saw each other.

"Is life here as good as we were promised?" I asked Gregoire when we had a few minutes alone.

"No, but we hope it'll get better," he said. "Only thirty houses were built when the first group of fifty families arrived. There are over 350 families here now and still very few houses."

I sighed. "I don't think I can take any more bad news. Where are we going to live? I thought a house would be ready for us."

"We thought that, too, but for now, most of us are living here in Châtellerault or other villages around Poitou, in temporary shelters, barracks, warehouses, and a few houses. Some unfortunate people have to live far from Poitou, where the rent is expensive. Everyone is helping to build houses; when that's finished, we'll start clearing the land and planting crops."

I looked around, suddenly realizing that some of the family was missing. "Where are Oncle Augustin and Tante Anne? Didn't you say they're here?"

"They were among the first Acadians to sign up to move here, so Tante Anne already has a house and Oncle Augustin's will soon be finished. Did you know that Oncle Augustin has four children now? We'll visit them later today, after you have rested a little."

I couldn't wait to see the new Acadian settlement that was supposed to be what we had all dreamed about, what we had prayed for, what would change our lives. We rode in a horse-drawn cart down a new road lined with neat houses. "This is called the King's Highway," said Gregoire. The bottom four or five feet of each house was stone, and above that wood and clay. The roofs were thatched with straw.

"Look at the big houses!" said Julien.

Gregoire smiled. "They're certainly bigger and nicer than anything we've lived in for a very long time."

We stopped in front of an unfinished house on a nearby street. Two people dropped their tools and rushed over to greet us. I fell into Oncle Augustin's arms, and then hugged his wife, Tante Marie-Madeleine. "I'm so glad to see you again. It seems like forever since we've been together."

"Let's sit down so we can visit for a few minutes," said Tante Marie-Madeleine.

"This house looks too big for just one family," I said.

"They're all the same size," said my uncle, "two rooms with a fireplace, a storeroom, a barn, and a shed, all for one family. Yours will be the same. We were also given animals, tools, and seeds."

I could hardly believe it. We had been in France for fifteen years and had always lived in tiny sheds and huts. I could hardly wait for my house to be built. It was wonderful to have something to look forward to again.

Much too soon Gregoire said, "We'd better let you get back to work. We'll be here to help tomorrow, and we'll visit on Sunday. Come, Pelagie, there's someone else you must see; then we'll go back to Châtellerault so that you and Marguerite can get settled."

We returned to the completed houses on the King's Highway. "I want you to see who lives here," said Gregoire, bringing the horse to a stop. He knocked, and a lady opened the door. She looked familiar, and when she cried, "Pelagie," I recognized Papa's sister Tante Anne. She had been working on her loom and had bread baking in the fireplace oven. The smell made me hungrier than I had been in a long time. After a few minutes, she said, "Let me go next door to get someone else you'll be happy to see."

A lady who looked a few years older than I (but it was hard to tell because we all looked older that our actual ages) walked in and hugged me with tears running down her cheeks. I didn't recognize her until she said, "I am Marie-Marthe, daughter of your Oncle Paul."

This was my cousin who survived the sinking of the ship *Duke William*, the only one in her family who didn't drown. I hadn't seen her since we left Île Saint-Jean when I was fourteen years old. We hugged and cried, and hugged some more. Then we sat and talked about the last eighteen years.

"Tell me," I begged, "what happened to you and your family."

With tears in her eyes, Marie-Marthe said, "When the English officers and soldiers came to Île Saint-Jean after the fortress at Louisbourg fell, we were forced to board the *Duke William*. Along with ten other ships, we sailed on November 25, 1758. I heard several sailors complaining that it was a dangerous time of year to cross the ocean, but they had to follow orders.

"The *Duke William* was the largest of the eleven ships, carrying almost 400 Acadians. The *Violet* was the next largest, with about 300 passengers. On the third night out, there was a terrible storm with sleet and violent winds. The only thing we could do was sit in the hold below deck and pray. We were tossed around from one side of the ship to the other, but the *Duke William* seemed to be strong."

I squeezed Marie-Marthe's hand as I relived the storm my family went through when we crossed the ocean to France. "I can still hear the howling wind and the pounding of the waves during our crossing," I said.

"After two days the weather improved a little," continued Marie-Marthe, "but the rest of the ships were nowhere to be seen. At the end of the following week, we came upon the *Violet*. When our ship pulled up close, their captain said they were taking on water, and their pumps were no longer working. Our guards were watching the other ship, and didn't realize, or didn't care, that the Acadians were on deck watching, too. The *Violet* was leaning, and after another violent squall, we stared in horror as the ship sank, taking all of the passengers and crew with her. There were a few cries, but everything and everyone just seemed to be swallowed up by the water."

Marie-Marthe shuddered as I wiped my eyes. "How terrible! I can't imagine seeing that happen," I said.

"They all drowned," said my cousin, "and there was nothing anyone could do to save them. To our shock, it wasn't long before the *Duke William* began to leak. All of the passengers, both men and women, helped the crew pump out the water. After four days we realized there was no hope for us. The *Duke William* was going to sink; we would soon be trying to survive in that icy water."

"Oh, Marie-Marthe, that had to be horrible, just waiting to die."

"By that time, there was much confusion. Some passengers were crying; all were praying and searching for people in other parts of the ship. I was frantic. I had been so busy doing what I could to keep the

Duke William from sinking, helping wherever I was needed, that I didn't know where my family was. They were somewhere on that ship, but it was a very dark night, with pounding rain and a strong wind. I don't know how it happened, but I was pushed into a small boat. I felt very much alone. We were drenched and freezing. I wondered if it would have been better to stay on the ship and drown quickly, instead of what was sure to be a slow death on a little boat in that vast ocean—nobody knew how far from land.

"The *Duke William* sank the following day, and our little boat reached England one day after that. I don't remember anything. I don't know who was on the lifeboat with me, or what happened. I heard later that only one other lifeboat made it to land; there were a total of twenty-seven survivors, but no one else in my family. The *Ruby*, another of the nine ships that left Île Saint-Jean, also sank, and over one hundred Acadians were lost."

We cried together, and then prayed for each member of her family—her husband, parents, three brothers, six sisters, a niece and nephew—and for Oncle Abraham, his second wife, seven children, and a granddaughter, who were also on one of the ships.

"Have you managed to find any peace and happiness?" I asked.

"It's been difficult," said Marie-Marthe. "For several years, I woke screaming every night, as I dreamed of the ships sinking, hearing the cries of the people. I always woke up shivering uncontrollably, both from fright and reliving the dreadful cold of the wind and water. But then I met Nicolas Albert, who is now my husband. He's a good man, and with his help I have finally accepted the trials that God sent to me."

That night after everyone was asleep, I thought about the family I had lost and the sufferings of our people. Everyone had lost family—to death, or scattered so far we couldn't find them. I thanked God for His blessings. I had my seven children, my sister, Marguerite, and my brothers, Gregoire and Daniel. King Louis XV understood our sufferings and wanted to help us by providing our subsidy. He also wanted to give us land so we could grow food for ourselves. I prayed that our lives would improve someday.

Marguerite, the children, and I were given a place to live with several other families in an old warehouse, but we were happy with that. We were used to living in sheds and knew this was only temporary; our house would soon be built. We had to pay rent, but we were luckier than the unfortunate families who lived miles from our worksite in Poitou, whose rent was very high.

We spent our days helping to build the remaining houses for the first fifty families that had arrived. The children and I were content because the future looked bright and we loved living near family.

Besides building houses, we cleared a small area of ground where we planted vegetable seeds. It was exciting to see the first leaves appear and watch them grow, until one day my plants turned yellow and no matter what I did, they all died. All of my neighbors' vegetables died, too. We had thought the soil was good, but it wasn't. And we didn't have enough water for our plants.

Still, I refused to give up hope. This had to work. We had nothing else to live for.

41

Another Decision

May 1774 was a month of joy and sorrow. My last gift from my beloved husband, our son John-Marin, was born on May 2, five months after Yves's death. He was a beautiful, healthy, happy baby, and I spent as much time as I could rocking and loving him, knowing I wouldn't have any more babies.

A few weeks later we learned that King Louis XV had died on May 10. He was our beloved king, our protector; I feared what our future would be without him.

The month that began with such joy with the birth of John-Marin ended in tragedy. My little Pelagie, who had reached her second birthday in February, died on May 29 and was buried the following day at St. Jacques Vienne Church in Châtellerault. Once again the pain was agonizing. I didn't know how I could go on living without my precious little girl; it was even harder because Yves was not there to grieve with me. But, as before, I knew I had to go on for the rest of the children.

Without the healthy lifestyle we had in Acadie, many infants and children were dying, including my brother Daniel's four-year-old son. My children had little time to get to know their cousin Daniel-Henry before he was suddenly gone. I feared for my little Jean-Marin. Would he survive?

While visiting me a few weeks later, Gregoire paced the floor. "Everyone I've talked to is afraid our next king won't treat us the way King Louis XV did," he said. "And it seems that we are correct. Before we moved here, the minister of finance promised that this land would be ours in a few years, and we would receive letters of guarantee soon after we arrived."

"Won't that happen?" I asked.

"No. Now we're told we won't receive title to the land until 1793, twenty years from the time we arrived! And our property will be under the feudal system."

I gasped. "But we thought we would only have to pay rent to the marquis for five years, and then the houses and land would be ours. We were told we wouldn't have to pay taxes to the government for thirty years. We'll owe much more than we were promised."

Gregoire nodded. "I'm afraid so. We don't know yet how much of our grain will be collected for rent, or how high our taxes will be for the church and the government. But it may be a large portion of what we grow."

"What will we do?" I asked.

"I don't know. Many of our people are tired of promises that are never fulfilled. They're refusing to clear land or plant more crops until we have title to the land."

* * *

By the end of July 1774, three hundred sixty-two Acadian families had arrived in Poitou, but fewer than fifty houses had been completed. We were all disappointed and disillusioned. I often heard the same question, "Why did we expect this project to work, when none of the others have been successful?"

Because of poor soil and lack of water, all of the vegetables in our gardens died in 1774, and again the following year. "I had so much hope," I said to Marguerite, "and everything is dying. What are we going to do?"

Everyone just sighed and shook their heads in disbelief.

By January 1775, when every Acadian family in Poitou was supposed to have its own house and a legal title to its farm, only fifty families lived in newly-built houses. Little land had been cleared.

"Why has this happened?" I asked Gregoire.

"The only thing we've been told is that prices for material continue to rise. The marquis can't get a loan from the government or anyone else, so he can't afford to finish the houses."

"And our rent continues to go up," I said, "so we're getting deeper and deeper in debt. We haven't received our subsidy in months. We'll be ruined!"

"Yes, all of us will. I don't know of any families that aren't in trouble. A Frenchman named M. Dubuisson who has a large farm in northern France recently visited a friend nearby. M. Dubuisson said this project will never work. Many Acadians believe it was a mistake to come here. They're hoping to go to Louisiana where many of our people live."

I shook my head. "Nothing will ever make me cross the ocean again. Even if everyone else leaves, I'm staying here."

Gregoire smiled. "We'll see."

Conditions continued to get worse. We wanted to work, but many Acadian farmers were afraid to, because the French people, our neighbors, were jealous. They worked hard, yet lived in poverty, and thought it wasn't fair for us to receive a subsidy—at least some of the time—when they never did. They didn't understand that King Louis XV had tried to help us because of all the troubles we had been through.

My sister, Marguerite, married Joseph Precieux in February 1775. They lived in a building close to us, but it was strange not being together. Except for the six months when Yves's and my home was our fisherman's hut, Marguerite and I had never been separated since she was born. I wanted her to be happy. She deserved to be happy, but I missed her very much.

After Mass one Sunday, Oncle Augustin invited me to his house along with Gregoire, Daniel, Tante Anne, Marie-Marthe, Marguerite, and our families.

As I walked into his house, I said, "It's good that you have a house, Oncle Augustin; we wouldn't all fit in our small section of the warehouse."

Oncle Augustin smiled, and then turned to the group. "Four convoys have been scheduled to bring everyone to Nantes—everyone who wants to leave. We'll be near the sea again so we can catch fish to feed our families, and not have to rely on vegetables that won't grow in the soil we're given. Do all of you want to leave?"

"I'd like to stay here," said Marguerite's husband, "but only fifty-eight houses have been completed, and they're telling us the marquis has run out of money. What are the rest of us, more than three hundred families, supposed to do? Continue paying high rent until we die?"

"I'm ready to get back to fishing and sailing," said Gregoire. "I was only six years old when we left Pigiguit. If we had stayed there, I'd be a farmer now, but I didn't have a chance to learn much from Papa before we left."

"What about me?" asked Daniel. "I was only two years old. We tried to grow crops during the five years we lived in Île Saint-Jean, but our land wasn't fertile, so I know next to nothing about farming. Only twenty-five of the Acadian men who moved to Poitou signed up as farmers; the rest are seamen or carpenters. It's no wonder we couldn't make this work. The organizers assumed that because we're Acadians and our ancestors were farmers, we'd be successful."

"Our troubles are not just because few of these Acadians are farmers," said Oncle Augustin. "I had a very productive farm in Acadie. But even though farming is in my blood and I've tried my best to grow vegetables, I can't do anything with rocky, dry soil."

* * *

The first Acadians departed from Poitou at the end of October 1775, sailing up the Vienne River to the Loire River. By this time I had almost given up hope that someday our lives would be better, but a tiny voice inside told me to continue to dream.

As my family and I left Poitou the following month, I looked around one last time. I had arrived so confident, looking forward to a nice house, land for farming, tools, and animals; that was everything we needed, except for fertile soil and water for crops. Unfortunately, we couldn't make anything grow in rocks.

My children and I sailed on the second convoy on November 15. We were joined by Marguerite, Daniel, Gregoire, Oncle Augustin, my cousin Françoise, and their families. I thanked God that I was with the closest members of my family. I needed to be surrounded by them so that, together, we could face whatever was in store for us.

I cried as I left my little daughter Pelagie buried in Châtellerault, but I knew there was no future for my family there. I prayed for the twenty-five families that had decided to stay in Poitou; since they were all farmers, maybe they would be successful. I prayed that life in Nantes would be better than anything we had experienced in France so far. If only I could provide enough food, warm clothes, and a place to live, my children and I would be happy. I prayed to Yves to intercede for us; maybe he could help us more from heaven than he had been able to on earth.

I knew I had to be patient and trust God and Yves while I waited to see what would happen next.

42

Nantes

We crowded the deck as we sailed down the Loire River. The water ahead of us was crammed with ships, large ones with two or three masts. "Look!" shouted Julien. "There must be hundreds of ships."

"Yes," said a Frenchman who stood nearby. "We're arriving in Nantes; it's a large city and a thriving port. The ships bring goods to and from eighteen manufacturing plants in Nantes. We even trade with America, the Indies, and Africa."

"What's made in Nantes?" I asked.

"Lots of products—cloth, pottery, steel, varnish, glass, rope, starch."

"Whoever heard of cloth being made in a factory?"

He smiled. "Many things will probably surprise you in Nantes."

Julian pointed to the shore. "Are those castles or palaces?"

The friendly Frenchman shook his head. "Neither. They're the ship owners' houses. Lots of money can be made by trading with other countries."

"I've never seen a house that big," said Julien. "Ship owners must have large families."

When we left the ship we were brought to a small hut. Since that was what we were used to, I didn't mind even though I hated having to pay high rent for it. I didn't want an immense house like the ones we saw along the riverfront, but I often thought of the house I was supposed to own in Poitou. That would have been nice, but it wasn't meant to be.

Soon after we arrived, our family had to face another tragedy; Marguerite's husband died from influenza. They had been married only a year and struggled to make a living, as all Acadians did, but they seemed to be happy. It was a terrible shock; she was alone again, so soon, and all of her dreams were gone. My dear sister moved in with my children and me again. I wished the circumstances had been different, but I was happy to have her back.

By March 1776 two hundred sixty-four Acadian families had arrived in Nantes from Poitou and Châtellerault. They settled in fifteen different church parishes around the city. Marguerite went to market one morning to buy flour, returning home very pale.

"What's wrong?" I asked.

She sighed. "Smallpox. Even with a medical school here, epidemics are a big problem. Diseases are probably carried by sailors who get sick after stopping in foreign ports. Remember the large number of Acadians who died of smallpox and other illnesses when we were brought here from Louisbourg?"

I shuddered. "Yes, including our poor little brother, Pierre. I'm afraid for Jean-Marin. He's so little; the very young and the old seem to die more often during epidemics."

"We'll do everything we can to keep all the children well," said Marguerite.

So many relatives and friends had died since my family had left Pigiguit. We had always been happy there, working, loving God, visiting family, singing, dancing, and laughing. In France we spent as much time as we could with family, but we never sang, danced, or played music. I couldn't remember the last time I had laughed. We lived with stress, constantly worrying about our children; we didn't have steady jobs or enough food. It was a sad life.

During one of his visits, Gregoire paced the floor. "Some of our people sent a petition to King Louis XVI to ask him to allow us to go to Louisiana. With taxes so high, we've all borrowed more money than we'll ever be able to repay. We must do something."

"But what?" I asked.

"I don't know. We can only hope and pray that someone will have an answer, and soon."

* * *

In the morning of the third day of June 1776, Jean-Marin whimpered softly when he woke up. He was pale and his skin almost burned my hand when I touched him. Marguerite and I spent that day and the next sponging him with cool water, but he was too weak to survive. Once again, my pain was almost unbearable. My baby was gone, and I felt that my heart had been ripped out of my body. I wished Yves had been with me so we could have comforted each other, but then I was happy he didn't have to suffer the loss of another child. I was numb, and didn't know if I would survive. But I had to pull myself together one more time for my children.

I couldn't think of any Acadian family in France that hadn't lost at least one child. I shed many tears, prayed for strength, hugged my children a little tighter than usual, and went on.

My oldest son, Jean-Guillaume, now a sailor working on a trading ship that traveled to other ports in France, often brought news from sailors returning from across the ocean. "The American colonists who helped England remove the Acadians from Acadie are now fighting *against* England to gain their independence."

My children, especially Julien, listened wide-eyed. "The colonists who fought the French when Maman was little?" he asked.

Jean-Guillaume nodded. "Yes, they've been ruled by England since they settled in the American colonies. Now they want to be independent and make their own laws. They rebelled against the high taxes imposed on them to help pay England's debt; much of the debt was a result of the battles the English fought to win control of land from the French."

One morning our neighbor Marie Girouard told me she had been exploring Nantes and wanted to show Marguerite and me some of the interesting places she had found. "You must see the gardens first," she said. "Medical and surgical schools were opened years ago, and the Garden of Pharmacists provides plants which are used to teach the students how to make different medicines. A French law requires the captains of trading ships to bring back seeds and plants from all foreign ports they visit. Plants from all over the world grow here, but you'll probably want to go to the public gardens to see magnolias first."

"What are magnolias?" I asked.

"Beautiful, large white flowers that grow on trees with shiny dark-green leaves; they were brought from land near the southern end of the Mississippi River."

"Where's the Mississippi River?" I asked.

"That's the exciting part. It flows into the Gulf of Mexico between Louisiana and the English-controlled land. When I look at a magnolia tree, I think that our Acadian relatives could be standing in the shade of another just like it."

Marguerite and I went to the public garden with Marie later that day. I couldn't stop looking at the tall magnolia tree with its beautiful flowers, as I thought about the Acadians who lived in Louisiana.

I was amazed at other things I saw as we walked around Nantes. It was hard not to stare at the men dressed in silk suits and white stockings who walked along the streets carrying gold-headed canes. "It's whispered," said Marie, "that these men are planters from Santo Domingo. They're supposed to be so well-off and their clothes are so expensive that they send them home to Santo Domingo to be washed, because the water there is so clear and pure."

We saw dresses made of beautiful cloth of countless colors. I thought of the effort it would take for me to make such cloth on a loom, even if I had the many shades of thread, and this was made by machines!

We stopped to look at great buildings built on the edges of the wharves, and carriages pulled by horses. "They are hired by people who can afford to pay for them," said Marie.

* * *

For over ten years, Acadians now living in Nantes had received letters from relatives who had spent years in the American colonies after deportation from Nova Scotia in 1755, and had finally arrived in Louisiana beginning in 1764. Our priest read one of the letters to us:

We miss Acadie but we have a good life in our new land. The Spanish government helped us get settled, and we are happy. Our soil is fertile, our farms are productive, we have plenty to eat, and our children are healthy again. We work hard, worship God, and have time to enjoy life. You must join us in Louisiana.

"Since Poitou didn't work out, we'll have to find a way to move to Louisiana," said Oncle Augustin. "That's the only way our children will have a better life."

Gregoire agreed. "From the many letters we've received from relatives and friends urging us to find a way to join them there, life in Louisiana must be better than this."

My children looked at me and nodded in agreement. Their excitement finally began to make me change my mind. "If everyone I know is determined to leave France, I'll probably have to go with you," I said one day. "But why do the Acadians talk about the Spanish officials helping them to get settled? I thought our people wanted to go to Louisiana because it's controlled by the French."

Gregoire said, "Before the end of the war between England and France, King Louis XV knew France could not win. To prevent England from taking control of Louisiana, he secretly gave it to his cousin King Charles III of Spain."

* * *

Toward the end of 1776 Jean-Guillaume came home from one of his sailing trips shouting, "You'll never believe what's happening in the American colonies now." We all stood still and looked at him, waiting for him to go on. "English troops were sent to America. At first there were a few minor battles, but that soon turned into war. Then on July 4 the colonists declared that they are independent and are no longer controlled by England!"

"Can they do that?" I asked.

"I've never heard of any country ever declaring its independence before. They have been fighting for over a year, and the war is still going on, but America seems to be winning."

In 1778, Jean-Guillaume brought the news that France had joined the American colonies in their fight against England. "France has been sending guns for some time, but now they're also sending troops and money. The ambassador to France from the colonies, Benjamin Franklin, helped convince King Louis XVI to fight with the colonists."

"But," I said, "when I was a little girl in Pigiguit, the American colonies fought *with* England *against* France. They helped the English deport our people. Why is France fighting with the colonists now?"

"The French government wants to defeat England. They're willing to help one former enemy if they can defeat another former enemy."

I shook my head. "What a strange world we live in."

The years passed slowly. It was a time of waiting and hoping to find a way to move our families to "*Nouvelle Acadie.*" I still didn't want to cross the ocean again but I realized I might have to for the sake of the children. I often wondered if any of our relatives were living in Louisiana. Two of Papa's sisters, Tante Judith and Tante Claire, had stayed in Pigiguit when we left for Île Saint-Jean in 1750. Unless they had escaped to Quebec, they had probably been deported to the American colonies. They could have made their way to Louisiana with hundreds of other Acadians.

I had promised Papa I would look for my lost relatives. I could only hope and pray that I would find some of them in Louisiana.

43

Waiting

Our subsidy had been cut in half—when we received it. We often heard whispered comments made by the people of France that their country would not be so deep in debt if it were not for *those Acadians* and the money that was being spent to fight with the colonists in the American Revolutionary War. How long would it be before our subsidy would have to be cut off altogether? How would we survive? Would King Louis XVI find a way to send us to Louisiana?

Returning from a sailing trip in 1779, Jean-Guillaume announced, "Spain entered the war for American independence and is fighting with the colonists and France—against England."

"Let's hope that helps to end the war," said Gregoire. "I don't think France can continue to spend money to help other countries."

* * *

By 1783 our family conversations centered on a man called Peyroux. "He's a Frenchmen who's been living in Louisiana," said Gregoire. "He recently arrived in France and went directly to the Spanish ambassador in Paris with an idea that could affect us."

"How?" I asked.

"Spain wants colonists in Louisiana to help protect its land from England. The leaders have been sending men there who don't know how to farm, giving them slaves to do their work. Peyroux's plan is to send *us* there instead. The rumor is that the Spanish ambassador liked this idea and will present it to the Spanish king, Charles III, if Peyroux gets our people to sign a petition asking to go to Louisiana."

"Yes," said Daniel. "Oliver Térriot, an Acadian shoemaker here in Nantes, is helping Peyroux. Térriot asked me to sign the petition, but I'm afraid to. If King Louis finds out about this, he might be so angry that he'll completely cut off the little help we're getting from France."

Jean-Guillaume nodded. "That's what I've heard many Acadians saying; they're afraid to do anything that might anger our king."

"But this might be the way for us to get to Louisiana," I said.

Daniel sighed. "We have to be careful."

Later in the year Daniel brought the news that only Térriot and four other Acadians had signed the petition. "But Peyroux sent it to the Spanish ambassador anyway. And the ambassador sent it to King Charles."

"How could he send it to the king?" I asked. "What will he think of us—only five signatures from several hundred families. I'm afraid the Spanish government won't be interested in working with us."

* * *

"The war in America is over!" shouted Jean-Guillaume as he dashed into our little hut at the end of 1783. "The peace treaty was signed in Paris in September. We won't have to worry about war when we live there."

"If we ever *get* there," I said.

Early in 1784 Daniel's news was even better. "Oliver Térriot received word from Peyroux; King Charles still needs colonists to help protect Louisiana from the English. He's willing to send us *and* pay for us to get settled near the Mississippi River."

"We're going to Louisiana!" shouted Julien, jumping from his seat near the fireplace, where he was making a net.

Daniel smiled at him. "Térriot has permission to tell the Acadians, but this has to be our secret. King Louis doesn't know about these plans yet. We can only hope he'll agree to let us go."

"Surely he'll be glad to get rid of us," said Julien. "He'll save lots of money."

As we waited, we heard many concerns that Acadians had about this venture.

"What about the money we owe, for rent and to merchants? We're all so deep in debt; surely King Louis won't allow us to leave without paying," said our neighbor M. Pitre.

"None of the other plans the government had for us worked. Why should this?" asked M. Bourg.

"I don't want to go all the way to Louisiana to starve to death. I'd rather stay here and take my chances," said M. Comeau.

Gregoire paced the floor as he told my family the latest news. "With all the uncertainty, a group of Acadians went to the French delegate in Nantes to ask if the French king will allow us to go to Louisiana and if Peyroux has permission to make plans for us. They should have waited for the Spanish officials to ask King Louis's permission for us to leave. He's sure to be angry and deny us now."

Things got worse. "Landlords and merchants refuse to give any more credit to Acadians with the promise that we'll pay when we can," said Daniel a few days later. "They're afraid we'll leave the country without paying our debts."

"What are we going to do now?" I asked.

He just shrugged and walked away.

A few weeks later Gregoire and Daniel ran into my hut with big smiles. "Good news from Oliver Térriot! King Louis will allow us to leave France because King Charles of Spain requested it. The Spanish ambassador's secretary advised us to send a petition to the French king, asking him to forgive our debts so we can leave for Louisiana. Peyroux is writing the petition."

"I'll sign this one," said Daniel.

Gregoire nodded. "So will I."

After sending the petition with thirty-five signatures, Peyroux received word that King Louis agreed to pay all our debts to the merchants and landlords.

"Thank God," I said. "Everything is working out well. This must be God's will for us."

Whenever groups of Acadians met, excitement surrounded us. People smiled and talked about the letters that continued to arrive from relatives and friends, telling how happy they were in Louisiana. We finally had something to look forward to. Remembering the first time I crossed the ocean, I dreaded doing it again, but I knew I had no choice; this would be for my children and the grandchildren I would have someday. Our lives *had* to be better in Louisiana. Didn't some of the letter writers call it *The Promised Land?*

By the end of May, Peyroux was given permission to get signatures of all Acadians who wanted to leave France for Louisiana. On August 10 he wrote to the Spanish ambassador saying that over thirteen hundred Acadians from Nantes and Paimboeuf wished to start a new life in America. The head of each family signed or put a cross next to his or her name. Peyroux promised to visit the towns surrounding St. Malo, where Acadians lived, to get more signatures.

The final number of individuals who hoped to travel to Louisiana was 1508. Peyroux hoped the first group of Acadians would sail at the end of 1784, but he still had to get bids from ship owners for the cost of transportation to New Orleans. This included food, water, coal, and vinegar for meals and disinfecting the ships.

One morning, Gregoire's wife, Marie-Rose, and my sister, Marguerite, baked bread while I knitted a pair of socks. Looking at the sock in my hand, I sighed. "I've dropped so many stitches, I'll have to rip this and start over again."

Marguerite laughed. "That looks like my first sock when you taught me to knit. What's wrong, Pelagie? You never drop stitches."

"I can't concentrate. The only thing I can think about is our voyage to Louisiana. We could be on a ship as long as three months—and in the winter. I don't think I could bear that."

Marie-Rose nodded. "We should refuse to travel then because of the bad storms in the ocean at that time of year."

"Yes," I said, "we had a terrible storm soon after we left Louisbourg in October. Except for flashes of lightening, it was so dark in the hold I couldn't see my hand in front of my face. The only sounds were the whistling wind, the roar of the water, and the screams of the passengers. And cold—it was so cold that my fingers were constantly numb. And October isn't the worst time to travel. I'm sure none of us will ever forget that the *Violet* and the *Duke William* sank in December."

Marguerite sighed. "Imagine, three months in a freezing, cramped ship! Our voyage from Louisbourg took five weeks, and that was bad enough."

We soon learned we had no reason to worry. The Spanish ambassador notified us that the first ship would sail in the spring of 1785. King Charles III promised to give us fertile land, tools, help building our homes, and a subsidy until we could take care of ourselves.

"It seems that the Spanish king is determined to do everything he can so our venture will succeed," said Gregoire.

I nodded. "I pray that it will."

44

Saying Goodbye

"Hurry, Julien," I said. "If we don't reach the dock before the Acadians board the ship, I might never see my brother Daniel again."

"But, Maman, we're sailing to Louisiana next month. We'll see him then."

"We can't be sure that's going to happen."

I hadn't swallowed a bite of my breakfast of day-old bread. I thought of the day we were forced to leave Louisbourg in 1758—twenty-six-and-a-half years before—when we were separated from Maman and Papa. Even though I had never stopped looking for them everywhere we lived and asking everyone I met, I hadn't been able to find them. I still didn't know if they were alive or dead. Would I lose touch with Daniel and Gregoire too when they sailed away?

"Come on, little brother, we're waiting for you," said Jean-Guillaume. He was standing near the gate with his brothers and sisters—François-Louis, Françoise-Pelagie, Marguerite-Perinne, and Yves-Jean. "Maman, everyone is excited about going to Louisiana; I heard that many more Acadians recently signed up for the voyage."

We greeted our neighbors as we hurried down the lane. It seemed that every Acadian in Nantes wanted to say goodbye to our people who were leaving on the first ship, *Le Bon Papa*. Even though almost all of us were scheduled to sail later in the summer, maybe, like me, they were afraid they'd never see their relatives and friends again.

The ship swayed gently as sailors loaded the clothes and household goods the Acadians were taking with them. They would travel down the Loire River to Paimboeuf and from there into the Atlantic Ocean.

Each family stood next to a small pile of mattresses, sheets, blankets, and trunks. Although every passenger was allowed to take a trunk, most families could put all their possessions in one or two. A little ache in my throat reminded me how sad it was to own so little after twenty-six years in France.

Near the dock, Daniel paced up and down. Henriette rubbed her arms as if she were cold. Their daughter, Henriette-Reine, stood quietly, staring at the water. Almost seven years old, she looked lost and scared.

I hurried up to them, hugging my brother for a long time. "Daniel," I said, but it sounded more like a sob, so I cleared my throat and tried again. "Daniel, how can I let you go? I've lost so many members of my family; I can't bear to lose you, too. It's hard to believe you were just ten years old when we left Louisbourg. I helped to raise you, and since you're grown, you've always been here when I needed you."

"Pelagie, my dear sister," he said, "I don't want to leave you, but I must go. I have to provide a better life for Henriette and our daughter. You'll join us soon. I'll never forget how you took care of me when we were deported from Acadie. You were only seventeen but you were a mother to me. We've had a hard life since then; it *has* to get better. *Adieu* (farewell), dear sister. Be as brave as you've always been. Pray for our safety, as we will pray for yours."

I hugged my sister-in-law, trying to contain my tears. Then I held my niece close and was rewarded with a slight smile when I whispered in her ear, "You're lucky. You're going to Louisiana first, so you'll find the best place to live."

With another hug for everyone, Daniel, Henriette, and Henriette-Reine were gone.

I stood near the dock with my children and my sister, Marguerite, and managed to say goodbye to everyone boarding the ship. Hugs and tears were plentiful, but smiles were few.

"I know the adults must be thinking about the terrible voyage when we were forced to come to France from Acadie," I said. "They're not in a hurry to travel across the ocean again."

Nearby, two Acadians in charge of the group had a list of the people assigned to *Le Bon Papa*; they checked off names as people boarded. One of them said, "Thirty-nine families, one hundred sixty-five people, were assigned to this ship. Three families are missing." He looked around and called the names, but no one responded. He shook his head and said, "We can't wait for them. Maybe they'll meet us in Paimboeuf."

As soon as everyone was on board, the ship sailed slowly toward the mouth of the river. We watched until we could no longer see the top of the white sails fluttering in the gentle wind. It was a beautiful day but no one seemed to notice. We were all deep in our own thoughts as we prayed for their safe journey. I walked home slowly with tears streaming down my cheeks. Would I ever see Daniel and his family again?

A few days later I was removing rocks from the ground that was supposed to be our garden. My efforts were a waste of time because the soil was hard and dry. Nothing grew there; nothing was ever going to grow there.

I heard footsteps and then, "Bonjour, Madame Crochet."

I looked up to see M. Olivier Terriot hurrying down the lane. I wiped my hands on my apron. "Good morning. Won't you come inside? It's so good of you to come. You must be very busy."

"Yes, my family will sail in a few days on the ship, *La Bergère*. I just received a letter from my cousin, who was deported from Acadie to New York and has been in Louisiana since 1767. He owns land and animals; his farm and garden provide grain, fruit, and vegetables of all kinds, enough for his family. He said the heat is terrible and the work never ends, but they are happy."

M. Terriot smiled. "In case I don't see you at the dock before we leave, I wanted to say good-bye and assure you that life will be better for us in Louisiana. You've made the right decision for your family. And, of course, everyone will help you get settled."

* * *

We continued to join the large number of Acadians who bade farewell to each departing group. Arrangements had been made for seven ships to sail to New Orleans. The third ship, *Le Beaumont*, was supposed to sail on the twenty-seventh of May but was delayed for two weeks because of unfavorable winds. One family canceled their trip and hundreds of Acadians begged to take their place.

A few days before the third ship sailed, I visited Gregoire. "None of our relatives were on the second ship," I said, "and I don't think any are scheduled for *Le Beaumont.*"

"No," said Gregoire. "But the *St. Remi. . .*"

"Please don't remind me. I know you're sailing on June 27."

"We have to go," said Gregoire. "I can't feed my five children here, and they're excited about sailing."

"Our dear cousin Françoise is also sailing on the St. Remi," I said. "Except for my children and Marguerite, Marie-Marthe will be my only family left in Nantes."

"We'll see you soon in Louisiana, Pelagie."

"Not soon enough. Our voyage has been postponed until August."

After Gregoire and his family sailed, I felt lost, just as I had when we arrived in Rochefort so many years before. My insides ached and I couldn't eat. I had a long wait before I would see my brothers again—if I ever did. The first ship, *Le Bon Papa*, had left France just three months before our ship was scheduled to leave, so I knew we wouldn't hear from any of the travelers until we reached Louisiana.

* * *

Since it would be a long time before I would be able to provide clothes for my family again, I filled my days with sewing and making cloth on a neighbor's loom. I also walked around Nantes, knowing I would never visit France again.

At the beginning of August, François-Louis twisted his cap as he sat at the table with me. "Maman, I've decided to stay in Nantes. I can get enough work on trading ships to support myself, and maybe a family someday. I don't want to be a farmer in Louisiana."

"Oh, François-Louis, am I going to lose you too?" I thought my heart would break, but my son was twenty-three—old enough to make his own decisions. Since I couldn't convince him to sail to Louisiana with us, I could only hope and pray that he would have a good life in France.

On August 12, my thoughts were with the Acadians who were departing from St. Malo on *La Ville d'Archangel*. This ship sailed to Nantes and Paimboeuf to pick up more passengers, then across the ocean to Louisiana.

When August 20 finally arrived, my stomach was in knots. I hated to leave Yves, Jean-Joseph, Jean-Marin, and my daughter Pelagie buried in France, but I had no choice. Saying good-bye to François-Louis was terrible, knowing I would never see him again. I took several deep breaths, trying to calm down before leaving our hut, but I soon realized I was the only one dreading the voyage.

Even though I felt very old at times, I was only forty-four. We had left Acadie for Île Saint-Jean thirty-five years before, and it was almost twenty-seven years since we had been forced to leave Louisbourg.

Jean-Guillaume, at age twenty-four, and seventeen-year-old Yves-Jean couldn't wait to cross the ocean, because they had worked on boats since they were old enough to follow Yves to work. Although the girls, Françoise-Pelagie, age twenty-one, and Marguerite-Perrine, nineteen, hated to leave some of their friends in France, they were looking forward to life in Louisiana. Julien, my youngest who was already fifteen years old, was so excited he couldn't keep still. Over and over he ran to the door saying, "Hurry, Maman, or they'll leave us."

We had packed everything for our journey in two small trunks. The one containing extra quilts and our few pots and dishes would be stored in the hold of the ship. The other trunk held quilts, sheets, towels, and an extra set of clothes for each of us; we would keep this one in our sleeping quarters.

Our ship, *l'Amitié*, waited at the dock for us. It rocked slowly in the water as its white sails waved in the breeze. Sailors loaded boxes and barrels of food and baggage, and made other last-minute preparations for the long voyage across the ocean.

"Look at the ship!" shouted Julien. "Jean-Guillaume, aren't you glad we're going to sea on a ship that big?"

"It would be big for a handful of fishermen and lots of dried fish," said Jean-Guillaume. "But with two hundred seventy passengers on a voyage that could take up to three months, it doesn't look so big."

The dock was crowded with Acadians who were planning to travel to Louisiana later in the year on the last ship, and wanted to see us off. I barely had time to say good-bye before we were told to board. As I left the dock, I thought of my long-ago voyage to France, when I was pushed into the hold, which was so crowded we had to take turns lying down at night.

"Maman, come see where we're going to sleep," said Julien.

The small sleeping quarters would be shared with several other families. "Cots," I said. "So this is where we'll put our mattresses. It's crowded, dark, and there's no privacy, but there's room for all of us to lie down at the same time. It might not be too bad."

I went out on deck to wave to our fellow Acadians on the dock. The captain raised a small flag and fired a shot to announce our departure. The sailors unfurled a topsail and raised the anchor. I gazed at the shore, watching the scenery, as our ship moved slowly down the Loire River past Paimboeuf, into the Bay of Biscay, and then into the Atlantic Ocean.

Marguerite stood beside me. As I looked back with tears in my eyes, she asked, "What's wrong, Pelagie? Are you sad to leave France?"

I shook my head. "No, but it's hard for me to leave François-Louis alone with no family, and Yves and my children—Jean-Joseph, Pelagie, and Jean-Marin—all buried in France. I'm also grieving for poor Oncle Augustin. He went through so much—losing three children on the terrible voyage to France; then his first wife and their fourth child died soon after they reached France. He was captured by the English and was in prison for three years. He looked forward to a better life in Louisiana. Unfortunately, he died less than two years ago, and his second wife, Tante Marie-Madeleine, died a short time later. I wish they had lived long enough to settle in Louisiana."

Marguerite hugged me. "They're at peace. They'd want you to look forward, not back."

* * *

"Good morning," said the captain as he came out on deck. "We're on our way to Louisiana."

"How long will it take to get there?" asked Julien.

The captain smiled. ""It depends on the wind. We're prepared for three months, but we hope to arrive in New Orleans sooner."

I remained on deck all afternoon as we sailed west. The air smelled clean and fresh, the ocean spray tasted salty on my lips, and a warm breeze ruffled my hair and skirt. A few clouds spread across the blue sky as the water sparkled in the sun. I took a deep breath, closed my eyes, and prayed. *Dear God, I'm not asking for anything for myself. I'll do my best to handle whatever problems you send me, but please make the lives of my children better. Give them a taste of the joy I had in Pigiguit. And please show me that we're doing the right thing—if this is Your will for us.*

After a long time, I opened my eyes and gazed at the sky, hoping for a sign. Up ahead were some thick clouds that seemed to be guiding us on our way. Suddenly, I saw what I had been hoping for. The sun was hidden by a large, dark cloud with bright, shining edges—a dark cloud with a beautiful silver lining. I fell to my knees with tears of joy streaming down my cheeks, and said out loud, "Thank you, God. Now I know this is what You planned for us. And thank you, Papa, for showing me that I'm doing the right thing. I'll look forward to a better life in Louisiana."

This move to Louisiana must be the silver lining Papa had often told me I would find someday when I needed it. "Even if it seems that your life is nothing but misery and sorrow," he had said, "keep praying and working hard, and someday you'll find that silver lining."

45

Another Ocean Voyage

After almost two weeks on the ship, I was finally accustomed to the constant swaying and the ringing of the ship's bells as the sailors changed shifts. One morning as Julien and I finished our breakfast on deck, Jean-Guillaume passed by. "Julien," he said, "I hoped I'd find you here. Come with me; look at the sailor who's holding that log. It has a weight attached to one end, and a rope with knots the same distance apart tied to the other end. Watch what he does." The sailor threw the wood into the water behind the ship.

"Why did he do that?" asked Julien as he rushed to the railing.

"The captain wants to know the speed we're traveling. As the ship moves faster, the sailor will count the knots as he lets out more rope. Another sailor with a sandglass will watch the time. They'll figure out our speed by the number of knots they let out in thirty seconds."

"I think I'm going to be a sailor," said Julien. "I watched them use a compass yesterday so they could be sure we're going in the right direction, and I saw the ship's boy turn the sand-glass to keep track of the time of day."

"When we get to the Mississippi River," said Jean-Guillaume, "you'll see how they figure out how deep the water is."

A few days later as I sat on my mattress mending a shirt, Julien burst into the makeshift room that was our sleeping quarters. "Julien, what are you doing?" I cried. "You know you shouldn't run on the ship. You could lose your balance, fall, and break your neck."

"Maman, come quick. Françoise-Pelagie and Marguerite-Perinne, you'll never believe it. Hurry!" He dashed out again as we stared at each other, then followed him.

When we reached the top deck, sailors were rushing around, shouting. "Captain! Captain Beltremieux, over here!"

Other sailors and male passengers surrounded a group of dirty, tired-looking men as Acadian mothers watched from a distance, holding the hands of their young children to keep them from getting too close. When we approached, Françoise-Pelagie gasped loudly while Marguerite-Perinne stopped in mid-step, appearing pale enough to faint. I looked from them to the men, then said, "Oh, no! It can't be."

Several passengers pointed, whispering, "Stowaways!"

A man said to anyone who was listening, "They hid in the hold behind boxes and barrels of food. They probably would have stayed hidden longer but the cook found them when he needed more flour."

Before I could stop my daughters, they pushed their way into the middle of the group of men, calling, "Joseph, Léonard." Tears ran down their cheeks as they reached two men whose faces suddenly lit up with smiles.

I shook my head. "Joseph? Léonard?" I said. "But how? And why?"

The captain reached the group and spoke to two sailors. "Bring the men down to my cabin along with the leaders who were chosen by the Acadians." He nodded to the rest of the crew. "Back to work. I'll talk to them individually and decide what to do."

They disappeared down the ladder and the rest of us were left with many questions. Françoise-Pelagie and Marguerite-Perinne, along with several other Acadian girls, couldn't stop smiling. They walked to the railing and stared at the water. Others milled around, talking softly, often glancing at the girls.

"Did you know about this?" I asked my daughters.

They both shook their heads, and replied, "Non, Maman."

After what seemed like forever, the captain returned to the deck followed by the stowaways and the Acadian leaders. He looked around and smiled. "Mesdames, Mesdemoiselles, don't be afraid. Your leaders know these young men and vouch for their good character. According to each of the stowaways, on this ship is a young lady who is very dear to him. They feared that, even if they sailed to Louisiana later this year, they might never see their beloved again. They were all willing to take the chance of being arrested.

"Since the Acadian leaders have assured me there is no danger, I'll allow the young men freedom on the ship. When we arrive in New Orleans, I'll turn them over to the Spanish authorities who will decide what action to take. Thank you for your understanding." He tipped his hat. "Good day."

With sighs of relief, two of the young stowaways left the group and joined our family near the railing of the ship. My daughters were crying again, but smiling through their tears. Françoise-Pelagie stood next to Léonard, and Marguerite-Perinne next to Joseph, as close as they could without touching. They couldn't take their eyes off each other.

"What are you doing here?" I asked.

"Madame Crochet," said Léonard, "you know the two of us have been courting your daughters for months, but without jobs we couldn't ask them to marry us. I decided I couldn't let Françoise-Pelagie leave me to move across the ocean."

Joseph nodded. "Even though we might have been able to sail on one of the other Spanish ships to Louisiana, we couldn't be sure we would find your family. So we hid until we were too far from land for the captain to turn back to France."

I almost smiled. "I guess I can understand that since I searched for my parents for twenty-six years without ever finding them or anyone who knew them. But what if the Spanish authorities punish you, or send you back when this ship returns to France?"

"We decided we had to take that chance. Otherwise we might never see our loved ones again," said Léonard.

For the rest of the voyage the girls walked on the deck with their young men as often as I allowed them to. They looked happier than I'd seen them in a long time.

* * *

When we lived in France, my work had never seemed to end—trying to grow vegetables, cooking, cleaning, sewing, spinning thread, making cloth on a neighbor's loom, and many more tasks. On the ship, our food was provided and I had little to do besides mending, knitting, and keeping our sleeping area neat. My sister, Marguerite, and I spent much of our time visiting with friends. With nearly three hundred Acadians on board, and freedom to move around as much as we wanted, there was always someone to talk to.

I was especially glad that my cousin Marie-Marthe was on this ship and also Jean-Charles, the brother of my favorite cousin, Françoise. Since Jean-Charles was five years younger than I, I'd never spent much time with him, and I was happy to get to know him and his family.

I rarely saw my sons. The two oldest, Jean-Guillaume and Yves-Jean, were seamen; they spent all of their time with the sailors, raising and lowering the sails, helping to raise the anchor, and mending the sails. Since they had traveled to different ports in France but never across the ocean, they seemed to enjoy the work, smiling a lot, even though they usually looked exhausted. Julien, my youngest, spent most of his time watching the crew work, and helping them whenever he could, running errands and assisting the cook.

Our sleeping quarters were small, with just enough room for our mattresses and those of several other families, but my children had never lived in anything except tiny sheds. They didn't complain, but I still reminded them that this was better than my first voyage. "When your papa and I were deported from Louisbourg," I said, "many people were crammed into each section of the hold. We were only allowed to go up on deck for a short walk every day. We were prisoners, and that's the way we were treated."

We enjoyed eating our meals on deck when the weather was pleasant, but we soon found our daily diet tiresome. "Maman," said Julien one day, "I want some of your soup. I'm sick of breakfasts of ship's biscuits, cheese, and dried fish. For dinner we have dried fish, dried beef, or beans and rice, and then more beans and rice or sweetened plums and rice for supper—day after day, week after week. And we could be on this ship for three months!"

I sighed. "Julien, you must learn to be thankful for what you have. King Charles of Spain is giving us as much as he can afford. I know you miss having soup and fresh, hot bread. But think about what your papa and I ate on our trip to France—ship's biscuits and dried fish or dried beef and water every day for five weeks. At least we have some variety now—cheese, and sometimes beans and rice instead of dried meat or fish. Be grateful for plums when we have them. And seasonings! Oh, olive oil and vinegar make everything taste so much better. And we have wine as well as water to drink. The Spanish king is treating us well. The sick are given fresh bread and even chicken soup."

Julien stared at me. "How does the cook make chicken soup in the middle of the ocean?"

"Jean-Guillaume told me he carried several cages of chickens into the hold of the ship before we left Nantes. The cook kills the chickens when they're needed to nourish sick people."

Days, then weeks passed as our ship slowly carried us to our new home. Unfortunately, people got sick even though the sailors swept all areas of the ship every day, cleaned with vinegar, and opened portholes and trapdoors to let in fresh air whenever the weather allowed. According to the captain, twenty-seven passengers were very sick and had to be isolated.

Six Acadians died. Following each death, the captain led a service of hymns and prayers, and the body was slowly lowered into the sea. I cried bitter tears each time, thinking of the struggles these people had endured, and their hopes for a better life in Louisiana—and, like Yves and Oncle Augustin, their hopes would never be realized.

Without our usual vegetables, exercise, and hard work, everyone appeared tired and pale. I looked forward to reaching Louisiana and walking on dry land. I didn't know what the future would bring, but I hoped and prayed for the kind of life we had in Acadie. I longed to see the many Acadians who had been deported to the American colonies in 1755 and were living in Louisiana now.

One morning the sky was covered with clouds; those in the front of the ship were dark gray—almost black. I spent the day watching the sky, hoping the clouds would move away, but they didn't. We continued to sail in that direction. "No," I said, even though no one was near enough to hear me. "I don't want to go through another storm at sea."

As the hours passed, the water became dark and angry-looking and the height of the waves continued to increase. Lightening flashed across the sky; thunder rumbled, getting louder as we sailed closer to the storm. Our ship plowed on as the water turned into a forbidding monster that appeared to be alive.

I could hardly stand up when the passengers were told to go to our sleeping areas; I didn't want to leave the deck. I was afraid if I didn't watch the storm, something terrible was sure to happen. Soon the crew was ordered to leave the deck too; that frightened me even more. "Who will sail the ship?" I asked Jean-Guillaume.

"Maman," he said, "do you want the wind to sweep the sailors away, or the waves to wash them overboard, never to be seen again?"

"No, of course not."

The storm lasted all night; no one slept or talked. Sometimes when it seemed that our ship might turn over, someone gasped or cried out, and we often prayed together. My misery brought back our family's terrible voyage from Louisbourg to France—the horrible storm, the sickness, and my little brother Pierre's death. I thought about my cousin Marie-Marthe, who had survived the sinking of the *Duke William* as all of her family drowned; she must be terrified. This storm had to be worse for her than for anyone else on board. I wished I could be near her to comfort her.

"Dear God," I prayed, *"did you keep me in France for over twenty-six miserable years so I would die in the middle of the ocean? Surely you had other reasons for keeping me alive. Please protect us. Give me the strength and courage to survive this storm and whatever storms you send in the future."*

In the morning, the water was calmer and sailors opened the trapdoors. Jean-Guillaume and Yves-Jean left to help clean and sweep the water off the deck. The sun wasn't shining but the sky had lightened. When we were allowed out of our sleeping quarters, the water was light blue again, with whitecaps moving across the front of the ship.

We were still alive! Thank God!

46

New Orleans

After two months on the ship with nothing to see but sky and water, Julien shouted one morning, "Land! I see land!"

"Those are islands," said the captain who was also on deck, gazing into the distance. "In a few days, we'll see America. In a few weeks, we'll be in New Orleans." Finally one morning he announced, "We'll enter the Mississippi River as soon as we check the depth of this passage. We don't want the ship to get stuck, as others have."

Julien, of course, stood as close as possible to the sailors, watching every move they made. As Jean-Guillaume joined his brother, a sailor dropped a rope over the side of the ship with a metal weight attached to the end. "What's he doing?" asked Julien.

"The sailors listen for the sound of the weight as it hits the bottom," said Jean-Guillaume. "Then they measure the rope to see how far down it went. They also check the suet—animal fat—they attached to the weight."

"What's the suet for?" asked Julien.

"When they pull the rope up, they look for sand or small rocks that stuck to the suet. Then they're sure it really hit bottom."

Seeing the captain near the railing, Julien asked, "When will we arrive in New Orleans?"

The captain smiled. "That depends upon the wind. We'll need strong, favorable winds to move our ship a hundred ten miles upstream against the current. I've heard of ships that have made it in five days, while others have taken three weeks. Sometimes captains have to dock on the side of the river for days, waiting for the wind to blow in the right direction."

We were lucky because the wind continuously pushed us along. The deck was always crowded with talkative, laughing Acadians, watching the scenery as we moved slowly toward our new home. After we docked, the captain announced, "My dear people, you are in New Orleans, Louisiana. Today is November 7; we made it in eighty days—a little less than the three months we planned for."

We held hands and thanked God for bringing us safely to America. With a smile on his face and a twinkle in his eye, a man boarded the ship as soon as it was tied to the dock. "Welcome, Acadians. I am Martín Navarro. I'm in charge of finances here in colonial Louisiana and I've been assigned to provide for your needs. I want to remind you of the kindness of our Spanish king, Charles III, who paid your travel expenses and will continue to provide for your needs until you can care for yourselves. He wants good people who are hard workers to live here, and he is confident that you Acadians are the kind of people he needs."

A number of men stood straighter, looked around, and nodded.

"In the last twenty years, hundreds of Acadians have come to Louisiana from the American colonies; they are doing well. Already this year, four ships loaded with Acadians have arrived safely from France; most of the families have selected their land and are getting settled."

Many people looked concerned and a few murmured, "But five ships left France before we did."

"Unfortunately," said M. Navarro, "the ship which left just before yours, *La Ville d'Archangel,* hasn't arrived yet." A few Acadians gasped before he continued. "I know you're concerned, but we know where the ship is. We received a message from the captain; their ship ran aground at the mouth of the Mississippi River four days ago. They've run out of food and many people are sick, but we've sent food and supplies to them. We'll do everything we can to get them here safely.

"Now we have to get you settled. We prepared several warehouses, and we built a large wooden hall to provide more room for you. You'll stay here for a month or so, until you have your strength back and are ready to decide where you want to live. I trust you'll be comfortable, as the Acadians who arrived on the previous ships were."

Several women smiled and breathed sighs of relief.

"Beginning today, the head of every family, male or female, will receive a subsidy of ten sols a day. Other adults will receive seven sols, and children two-and-a-half sols. With this you should buy necessities, such as wood and tools."

"So much money," I whispered.

Navarro continued. "I'll now introduce Pedro Aragon y Villegas, who has been appointed commissioner for the Acadians in New Orleans. He'll see that your immediate needs are taken care of, and when the time comes, help you choose your land and give advice about the houses you will build.

"Because many Acadians on the first ships took sick after their arrival, due to a change of food and climate, we built two small hospitals—one for men and another for women. You'll be more comfortable there than in the city hospital. However, I beg you to obtain permission from the commissioner if you need medical care. The royal treasurer complained about problems when this process is not followed. Thank you for your cooperation. Commissioner Villegas will take you to your lodgings now. Enjoy your supper and get a good night's rest. I'll return in a few days to tell you what you should expect in Louisiana."

It was wonderful to walk on land again after almost three months aboard a swaying ship, and to eat a meal of freshly cooked meat, vegetables, and bread, hot from the oven.

I couldn't stop crying when my brother Gregoire rushed up to hug me. His ship, *St. Remi,* had arrived in New Orleans two months before, but because it was a large ship with many passengers, smallpox and other diseases broke out during the voyage. A large number of people were sick, and twelve died before they arrived in Louisiana. Many other passengers became sick after landing; for the good of all, it had been decided that the group would stay in New Orleans until everyone regained their health. I was thrilled to have time to spend with Gregoire and his family, and hoped to live close to them.

Marie Rose and Gregoire's new baby, Martine, was born soon after their ship docked in New Orleans. My happiness increased when Gregoire told me that my favorite cousin, Françoise, her husband, Honoré Caret, and their son Pierre-Marin, also arrived in New Orleans on the *St. Remi*. It was wonderful seeing them; I looked forward to living close to them and visiting often.

Six families that had traveled to New Orleans on *La Bergère*, the second ship to leave France, remained in New Orleans. These people had been too sick to go to their new land with the rest of their group, but the week after we arrived, they were healthy and anxious to depart.

A few days after our arrival, M. Navarro came to the building that was our temporary home with an announcement. "I've been told about a number of young ladies on your ship who are the proper age for marriage, as well as twelve stowaways who followed the young ladies. Knowing that King Charles desires to fill this land with your people to protect it from the enemy, I won't punish these young men, but will speak to them about their intentions. I'll let you know my decision."

We spent the next few weeks recovering from our voyage, regaining our health, walking around the city, and looking forward to our new lives. We walked on narrow wooden sidewalks near the Mississippi River on our way to Mass at St. Louis Church. We enjoyed standing on the levee and watching the rushing water moving down to the Gulf of Mexico, amazed that we had sailed upriver on that magnificent waterway.

* * *

I learned that my brother Daniel and his family had moved up the Mississippi River to St. Gabriel with almost all of the Acadians who had sailed to New Orleans on the first ship, *Le Bon Papa*. The Acadians on the second ship, *La Bergère*, had moved to La Fourche (the fork). Almost all of the passengers on the third ship, *Le Beaumont*, chose to live in Baton Rouge, while most of those on the fourth ship, *St. Remi*, which was Gregoire's ship, also chose La Fourche.

240

Navarro's next announcement brought bright smiles to my daughters' faces. "I have spoken to the twelve stowaways and also several sailors who want to marry Acadian girls. Some feared they would be unable to find the Acadian ladies if they traveled across the ocean on a different ship. Others were afraid that the young ladies would lose their government subsidies if they married someone who is not an Acadian. I told them, and I'm telling all of you now, I promise to allow the sailors and stowaways to live in Louisiana, and I will give the subsidy for head of family to anyone who marries an Acadian girl. The young ladies will continue to receive their government subsidy of seven sols a day until the families can support themselves.

"Twenty-three young men desire to marry, and the bishop has agreed to dispense with the three banns of marriage so the weddings can be performed and everyone can move to their chosen land. We will enjoy these ceremonies with dancing and games. I will provide beer, cider, and coffee."

Françoise-Pelagie and Marguerite-Perinne burst into tears as everyone around us shouted and clapped. Soon Joseph and Léonard stood next to my daughters with smiles so wide I feared their faces would split. I sighed a great sigh of relief. My daughters would be happy.

It was soon time for the families from our ship to pick men who would inspect and recommend land for our homes. They traveled to La Fourche and suggested that area as a good place for a settlement. There was plenty of available land on the water, many Acadians already lived there and were doing well, and crops were growing. M. Navarro reminded us that our group wouldn't be forced to move together. Each family would be allowed to select its own area to live. The Spanish government wanted us to be happy.

"Nothing would make me happier than to live near Gregoire and his family," I told my children.

"Then that's where we'll go," said Jean-Guillaume. "I think we can make a good living there."

Seventy-one families selected La Fourche, and plans were made for us to leave New Orleans in mid-December. The rest of the families would move later to other areas in Louisiana.

Françoise-Pelagie, Marguerite-Perrine, and I made the few preparations necessary for their double wedding celebrated on November 24, 1785 in the Church of St. Louis. I was thankful that I had made a new dress for each of them during the long months in France while we waited to leave for Louisiana—their only good dresses. We just needed to iron out the wrinkles and freshen their caps.

It was a month of celebration. Every Acadian from France who was still in New Orleans and able to walk, attended the twenty-three weddings, which were held between November 20 and December 19—seventeen from our ship and six from the *St. Remi*. We forgot the sadness of our lives in France and toasted the futures of these young couples, and our own, with hope. We prayed our lives would finally begin to improve.

47

River Voyage

One morning Jean-Guillaume hurried into our area of the warehouse. "Maman," he said, "please come for a walk with me. I must talk to you."

Outside, he said, "Maman, you know that I've been seeing Marie-Marthe Boudrot for some time, and her family was on *L'Amitie* with us. I love her, but since I was unable to find steady work in France, I couldn't provide for her. However, since the Spaniards want more people to populate the area, I can get my own land grant and head-of-the-house subsidy. I've spent many hours thinking about it. Yves-Jean and Julien can farm your land, and if my land is close to yours, we'll help each other and we'll all have a good living. What do you think?"

"I know you're old enough to get married and have your own farm. With your help, I think we'll manage. I can't keep you tied down any more than I could keep the girls from getting married. Go; be happy."

With a smile and a hug, Jean-Guillaume dashed off. Looking over his shoulder, he said, "Thanks, Maman, I'm going to talk to M. Boudrot. Wish me luck."

* * *

The ship that had been grounded at the mouth of the Mississippi River, *La Ville de Archangel,* finally arrived on December 3, its passengers weak and exhausted after one hundred thirteen days on board. It was followed quickly by the last ship, *La Caroline,* on December 17. After M. Navarro welcomed the passengers, those who were well enough joined us in the village camp, which had been set up for the Acadians. We were crowded, but no one seemed to mind because we were overjoyed to be with a large group of relatives and friends.

On December 14, we celebrated the marriage of Jean-Guillaume and Marie-Marthe Boudrot. It was another beautiful wedding, but I had mixed feelings. Only a month before, my five children lived with me, and after three weddings only my two youngest sons were left—Yves-Jean, now age eighteen, and Julien, age fifteen. My heart ached, because even though I hoped we would all live close together, they were no longer mine, but belonged to someone else. I had to remember they were happy at last and had good futures to look forward to, the answer to my prayers. I often wondered how long my two youngest boys would be with me.

Our family celebrated one more wedding. My sister, Marguerite, married Claude-Bernard Dugas, who was also a passenger on *L'Amitie*. I said many prayers for them. Marguerite had spent her life helping me, and she deserved happiness. I also prayed that they would live close to me, because I couldn't bear to lose my sister now.

The day after Jean-Guillaume's wedding, Juan Prieto, who was in charge of the royal warehouse and supplies, entered our living quarters followed by several men carrying large, heavy boxes. "I have tools for you," he announced. Each family was given meat cleavers, axes, hatchets, hoes, spades, and knives, many of the things we would need to begin our lives in this new land. "Boats have been arranged to transport seventy-one families to La Fourche, and also guides, barges for luggage, and deck-hands."

A large number of Acadians from France had already settled in La Fourche, sixty-eight families from *La Bergère*, and three from *Le Beaumont*. They would soon be joined by eighty-five more families from the *St. Remi* and seventy-one from *L'Amitie*, who were ready to leave New Orleans. Anselmo Blanchard had accompanied the families from the *St. Remi* to La Fourche and would remain there as commanding officer. Lieutenant Nicolas Verrett was appointed officer in charge of the area. He would help us choose our land, advise us in building our homes, and provide help when we needed it.

At last the day arrived for us to start our journey up the Mississippi River. Again, we needed favorable winds to push us upriver, but God must have been watching over us because we never had to stop to wait for the wind to blow in the right direction.

Our small boat seemed lost on the wide river that wandered and curved between thick woods on both riverbanks, broken occasionally by small cabins. Since it was December, many trees were bare; however, they were nearly covered with something gray and stringy hanging from the branches. No one from Louisiana was on deck with us, but I knew I had to ask a question—*what is that?*

Early on the second morning a small church surrounded by neat farms and houses attracted our attention. "Is this where we're going to live?" asked Jean-Guillaume.

"No," said the captain. "This community is called the German Coast; there isn't any available land left. Germans were brought here to provide food for the people in New Orleans who don't have enough land to grow crops."

The next day the captain said, "We'll soon see the settlement called the Acadian Coast. The first Acadians arrived from the American colonies in 1764. During the next few years, hundreds more settled here and farther upriver."

"Is *this* where we're going to live?" asked Jean-Guillaume.

The captain smiled. "No, there's no available land here either."

"The crops appear to be thriving," said Yves-Jean.

"Yes, these people have been here long enough to grow almost everything they need, and they can trade for anything they can't grow. Their lives are finally good."

The following afternoon, the captain and deckhands took down the sails and picked up long poles, pushing along land on the side of the river, as our little boat turned south into a slow-moving, narrow waterway. "This is Bayou La Fourche, named because of the fork in the river," said the captain. "The bayou is narrow, and with so many trees along the banks, it's difficult to catch any wind, so we push our way along the bottom with poles instead of using the sails."

"Bayou? What's a bayou?" Julien asked.

"It's a very slow-moving stream which flows in either direction depending on wind and rainfall," said the captain. "Since 1769 many Acadians have moved here from the Acadian Coast, because there's more unclaimed land here. You will see how prosperous their farms are. We'll soon reach the area where you're going to live."

For the rest of our journey, whenever people saw our boat, they dropped their hoes and rushed to the river to wave and shout, "Bienvenu. We're happy you're here."

I wondered if *I* would be happy. I watched the water and the logs near the bank as we floated past. Suddenly, one of the logs moved. When it opened its big mouth and I saw rows of sharp teeth, I shouted, "What is *that?*"

"Oh, just an alligator, madame. If we don't bother them, they usually leave us alone."

Usually, I thought. I was almost afraid to breathe for the rest of our trip, and stayed far from the sides of the boat.

When we docked late in the evening, Lieutenant Nicholas Verrett boarded our boat. "Bienvenu. It's good to have more Acadian settlers in La Fourche. I have arranged for you to stay with Acadians in their homes, or if there isn't room, in their barns until you build your temporary huts. Don't worry—you'll be comfortable. Before you go ashore tomorrow morning, I'll give you more information about life here so you'll know what to expect. You *will* be happy. Have a good night."

My prayer before going to sleep that night was: *God, let this be the place where we'll finally have a better life. Our children have suffered so much and deserve to have the happiness that my family had in Pigiguit. Please bless us and give us peace so we'll have the energy to do good for others. And protect us from alligators. Amen.*

48

Clearing the Land

The next morning I was awake long before the sun began to light the sky, to find many of my fellow passengers already awaiting Lieutenant Verrett's arrival, all anxious to learn more about our future. I was finishing my shipboard breakfast of bread and cheese when the lieutenant came on board and greeted us with a big smile. "Good morning. I see you're ready to start your new life. Each family will receive a land grant along Bayou La Fourche—six arpents on the bayou and forty arpents deep."

Murmurs were heard throughout the boat.

"Why is the French measurement used in Spanish territory?"

"So much land."

"We'll have our own land."

"I hope this is finally a place for us to settle down."

"How will Yves-Jean, Julien, and I farm that much land?" I whispered.

Lieutenant Verrett smiled as he answered questions. "The French measurement is used in Louisiana because their government originally owned this land and gave land grants. Each family will be required to clear and plant at least two arpents, and build a temporary cabin, a levee, and a road along the bayou. If you do that in the next three years, the land will be yours. The Spanish government will continue to help you until you can support yourselves, because we want you to succeed, but you will have to work very hard."

"What's a levee?" asked Jean-Guillaume.

"You might have heard people from Acadie talk about building dikes," said Lieutenant Verrett.

"Yes, Maman told us about the dikes on their wheat farm in Pigiguit. Her grand-père and great-grand-père helped build them when they received their land grants."

"We call them levees; they're needed to protect the land from flooding," continued the lieutenant. "In Acadie, the Bay of Fundy flooded the marshland twice a day at high tide. The farmers wanted to use the land for their wheat fields, so they built dikes. But since the floodwater was salty, they built gates, called *aboiteaux*, under the dikes. The gates opened to let rainwater flow into the bay, but they didn't allow the saltwater to flow from the bay to the land.

"Don't worry," he said. "Your job will be easier. You'll build levees but you won't need the gates, since your land doesn't have to be drained. Your neighbors will show you how to build them."

"Is this land fertile?" asked Yves-Jean. I smiled because he already sounded like a farmer instead of a sailor.

"Yes, the land near the bayou is rich, and your crops will thrive."

"What about the rest of the land?" asked Jean-Guillaume.

"In two or three years, you'll have a temporary home, a levee, a road, and a small plot of land to grow vegetables. Then you should clear more land to plant crops to feed your family and some to sell in New Orleans. The land farther back from the bayou doesn't drain well enough for growing crops, but it's a good place for farm animals to graze in the underbrush. Behind that is swampland, where you can hunt wild animals for food, and use their fur for trading."

Jean-Guillaume nodded at his brothers. "*All* of the land is useful."

Lieutenant Verrett continued. "The Spanish government hopes to keep families together as much as possible, so in a few minutes those who have relatives nearby will leave the boat. You'll select your land and start to clear the trees and brush with the help of your neighbors."

M. Verrett pointed to the land where we were docked. "This is Gregoire Benoist's land; farther south is forestland waiting to be chosen. Gregoire's sister and the adult members of her family will choose the first land in order to be near their relatives."

"Oh, I can hardly believe it," I murmured. "I'll live near Gregoire and his family again."

The lieutenant smiled at me. "Yes, Madame Crochet, if that meets with your approval, your family may leave the boat now. Josef de la Puente, one of our guides, will accompany you to your brother's land, and I'll go with the rest of the passengers a little farther down the bayou so they can choose their land. I'll come back later to see how you're getting along, and give you your supply of food."

"Merci." I quickly went ashore with my five children, two sons-in-law, one daughter-in-law, my sister, Marguerite, and her husband, as the deck hands removed our mattresses, trunks, and other baggage from the barges. I stopped walking, looked around, and sighed. "I know I should be happy to own this land, but how are we supposed to grow crops here? The trees, brush, and vines are so thick, we can hardly move. This will never work."

Jean-Guillaume looked at me. "Maman, did you see how well the crops are growing all the way down the bayou? We know the land is fertile, and not dry and barren like the land we tried to farm in France. We'll pray and do our best."

I shook my head and smiled. "You're wiser than I am, son."

Since we had docked very close to Gregoire's land, it didn't take us long to find him. He and his family were hard at work building their first cabin in Louisiana with the help of several Acadian families who had been passengers on *La Bergère*, which had arrived in New Orleans three weeks before Gregoire's ship.

Gregoire and his wife, Marie-Rose, hugged us and introduced the neighbors who were helping them. After greeting us, Jules LeBlanc put his ax down and wiped his forehead. "We arrived here two-and-a-half months ago," he said. "All of us who sailed on *La Bergère* already have a temporary cabin and a small vegetable garden. We're helping the Acadians who recently arrived on the *St. Remi*, and then we'll help you."

I smiled at him. "Merci. We'll be happy to have your help. But now we'd better walk around and choose our land."

A short time later I thought I would never stop smiling because my prayer was answered. Going down the bayou our families would live as follows: Gregoire; my daughter Françoise and her husband, Léonore; my two unmarried sons and I; my daughter Marguerite-Perinne and her husband, Josef; my sister, Marguerite, and her new husband, Claude-Bernard; and my son Jean-Guillaume and his wife, Marie.

When I pictured my family as my neighbors, I thought I couldn't be happier until Marie-Rose said, "Pelagie, I can't wait to tell you who lives on the other side of us."

I took a deep breath. "Can it be my cousin, Françoise? I know she traveled on *St. Remi* with you."

"Yes, it's Françoise. I knew you'd be thrilled."

I couldn't say a word as tears of happiness rolled down my cheeks, and I whispered a quiet prayer of thanks.

After watching Gregoire's family and their neighbors for a few minutes, my children knew what they had to do. "We'll build your cabin first, Maman, so you won't have to sleep in the barn many nights," said Jean-Guillaume.

My new life was beginning! My sons and sons-in-law used their axes to chop down trees while the girls and I pulled up underbrush and vines. By the time we had a clearing big enough for a temporary cabin, it was getting dark and Gregoire called us. *"Viens ici. Regarde ma maison."* (Come here. Look at my house.) It was small but would be enough for his family until they had time to build a larger cottage.

We went to Jules LeBlanc's cabin for supper. His neighbors brought platters and dishes piled high with meat and vegetables that smelled so good my mouth began to water. I almost burst with happiness when my cousin Françoise and her husband, Honoré, joined us. We could have talked all night, but we had to stop long enough to eat.

Home-cooked food tasted wonderful after our months on the ship. I had much more to talk about with Françoise, but I was so tired I could hardly keep my eyes open, and was happy when M. LeBlanc brought us to his barn. "You may sleep here for a few nights until you finish building your cabin. I'm sorry we don't have room for you in our cabin, but we built it quickly, as you will, and it's very small."

"Your barn is larger and looks more comfortable than some of our huts in France," said Julien.

M. LeBlanc chuckled. "That's true." His children followed us into the barn, their arms loaded with the gray, stringy plants that hung from most of the trees. "What *is* that," I asked.

This time he laughed out loud. "It's moss. Acadians call it Spanish moss because it reminds us of the Spaniards' beards. It is used for stuffing mattresses, cushions, and pillows. It makes a comfortable bed, and I don't think we'll ever run out of it."

"How will we ever get two arpents cleared for a cabin and crops?" I asked. "This land is covered with underbrush, trees, vines, and bushes."

"You're right. It looks like an impossible job, but did you see the Acadian Coast as you came up the Mississippi River?"

"Yes, it's a clean, neat settlement. And it looks prosperous."

"Those Acadians are doing well, but it took determination and lots of hard work," said M. LeBlanc. "When they arrived, the land looked just like yours. Each farmer had to do what we will do—clear at least two arpents, build a cabin, plant vegetables and corn, and build a road and levee. They did that and more, just helping each other. They'll tell you that ten years after they arrived, they had as good a life as they did in Acadie—as many animals and the same amount of crops."

Jean-Guillaume nodded. "We're willing to work; no, we're *eager* to work. After our years in France, we're ready to prove that we're not lazy; we just didn't have fertile land. We want to show the Spanish king that he didn't make a mistake by bringing us here. We *will succeed*."

I smiled. "Once more, son, you're proving that you're wiser than I am."

The next morning after a quick breakfast of bread and milk, we gathered our tools and walked to our land. *Our land,* I thought. But when I looked around, I was overwhelmed—again. "How are we going to do this?" I whispered.

"Maman, didn't the first Acadians have to clear their land the way we're going to?" asked Julien.

It had been years since I'd thought about the stories Grand-père told me before I left Pigiguit when I was nine years old. "My great-grand-père and great-grand'maman sailed to Acadie from France in 1671. Most of their land was covered with trees, but they didn't want to cut them down for their farms because the Mi'kmaq Indians hunted and trapped in the forest. The Acadians wanted to use the marshland near the water for their farmland. But to do that, they had to build high dikes, drain the land, and wait for the rain to wash away the salt that was left by the water from the bay. They also had to build houses and plant vegetables and wheat."

"They did as much work as we'll have to do," said Julien.

"Yes, I'll keep reminding myself that the Acadians who arrived here before we did will help us. Our ancestors made a good life for themselves and we can too."

I started pulling up small bushes and underbrush, and soon had a pile almost as high as my head. It wasn't long before several small boats arrived, carrying Gregoire, Honoré, Jules LeBlanc, a few other neighbors, and their sons. They climbed out of the boats, their arms loaded with tools. "Bonjour," said Jules. "Gregoire has a cabin to live in and a small bit of land cleared to plant vegetables, so we're ready to help you."

"We're happy to have your help," I said.

"More Acadians probably will move here, and you'll help them, I'm sure."

We worked until we heard voices on the bayou, and saw a group of ladies and girls in boats. They pulled to shore and joined us with their arms laden with food—pork, beef, carrots, turnips, and greens. They spread the food on a cloth in a spot with enough room for us to relax and eat. I didn't realize how hungry I was. Madame LeBlanc passed around a plate of something yellow and slightly brown on top. "Try the cornbread," she said.

"We ate some in New Orleans," I said, taking a piece. "But I thought you'd make bread out of wheat—the kind Acadians are used to eating."

"No, this is made of ground corn," said Madame LeBlanc. "You've probably heard that wheat doesn't grow well here, but corn does. The Spaniards gave us seed corn so we can grow our own. Friends of ours who live on the Acadian Coast taught me how to make cornbread. It's different from the bread made with wheat that we used to eat, but we like it. Try it."

Julien took a big bite and smiled. "Good," was all he said as he finished that piece and took another.

The rest of us enjoyed it too, and I asked Madame LeBlanc to teach me how to make it. "I will, as soon as you have a little free time," she said. "You must also try this fruit, called oranges, because of their color."

"Juicy and sweet," said Julien, and we all agreed.

We were soon back at work with the help of the ladies and girls. By the time I thought I would drop from exhaustion if I had to pull one more vine or drag one more branch to the huge pile near the bayou, Madame LeBlanc said, "We've done enough for today, and it will soon be dark. Some of the ladies and I will leave to prepare supper. Everyone, please come to eat with us."

I breathed a sigh of relief as I watched the men gather their tools. We had a nice space cleared near the bayou. "This should be enough for a cabin the size of Gregoire's and a small garden," I said.

Jules LeBlanc nodded. "Yes, we'll build your cabin tomorrow. If everything works in our favor, you'll sleep in it tomorrow night."

That was the best news I'd had in a long time. As I fell asleep in the barn that night, I couldn't stop smiling. A cabin of my own—at last! I was too exhausted for a long prayer, so I just said, "*Merci, mon Dieu.*"

49

My Cabin

Even though I was exhausted, I was too excited to sleep well. The last time I could say *my house* I was only seventeen years old, when Yves and I lived in our cozy little fisherman's cottage in Louisbourg after we were married. That had been twenty-seven years ago, and we lived there for just six months before our nightmares began, and we were deported to France.

The men and boys who had worked so hard the day before, helping us clear the land, soon joined us along with Gregoire's wife, Marie-Rose, my cousin Françoise, and many of the neighbors' daughters. "While the rest of the ladies prepare dinner for all of us," said Marie-Rose, "we'll show you how you can help with your cabin."

"We have a pile of trees that we cut yesterday, but we'll need more," said Jules LeBlanc. Soon the sound of axes and saws rang through the forest as some of the men cut small willow trees and others hammered them into the ground, standing on end side by side after the boys stripped the branches from them. My girls and I helped other boys weave the smaller branches crossways through the poles to hold them together.

We didn't stop until the ladies brought dinner. I breathed a sigh of relief as I sat on the grass near the bayou and leaned against a tree. "Oh, it feels so good to relax for a few minutes. This is hard work!"

Jules LeBlanc nodded. "Be glad we're doing this during the winter. My cousin, who lives on the Acadian Coast, arrived at the beginning of summer and did all of this work in the summer heat. He told me there's nothing like Louisiana's heat and humidity. We haven't felt it yet, since we arrived just a few months before you did."

When it was time to get back to work, Madame LeBlanc said, "Pelagie, instead of helping the boys with the walls, we should cut palmetto fronds for the roof while the children collect moss for your beds. Be sure to watch for snakes when you're walking through the woods. We probably won't see any alligators."

I shuddered. "I hate snakes. They also live in Acadie and in France, but we rarely saw them. An alligator was in the bayou on our trip here, and I don't want to see any more of them."

Jules LeBlanc smiled, "Don't worry; they're more likely to be in the water or the swampy area than this dry land."

Just as I thought I would collapse from exhaustion, we put the last palmetto frond on the roof, and our temporary cabin was finished. From the outside it looked similar to an Indian hut. I walked inside, looking at the dirt floor and the rough walls with no windows, but I couldn't have been happier. It was a place to live, and it was mine!

Everyone waited outside for me. "What do you think, Maman?" asked Julien.

I smiled at my family and new friends. "It's wonderful! It reminds me of the hut my papa built when we arrived in Île Saint-Jean when I was nine years old. It is nicer and will be a lot more comfortable than some of our huts in France. Not as nice as Yves's cottage in Louisbourg where we lived after we got married, but I like it."

"We'll build a cottage for you, bigger and better, as soon as we have time," said Jean-Guillaume. "But we have a lot to do before that."

I hated to leave my new cabin, but we had to eat supper, and Yves-Jean, Julien, and I had to collect our clothes and other belongings so we could settle down in our own home. I slept better that night than I had in years.

Early the next morning we were back at work. Jean-Guillaume, my sister, and my two daughters needed their land cleared and cabins built. We were so busy that we didn't hear Lieutenant Verrett's boat when it docked near our land. "Bonjour," he called. "I see you've been working very hard."

I smiled and nodded. "Yes, you must come to see my cabin."

"Let me get your food first." He went back to the boat and returned with two of his men who carried heavy-looking boxes. "This should be enough until I come back in a few weeks. I brought food for each family."

The men carried the boxes inside. I hurried to open them and was delighted with what I saw. "Smoked ham, dried beef, cabbage, carrots, turnips, and greens. What a treat!"

"I'll bring your animals the next time I come. You should be ready for them by then."

"Animals, too?" I asked.

"Yes, we'll give each family six hens, a rooster, a cow, and a calf. We want to help you until you can care for your family yourself."

I couldn't stop smiling. "Then we'll have butter, cheese, and eggs. The Spanish king promised to take care of us, but this is far more than I had hoped for."

After many long days my sister and each of my married children had a cabin and a chicken coop, and we had an outside oven that we could all use. But we still had no time to rest because we couldn't forget the long list of things we had to do before the land would be ours.

"The first thing each of you should do is clear enough land for a vegetable garden," said Jules LeBlanc. "It will soon be time to plant spring crops so you can start eating your own food in a few months. Since my group arrived at the beginning of October, we planted carrots, cabbage, and mustard greens as soon as our cabins were completed. It will probably be close to two years before we can supply all the food we need, but it feels very good to eat vegetables from our own garden."

More trees had to be cut down, more vines and underbrush removed, but each family finally had a small space cleared for a garden. On one of his visits to see how we were getting along, Lieutenant Verret brought vegetable seeds for us to plant as soon as the ground was ready.

"What kind of seeds do you have?" I asked.

"I'm sure you're familiar with string beans and peas."

I smiled. "I helped Maman plant and harvest those when we lived in Pigiguit."

"Yes," he said. "We ate lots of beans and peas in Acadie. I'm also going to give you seeds for vegetables and fruit you've probably never eaten—lima beans, collard greens, sweet corn, pumpkins, and squash. You still have time to plant mustard greens, and you can plant sweet potatoes soon. I'll give you cantaloupe and watermelon seeds too. You should also plant grape vines. I think you'll enjoy all of this good food."

We had enough to eat since we still received supplies from the Spanish government, but I remembered the joy of harvesting our own food in Pigiguit, and I couldn't wait to pick vegetables and fruit from my garden. The soil was rich and water was plentiful; I knew my plants would grow and provide us with an abundance of food. I smiled, thinking about having all we wanted and not limiting portions, so everyone in the family could grow strong and healthy.

While I planted vegetables and fruit, the men built a levee with a road alongside so wagons could travel from one farm to another. Not that any of us had a wagon, but the Spanish government required a road before the land would be ours.

We walked wherever we wanted to go, and the Acadians who had lived along Bayou La Fourche for several months paddled their boats down the bayou to visit. I wasn't in a hurry to have a boat, because except for my brother Daniel, all of my family lived on either side of me. But I hoped that someday soon, when we finished the biggest jobs, my sons would build a boat so we could visit Daniel.

I was always busy. Gregoire had made a small loom for Marie-Rose, and Honoré had made one for Françoise, and they let me use them as often as I wanted. A trader came down the bayou from the Acadian Coast every week or so, and whenever I had a few extra eggs, I traded for cotton. His wife came with him a few times to teach us how to remove the cotton seeds from the bolls, spread the cotton out slightly, put a small piece on the spindle of the spinning wheel, and then twist and twist until a thread began to form. It took a while for us to learn how to get the thread even, instead of in clumps, but once we learned, we used the thread to make cloth on the loom.

Finally we could make sheets, towels, and covers for pillows and mattresses, which we would stuff with moss after we cleaned it. That was another thing we had to learn—to pile up the moss and soak it in water for about six weeks until it lost its gray covering, leaving the strong inside strand that would withstand lots of use.

I fell into my bed of moss at night, exhausted but happy. I had so much to be thankful for. I had a small but comfortable cabin to live in. My children, sister, brother, and favorite cousin lived close to me, and we could visit often. We had enough to eat, and would soon be eating food from my garden. I enjoyed visiting with my neighbors and working with them. Since they all spoke French and the ones my age and older had all lived in Acadie, we had much to talk about.

I still missed François-Louis, who stayed in France, Yves, my deceased children, and my lost relatives. Having them with me again was the only thing that would have made my life better than it was.

50

Adapting to a Strange, New Land

Shortly after we arrived, Jules LeBlanc invited us, along with our neighbors, to a get-together on Saturday evening. "We'll meet in my barn. It's big enough for all of us."

Everyone brought food; we sang and danced as several of the men played their fiddles. It reminded me of get-togethers we had when we lived in Pigiguit; I had always looked forward to Saturday evenings. It was a time to spend with our neighbors, relax, and have fun after working hard all week. I had missed this when we lived in France, but we didn't have the time or energy for dancing.

"Do you get together to pray on Sundays?" I asked.

Jules LeBlanc nodded. "Come back tomorrow morning; we'll say prayers and sing hymns. There's a Catholic Church, Ascension of Our Lord, on the Mississippi River. A missionary priest travels up and down the river to say Mass, baptize babies, and bless marriages that have taken place since his last visit. I hope he'll have time to say Mass here several times a year."

When I wasn't spinning, making cloth on my new loom that the boys made for me, or sewing, I was cooking, baking, or making butter and cheese. I had to plant vegetables, weed the garden, make candles, and clean the hut. My family and neighbors often helped with these chores. We talked, laughed, and sang as we worked.

The men were constantly busy outside, building a barn and fences, working on the levee and road, cutting trees, and clearing land to plant cotton and additional corn. Somehow they found time to make a table, benches, and a bed for me, so we would be a little more comfortable.

One evening when Yves-Jean came in for supper after a long day in the fields, I said, "You're working too hard; you look exhausted."

He wiped his sweaty forehead on his sleeve. "We want enough corn to trade for more cows, pigs, and chickens, and I know you need more cotton for your sewing projects."

"Yes, we need so much now. It seems that it'll take forever to get everything done."

"Maman, we'll just keep working. That's all we can do."

Just as our ancestors had adapted to their new land when they left France and learned to make a good living in Acadie, we slowly adapted to our land in Louisiana. The men provided extra food by hunting ducks and geese in the marshes. They also trapped animals for food and their fur. The young people helped with the work in the house and garden from the time they were old enough to understand what needed to be done. They spent their free time fishing and catching crabs in the bayou.

Since we were so busy, time seemed to fly. My sister and I sat near the bayou one evening watching the sky darken over the water. "Look at my children," I said. "They were so pale and thin when we lived in France, but now they're blossoming with health."

Marguerite nodded. "Yes, they're healthy and happy, as they should be. Their pinched looks have been replaced by smiles and pink cheeks."

"With the food supplied by the Spanish government, the vegetables in my garden, and those given to us by our neighbors who arrived in La Fourche several months before we did, no one is ever hungry. Good food, fresh air, sunshine, and not having to worry about where our next meal will come from have worked their magic. Everyone's happiness seems to grow by the day. I don't think our lives could possibly get better."

I thought my world was complete, but in 1787 Françoise-Pelagie and Léonard had a baby boy, Yves Surge, my first grandchild. Such a joy he was! How I loved rocking him and singing to him! They lived close enough that I could visit them every day. "I'll take care of the baby so you can rest," I'd say. Françoise-Pelagie always gave me a smile, knowing that I was doing it for myself as well as for her.

Soon after this, Yves-Jean married Anne Dugas, who had arrived from France on *Le Bon Papa* and lived with her family on the Mississippi River. After their wedding the couple was given a land grant on the west bank of Bayou La Fourche, across the bayou from us. I missed Yves-Jean, but I consoled myself with the thought that he was happy, and the boys would soon have time to build boats so we could cross the bayou to visit.

By 1788 we had lived on Bayou La Fourche for three years and had completed the work required by the Spanish government, so the land was ours. We were supporting ourselves, growing enough crops for our use, as well as some additional corn that we traded for cows and pigs.

As they had promised, my sons built a cottage for me. I didn't need much room—just Julien and I were left—but I looked forward to having a bigger, sturdier home. When they started hammering a row of small trees side by side into the ground, I shook my head. "This looks like the one you built before. I don't need another cabin."

As usual, all of our neighbors were helping. Jules LeBlanc smiled at me. "Be patient. You'll see that it's different. It will look just like the rest of the new cottages we've built. We'll use two rows of saplings instead of one, and put planks on the outside to make it look like a real house."

"And *bousillage*," said Jean-Guillaume. "It's a mixture of mud and Spanish moss; we'll put it behind the planks to keep the cottage warm in winter and cool in summer."

I smiled at my oldest son. "You sound like you've been doing this forever."

"I've been working and learning. We'll also put windows in the front and back to catch the breeze in the summer, and shutters to cover the windows in the winter. You'll like it."

When my cottage was finished, it was larger than the cabin, and more comfortable because of its windows, thick walls, and roof made of boards. Like the cabin, it sat directly on the ground with a dirt floor, but I was happy. What I liked best was to sit in my rocking chair just outside the front door at the end of the day, watching the sky darken and the stars peek out. I loved to listen to the night sounds, crickets and frogs singing their evening songs. And I enjoyed watching children catch lightning bugs and play tag.

One day as I rocked my newest grandbaby, I looked closely at him; he was pink, healthy and playful. I thought about my own children at his age; they had been pale, thin, and listless. I thought about my babies who had died, and I knew it was only by the grace of God that six of my children had lived to adulthood.

Years ago, in St. Servan in 1764, I had said, "I hope to find a place to live where we'll have lots of family nearby, enough food, a warm, comfortable house, and clothes that aren't so raggedy they're falling off our backs. That would be heaven for me. That's all I want and need."

Another time I had said, "If only I could provide enough food, warm clothes, and a place to live, my children and I would be happy."

My grandson cooed and smiled at me. I looked at him and realized I had everything I had wished for, and much more. At that moment, I was sure I had done the right thing when I made the decision to come to Louisiana. It had been extremely difficult as a widow with a family to leave France, sail across the ocean, and begin again in a new, strange land, not knowing what our life would be like. All I could do was trust in God and the many friends and relatives who had written to the Acadians in France to urge us to join them in Louisiana.

But finally I knew that my children, my grandchildren, and all of my descendants had a bright future in Louisiana. We were happy and healthy. My life was good. I had a comfortable cottage, and family and friends close by. We worked hard but also enjoyed life. Yes, at last I had found my silver lining. Holding the baby very close, I whispered a prayer. *Thank you, Papa, for telling me that if I prayed and worked hard, I would find my silver lining. Thank you, God, for all you have given me. You have truly blessed my family.*

Epilogue

Pelagie Benoist, a strong and courageous woman, lived a long life. She died in Thibodaux, Louisiana on August 7, 1824 at the age of eighty-three. Her funeral services were held that day at St. Joseph Catholic Church in Thibodaux.

At least twenty-four grandchildren, including one set of twins, and twenty-two great-grandchildren were born during Pelagie's lifetime. Two more grandchildren and many more descendants were born after her death.

Pelagie experienced many changes in Louisiana. The Acadians' cabins and cottages weren't meant to be permanent since they were built quickly for shelter while more important jobs were completed, such as clearing land, planting crops, and building a levee, barns, and fences. After a few years in Louisiana the Acadians had time to build houses that were more comfortable than the first ones.

After 1790 the new houses were similar to the French Creole houses the Acadians had admired when they arrived in New Orleans. Each house, two rooms wide, was raised above the ground for ventilation and for protection from flooding. Windows and doors in the front and rear allowed breezes, which helped to cool the house. A porch across the front, called a gallery by the Acadians, provided a comfortable place to sit and visit as family and friends enjoyed the cool evening air. Along Bayou La Fourche and the Mississippi River, a loft, used as a bedroom for the older boys, was usually reached by a steep set of stairs in a room at the back of the house (unlike the Acadian houses built in western Acadiana, with stairs to the loft on the front porch).

The early settlers in Acadie in the 1600s had had to adjust to a shorter growing season than they were used to in France, and had to learn to build dikes so they could grow crops in the marshland. In Louisiana the settlers adjusted to the heat, the excessive rain, and the types of crops they could grow.

Many other changes had to be made by the Acadian settlers in Louisiana. Since the weather was too hot for them to wear wool clothing except for a short time in the winter, and they couldn't grow flax in Louisiana, they learned to grow and spin cotton for cloth.

Since wheat, oats, and barley didn't grow well in Louisiana, the Acadians grew corn, and made cornbread instead of the wheat bread they ate in Acadie. They had grown turnips and cabbage from spring through fall in Acadie, storing the turnips in their root cellars. They cut the cabbage, turned it upside down, and left it in the fields for the snow to cover and protect it. In Louisiana cabbage and turnips could only be grown in winter, so the Acadians grew and ate more peas and beans. They still enjoyed field peas as they had in Acadie, but added red beans, butter beans, and sweet peas to their diets.

Since the Louisiana Acadians didn't need large flocks of sheep for their wool, they raised only a few, but bred more chickens than they had in Acadie. Despite the difficulty the Acadians faced in clearing the abundance of hardwood trees from the fertile land they needed for planting their crops, they slowly got the work done. After three years in Louisiana, almost all Acadian families had at least two arpents of land that were producing food (as required for their land grants), and several more arpents fenced in for their animals. Whenever they were able to grow more corn than was needed by their families, the Acadians sent the excess to New Orleans to be sold. This allowed them to buy goods they weren't able to produce.

The Louisiana Acadians' usual meal was salt pork, corn bread, and vegetables and fruit that were in season. They also enjoyed eggs, bacon, fish, and wild game. For weekend get-togethers and special celebrations they often made corn soup. Many farmers grew a small amount of rice in case their corn crop failed.

The first Acadians on Bayou La Fourche, who moved there from the Acadian Coast on the Mississippi River in the late 1760s and 1770s, settled on the upper bayou on the west bank because there was less danger of flooding. The Acadians who came from France in 1785 settled on the unclaimed land farther south in the area that is now between Labadieville and Raceland. Pelagie's family, except for Yves-Jean, settled on the east bank.

A 1788 La Fourche census shows that Pelagie, along with Yves-Jean and Julien, owned six arpents of land, twenty-five quarts of corn, and two hogs. By 1791 Pelagie and Julien had twelve quarts of corn, four hogs, and two cows. The other members of her family also seemed to be farming successfully. The following censuses through 1798 listed only names of people.

By 1795 Pelagie had been in Louisiana for ten years. The Acadians in Grand Pre, Pigiguit, and other towns near the Bay of Fundy had been forced to leave their homes forty years earlier. It had been thirty-seven years since the British had captured the fortress in Louisbourg and the Acadians there and in Île Saint-Jean were sent to France. Acadians who were old enough to have owned farms in Acadie before the deportation often told their children and their younger neighbors that their lives were finally every bit as good along Bayou La Fourche as they had been in Acadie. They had cleared approximately the same amount of land as they had farmed in Acadie and owned roughly the same number of cattle and pigs as they had in Acadie.

* * *

Pelagie lived to see many of her grandchildren get married. Unfortunately there were also deaths among the younger members of the family. After losing three of her young children in France, two more of her sons died in Louisiana before she did—Yves-Jean in 1811, and Jean-Guillaume in 1821. One of Yves-Jean's daughters passed away at the age of four months, and one of his grandsons died at the age of sixteen months.

Julien married Marguerite Belanger of Pointe-Coupeé in May 1798. For a short time they lived near Baton Rouge, and then moved to Bayou La Fourche to be near his family.

Pelagie's daughter Françoise was just twenty-six with three young children—Yves Surge four years old, Jean two years old, and Joseph one year old—when she was listed as a widow on the 1791 census. The following year she married Philippe Bruze of Genova.

Pelagie died at the home of her grandson Similien Adam, her daughter Marguerite-Perinne's son. After Pelagie's death her estate listed the following possessions: a feather bed, a straw mattress, a pillow, a sheet, two blankets (one of them old), a mosquito-bar, a basket, four old shirts, a pair of shoes, a dress, two bathrobes, two pairs of stockings, a shawl, one skirt, a small pot, a chamber pot, five plates, a coffee box, and knitting needles—for a total value of fourteen dollars. These goods were sold at public auction for twenty-seven dollars to pay her debt of fourteen dollars for "care and board in the last illness," two dollars and fifty cents to pay for "5 planks which served to make a coffin," one dollar for the auctioneer, and seventy-five cents for rum for the auction. This left eight dollars and seventy-five cents, which may have been her legacy for her family.

Even though Pelagie's material goods were few, her living legacy was large. Her bravery sustained her family through their difficult years in France, and brought them to Louisiana. She was a widow with five children who spent eighty days on a sailing ship, not knowing what their lives would be like when they reached their new land. She lived thirty-nine more years and had many descendants in Louisiana, who now probably number in the thousands. We can only appreciate and admire her courage, and hope that her years here were happy and that she did, indeed, find her silver lining.

Cajun Cabin, Destrehan Plantation, Destrehan, LA

Afterword

The first permanent white colonists in North America were the Spanish, who settled in St. Augustine, Florida, in 1565. The French settled on Sainte-Croix Island, New Brunswick, in 1604; this led to the first permanent French settlement of Port Royal (now Annapolis Royal), Nova Scotia, in 1605. The English arrived in Jamestown, Virginia, two years later.

Because the English rulers wanted the Acadians' land, which was originally controlled by the French, many battles were fought. Sometimes one country was in control, sometimes the other. The Treaty of Utrecht in 1713 finally turned Acadie over to the English, and it was renamed Nova Scotia. France remained in control of Île Saint-Jean (now Prince Edward Island) and Île Royale.

As early as 1713 French officials encouraged Acadians to leave Acadie for French-controlled land. A few moved to Île Saint-Jean to join the first settlers from France in 1720; the migration of the Acadians continued slowly through the 1720s and 1730s. When Halifax was founded in 1749, French officials *urged* the Acadians to leave English-controlled Nova Scotia and move to Île Royale or Île Saint-Jean. The officials promised to supply tools and food for a year, until the families could take care of themselves. Larger numbers of Acadians began moving to Île Saint-Jean because of unrest and threats of deportation when the Acadians refused to sign an oath of loyalty to the king of England.

In 1749 the population of Île Saint-Jean was about 735, and by 1755 it had increased to approximately three thousand. But unlike Acadie where farmers usually had extra grain, vegetables, and animals that they sent to Louisbourg to feed the people in the fortress, the farmers in Île Saint-Jean often had poor harvests and other problems with their crops. With the increasing population in Île Saint-Jean and fewer farmers in Acadie to supply food, the officials in Louisbourg were unable to provide enough food for the people of Île Saint-Jean, leaving many near starvation.

Historians tell us there could have been as many as eighteen thousand Acadians in Nova Scotia in 1749; there were still approximately fourteen thousand in 1755. Following the fall of Fort Beauséjour to the English in June 1755, more Acadians escaped to Île Saint-Jean. In other parts of Acadie, many fled into the woods and made their way to New Brunswick, Quebec, or the fort at Louisbourg on Île Royale. The Mi'kmaq Indians often gave food to the Acadians and helped them hide from the English as they tried to reach a safer place to live. The Acadians continued to flee until *Le Grand Dérangement* (The Great Upheaval) at the end of 1755.

From October to December 1755, at least seven thousand of these French-speaking people were forcibly removed from their homes from the areas around Port Royal (which had been renamed Annapolis Royal by the English), Minas Basin (the area around Grand Pré), Fort Beauséjour (renamed Fort Cumberland), Fort Edward at Pigiguit, and surrounding areas. The Acadians were sent to the following American colonies: Virginia, Maryland, Pennsylvania, Massachusetts, South Carolina, New York, Georgia, and Connecticut.

Thousands died as a result of the deportation, either on the ships or in the following months. There were smallpox epidemics on many of the ships. The governors and the people in the areas where the Acadians were forced to settle didn't want Acadians in their colonies any more than the Acadians wanted to be there. In some of the colonies, the authorities gave Acadians leaky ships to return to Nova Scotia. In others, the people collected money to send the Acadians back to Nova Scotia. Many Acadians made their way to Louisiana after ten or eleven miserable years in the colonies. Others had to remain where they were.

About twelve hundred Acadians who were transported to Virginia in 1755 were sent to England the following year by the governor and council of Virginia. They lived there until 1763, when they were sent to France.

* * *

Before the deportations began, Lieutenant-Governor Charles Lawrence wrote to the British authorities to tell them he planned to remove the Acadians from Nova Scotia. They neither approved nor tried to prevent his actions. Several months later, Lawrence wrote again to inform the authorities that the Acadians had been dispersed. In October 1756 Lord Halifax of Great Britain wrote to Lawrence to commend him and to notify him that he had been named governor of Nova Scotia.

Determined to take control of the entire eastern part of North America following the deportation, the English planned the 1758 attack on the fortress of Louisbourg on Île Royale. That island and Île Saint-Jean were still controlled by France.

The English soldiers also continued to search for runaway Acadians in Acadie and New Brunswick until 1759.

* * *

In the two months after the fall of the fortress at Louisbourg to the English in July 1758, more than three thousand civilians living in Louisbourg were deported to France. Wounded and sick officers were also sent to France while wounded and sick soldiers and sailors remained in the fortress hospital. The rest of the troops were sent to English prisons.

While the deportation of these people was taking place, the English commander of Louisbourg, thinking only a few hundred Acadians lived in Île Saint-Jean, sent five ships carrying five hundred soldiers to the small island. They were to notify the French officers and the Acadians of the defeat of Louisbourg, accept the surrender of the island, build an English fort, and take the Acadians to Louisbourg. From there, they would be sent to France. But with the arrival of many Acadians who had escaped from Acadie, the population of Île Saint-Jean had risen to approximately forty-six hundred civilians.

At the end of August 1758, the first ships left Île Saint-Jean for Louisbourg with nearly seven hundred residents—now prisoners—who were soon deported to France. Realizing that many more Acadians lived in Île Saint-Jean than they thought, the English commanders sent fifteen more ships to transport the Acadians first to Louisbourg, and then to France.

Less than one hundred French soldiers were in Île Saint-Jean at the time the English took over the tiny island. They were sent to England along with roughly three thousand military from Louisbourg and other parts of Île Royale. Some of them remained in England until the end of the Seven Years' War in 1763, when they were sent to France. Others remained in England only a short time before being sent to their mother country.

By the end of October 1758, fourteen hundred to fifteen hundred Île Saint-Jean civilians had escaped to Quebec and Miramichi, New Brunswick. Between one hundred and two hundred people hid until the soldiers stopped searching for them; these Acadians remained on the island. Another three thousand had been removed from their homes and were sent to Louisbourg.

On November 25 eleven ships left Louisbourg carrying the Île Saint-Jean Acadians on their voyage to France. The captains knew of the danger of storms when crossing the ocean at that time of year, but they followed orders. The ships were soon separated by stormy weather. Eight of the eleven ships finally reached France. The *Violet* and the *Duke William* sank during the crossing; between five hundred and six hundred people drowned. The *Ruby* ran ashore in the Azores, began to leak, and soon sank; over one hundred people drowned.

Prince Edward Island historian, Earle Lockerby, states that of the three thousand Acadians deported from Île Saint-Jean, 1518 died—30% from sickness and 20% from drowning.

Due to the terrible conditions on board, nearly nine hundred people died of illness during the voyages and 205 more (14% of those who completed the trip) died from sickness in the two or three years following the voyage.

* * *

To prevent France from attempting to take over the Fortress of Louisbourg again, the English demolished it during the summer of 1760. Two hundred years later, wanting to provide jobs for out-of-work coal miners, the Canadian government financed a partial reconstruction of the fortress town as a tourist attraction. The coal miners were taught the skills necessary for the rebuilding of about one-fifth of the town. Costumed people now reenact the lives of the residents of Louisbourg in the peaceful year of 1744.

* * *

About three hundred thousand descendants of the 1755 Nova Scotia Acadians now live in the four Atlantic provinces in Canada (New Brunswick, Nova Scotia, Newfoundland, and Prince Edward Island), where French is spoken and the people call their land l'Acadie. Several hundred thousand descendants of the Nova Scotia Acadians also live in Louisiana, where they are called Cajuns. Others live in Quebec, New England, and France.

In 2003, Queen Elizabeth II's Canadian representative issued a royal proclamation acknowledging the "tragic consequences" of the expulsion of the Acadians by the English, "including the deaths of many thousands of Acadians."

Author's Notes

Although quite a lot of general information is available about the Acadians in the seventeenth and eighteenth centuries, specific information about Pelagie and her family is limited to births, marriages, deaths, census records, ship records, and land holdings. Following is a list of some records that I found. I was unable to find other information that I needed; in those instances I used available Acadian history and my imagination to complete the story.

Claude Benoist and his brothers were included in the 1752 census of Île Saint-Jean; it stated that they had been there for two years. There is a record of Pierre's baptism at the church in Port-la-Joie; his name appears once more, saying only that he died at sea on the way to France.

I was unable to find any records of Claude Benoist's family between Pierre's baptism at the church in Port-la-Joie, Île Saint-Jean, in September 1754 and the baptism of Sébastien-François in October 1757 in the chapel in Louisbourg. Since no information was available to show how long they stayed in Île Saint-Jean, I picked a time for them to move.

Claude Benoit and Elisabeth Terriot are listed on the record of Pelagie's marriage as her parents, not her late parents. I couldn't find any further information about either of them. The only information I found for Pelagie's sister Marie Josephe and her brother Sébastien-François were baptismal records. Marie Josephe was born in 1748 in Pigiguit, and Sébastien-François in Louisbourg in October 1757. I found no ship's records or death records for any of the preceding four people.

Available data about Pelagie's other siblings is reported in this story.

François-Louis was listed with Pelagie on the second convoy from Châtellerault to Nantes on November 15, 1775 when he was fourteen years old. He was not included with her on the ship's list to Louisiana. I was unable to find any other records of him.

Census records show that Pelagie's father and uncles were farmers in Acadie and Île Saint-Jean, and Guillaume Benoist owned a sawmill on Île Royale. However, I was unable to find information about jobs held by Yves Crochet or by Pelagie's father and her uncle Augustin after they moved to Louisbourg. And I could only guess about the reason for Yves and Pelagie's many moves in France, which are documented by birth and death records of their children.

In official records, Pelagie was referred to as Pelagie Benoist, wife of Yves Crochet. After his death she was Pelagie Benoist, *veuve* (widow) of Yves Crochet.

Pronunciation Guide and Glossary

Acadia – The English word for Acadie.

Acadie (ah cah DEE)– A French colony in eastern Canada from the 1500s to the 1700s. Today, the areas of Nova Scotia, New Brunswick, Prince Edward Island, and Newfoundland where French-speaking people live.

Angelica – A tall plant with flowers that are white or slightly green. The seeds, stems, leaves, and roots were used for flavoring and as medicine by the Acadians.

Bann – An announcement in church of a forthcoming marriage so anyone knowing of a reason why the wedding shouldn't take place would notify the priest. Three banns were required to be read at Mass on consecutive Sundays. A dispensation could be obtained if there was a good reason for the marriage to be performed sooner.

Bayou La Fourche – Now Bayou Lafourche. A branch of the Mississippi River that was dammed in 1905 at Donaldsonville.

Benoist (ben WAH) – Also spelled Benoit, Benoi, Benois.

Bon – Good.

Bonjour – Good day, good morning, good afternoon

Breeches – Men's pants which reached the knee or just below the knee.

Cajun – The name for Acadians living in Louisiana. The word Acadian is pronounced *A KAH zhahn* in French. After the Acadians reached Louisiana, the first syllable was dropped. The local

French pronunciation was *KAH zhehn* in the late 1700s and 1800s. The English pronunciation *KAY jun* is now used.

Chignecto – A narrow strip of land connecting Nova Scotia and New Brunswick.

Cobiquid – The name for Acadian settlements spread over an area from Pigiguit to Chignecto.

Cornwallis, Edward – Governor of Nova Scotia from 1749 to 1752.

Dike – A mound of earth and rock built to hold water back from the land.

Dinner –Noon meal.

Fort Beauséjour – French fort which was renamed Fort Cumberland after it was captured by English soldiers. It is on the Isthmus of Chignecto in New Brunswick.

François (frahn SWA) –The male French name for Francis.

Françoise (frahn SWAZ) – The female French name for Frances.

Grand'maman – Grandmother

Grand-père – Grandfather

Grand Pré – A village in Acadia. Grand Pré means "great meadow."

Halifax – The capital of Nova Scotia.

Hold – The inside of a ship, below the deck, where goods are stored.

Île (ill) – The French word for island.

Île Royale – A large island on the northeastern side of the mainland of Nova Scotia. It is now called Cape Breton Island.

Île Saint-Jean – French-controlled island where Acadians lived until it was captured by the British in 1758 and was renamed Prince Edward Island.

Jacques Cartier – A French explorer who explored the St. Lawrence River and claimed the area for France in 1534.

Josephe – Female French name for Joseph.

La Bergère – (The Shepherdess). The second of the seven ships bringing Acadians from France to Louisiana in 1785.

La Caroline – The seventh and last of the seven ships bringing Acadians from France to Louisiana in 1785.

l'Amitié – (Friendship). The fifth of the seven ships to leave Nantes, bringing Acadians from France to Louisiana in 1785.

La Ville d'Archangel – (The City of the Archangel). This ship sailed from St. Malo to Nantes, the sixth of the seven ships leaving Nantes, bringing Acadians to Louisiana in 1785.

Lawrence, Charles – British military officer who was named lieutenant-governor of Nova Scotia in 1753. He ordered the expulsion of the Acadians from mainland Nova Scotia to the American colonies in 1755; he was named governor of Nova Scotia in 1756. He commanded the capture of Louisbourg in 1758, and ordered the expulsion of the Acadians to France.

Le Beaumont – (The Beautiful Mountain). The third of the seven ships bringing Acadians from France to Louisiana in 1785.

Le Bon Dieu – The good God.

Le Bon Papa – (The Good Father). The first of the seven ships bringing Acadians from France to Louisiana in 1785.

Le Saint-Remi – The fourth of the seven ships bringing Acadians from France to Louisiana in 1785.

Louisbourg – A French fortified town near the northeastern tip of Île Royale. It was captured by the British in 1745, returned to France in 1748, and then captured again by the British in 1758.

M. – Abbreviation for Monsieur, the French word for Mr.

Ma chère enfant – My dear child.

Madame – The French word for Mrs.

Malouines – The French name for the Falkland Islands, near the southern tip of South America in the Atlantic Ocean.

Maman – Mother

Megrit – A town in northwestern France.

Merci – Thank you.

Mi'kmaq – A tribe of Indians in Nova Scotia at the time of the Acadians. Also spelled Micmaq or Micmac.

Mon Dieu – My God.

Northumberland Strait – A body of water between Nova Scotia and Prince Edward Island.

Nova Scotia – A province in southeastern Canada.

Oncle – Uncle

Papa – Father

Pelagie (pell ah ZHEE)

Pigiguit– An Acadian settlement which is now called Windsor. Also spelled Pisiquid, Pisiguit, or Pisiguid.

Port-la-Joie – The first permanent European settlement on Prince Edward Island, settled by the French in 1720. Also spelled Port-la-Joye.

Port Royal – First permanent French settlement in North America, founded in 1605. The name was changed to Annapolis Royal when captured the final time by the English in 1710.

Poupeé (pou PAY) – Doll.

Sister Saint-Arsène – One of the nuns of the Congregation of Notre-Dame who taught school in Louisbourg.

Sister Saint-Thècle – One of the nuns of the Congregation of Notre-Dame who taught school in Louisbourg.

Sol (or sou) – An old French coin. Twenty sols equaled one livre. According to Bernard Pothier, a pound of butter cost tens sols, and an ax cost six livres in Acadie in the 1740s.

Spruce beer – Beer made from young shoots, the new growth, of spruce trees.

Supper – Evening meal

Tante – Aunt

Tatamagouche – A village in Nova Scotia on the Northumberland Strait.

Te Deum – A service in the chapel for the purpose of thanking God for a military victory or a blessing received by the royal family.

Thériault (terr e OH) – Also spelled Terriot, Thériot,

Yves – (sometimes spelled Ives)

Bibliography

"Acadian Deportation of 1758." Port-la-Joye—Fort Amherst National Historic Site of Canada.

www.pc.gc.ca/eng/lhn-nhs/pe/amherst/natcul/natcul3.aspx

"Acadian Emigration to Spanish Louisiana." The Southwestern Louisiana Journal, Southwestern Louisiana Institute, Lafayette, LA. January, 1958, Vol. 2, No. 1.

"Acadian Families on the Second Convoy from Châtellerault to Nantes on November 15, 1775."

http://www.acadian-home.org/Chatellerault.html.

"Acadians Who Found Refuge in Louisiana, February 1764-early 1800s."

_____. www.acadiansingray.com/Appendices-ATLAL-BENOIT.htm.

_____. www.acadiansingray.com/Appendices-ATLAL-CARRET. htm.

_____. www.acadiansingray.com/Appendices-ATLAL-CROCHET. htm.

Albert, Linzy D. The Alberts of Lafourche, a Profile of Acadian Heritage, Genealogy and Historical Sketch of the Nicholas Albert Family of France, Acadie, and Bayou Lafourche in Louisiana 1726-1785.

_____. Genealogy Revisited: The Nicolas Albert Family of France, Acadia, Bayou Lafourche in South Louisiana 1670-1994. Linzy D. Albert, 1994.

Ancelet, Barry Jean, Jay Edwards, and Glen Pitre. Cajun Country. Jackson, MS: University Press of Mississippi, 1991.

Arsenault, Bona. *History of the Acadians*. Gaspé, Quebec: La Fondation de la Société Historique de la Gaspésie, 1994.

Arsenault, Georges. *The Island Acadians*. Charlottetown, P. E. I., Ragweed Press, 1989.

"Behind the Scenes of Special Events at Louisbourg: the Costume." http://fortress.uccb.ns.ca/behind/cost.html.

"Behind the Scenes of Special Events at Louisbourg: The Gardens." http://fortress.uccb.ns.ca/behind/garden.html.

Benoit, Louis. *History, Notes, and Genealogy of the Acadian Family Benoit*. Quebec, Canada: Les Éditions Faye, 1997.

Bernard, Shane K. *Cajuns and Their Acadian Ancestors: A Young Reader's History*. Jackson, MS: University Press of Mississippi, 2008.

Blanchard, J. Henri. *The Acadians of Prince Edward Island-1720-1964*. Charlottetown, P.E.I., 1964.

Bourg, Leola Tullier. *The Genealogy of Antoine Bourg and Yves Crochet*. Baton Rouge: L.T. Bourg, 1988.

Brasseaux, Carl A. *The Founding of New Acadia: the beginnings of Acadian Life in Louisiana 1765-1803*. Baton Rouge, LA: Louisiana State University Press, 1987.

_____. "Metamorphosis of Acadian Society in Late-Eighteenth-Century Louisiana." Acadian Memorial Archive. Ensemble Encore: Together Again! Essays.
www.acadianmemorial.org.

Braud, Gerard-Marc. *Les Acadiens en France: Nantes et Paimboeuf 1775-1785*. Nantes: Ouest Editions, 1994.

_____. "The Deportation of the Acadians." Canadian Encyclopedia.
www.thecanadianencyclopedia.com/featured/the-deportation-of-the-acadians.

_____. *From Nantes to Louisiana: The Odyssey of an Exiled People*. Lafayette, LA: La. Rainette, 1999.

_____. *The Story of Acadia: The Odyssey of an Exiled People*. Lafayette, La: La Rainette, 1999.

"Cajuns in the 18th Century."

http://www.acadian-cajun.com/hiscaj2c.htm.

Ditto, Tanya Brady. *The Longest Street: The Story of Lafourche Parish and Grand Isle*. Baton Rouge, LA: Moran Publishing, 1980.

"The Drummers of Louisbourg."

http://fortress.uccb.ns.ca/LCFMarine/drummersE.htm.

Faragher, John Mack. *A Great and Noble Scheme*. New York: W. W. Norton, 2005.

"Food and Cooking in Louisbourg."

http://fortress.uccb.ns.ca/LFood/foodE.htm.

Gateway to the New World CD-ROM.

Gerrior, William D. *Acadian Awakenings., Vol. I & II*, Canada: Port Royal Publishing, 2003.

Harvey, D. C. *The French Régime in Prince Edward Island*. New York: AMS Press, 1970.

Hebert, Donald. *Acadians in Exile, 1785*. Crowley, LA: Hebert Publications, 1980.

Hebert, Timothy, ed. *Acadian Church Records: Port La Joye, Île St Jean, 1749-1758: St. Jean l'Evangeliste Parish*, 2000.

"Hundreds Perish at Sea While Being Deported."

http://www.acadian-home.org/acadians-die-at-sea.html.

"Inventory & Verbal Process of Sale of the Estate Left by the Deceased Pelagie Benoit, Widow of Ives Crochet," *Terrebonne Life Lines*, Vol. 5, no. 2, Houma, LA: Terrebonne Genealogical Society, 1986, pp. 66-67.

Jaenen, Cornelius. *The Role of the Church in New France*. Toronto: McGraw-Hill, 1976.

Johnston, A.J.B. *Control and Order in French Colonial Louisbourg, 1713-1758*. East Lansing, MI: Michigan State University Press, 2001.

_____. *Endgame 1758: The Promise, the Glory, and the Despair of Louisbourg's Last Decade*. Sydney, Nova Scotia: Cape Breton University Press, 2007.

_____. *Religion in Life at Louisbourg 1713-1758*. Kingston, Ontario: McGill-Queen's University Press, 1984.

_____. *The Summer of 1744: A Portrait of Life in 18th-Century Louisbourg*. Gatineau, Quebec: Parks Canada,1983.

Johnston, A.B.J., Kenneth Donovan, B.A. Balcom, and Alex Storm. *Louisbourg: An 18th-Century Town*. Halifax, Nova Scotia: Nimbus Publishing, 1991.

Jonah, Anne Marie Lane, Ruby Fougère, and Heidi Moses. "A Necessary Luxury: Chocolate in Louisbourg and New France." *Chocolate: History, Culture, and Heritage*. Hoboken, New Jersey: John Wiley & Sons, 2009.

"La Ligne Acadienne." www.acadian-cajun.com/ligne.htm.

Landry, Don. "The Ships of the Acadian Expulsion, 1999. www.acadian-cajun.com/landryships.htm.

LeBlanc, Dudley. *The Acadian Miracle*. Lafayette, LA: Evangeline Publishing, 1966.

Lockerby, Earle. *Deportation of the Prince Edward Island Acadians*. Halifax, Nova Scotia: Nimbus Publishing, 2008.

Macpherson, Catherine. "Chocolate's Early History in Canada." *Chocolate: History, Culture, and Heritage*. Hoboken, New Jersey: John Wiley & Sons, 2009.

McFadden, Christine and Christine France. *Chocolate*. London: Hermes House, 2003.

McLennan, John Stewart. *Louisbourg, from its Foundation to its Fall, 1713-1758*. London: Macmillan and Company, 1918.

Pitre, Verne. "Poor Woman Revisited." *Terrebonne Life Lines*, Vol. 11, no. 2 (1992): 1-8.

Pothier, Bernard. *Course à L'Accadie: Journal de Campagne de François Du Pont Duvivier en 1744.* Moncton, New Brunswick: Editions d'Acadie, 1982.

Proulx, Gilles. *Between France and New France: Life Aboard the Tall Sailing Ships. Toronto:* Dundurn Press, 1984.

Rieder, Milton and Norma. *The Acadians in France: Archives of the Port of Saint Servan.* Metairie, LA: Rieder, 1967.

—————. *The Acadians in France 1762-1776.* Metairie, LA: Rieder, 1973.

Robichaux, Albert J., Jr. *The Acadian Exiles in Chatellerault 1773-1785.* Eunice, LA: Hebert Publications, 1983.

———. *The Acadian Exiles in Nantes 1775-1785.* Harvey, LA, 1978.

———. *The Acadian Exiles in Saint-Malo 1758-1785.* Eunice, LA: Hebert Publications, 1981.

———. *Acadian Marriages in France: Department of Ille-et-Vilaine, 1759-1776.* Harvey, LA, 1976.

———, ed. *Colonial Settlers along Bayou Lafourche, 1770-1798*, Vol. II. Harvey, LA, 1974.

"The Seven Ships Passenger Lists."
www.acadian-cajun.com/7ships.htm.

"The 1758 Exile."
www.acadian-cajun.com/1758ex.htm.

"Sieur de la Roque 1752 Census for Prince Edward Island/Ile Saint Jean."
www.islandregister.com/1752_page11.htm.

Stacey, Truman. *Louisiana's French Heritage.* Lafayette, LA: Acadian Publishing House, 1990.

Uzee, Philip D., ed. *The Lafourche Country: The People and the Land.* Lafayette, LA: Center for Louisiana Studies, 1985.

Warburton, Alexander B. *A History of Prince Edward Island.* St. John, New Brunswick: Barnes & Company, 1923.

Westerman, Audrey B. "Pelagie Benoit, A Poor Woman." *Terrebonne Life Lines,* Vol. 8, no. 3 (1989), 65-68.

White, Stephen A. *English Supplement to the Dictionnaire Généalogique des Familles Acadiennes*. Moncton, New Brunswick: Centre d'études acadiennes, Université de Moncton, 2000.

White, Steven A. "Hundreds Perish at Sea While Being Deported." www.acadian-home.org/acadians-die-at-sea.html.

Winzerling, Oscar William. *Acadian Odyssey*. Eunice, LA: Hebert Publications, 1955.

Genealogy

Martin Benoist --------- m. 1671 ------------- Marie Chaussegros
     b. 1643 --------------------------------- b. about 1656
     d. after 1714 ---------------------------- d. after 1714

1) .Jacqueline
     b. 1672 or 1673, Port Royal
     d. 1755, Virginia

2.) Pierre, the Elder
     b. 1675, Port Royal
     d. before 1755, Pigiguit

3.) Clement
     b. 1677, Port Royal
     d. 1748, Pigiguit

4.) Marie
     b. 1678 or 1679, Port Royal
     d. 6/11/1714

5.) Jean
     b. 1681, Port Royal

6.) Pierre, the Younger
     b. 1683, Port Royal
     d. before 1751, Pigiguit

7.) Claude
     b. 1686, Port Royal
     d. 1743

8.) Catherine
      b. 1689, Port Royal
      d. 1/26/1760, France

9.) Jeanne
      b. 1692, Port Royal

10.) Françoise
      b. 1693 or 1694, Port Royal
      d. 1755, Maryland

Pierre Benoist, the Younger ------- m. 1703 --------- Elizabeth (Isabelle) LeJuge
      b. 1683 -- b. 1689
      d. before 1751 ------------------------------------- d. 1759, France

I. -- Paul
      b. 1704

II.--Marie
      b. 1705

III. -- Guillaume
      b. 1707

IV. -- Abraham
      b. 1709

V. -- Marguerite
      b. 1710

VI. – Charles
      b. 1713

VII. -- Judith
      b. 1716

VIII. -- Claire
      b. 1719

IX. -- Claude
        b. 1721

X. -- Helene
        b. 1725

XI. -- Augustin
        b. 1728

XII. -- Anne
        b. 1730

I. -- Paul Benoist- ---------- m. about 1725- ------- Anne Trahan
        b. 1704, Pigiguit ------------------------------ d. before 7/1750
                        2nd m. 7/27/1750 ----- Marie Joseph Viger
        d. 12/13/1758 ---------------------------- -----d. 12/13/1758

1. Paul ---------- m. 10/8/1748 ---------- Magdelaine LeBlanc
        b. 1727
        d. 12/13/1758

                1-A. Joseph ------------------------------- 1-B. Agathe
                        b. 1749 -------------------------------- b. 3/14/1751
                        d. 12/13/1758 ------------------------ d. 12/13/1758

2. Marie-Joseph
        b. about 1730
        d. 12/13/1758

3. Anne Gertrude ------ m. 1/23/1752 ------- Charles Doiron
        b. about 1733 ---------------------------- (Douairon)
        d. 12/13/1758

4. Françoise
        b. about 1735
        d. 12/13/1758

5. Marie-Marthe -------------- m. about 1753 ----------- Jean Clement
      b. about 1737 --------- 2nd m. 1/12/1761-------- Nicholas Albert
      d. about 1790, Louisiana

6. Elizabeth
      b. about 1739
      d. 12/13/1758

7. Antoine
      b. about 1741
      d. 12/13/1758

8. Jean
      b. about 1743
      d. 12/13/1758

9. Rose
      b. about 1745
      d. 12/13/1758

10. Scholastique
      b. about 1747
      d. 12/13/1758

III. Guillaume Benoist ----- m. about 1729 ------ Marie-Josephe Gautrot
      b. about 1707

1. Pierre
      b. about 1730
      d. 1811

2. Michel
      b. about 1732

3. Judith
      b. 1734

4. Boniface
> b. 1737

5. Simon
> b. 1739

6. Genevieve
> b. 1743

IV. ---Abraham Benoist --------- m. 9/23/1732 ------------- Angelique Vincent
> b. 1709 -- d. 1750
>
> 2nd m. 9/21/1751 ---------- Marie Josephe Lejeune
> d. 12/13/1758 --- d. 12/13/1758

1. Jean -------------------- m. 1756 -------------------- Rufine Doiron
> b. 1734
> d. 12/13/1758 ------------------------------- ----- d. 12/13/1758

> > A. Marie-Josephe
> > b. 1757
> > d. 12/13/1758

2. Marguerite
> b. 1736
> d. 12/13/1758

3. Marie-Josephe
> b. 1738
> d. 12/13/1758

4. Marie-Madeleine
> b. 1740
> d. 12/13/1758

5. Pelagie
> b. 1742
> d. 12/13/1758

6. Marie
>b. 1747
>d. 12/13/1758

7. Joseph
>b. 7/5/1752
>b. 12/13/1758

8. Charles
>b. 2/20/1754
>d. 12/13/1758

VI. ---Charles Benoist ----- m. 10/24/1735 -------- Madeleine Thériault (Terriot)
>b. 1713
>d. 1760, France

1. Marie ---------------- m. 10/3/1757 ----------- René Rasicot
>b. 1736 -------- 2nd m. 1/7/1766 --------- Joseph Hébert
>d. 1806, Louisiana

2. Anne ----------- m. 1758 --------------- Charles LeBlanc
>b. 1739
>d. 1761, France

3. Françoise -------- m. 3/6/1759 --------- Honoré Caret
>b. 1741
>d. 1788, Louisiana

4. Judith
>b. 1744
>d. 1760, France

5. Jean-Charles ------ m. 1770 ------- Anne-Marie Haché
>b. 1746
>d. 1787, Louisiana

6. Pierre Paul
   b. 10/21/51
   d. on way to France, 1758

VII. --- Judith ------------- m. 1738 ------------ Claude LeBlanc
      b. 1716
      d. 1763

VIII. --- Claire ------------- m. 1742 ------------- Pierre LeBlanc
      b. 1719
      d. before 2/8/1776

IX. -- Claude Benoist ------ m. 1740 --------- Elisabeth (Isabelle) Theriault
      b. 1721

1. Pelagie ------ m. 2/6/1758 ----------- Yves Crochet
      b. 1741 or 1742 --------------------- b. 9/1/1732
      d. 8/7/1824, Louisiana ------------ d. 11/23/1773, France

2. Gregoire ------------------m.1770---------- Marie-Rose Caret
      b. about 1744
      d. 1/21/1829

3. Anne ---------- m. 2/5/1765 ------------- Louis Haché
      b. 1746
      d. 9/25/1767

4. Daniel ------------------m.1768----------------- Henriette Legendre
      b. about 1748 ----- 2nd m. about 1799 ---- Madeleine-Ursule Doiron
      d. 1825

5. Marie Josephe
      b. 1748

6. Marguerite ------------m.1775----------------- Joseph Precieux
      b. 9/4/1752 -- 2nd m. 1786 --------------- Claude-Bernard Dugas
      d. 9/8/1837

7. Pierre
      b. 9/1/1754
      d. 1758 on the way to France

8. Sébastien-François
      b. 10/20/1757

XII. --- Augustin -------- m. 2/9/1750 ----------- Marguerite LeJeune
      b. about 1728 -------------------------------- b. 9/27/1730, Acadie
                                             d. 5/17/1759
                2nd m. 7/19/1763------- Marie-Madeleine Gautrot
                                  b. 5/20/1741
      d. 9/8/1783, Nantes ------------------------ buried 1/1/1784, Nantes

1. Marguerite
      b. about 1751 ---------------------- d. at sea 1759

2. Simon
      d. at sea 1759

3. Elizabeth
      d. at sea 1759

4. Perinne-Jeanne
      b. 5/15/1759 ---------------------- d. 5/20/1759

5. Mathurin
   b. 5/10/1764

6. François-Jean-Baptiste
   b. 10/7/1765

7. Jean-Marie-Augustin
   b. 1/2/1767 ----------------------- d. 12/14/1768

8. Marie-Jeanne
   b. 1/2/1769 ----------------------- d. 3/20/1770

9. Françoise-Apollonie
   b. 10/19/1770 --------------------- d. 9/5/1772

10. Victoire-Marie
    b. 11/11/1772

11. Anne-Marie
    b. 1/8/1773

12. Joseph-Marie
    baptized 11/4/1774 ---------------buried 7/26/1777

13. Jean-Marie-Augustin
    baptized 6/16/1777 -------------- buried 6/23/1777

14. Jean-Augustin
    baptized 1/16/1783

Pelagie Benoist ---------- m. 2/6/1758 -------- Yves Crochet
        b. 1741 or 1742 ---------------------------- b. 9/1/1732
        d. 8/7/1824, Louisiana -------------------- d. 11/23/1773, France

1. Jean-Guillaume ------ m. 12/14/1785 ---------- Marie Marthe Boudrot
        b. 9/9/1760, Megrit
        d. before July 1821, Louisiana

2. François-Louis
        b. 12/14/1761, Megrit

3. Jean-Joseph
        b. 3/25/1763, St. Servan
        d. 4/4/1763

4. Françoise-Pelagie ---------------- m. 11/24/1785 ------ Léonard de la Garde
        b. 5/20/1764, St. Servan --- 2ⁿᵈ m. 6/1792 ------- Philippe Bruze
        d. 2/25/1836, Louisiana

5. Marguerite-Perinne ------ m. 11/24/1785 ------- Joseph Adam
        b. 5/23/1766, Megrit
        d. 11/26/1830

6. Yves-Jean --------- m. early 1790s ---------------- Anne Dugas
        b. 12/3/1767, Megrit
        d. early 1810s, Louisiana

7. Julien ------------- m. 5/8/1798 ------------ Marguerite Belanger
        b. 3/4/1770, Megrit
        d. 9/24/1829, Louisiana

8. Pelagie
        b. 2/7/1772, Megrit
        d. 5/29/1774, Châtellerault, France

9. Jean-Marin
        b. 5/2/1774, Châtellerault, France
        d. 6/3/1776, Châtellerault, France

Ollie Ann Porche Voelker's Family Line

Martin Benoist & Marie Chaussegros

Pierre Benoist & Elizabeth LeJuge

Claude Benoist & Elisabeth Theriault

Pelagie Benoist & Yves Crochet

Julien Crochet & Marguerite Belanger

Paulin Crochet & Clementine Bonvillain

Elise Crochet & Louis LeGrand

Emily LeGrand & Henry Porche

Roland Porche & Annie Erick Giroir

Ollie Ann Porche & William Voelker

Cynthia Voelker & Stan Bonis

Blaine Bonis

Annie Bonis

Eric Voelker

Heidi Voelker & Shawn Davis

Brynn Davis

Tess Davis

Rhett Davis

Kathryn Voelker & Steve Walker

Ethan Walker

Kaitlin Walker

CPSIA information can be obtained
at www.ICGtesting.com
Printed in the USA
FFOW03n1219221014
8253FF